BROKEN COVENANT

Charles M. Sennott

SIMON &
SCHUSTER

New York
London
Toronto
Sydney
Tokyo
Singapore

SIMON & SCHUSTER
SIMON & SCHUSTER BUILDING
ROCKEFELLER CENTER
1230 AVENUE OF THE AMERICAS
NEW YORK, NEW YORK 10020

DESIGNED BY NINA D'AMARIO/LEVAVI & LEVAVI
MANUFACTURED IN THE UNITED STATES OF AMERICA

1   3   5   7   9   10   8   6   4   2

LIBRARY OF CONGRESS CATALOGING-IN-PUBLICATION DATA
SENNOTT, CHARLES M.
BROKEN COVENANT / CHARLES M. SENNOTT.
P.   CM.
1.COVENANT HOUSE (NEW YORK, N.Y.)   2.SOCIAL WORK WITH
YOUTH—NEW YORK (N.Y.)   3.CHURCH WORK WITH YOUTH—NEW
YORK (N.Y.)   4.RITTER, BRUCE, DATE.   5.CATHOLIC CHURCH—
UNITED STATES—CLERGY.   6.SEX CRIMES—UNITED STATES—
INVESTIGATION.   I.TITLE.
HV1437.N5S46   1992
362.7'4'06073—DC20   92-26312
                                                   CIP

ISBN 0-671-76715-1

FOR MY MOTHER;
IN MEMORY OF MY FATHER.

AND FOR JOHN COTTER.
CHEERS, MATE.

Acknowledgments

This book would not have been possible without Julie Klapper, who held the light of understanding while I explored the darkness. It was her love, patience, and sound advice that saw me through.

To my agent, Elizabeth Kaplan, I will be forever grateful. She understood the depth of this story before I did, and had enough faith to let me get to the bottom of it myself. She also offered hours of calm counseling to a first-time author.

Gail Winston, my editor at Simon & Schuster also deserves credit for her patience and diligence. She helped transform a rough manuscript into a polished book.

But this story would never have been told at all were it not for John Cotter and the *New York Post*. Cotter, a great friend and a great editor, who first assigned this story to me, died just a few days after I finished the first draft. I'd like to recognize my friends and colleagues Paul Schwartzman, Mark Kriegel, Mike McAlary, Jim Willse, Lou Colasuonno, and Steve McFadden, with whom I shared the painful task of burying Cotter and inherited an obligation to keep his flame alive.

To all of the men and women who participated in the 1990 *New York Daily News* strike, thanks for your inspiration. And to James Hairston and Matthew Storin who gave me the time to finish what often seemed like an endless task.

It would be impossible to name all of the family, friends, and fellow journalists who offered their advice and encouragement and whose companionship I missed while locked away in my apartment writing. A few to be noted are: Jack Levine, Molly Fowler, Jerry Klapper, Pete Hamill, Ben Terrall, and Lyle Harris.

But finally, I'd like to recognize my mother, Virginia, my brother, Mark, and my two spiritual advisers, Joseph Lagan and Father Bill, all of whom took the time to read the manuscript and offer their trustworthy opinions.

Contents

Part V THE FLOOD

Part VI THE NEW COVENANT

Author's Note

"I have no way of proving my innocence. My accusers cannot establish my guilt."

With those unsettling words, Covenant House founder Father Bruce Ritter stepped down in February of 1990 in the wake of allegations of sexual and financial misconduct. The question of Ritter's guilt or innocence was left unanswered for the hundreds of thousands of people who contributed to his mission and for the millions more who simply wondered if it was possible that a man many regarded as a living saint could truly be a slayer of the soul. How could a man who claimed to save so many victims be a victimizer himself?

There was never a criminal conviction of Father Ritter. In what was widely viewed as an implicit deal between the Catholic Church and the Manhattan District Attorney's office, the charges against Ritter were dropped the day after he resigned. To its great credit, however, Covenant House decided to commission an independent investigation. To get to the bottom of the swirling allegations against its founder and spiritual leader, the national board of directors hired a world-renowned private investigative firm, Kroll Associates, and one of the top law offices in the country, Cravath, Swaine & Moore. The nearly $1 million report, half of which was provided pro bono, was the product of a five-month investigation, 150 interviews, and the poring over of thousands of pages of documents. The purpose of the report, it stated, was not "to make a legal determination of guilt or innocence concerning the allegations" against Ritter. The report also noted that "[n]one of the allegations, when viewed individually, can be proved beyond any question." Nonetheless, the report confirmed, the "cumulative evidence" against Ritter was "extensive." It documented the cases of fifteen young men who claimed to have been sexually abused or sexually approached by Ritter, including young residents and members of the organization's live-in Faith Community. The fifty-two-page summary of the report also concluded that some of Ritter's financial practices were "questionable at best."

This book relies both on the charity's own findings in the Kroll report and on original reporting, based on nearly 100 interviews, trips to most of the Covenant House subsidiaries throughout the United States, data collected from several other facilities in Latin America and Canada, and research trips from Rome to the small New Jersey town where Ritter grew up, and many stops in between. Regrettably, there were people who declined to be interviewed for this book, including Father Ritter, many key Covenant House staff executives, and Cardinal O'Connor. But scores of others did take the time to talk to me and help bring understanding to a painful chapter in the charity's history.

I have tried to make the book as fair and accurate as possible. In every instance in which dialogue is used or scenes are re-created, I interviewed at least one person who was present and—where possible—tried to confirm the accuracy of the account through other sources. Much of the specific sourcing is obvious in the text, but it is also explained in further detail in the source notes.

Despite its careful wording, the Kroll report was widely viewed as confirmation that Ritter was guilty of sexual misconduct. And, like much of the press coverage at the time, this book concludes that the charges against Ritter were true. There are no criminal or civil charges pending against Ritter and, to this day, he continues to maintain his innocence.

Prologue

THE last light of day sliced through the folding shutters of the French windows, casting thin bars of darkness and light in the sacristy of the Covenant House chapel. Through the shadows, Father Bruce Ritter moved slowly, laying out his black and white vestments and marking the liturgical readings in his lectionary. The Catholic priest was preparing to say mass before a congregation of faithful followers at the charity's shelter, located on the sultry fringes of the French Quarter.

It was 4:25 in the afternoon and Father Ritter had just flown in from the New York headquarters of his charitable empire, which cared for some 25,000 kids annually in cities throughout the world. Ritter planned to be in New Orleans for only a few days to attend a board of directors meeting and a fund-raising event. The sixty-two-year-old Franciscan was proud of his latest franchise—a handsome complex of three new brick buildings designed with attention to the ornate detail of the Quarter's Spanish and French architecture. Like all of his Covenant House programs across the country, the New Orleans site was noticeably clean and efficiently managed—providing beds, hot meals, and counseling to some two hundred young people a night who would otherwise be struggling to survive somewhere on the streets. This was no ragged Catholic charity in a dusty old building. This was Covenant House—the private charity of the 1980s, the perfect mix of free enterprise and compassion.

The telephone rang in the sacristy—a small room behind the chapel that doubled as an office—breaking the silence of Ritter's preparation for mass. Ritter picked up the receiver and sounded annoyed with the interruption. "Hello, Father Bruce," I said, and paused. The newsroom at the *New York Post* was buzzing near deadline. I had to cup my ear to concentrate on the call. How was I going to tell the revered Franciscan priest what I had been investigating for the last month and a half? It was a blockbuster exclusive, and my editors were pushing hard to get the story in the paper. I had been stalling for weeks to firm up details, though caution was not what the feisty tabloid was all about. I knew that once the story broke and the attorneys and public-relations experts got in the way, I'd never get to Father Ritter. I wanted to hear his voice with my own ears. Frankly, I didn't believe the allegations—or at least I didn't want to believe them. The man was legendary among those who knew his tireless work on behalf of troubled young people nationwide. It had also crossed my mind that the story might be a career ender for me—a radioactive scandal perhaps too volatile even for the *New York Post*. Give me a good clean mob hit, an undercover report on Colombian cocaine cartels, the "troubles" in Northern Ireland—anything but the far more treacherous terrain of darkness and disillusion that needed to be traveled in this assignment.

"Hello?" demanded Father Ritter, sounding more impatient with the long pause.

"Father Ritter, I'm Charlie Sennott, a reporter with the *New York Post*. We've never met. But I had to reach you."

"Sure. How did you find me here? Oh, New York must have told you, right? What's going on, man? What's up?" asked Father Ritter, rather self-consciously using the informal rhythms of the streets.

I explained in slow, halting words that he was the target of an investigation by the Manhattan District Attorney's office into allegations that he had misused Covenant House funds to maintain a sexual relationship with a nineteen-year-old former male prostitute who had come to Covenant House for help.

"Oh, come on, this is crazy," said Ritter.

"Father Ritter, the D.A. is pretty deep into the investigation," I said. "There's a lot going on."

"All right, go on," he said.

For a reporter the questions were simple and direct. But for a Catholic, they were more than just embarrassing, they were disturbing. My Irish Catholic roots were showing, and years of learned deference to men of the cloth were hard to overcome. I had to ask a man revered by presidents and praised throughout the country for his good works about allegations brought against him by a self-described former hustler. I had to ask a priest if he had broken his vow of celibacy and engaged in a homosexual relationship. I had to ask if he had broken an equally sacred bond of trust between a youth-care counselor and his client. I had to know if Father Ritter under-

stood these young victims of the streets so well because he himself
was a victimizer.

"Did you have a sexual relationship with Tim Warner?" I asked,
almost choking on the words. To be discussing sex with a priest
brought back some childhood images—dark confessional booths and
stern warnings about eternal damnation for impure thoughts. But
the roles seemed reversed. Had I become a priest's confessor? What
right did I have to be asking this man these questions?

"God help me, it's not true. Oh, God, no," said Ritter.

Throughout the phone interview, Father Bruce Ritter confronted
the first hint of public revelation of his secret life with adamant denials
and conspiracy theories. He said it was the Mafia setting him up; he
implied that maybe it was militant gay activists or other "enemies of
the Church." But soon it would all be unearthed—more than a dozen
young men would ultimately come forward with similar allegations
of sexual misconduct.

Then there was what seemed a long pause on the other end of the
phone, followed by words that were repeated in a way that was haunting and slow, as if he were talking to himself. "I'm so careful," said
Ritter. "I'm so careful. . . . I'm so careful."

I

In the Garden

"God created Man in the image of Himself . . ."

The Jerusalem Bible, Genesis 1:27

Chapter 1

The Priest, the President, and the Prostitute

Tuesday, November 14, 1989
New York City

THE motorcade rolled down Ninth Avenue in Manhattan—a stream of black limousines, shiny chrome, and flashing blue lights—to Sixteenth Street. It stopped before a large, oddly shaped building, which had originally been home to the National Maritime Union. The eleven-story white-washed leviathan looks like an abstract interpretation of a great ship, with its sloping façade that resembles a bow and its mock portholes for windows. COVENANT HOUSE proclaimed the three-foot block letters above the rounded portals at the entrance.

Four men bounded out of the lead limousine. Dark sunglasses. Trenchcoats. Hands hidden inside lapels. Their heads moved mechanically, like surveillance cameras, over the crowd of people gathering in front. One of them opened the double doors on the passenger side of the second limousine.

There he was: former President of the United States Ronald Reagan stepping out into the flash of cameras and the rush of television crews. He smiled and waved, still basking in the glory of the decade that was his. The Secret Service men formed a circle and ushered

Reagan through the crowd. Camera crews jostled for position. They walked backward and then spun to the side for a wider shot of Reagan entering the building. He walked straight through it all—the choreography of power.

Father Bruce Ritter waited for Reagan just inside the doorway. The Franciscan priest stood before a large wooden plaque that depicted a dove in an open palm, or as the kids put it, "a bird in the hand": the symbol of Covenant House.

This was not Reagan's first visit to Father Bruce Ritter's charity. But the occasion was, nevertheless, a major media event. Clearly, it was not as celebrated as the visit by President Bush and his wife, Barbara, over the summer. The first lady held a child of a teenage mother in her arms and the photograph ran on the front page of *The New York Times.* Bush had chosen his visit to Covenant House as the platform to launch his "thousand points of light" initiative that day. It was a lead story on every network.

But on this crisp fall day, Ritter relished the timing of the visit. It was just what the charity needed: national publicity on the advent of the holiday season, a televised reminder to millions of Covenant House donors that the time to give was once again upon them. "Providence," Ritter always called it. The priest smiled and held out his hand.

"Hello, Father Bruce," said Reagan in the folksy and familiar voice. Ritter and Reagan were of the same stock, brought up poor and Irish during the Depression. They understood each other.

"Welcome back to Covenant House, Mr. President," said Ritter, shaking hands with Reagan for an unnaturally long time, while the cameras clicked like automatic gunfire. Then the president and the priest walked side by side—Reagan with his hair slicked back, in a blue pinstripe suit, and his Hollywood posture; Father Bruce with his bald head shining in the klieg lights, in black clerical garb, and with an impish grin.

The Covenant House building they walked through was a standing testimony to the power and the glory of Father Bruce Ritter. If it was a great ship, then Ritter was its captain. A fierce taskmaster, Ritter always made sure it was scrubbed spotless. For the crew on board, there were dreaded spot inspections weekly. But today it had a special shine. Freshly potted plants and flowers brightened the building. Newly painted hallways were filled with scores of runaways. The kids, most of them between eighteen and twenty-one, were from Covenant House's "Rights of Passage," an eighteen-month-old program, based in the building, that was helping street kids finish high school, start college, or find a job. This was separate from the main crisis center, or "Under 21" program, as it was called, which provided overnight shelter for street kids near Times Square. The crisis center was still the first step in getting kids off the street, but the Rights of Passage program was devised to help them stay off the streets.

Rights of Passage was the future of Covenant House, a shift from providing only short-term crisis care to a long-term vision of hope and promise. Ritter's plan was to slowly build these long-term facilities across the country.

Ritter loved the shiplike building for the simple fact that it was a prize. He had pirated it away from Mayor Edward I. Koch in 1988, in a bitter political battle between the Mayor of New York City and the Saint of Times Square. Koch wanted to build a prison release program. Ritter wanted to establish Rights of Passage. The city tabloids had a feast. The people sided with Ritter against Koch, voting for compassion over incarceration.

But that was history in the halls of Covenant House. The young kids only understood the moment. They stared in awe at the presidential and sacerdotal power that stood before them.

"Damn," said one kid in stone-washed jeans and a leather jacket, after the entourage passed. "You see that? That's the man. Yo, Ronnie."

The television crews set up inside a large auditorium. There was a podium and the kids fanned out around it, impatiently waiting for the former President.

In the wings, there was a reception, where Reagan shook hands with the staff. Then the former President and Ritter talked quietly together. They had become important allies over the years. Reagan named Bruce Ritter one of America's "unsung heroes" in his 1984 State of the Union Address, marking a watershed for Ritter by ushering the organization into national attention. The charity's annual budget tripled within four years after the speech, from $27 million in 1985 to more than $90 million by 1989. Covenant House had become a phenomenal success in no small part because Reagan and Bush had chosen it as the paradigm of social service in the age of privatization. In April of that year Ritter had been honored with the Presidential Volunteer Action Award and the Bush administration's first annual Ronald Reagan Award for Excellence. All of the acclaim meant more dollars and a bigger program. In fact, the current issue of the *Non Profit Times* had listed Covenant House as the third-largest charity in the United States in terms of public financial support. It had nearly twice as much public funding as CARE and three times as much as Save the Children. Covenant House was becoming one of the most prominent charities in the world.

Ritter's work fit neatly into the conservative agenda. He raised 95 percent of his funding through private donations, relying on government funding for only 5 percent. Covenant House was a private-enterprise charity that on the surface seemed remarkably more efficient than the bloated social-service bureaucracies that relied primarily on government funds. With charities like this one, the Republicans were asking, who needed government spending? Bruce Ritter's business sense was so keen that *The Wall Street Journal* profiled him on its front page. Conservative columnists all around the country asked, "Why can't more people run programs like Father Bruce Ritter's?"

A strict moralist with a background in medieval theology, Ritter's Catholic views wedded perfectly with the growing conservatism of Reagan America. Ritter was even named a Republican appointee to the Meese Commission on Pornography. In line with the Roman Catholic Church, Ritter was vocally opposed to abortion, gay rights, and contraception. But he went even further, pontificating his opinions about the inefficiencies of government bureaucracies. His work was perceived by the far right as a Catholic blessing for a historic shift of the burden of social responsibility from the government to the private sector.

His colleagues in the area of social work questioned how Ritter could applaud men who were gutting the same federally funded programs they relied upon for survival. They felt Ritter's symbiotic relationship with the Reagan and Bush administrations was an unforgivable betrayal. Ritter dismissed their criticism as jealousy.

The money brought in by the attention begot a booming expansion of programs. In its twenty-year history, the charity had grown from humble beginnings in a Lower East Side tenement to an international organization with seventeen centers in eleven American cities as well as in Panama, Honduras, Guatemala, Mexico, and Canada. Covenant House was in the process of beginning new programs in Los Angeles, Washington, Trenton, Newark, and other American cities. It expected to get a foothold in the Pacific Rim, by the end of the following year, beginning with a program in the Philippines.

Covenant House had an operating budget of more than $90 million for fiscal 1989 and was planning a projected $95 million budget for the upcoming year. This private charity's annual spending was more than three times what the federal government budgeted for all similar programs nationwide. Covenant House's wealth was fueled by one of the most sophisticated direct-mail marketing departments in the country. It pumps money into a legal-advocacy department that worked on the legislative and judicial levels and seemed to dovetail in many respects with the interests of the far right. While most advocacy departments for such charities fought for better housing, job placement, education, and government funding for urban child-care centers or drug-rehabilitation centers, Covenant House focused primarily on pornography, the apolitical obsession of the far right.

Ritter was a corporate Saint Francis of Assisi, a CEO with God and the Republican party on his side. He had also become a great story. The national media were in love with the street-smart priest. The same week as the Reagan visit, ABC's *World News Tonight* made Ritter "Person of the Week." The piece recounted the mythology of Covenant House, from the grainy black-and-white footage of the early years in the East Village to the sultry color video of Times Square. Ritter was asked about the prestigious Father Flanagan Award, which was to be bestowed upon him later that month. He stared straight at the camera and replied: "I would rather be remembered in some secret, remote corner of the heart of a street kid who knew I loved him."

Ted Koppel, who was sitting in for Peter Jennings, closed out *World News Tonight* by praising Ritter: "And so tonight we choose Father Bruce Ritter. He's seen how tough life on the street for a kid can be and he's found a way to reach them. If you want to make a street kid cry, he says, offer them a place to live."

World News Tonight was the top of that week's coverage. A *Time* photographer was also at the Reagan media event, taking shots for a planned Christmas issue that was going to include an interview with Ritter. What better story was there for the holiday season than a priest cut from the same cloth as Bing Crosby saving street kids from the world of drugs and prostitution? CBS *Morning News* was working on signing a contract with Ritter that would guarantee an exclusive live shot from Covenant House on Christmas morning. Even Walt Disney Studios, the great American mythmakers, were negotiating with Covenant House executives to buy the exclusive rights for a feature-length film on the life story of this Father Flanagan of the 1980s.

Ritter was a marketable icon: America's answer to Mother Teresa. He was the brightest of the "thousand points of light," and on this day that light was shining as brightly as it ever had.

In the large auditorium at Covenant House, the crowd applauded as Reagan approached the podium. "I care about you and that's why

I am here," Reagan said, as the crowd of mostly black and Hispanic faces looked up at him. They were young homeless adults, teenage mothers with no place to turn, street hustlers, and recovering drug addicts. They were kids mostly over the age of seventeen, who had outgrown foster care and fallen through the cracks of the city's social-service institutions.

"At times you must have wondered why you were born, at times you must have hated the world, you must have wondered where you'd find food and a place to live and whether anyone at all cared about you," said Reagan. The great communicator had the crowd mesmerized. There was a hush of emotion.

"I know how big and bad the world can be; my father was an alcoholic, and I was frustrated and angry. We were poor," Reagan said. "But my mother taught me that everything bad happens for a reason. Know that if you bear with it and go on down the road something good will happen."

Ritter sat behind the podium, watching over his kids. They were respectful. There were faint cries from the infants of teenage mothers. Some of the kids jostled with each other. But most of them listened. A few even shook their heads at what the former President was saying. They might not have been educated, but they knew first-hand the contradictions of Reagan's policies. They were street-smart enough to know when they were being hustled by a politician.

Reagan took some questions from the audience. One resident, a seventeen-year-old girl named Melissa Adams, raised her hand. She stood up and asked the former President, "Why did you just realize there was homeless people? We've been around for years."

Reagan cupped his ear and shook his head, the same way he had at so many press conferences in front of helicopters or as he was whisked across the White House lawn into a limo with its motor running. He was the President who couldn't hear. Ritter leaned over and spoke into the tiny hearing device in Reagan's ear.

The former President nodded his head in recognition. He had the answer.

"Yes, I did know, but I had a philosophy about government weaknesses, and I found that there were programs in which the administrative overhead was two dollars for every one dollar that reached the needy, and that had to be changed. A program like this would cost four times as much if the government were to do it."

Ritter smiled. He liked it that one of the young people in his care had posed such a hard question. This was the deal, the political covenant between Father Bruce and Ronald Reagan. There was no better forum for Reagan to vocalize his message of privatization, of free-enterprise compassion, and of getting the government off people's backs while still showing that he cared about the homeless and society's throwaways. It couldn't have been a better platform if it had been scripted by a speechwriter.

Reagan handed out some gold pens with his name on them and then waved goodbye. The kids clapped. On the way out, he handed Ritter an envelope. Enclosed was a personal check from Ronald and Nancy for $5,000 made out to Covenant House.

Father Bruce took the envelope and looked Reagan in the eye. "God bless you, Mr. President," he said.

That same afternoon, as the presidential motorcade pulled away from Covenant House, Kevin Lee Kite was drinking Diet Coke and chain-smoking Marlboro 100s in a cramped office at St. Luke's–Roosevelt Hospital's Crime Victims Unit on the Upper West Side of Manhattan.

Kite, a handsome young man with a crop of strawberry-blond hair and a boyish smile, was going by the name "Tim Warner." He looked to be the age he said he was, nineteen. He was actually twenty-five. He fidgeted nervously in the waiting room, flipping through stacks of psychology journals and other magazines on a coffee table. One cover had a photograph of a battered woman with the headline YOU DON'T HAVE TO TAKE IT.

This was Kite's second visit to the St. Luke's Crime Victims Unit after being referred to the center by an 800 number for counseling on sexual abuse. St. Luke's specialized in counseling victims of sexual as well as mental abuse. It also helped victims of antigay violence. A counselor, Jane Seskin, had first heard from Kite on November 12. He sounded frightened on the phone and said that he was in a "very bad situation" and wanted to talk to her in person.

Kite arrived the next day to tell his story. He claimed to have been having a sexual relationship with Father Bruce Ritter. Kite told of his past as a male prostitute with a Houston-based escort service. He said that he had met Ritter in New Orleans and that the Franciscan priest had brought him to New York with the promise of a way to start his life over. Kite wanted to get out of "the male-escort business," as he always insisted on calling it. He put all his faith in the priest.

But soon Kite found himself doing what he had always done. As far as he was concerned, Ritter had become just another john. The only covenant he had with Ritter was a silent exchange of sex for money and special privileges. As Kite told it, he was given a one-bedroom apartment, a computer, a college scholarship, spending money, new clothes, and nice dinners at restaurants. In exchange, Kite said, Ritter had his way with him on Sunday night trysts in his apartment or on weekends at a secluded cottage on the estate of a Covenant House board member.

Kite complained to Seskin how the lies and hypocrisy of the famous Franciscan had infuriated him. But he said he was worried about ending a relationship with a powerful man like Bruce Ritter. He'd been around enough powerful men to know what happens when their dirty secrets get out. He looked frightened.

She was skeptical, but Kite had names, addresses, and documents to prove the elaborate expenditures. He had come to the right place.

On his second day at St. Luke's, Seskin picked up the phone and called the Manhattan District Attorney's office. She reached the office of Assistant D.A. Linda Fairstein, who had cooperated with the staff at St. Luke's on other investigations. As head of the Sex Crimes Unit, Fairstein was a maverick prosecutor, in the forefront of defining date rape and bringing new muscle to the legal advocacy of rape victims.

Fairstein, in her early forties, is a tall blonde who favors smart blue blazers. She exudes the kind of confidence and caution, the passion and the moral outrage that make for a great prosecutor. She had tried more than thirty-five cases since joining the Manhattan District Attorney's office in 1972. Only two resulted in acquittals.

In 1986, she gained notoriety for the "preppie murder" case, in which a handsome prep-school student named Robert Chambers was accused of killing his classmate Jennifer Levin while having "rough sex" in Central Park. The trial lasted thirteen weeks, before Chambers pleaded guilty to manslaughter in the first degree.

On this day, Fairstein was in the middle of preparing for pretrial motions in what was the latest New York City horror story: the "Central Park jogger" case. The jogger, a successful white female executive, had been beaten, raped, and left for dead by a group of black teenagers who were "wilding" in Central Park. The case had rocked the city. Fairstein was under a lot of pressure.

After checking her messages, Fairstein contacted Seskin and told her that she would be able to meet with Kite the following day. Fairstein had run into Ritter before, had observed his arrogance and the power his charity had brought him. She knew how big this case could be. She told Seskin to make sure that Kite brought the documents. On November 15, shortly before 11 A.M., Linda Fairstein met Kevin Kite.

"I trusted her right away," Kite remembers. "She was so confident and calm. She listened and I got the feeling she believed me. She has a way of protecting you and making you feel like she trusts you."

Linda listened to Kite's story and studied the documents he had brought with him. She asked him questions over and over about what had happened, how it happened, how much money was involved. His story remained consistent. None of the allegations seemed to shock Fairstein. She'd heard just about everything in fifteen years with the Sex Crimes Unit. She was tough on defendants who were inconsistent. But once she latched onto a case, she was a fierce defender of victims' rights. Fairstein had earned a reputation as a tireless prosecutor, breaking new ground by convincing juries that proof of physical force was not necessary for a rape or sexual-harassment conviction. Her closing arguments had helped to broaden the legal definition of a sexual crime to include any use of power—moral, political, financial, or physical—to manipulate another person into having sex.

Fairstein explained the prosecutorial purpose of the District Attorney's office and warned him about the seriousness of his allegation.

"Look, there is time for you to get out of this," Fairstein said. "But there will come a point when you can't back out. We'll be on your side all the way, but once you're in it, you're in it. Do you want to back out?"

"No," he said, just beginning to realize what he had gotten himself into.

Chapter 2

If God Doesn't Like Me the Way I Am . . .

INVESTIGATORS from the D.A.'s office used masking tape to secure the Nagra SN tape recorder—a small, metallic box about the size of a deck of cards—inside a blue canvas pouch that Kevin Kite often wore around his waist.

They taped the wires on two finger-sized microphones so that they strategically pointed out of the left and right corners of the flap of the pouch. Kite was practicing opening it to press the record button without untaping the microphones. It was a maneuver the investigators had him repeat several times.

It was only a few days after Linda Fairstein's first meeting with Kite. But she had called in the "wire team" because Kite was going to meet Father Ritter that afternoon. Although she had intended only to interview Kite for more details, she was too aggressive a prosecutor to pass up a shot at tape recording a conversation between Ritter and his accuser. One of the detectives, Maureen Spencer, reminded Kevin to speak clearly and slowly during the taping.

"Just go with the conversation. Don't try to lead it," said Spencer, a New York City detective who had served as Fairstein's right-hand woman for years.

Spencer told Kite that if at any time he was nervous and didn't want to go through with the taping he should simply forget about the record button and get the machine back to them as soon as possible.

"The main thing is your safety," said Spencer. "If worse comes to worst, throw it out the window."

"Wait a minute," another detective said sarcastically. "Keep in mind these things cost a few thousand dollars."

This kind of attention seemed to be filling a void in Kite's life. Finally, someone believed in him. At about 3 P.M., he took a cab down to the Covenant House headquarters at Forty-first Street and Tenth Avenue in Manhattan, where he was scheduled to meet Ritter. For the last two weeks, Kite had dropped out of sight and Ritter was worried about him, leaving persistent phone messages on his machine, and promptly cutting off Kite's spending money by canceling his twice-monthly checks.

Ritter was driving out to the vigil for a fellow Franciscan priest in New Jersey who had passed away, and Kite was to accompany him. They would talk on the way.

Father Bruce was adjusting his white collar when Kite walked into his office. Ritter looked at him, almost through him, with a mixture of disapproval and concern. It was a practiced look, one that he had used many times throughout his life with hundreds of thousands of kids he had tried to help. Ritter, not quite six feet tall, is almost completely bald, with unstylishly long sideburns and only a patch of silver hair, which falls from the back of his head just over his collar. Across his forehead run deep horizontal ridges. But there are other features that seem incongruous—the slightly upturned corners of his mischievous eyebrows, and a rounded, boyish face that can break into an impish grin. Most perplexing, perhaps even disturbing, are his liquid blue eyes—as penetrating and reflective as the edge of a stainless-steel razor.

Kite couldn't handle the eyes when he walked in, and quickly excused himself to the bathroom. He stared at himself in the mirror and wondered what in the world he was getting into. He was in the middle of a sting operation on a saint. Delicately opening the flap of the pouch, he pressed the record button and the two-hour tape began running. He closed the flap, took a deep breath, and walked out.

"Let's go, we're going to be late," Ritter said.

They took the elevator down to Ritter's gray 1990 Toyota Cressida, parked in front of the Covenant House headquarters. Ritter threw a blue canvas bag into the backseat, and the two of them hopped in the car.

They pulled out past the mostly black and Hispanic kids milling about in front of the crisis center. Kite always took notice that he was about the only white kid of some five hundred in the New York City program. A young woman with a baby carriage waved to Father Bruce. He waved back. It was beginning to rain, and he turned on the windshield wipers.

"Why are you avoiding me?" Ritter asked Kite.

Kite greeted the question with obstinate silence.

Ritter's voice rose in anger: "What's wrong, why haven't you come to see me? Tell me."

Finally, Kite broke his silence: "I don't know, I'm just not happy."

"Well, what's not making you happy? Why are you doing this to me? What's going on? You've gotta tell me, you've gotta tell me what's going on?"

"I don't know," Kite said. "Things are just bothering me."

"What things?"

"I don't know."

Then Ritter slammed the steering wheel: "Well, damn. Come on, man." He fell silent for a long while.

"I've checked at school. You haven't been there. Where are you these days? Damn. Why aren't you going to school?" Ritter asked.

There was silence except for the sound of the windshield wipers. Kite was numb with fear. He could almost feel the tape moving around the reel in his pouch.

"I've been thinking about our relationship," Kite said.

"Okay. What about it?" asked Ritter.

"The sexual part of our relationship," said Kite, mumbling the words. "I'm not comfortable with the sexual part of our relationship," he said, remembering that the detectives had told him to speak clearly.

"You know, I decided twenty years ago, if God didn't like me the way I was, that's His problem," said Ritter.

There was another silence. It seemed interminable. Kite was thinking about the tape. He was wondering if the conversation was substantive enough to prove that they had been involved in a sexual relationship. He continued just in case.

"I'm not happy. This relationship is bothering me. We've been involved for a long time. It's one of the longest relationships I've ever had," said Kevin.

"This has been one of the longest relationships I've been in also," said Ritter.

"Well, the whole thing just bothers me," Kite replied.

There was another long silence, and then Ritter changed the subject. The conversation trickled off into a discussion about the possibility of Kite's getting a job as the car turned off the highway. In a few minutes they pulled up to a side street near the church where the priest's wake was being held.

He was told to wait in the car while Father Bruce attended the vigil. They drove home in silence. The two-hour tape had already run out, so Kevin saw no point in carrying on any conversation. He asked to be dropped off at his apartment on Eighth Avenue at Forty-fourth Street.

Ritter had a disappointed look in his eye when he pulled to a stop, but Kite insisted on going home. Tired of the lies and compromises, Kite wanted to take a stand for the first time in his life. He was a bright young man but had done little in the way of accomplishments. Exposing Ritter might have been a way for Kite to distract himself from the ruin and compromise of his own life.

Kite returned to the one-bedroom apartment that Ritter had provided for him. He removed the canvas pouch and called the District Attorney's office to tell them the recording was completed. He was told to be at the office early the next morning to return the recorder and hand over the tape.

Kite popped a can of Diet Coke and lit up a Marlboro 100, and played his conversation with Ritter over in his mind. He thought about Ritter saying "If God didn't like me the way I was, that's His problem." They were powerful words. Had Ritter in some way accepted his homosexuality? The arrogance of the statement had, at first, escaped Kite. He believed it was solid confirmation for the investigators that he was telling the truth. But they were also classic Ritter: powerful, forceful, and yet intentionally vague and open to interpretation.

Early the next morning Kite walked into Fairstein's office in lower Manhattan, and handed the metallic tape recorder over to her assistant, who sent it over to another part of the D.A.'s office for processing and transcription. It was the first of two wires. Kite had quickly arrived at the point where he couldn't turn back.

Linda glanced at him over the mountain of paperwork spread across her desk. She didn't have much time, but she gave him a reassuring look.

"You've got to hang in there," she said. "You should know right now that this whole thing could get very ugly."

Chapter 3

Congratulations, America

THROUGH the December darkness, a spotlight shone down on the entrance to the main Covenant House crisis center, at the edge of a section of Manhattan once called Hell's Kitchen. The three-building complex at the corner of Forty-first Street and Tenth Avenue formed the nucleus of Ritter's sprawling charitable empire and the model on which the other Covenant House crisis centers were designed—from Houston to Toronto and New Orleans to Fort Lauderdale. Every night, the main intake center, "Under 21," sheltered more than three hundred young people ranging in age from twelve to twenty-one. Sometimes they were older, if they were in enough trouble or knew how to lie well enough to fool the intake counselors.

Inside the eight-story brick shelter, four floors housed the youths for an average stay of a few weeks. They were there for every reason imaginable—a family crisis, a drug problem, death threats in their neighborhood, the fear of being beaten to death by their parents, or perhaps an unexpected eviction that left them temporarily homeless. The kids were in crisis, most of them, and Covenant House did what it could. Few were actually reunited with their families, because most didn't have functional families. About 90 percent were minority, poor, and from the inner city. The majority were homeless or from households shattered by drug addiction or physical, sexual, and psychological abuse—the full array of destructive forces that accompany poverty and hopelessness.

There were two large first-floor reception areas—one for males, the other for females—where young people came in off the street to spend the night sleeping on couches or rubber mats for a few days until they could get a bed on one of the crowded dormitory-style floors upstairs. Those under the age of seventeen were usually taken by state officials and placed in foster care. Some were placed in specialized Covenant House programs, such as the drug-counseling unit or the group homes for teenage mothers. Others would eventually be referred to outside agencies. A cafeteria served hot meals three times daily, and there was always someone on staff to dig up something to eat at any time for a hungry kid just off the streets.

A range of social services was offered, from the Special Needs Unit for young people with the HIV virus, to classes for teenage parents about nutrition, health care, and how to find a job or an apartment. A free twenty-four-hour clinic for the multitude of health problems, ranging from exhaustion and malnutrition to knife wounds and drug overdoses, was also offered.

At the corporate offices on the eighth floor, Ritter's executive staff oversaw Covenant House's national and international operations. Ritter himself had an office there and a studio apartment. The entire building was a towering testament to Father Bruce Ritter's compassion for the young and the lost in New York City.

On this raw night in the first week of December 1989, the young street people had abandoned the summertime practice of sleeping out by the West Side piers or just hanging out till morning on the "Deuce," as they call Forty-second Street. It was below freezing. Covenant House was getting crowded. A blue Covenant House "outreach van" was cruising the streets, first around Times Square and then stopping across town to talk to a few kids in front of the Port Authority Bus Terminal. A six-foot-two staff member named Claude, whom the kids on the street called "Big Guy," was handing out ham sandwiches and paper cups of juice.

He talked briefly with the kids, not much preaching, just telling them to "take care" and "watch yourself." He told them that the doors to Covenant House were always open should they want to come in. From there, the van headed along the West Side piers, where young boys lined a concrete wall overlooking the Hudson River. Johns cruised by in Cadillacs and station wagons. The kids looked scared and glad to see the familiar blue Covenant House van. They took some sandwiches while Claude filled out a "contact sheet" on some of the regular Covenant House kids, describing briefly how they were doing and how they looked.

The van headed for "The Loop," another active area for male prostitutes, around East Fifty-third Street, and then to the meat-packing district, with transvestites shivering in miniskirts on the back-streets where they turn tricks. Then it was back up to Times Square. All night, the van crisscrossed Manhattan's seediest pockets, looking to help any young persons in crisis and hopefully persuade them to come back to Covenant House.

By the time the van circled back toward Covenant House, a dozen young people were waiting to be processed at the entrance. First greeted by a security staff, they were cleared on a computer, and then buzzed into a set of double doors that led to the warm environs of the Covenant House lounge, with its plush sectional couches, a television, potted plants, and tables covered with magazines and books. Inside, there were about twenty-five young people—most of them black and Hispanic and a near even mix of males and females. Two of the girls were pregnant and another was cradling an infant. There was a kind of buzzing sexuality to the place. With all those young teenagers under one roof, it felt as giddy and awkward as a high school dance.

Most of the twenty-five in the lounge were waiting for "intake interviews," in which a counselor logs into a computer their names, addresses, and basic information on how they wound up there. A policy of "open intake" means no kid would be turned away. For the ones who were under eighteen, a phone call would be made home, if they had one. The older ones were on their own. Complete con-fidentiality was assured. The counselors and the street kids agreed upon what the staff workers called a "covenant," which was basically a promise to respect each other and be honest. That's about all, in terms of a social contract, that bound the community. But somehow it seemed to work. The place was clean, the kids respected the en-vironment, and they seemed to care about each other.

Mohammad, who was stretched out on a couch watching television, wound up at Covenant House after he dialed the Nineline, a Cove-nant House hotline for teenagers in crisis, which he had seen adver-tised on a billboard. That week, he had been staying on the floor at Under 21. Mohammad, 19, left his home in Newark, where, he said, his mother was addicted to crack. He ended up in New York City and said the hotline was the only number he could think to dial. He claims he was contemplating suicide before he made the call and a blue Covenant House van picked him up and brought him to the shelter. Thin, with a long single braid of hair that fell down his back, Mohammad wore a down jacket that had been given to him by one of the counselors from the roomfuls of donated clothes they keep at Covenant House. He was hoping to be moved within the next few days to one of the rooms on the upstairs floors.

Eventually, he said, he wanted to get a job and an apartment. But for now he was just thankful for the chance Covenant House had given him to get off the streets.

"It saved my life, man," he said. "I mean I was thinking about taking the elevator up the Empire State Building. I was ready to push the button, but you know you can get by with help. I'm getting by."

Outside there was a lot of loud noise, and some of the youths were pressing their noses against the glass doors to get a look at a teenager named Ronnie, who was drunk and fighting with the security guards at the entrance.

"Yo, man, let me the fuck in," Ronnie said to several stocky men in blue blazers who were surrounding him near the entrance guardhouse. Some of them were off-duty police officers and armed with handguns. They held their hands near bulges in their jackets, a subtle gesture that's well understood on the streets.

Ronnie's name came up on the computer as having had his "card pulled," which in Covenant House counselors' jargon meant he had already been involved in more than three violent disturbances at the facility. Ronnie had broken his part of the covenant, and that's where the open-intake philosophy ends. Even with a "pulled card," some counselors intervene, giving some kids fourth and fifth chances at staying in the program.

"Fuck the card, let me in. Too cold," said Ronnie, walking straight past the guards toward the door, where they stopped him and pointed him back toward the darkness, beyond the spotlight at the entrance to Covenant House. It always bothered Ritter that he never knew what was going to happen to the kids who got turned away. He insisted on open intake, but it didn't always work. Ronnie walked away, yelling at the guards, and disappeared around the corner.

Felipe, twenty, who grew up in the Bronx, had spent three years at an upstate correctional facility; he had been convicted on a robbery charge. When he was released, he had nowhere to go and ended up at Covenant House. For the last few months, he'd been living on one of the residential floors in the Under 21 program. Sometimes the floors were dangerous, with too few staff members and scores of often violent young kids thrown together. Always overcrowded, the shelter normally had up to triple the city-recommended capacity of 110 youths a night. There were organized gangs in the shelter and some teenage drug dealers peddled their wares inside the building. The word on the street was that Covenant House was a dangerous shelter—a place to watch your back. But for the most part, the kids agreed that a clean bed, a warm room, and a roof overhead was at times a better alternative than the streets.

"I realized I was heading in the wrong direction," said Felipe. "I had heard of Covenant House. I came to the place with no direction except knowing I wanted a change in life."

After weeks of an intense job search and work with his counselors, Felipe landed a full-time carpenters' job and was about to move to his own apartment.

"I am amazed at the difference I see in myself," he said. "Without Covenant House, I wouldn't have had the chance."

There were others who were long-time residents of the program, like Lawrece. Raised in Queens, Lawrece saw her home broken up by the state's social services after her mother had a nervous breakdown. She ended up being bounced around between foster homes until she got pregnant at the age of seventeen. She dropped out of high school and came to Covenant House with her son in her arms and nowhere else to go. For a year and a half she lived in Covenant House's mother-and-child program. In the fall she had been accepted by Rights of Passage, a long-term residential program in which young men and women are given a chance to complete high school, find a job, or even enroll in college courses. If Lawrece, nineteen, stayed on track, she'd get her Graduate Equivalency Diploma for high school by the end of that year, and she was hoping to go on to take college courses.

"This building carries within it unconditional love and hope," she said. "The kind that rubs on and never rubs off of you when you leave."

This was the day-to-day reality of Covenant House, where young lives were being saved and sometimes lost. It was this kind of heroic work that was threatened as Kevin Kite moved forward with his allegation against the charity's founder. The Mohammads and Felipes and Lawreces were the people who stood to lose as the scandal that Kite ignited threatened to engulf the charity.

By the late 1980s, Ritter had little to do with the day-to-day functioning of Covenant House—he mostly traveled on a national fundraising circuit that paid the bills and kept the charity functioning at its different centers worldwide. Ritter counseled only what he called "high-risk" cases—like Kevin Kite. But many of the kids in the crisis center did not even know who Ritter was. By 1989, the charity had become much bigger than its founder. But it was still so closely associated with Father Bruce that the bad publicity threatened to destroy everything he had built over twenty years—or at least that's the way he and his loyal staff saw it.

On December 12, 1989, the headline in the *New York Post* exploded on the newsstands: TIMES SQUARE PRIEST PROBED. FORMER MALE PROSTITUTE CITES 'GIFTS.'

The story blew the roof off Covenant House and detailed the Manhattan District Attorney's investigation of Ritter and the use of Kite, or "Warner," as he was still calling himself, as the star witness. With just one newspaper story, the entire charity's future was suddenly in question—hit with a roaring scandal at the height of the Christmas fund drive. From that point on, Linda Fairstein's warning to Kite came true. The story had indeed gotten "very ugly."

At first Ritter adamantly denied the charges. The story twisted and turned for two months, with more and more allegations of impropriety surfacing at Covenant House. Then everything began to unravel in early February as Ritter's own Franciscan Order also moved to investigate a series of allegations of sexual misconduct against Ritter that stretched over many years.

On February 6, 1990, just past midnight, Ritter put on his black peacoat and a black skullcap and headed out to get copies of the early editions of the morning's papers. He knew that the allegations against him were mounting—that more young male accusers had come forward with new allegations—and that to continue running the charity was becoming impossible.

Out the doors of Covenant House and due east on Forty-first Street, Ritter walked past the entrance to the Lincoln Tunnel and the old men camped out near the heating vents in the back of the Port Authority Bus Terminal. He kept his head down and his collar up against the cold as he walked past the neon marquees for movies rated XXX, with names like *Rough Stuff* and *Nasty Boys,* past the peep shows and prostitutes arguing with pimps over fistfuls of dollars, past a man dressed in pink hot pants and a short fur coat. In a second-floor window on the corner of Forty-first Street and Eighth Avenue, a blinking red neon sign flashed the words JESUS KNOWS through the smog of traffic.

Ritter pushed open the doors to the bus terminal. In the entrance-way, a dozen young kids stood close to a rusted heating duct. Young studs swaggered and preened in tight jeans, cowboy boots, short leather jackets, and expensive air-pump sneakers. One of them, wearing a black hooded sweatshirt, was peddling crack at $10 a vial; others were offering to sell their bodies for a few dollars more.

In a litter-strewn stairwell off to the side, a young boy wearing a wig was crouched in a corner. He was either sleeping or strung out. The kids looked dirty, tired. The neon wilderness of "Forty Deuce" was a cold blur outside. They ignored the smell of urine, the bus fumes, the cops with nightsticks telling them to move on. On this forbidding February night in New York City, the Port Authority Bus Terminal was what they called home. Most of these kids had been in and out of Covenant House for months, some were out on "cards," some couldn't abide the curfew and make a living, and a few either hadn't yet found Covenant House or didn't care to. These were the kids whose life stories hadn't been turned around, and probably never would be.

Ritter kept on walking past them, and past the drug dealers working pay phones, past the steel-shuttered shops in the terminal, past the glassed-in gallery dubbed "the fish bowl," where chickenhawks meet young boys and desperate deals go down at night.

Ritter just walked on, silent and brooding, toward the newsstand. Stacks of the early editions of the tabloids screamed more scandal. NEW RITTER BOMBSHELLS, proclaimed the *New York Post.* Even *The New York Times,* cloaked in its own cautious idioms, heralded the scandal on the top left-hand corner of its front page: SEX CHARGES ERODE IMAGE OF COVENANT HOUSE.

By the next morning, it had become painfully clear that it was all over for Father Bruce. He would have to announce his temporary resignation—a precipitous fall from grace for an American icon. Although Ritter would try to hang on to power for three confusing weeks, in which more allegations of sexual misconduct and financial wrongdoing would boil to the surface, he would never return to the organization he had founded.

And as he walked slowly with the newspapers under his arm through the Port Authority, Stan Ford, his bodyguard and confidant, walked about ten yards behind him. Ford had followed Ritter to make sure he was okay. He was worried about him in light of the scandal. They didn't talk; Ford kept his eye on his boss. Ford walked with a slight limp. His leg had been injured in a 1965 search-and-destroy mission in Vietnam. He came home to Newark and riots and eventually worked for the police department. But he met Ritter in the late 1970s, and Ritter made him the head of security. Ford carried an intense, almost military loyalty to Ritter. And he, like just about everyone on the staff, was struggling to figure out how all this had happened.

Ford likes to say that his "position to Bruce was like Ollie North to Reagan," and he talks about Ritter's "intestinal fortitude" and often ends his sentences with phrases like "I'd go over any hill for that man."

That night, as Ritter was meeting the sad trajectory of his fate, Ford grew furious when he caught a few of the drug dealers and hustlers laughing at the fallen priest.

"You sons of bitches," Ford muttered to himself as he glared at the hustlers and their customers: sleazy men who hovered nervously around the hallways of the Port Authority. Those men used to fear Bruce Ritter, Ford thought. Father Bruce was often the only thing that stood between the kids and the temptations of the streets, the quick money, the drugs, the prostitution.

Later, Ritter tried to tell Ford that he was only stepping down temporarily while they did the investigation. But Ford knew that when they tell a man to step down they rarely tell him to step back up.

"I don't think we'll ever see another man like him. If I had it to do all over again, I'd follow the man straight into hell," said Ford afterward. "America has lost something. I wish I could take his pain for him. Well, we destroyed another one. Congratulations, America."

II

The Tree of Knowledge

You may eat indeed of all the trees in the garden. Nevertheless of the tree of the knowledge of good and evil you are not to eat, for on the day you eat of it you shall most surely die.

The Jerusalem Bible, Genesis 2:17

II

The Tree of Knowledge

Chapter 4

The Cloth

WHEN he came into the world, America was in the midst of a booming but unpredictable economy that would soon collapse into the Great Depression. Born February 25, 1927, in Hamilton Township, New Jersey, he was baptized with the name John Ritter. Throughout his childhood, family and friends called him "Jack." Only after taking his vows as a Franciscan priest did he adopt the name "Bruce."

Hamilton was a dusty farming community on the outskirts of Trenton, where most of the townspeople worked in the factories or on the outlying dairy and vegetable farms that fed its populace. The Trenton-Morrisville bridge, which spans the Delaware River, featured a motto in block letters fashioned from sheet metal: TRENTON MAKES. THE WORLD TAKES.

His father, Louis Charles Ritter, was a general supervisor of the Trenton Potteries, one of dozens in the area that used the abundant supply of clay from the banks of the Delaware River.

Ritter was four years old when his father died after suffering an illness that neighbors remember as a brain tumor. That left Julia Agnes Morrissey Ritter to be "both mother and father" to a family of five at the height of the Depression. Ritter was the middle child, with two brothers and two sisters. They were raised in a small four-room house at 34 Wesley Avenue, where the tracks for the old Johnson Trolley Line wound past, and where they could hear the clanging of the trains on their way to New Brunswick. A wooden fence in the backyard marked the boundaries of home. Past the fence there were chicken coops and a melon patch.

His mother was meticulous in everything, especially her planting and gardening. The neat line of four pine trees that she planted as seedlings are now thirty-five feet tall and still give shade and shelter to the southern exposure of the small wood-frame home. From the front porch, across a patchwork of vegetable gardens and small wooden bungalows that stretched acre after acre, just barely visible was the spire of Saint Anthony's Catholic Church, where his mother played the organ and the priest-to-be and his brothers and sisters attended service.

Mrs. Ritter had only a $45-a-month widow's pension. But she was an accomplished seamstress and made extra money doing piecework for Manhattan's garment district. The whirring of her White sewing machine and the pumping of the treadle were familiar sounds in the neighborhood. She was able to scrape together enough money through the piecework and her pension to keep her children well groomed and well fed.

The kids also took on jobs to help pay for the groceries. Young Jack worked on the nearby farms, painted houses, and helped at a bakery across the street. A thin boy with a crop of dirty blond hair that stood up in a cowlick, he had an all-American smile. But he is remembered as quiet and a little bit removed.

As an adolescent, Ritter sometimes suffered from a deep brooding spirit. In later years, he would often tell his colleagues that he identified with the awkward and fragile street youths he cared for. He would make veiled references to how he "understood their pain," but he would never expound on it.

At five foot two and about ninety pounds, Mrs. Ritter wore round spectacles and arranged her hair neatly in a bun. But what neighbors remember most was a long switch she fastened to her apron strings. It was rarely used in public, but perhaps the reminder of the stick dangling from that apron was all she needed to keep her kids in line.

"She raised us on good old-fashioned Irish Catholic guilt," Ritter remembered. "If everyone in the world turned against the Church, my mother would remain the last Roman Catholic. The area we lived in was hit hard by poverty, but the families, schools, and neighborhood stayed united and strong. Such is not the case today."

"Mrs. Ritter was a very strong, determined character. She had a lot of iron in her, that's for sure. Ritter himself had the same iron, there was no doubt about that. He had a lot of his mother in him," said James Fitzgibbons, who has known Ritter almost all of his life.

Their paths have intertwined at key points for more than a half century. They grew up only a few miles from each other; they studied together in seminary, did their doctoral studies in Rome, and were ordained the same day.

"For Mrs. Ritter, sex was the big sin. Some of that was the times, but she was certainly very strict about it," said Fitzgibbons, remembering when he and Ritter were in seminary together in the 1950s and Ritter came home with a copy of *Catcher in the Rye* under his arm. She stopped her son and asked him, "How in the world can you read that book? It has swear words and sex in it."

"Ritter tried to talk with her about it, but she was not to be swayed," said Fitzgibbons.

Ritter was very close to an aunt named Elizabeth, who used to make large pots of soup and beef stew for poor families struggling through the Depression. Fitzgibbons said that Ritter learned a great deal about compassion for the poor from her and that he frequently mentioned her in his work.

He attended public schools, the Kuser School in Trenton and Hamilton High School, where he graduated in 1945. He worked as a freight-car loader through high school and for the first part of the summer after he graduated. Then he volunteered for the United States Navy in the closing months of the war and ended up assigned to a base in Mississippi.

In the Navy, most young sailors were "looking for a good time." They couldn't wait to get passes for leave. Their talk was of dames and booze and big bands. But not Ritter. He was beginning to navigate his faith, to explore spirituality. He began to read a lot, checking out books on Saint Thomas Aquinas and Saint Francis of Assisi from the base library. The other sailors had Betty Grable movie stills, but he had Aquinas. He was at home in the dusty smell of the leather-bound volumes, pondering the historical weight of these great theologians.

Discharged from the Navy in July 1946, Ritter went back to New Jersey and back to his old job loading freight cars for a year. The work was hard, dirty, and loud. For a poor kid raised in the Depression, the pay wasn't bad. But Bruce knew he could do better. He was deepening his understanding of faith, continuing to read the works of the Catholic saints and searching for a spiritual life. Ritter thought through the call to the priesthood, which became persistent and finally undeniable.

His brothers and sisters were surprised. They had had no idea their brother Jack had "the calling." His mother was thrilled. Her Jack was going to be a priest.

In postwar America, the priesthood was an honored vocation for young men from poor backgrounds who showed intellectual promise or who wanted to display their "God-given qualities for leadership." This was the golden age of the immigrant Church in America. It was thriving and vibrant. The young men drawn to the seminary were among the best and the brightest of their high school classes. The slightly older ones were often decorated veterans of the war. These were all-American boys from working-class families of first- and second-generation Irish and Italian and Polish immigrants. They were the sons of cops and construction workers, of shoe salesmen and dock workers. They loved Benny Goodman and Joe DiMaggio, Broadway shows and Bing Crosby. They thought of themselves as cut from the same cloth as Spencer Tracy and Humphrey Bogart. They were tough when they needed to be, but still on their way to "the vocation," as it was called, which was greeted at every corner in every hometown with approval and respect. Ritter wanted to be a part of this consecrated American dream.

In early 1947, he applied to the Order of Friars Minor Conventual and was accepted by the Saint Francis Seminary on Staten Island in New York City, beginning in the fall of 1948.

Ritter loved Saint Francis, probably the most popular saint of the Roman Catholic Church. Saint Francis's romantic story spoke of sacrifice and commitment. Born the son of a wealthy cloth merchant in the Italian town of Assisi in the thirteenth century, Francis was an average young man until he heard the words of Christ telling him to leave all of his possessions and follow Him in a life of poverty.

The Franciscans embraced the deep but pragmatic spirituality that Ritter sought. Of all the orders, the Franciscans have the most freedom from spiritual restraint, from systems and routine. Their uncompromising belief is tempered by a kind of joyous madness in throwing away everything to walk around penniless in sandals. They maintain absolute confidence that if they ever get into trouble God will be there to get them through. They're risk takers, rebels fiercely independent, and uncompromising. So was Ritter.

He joined the Order of the Friars Minor Conventual—one of three distinct branches of the Franciscans, each one having a different interpretation of the vow of poverty. Ritter's choice was more lax in its interpretation.

At Saint Francis on Staten Island, Ritter quickly showed promise as a student. Seminaries like this one and hundreds of others throughout the country were brimming with a bumper crop of eager young men. They were on the ball, clean, sharp, and rugged. And among this gifted clan, the young postulant from New Jersey shone above his peers.

The seminarians lived by The Rule, a set of centuries-old doctrines that governed their studies and their daily schedule. It was strict but nowhere near the ascetic routines of the contemplative orders, such as the Trappists and the Benedictines. They lugged around weighty volumes of thirteenth-century scholastic philosophers like Bonaventure and Scotus. But of all the books they studied, Saint Thomas Aquinas's *Summa Theologiae* was the central text for every seminarian. The young men feverishly memorized Saint Thomas's Five Proofs of the Existence of God, and later regurgitated them in exams.

In the language of Thomist medieval scholasticism, there were *quaestiones,* or questions, which were posited and then followed by *responsiones,* or logical answers to the questions, all of which confirmed the thesis presented in the *disputationes.* A wonderfully comforting system of logic, Saint Thomas's *Summa Theologiae* became the spiritual atlas for a generation convinced it knew exactly where it was going.

In an era when most of their contemporaries were buying prefab homes, Sears appliances, big Buicks, and other baby-boom accessories, they wanted to be the soul of America, not just its consumers.

But as much as he was born and bred to fit this mold, Ritter was beginning to realize he was different. He felt apart from it all and not sure why. He liked to ask questions that had no answers. He sometimes got annoyed with all the good-natured jocularity and the conformity and rules that came with seminary life.

One fall afternoon, in his first year at seminary, while Ritter was absorbed in his reading, one of his superiors marched through the corridors, demanding that all friars immediately report to the study hall and remain there until further notice. He and the other first-year friars wondered what was happening. The word came back from the older seminarians who'd been through the exercise before. Two young men, who had been discovered committing "unnatural acts" in a back room, were being removed from the seminary. The students were kept in the study hall while the young men's bags were quickly and quietly packed. They were promptly shown the gates of the seminary and told never to return. The seminarians saw their fallen brethren from the window of the study hall as they walked through its gates. They might as well have been walking into hell—like the frightening images of cowering Christians in a Bosch painting.

The message was clear to the young seminarians that, as one of Ritter's classmates put it, "Any kind of sexual acting out meant you were zapped practically on the spot."

"In those days, everybody kept their sexuality tightly under wraps," remembers Fitzgibbons. "It was like being in the Marines. You were training for celibacy and giving up sexuality."

Although Ritter was somewhat older, most of the young men were suffering through the preparation for the vow at the age of eighteen or nineteen, referred to in their biology textbooks as "active hormonal years." There was a pervasive homophobia that creaked through the corridors of Saint Francis and every other seminary in the country. The young men were constantly on guard, policing every relationship with faculty and fellow seminarians. They developed a sexual sonar that gauged any emotion, any hint of intimacy that they felt for or from the other men with whom they lived and worked. It was a psychological struggle that few discussed, but that often became a form of insidious torment. It kept a kind of permanent distance between the seminarians and encouraged a deep void that prevented them from ever becoming too close to anyone. Eunuchs for the kingdom of God is what Saint Paul called them. But the vow of celibacy was not all that was emasculating about seminary life. The orders practiced a blanket obedience to the hierarchy of the Church and the order. This, above all, was The Rule. Within the patriarchy, individual success was frowned upon. The seminarians were expected to understand their rank. To question was natural, but to challenge unacceptable. To do well in studies was admirable, but arrogance with success was unforgivable. There was a fine line between humility and insecurity, between strong faith and false piety. And the would-be priests were expected to know precisely where that line was drawn.

Frustrated by the holy mediocrity this system perpetuated, Ritter seemed consumed by a desire for success, especially his own. He was the leader of his class, the most intelligent, the most spiritual, the prefect in his dormitory, the editor of a school magazine called *The Troubadour*. Despite his frustration with the hierarchy, there must have been a side of Ritter that admired or at least aspired to it, for he eagerly enforced The Rule with his fellow friars. For example, he proclaimed himself the head of the clean-up detail at the dormitory and in the dining hall. He would assign his fellow seminarians

tasks, like sweeping, mopping, washing windows, cleaning bath-
rooms, and emptying trash.

Ritter was also developing a reputation as the "power broker" for
any fellow seminarians who wanted something from their superiors.
If they needed day passes to see friends or family, or special permission to go to the city to see a play or visit a museum, they went
to Ritter. His political agility with the higher-ups gained him respect
and popularity among his classmates. Knowing how to manipulate
power was a skill that he would hone over the years.

Despite his more shrewd qualities, he was also regarded as deeply
spiritual, known for going into contemplative meditations well past
10 P.M., the mandatory time for lights out in the dormitory.

During his first two years at Saint Francis, Ritter went through an
intellectual exploration of a more dynamic movement within the
Church. He developed an interest in the teachings of Thomas Merton. The popular, modern spiritual writer was gaining attention at
the time, and his best-selling autobiography, *The Seven Storey Mountain*
(1948), was a breakthrough at a time of crippling conformity. Merton
was the Holden Caulfield of Catholicism, asking awkward and puzzling questions about his own journey of faith that ultimately led him
to become a Trappist monk.

Merton had a profound impact on Ritter, offering a depth of
reflection that wasn't in the core courses on theology and history. He
was alive, questioning his belief, questioning his motivations, explor-
ing the inner conflict of doubt and faith. Like Merton, questions
ultimately served to confirm his faith.

Merton's essay "War and the Prayer for Peace" is a classic example
of his modern, self-effacing theology:

> It is not only hatred of others that is dangerous but also and
> above all our hatred of ourselves: particularly that hatred of our-
> selves which is too deep and too powerful to be consciously faced.
> For it is this which makes us see our own evil in others and unable
> to see it in ourselves.
>
> When we see crime in others, we try to correct it by destroying
> them or at least putting them out of sight. It is easy to identify the
> sin with the sinner when he is someone other than our own self.
> In ourselves, it is the other way round; we see the sin, but we have
> great difficulty in shouldering responsibility for it. We find it very
> hard to identify our sin with our own will and our own malice. . . .
>
> We must try to accept ourselves, whether individually or collec-
> tively, not only as perfectly good or perfectly bad, but in our mys-

terious, unaccountable mixture of good and evil. We have to stand
by the modicum of good that is in us without exaggerating it.

Ritter's interest in Merton led him to what he called a "brief foray
into the monastic life." He dropped out of Saint Francis in 1949,
during the spring semester of his second year, to join the same Trappist abbey in Gethsemane, Kentucky, where Merton lived. In fact,
Merton had originally been a Franciscan, and perhaps Ritter related
to the writer's frustration with the order.

Through his writings, Merton made the Trappist monastery something of a religious fad, attracting thousands of postulants. He entered the monastery in 1941 and was ordained the same year that
Ritter arrived.

The abbey, located deep in the heart of Kentucky, adhered strictly
to the ancient traditions of the Cistercian Order, or Trappists, as they
are commonly called. Founded in the eleventh century, its monks
are known for living in deep seclusion under the principle of strict
observance. They emphasize manual labor as an important part of
the daily round of work and prayer.

Ritter lasted only about three months. When he returned to Staten
Island, his Franciscan superiors expressed concern about his commitment to the Franciscan order.

They saw it as self-indulgent that he went off to Merton's monastery, and Ritter himself later admitted it was "a mistake." His superiors even questioned whether he was right for the vocation of the
priesthood. Finally, after much discussion, prayer, and humility, he
was permitted to return to Saint Francis to finish his last semester.

After returning to Saint Francis, Ritter was more involved with his
classmates, more friendly, but still fiercely competitive. With his muscles toned from working on the Abbey's farm, he would challenge
his fellow friars to arm wrestle.

He'd clear off a long wooden table in the kitchen after dinner, roll
up his sleeve, and wait for anyone to challenge him. No one could
last more than a few minutes before his arm would buckle and fall
back against the table.

Ritter also exhibited exceptional mental strength and a remarkable
ability to read people. Just before they graduated, he made a hu-
morous exhibition of his powers of intuition during a carnival the
seminarians held to raise money on behalf of the poor. It was an
elaborate event, which the students took seriously. The competition
was fierce to come up with the best carnival act. Ritter topped the
list with his infamous "swami routine." Using a towel wrapped around

his head and tied like a turban and a shiny blue curtain as a cape, Ritter transformed himself into a mind-reader.

"It was strange. He really took on the character," remembers Fitzgibbons. "Everybody was amazed at how much he knew about them. He could read you. . . . I think it was that he was so intuitive."

Ritter was also an avid reader, with a passion for a literary genre that seemed, on the surface, incongruous with his scholarly pursuit of medieval dogma: American Westerns. He loved dime-store novels about the wild West, and he loved the Hollywood heroes who rode in from the sunset to save the day. During the summer, the seminarians would travel up to the Adirondack Mountains to a campground on Raquette Lake. Away from the excruciating study of systematic theology and the memorization of Latin declensions, the young men would take to canoes, hike the nearby trails, and swim the lake. Ritter, however, would keep to himself, preferring to retire to his bunk and burn through a stack of paperbacks in the cool shade of the wooden cottages where they stayed.

One of his favorite books was *Shane,* the best-seller by Jack Shaefer. He read it several times before the classic George Stevens Hollywood production was released. Shane was a simple metaphor: the good guys in white hats and the bad guys in black.

Being inveterate nicknamers, his fellow seminarians dubbed Ritter "Shane," or sometimes "Tex." The monikers stuck with him, but Ritter and his schoolmates eventually had to shed their nicknames and come up with their own religious names, which they would carry with them as long as they remained priests. It was a famous Franciscan tradition to choose the name of a Holy Roman emperor, a saint, or a classical Latin poet—names like Maximilian, Juniper, and Seraphin—which they would then assume as their own upon beginning their novitiate in the order. The young friars would spend weeks choosing. The formal Latin name that Ritter selected was "Brutus," the name from which he derived the English variation, "Bruce."

Ritter's choice was unique. Even his fellow Franciscans thought it a little strange that a friar would pick a name that conjured up such a controversial and complicated hero in ancient history.

By the fall of 1950, young Brother Bruce Ritter moved on from Saint Francis Seminary to begin his one-year novitiate at Our Lady Queen of Peace in Middleburg, New York. For the first time Ritter was wearing the black robes of the Order Minor Conventual, but without the thick white sash that signifies an ordained friar. He would still have to wait several years for that.

The religious life in Middleburg was ordered, with the seminarians

rising every day at 5:30 A.M. to spend two hours in chapel, followed
by meditation and the recitation of the divine office in Latin. When
the seminarians weren't praying, they were working on a farm or
renovating the former nursing home that had been purchased by
the Church as a seminary.

From Middleburg, he went on to Assumption Seminary in Chaska,
Minnesota, to study theology and received his B.A. after two years.
He did well in his classes at Assumption and was continuing to develop
confidence in his intellectual abilities. In fact, he was given a position
as a professor's assistant in the philosophy department. He was also
the leader of his study group. But he did not suffer fools gladly. In
fact, he could be impatient and arrogant with fellow students who
didn't understand, say, the Thomist interpretation of the Aristotelian
system of epistemology.

One afternoon after Ritter had been boasting of his accomplishments on a final paper, one of his superiors, Father Robert Bayer,
walked into the dining hall and jokingly reprimanded Brother Bruce
before his fellow seminarians.

"We are all unprofitable servants of God, Brother. You should not
forget that," said Bayer.

After Minnesota, Ritter began his graduate study of theology at
Saint Anthony-on-Hudson Seminary in Rensselaer, New York. But
he was there only briefly. In 1953 Ritter was accepted to a five-year
doctorate program at the Franciscan Pontifical Faculty of Saint Bonaventure in Rome.

The Eternal City was a long way from his sleepy hometown in New
Jersey. Saint Bonaventure was an exciting community of some eighty
Franciscan friars from Italy, Holland, Japan, Britain, Germany,
Spain, the United States, and other countries. The doctoral students
would have lengthy intellectual discussions on theology, morality, and
politics—heady days for a guy from a dusty blue-collar town. He was
in his late twenties, a little bit older and, he felt, a lot wiser than his
fellow students. Assuming the role of the captain among the friars,
Ritter was sometimes surly but always intellectual. He commanded
respect.

Despite Saint Francis's romantic lessons about living in poverty, he
was not thrilled by the poor physical conditions at the seminary. The
building's faded, cracked red-clay façade looked out on Via San Teo-
doro in the middle of a working-class neighborhood. The narrow,
cobblestone street cut along the back wall of the Roman Forum. The
building was as drafty and dirty as an "old car barn" with wide,

Roman-arched hallways that needed paint, and an orange-tiled floor that was cracked and buckled. The seventy seminarians shared one shower. The boiler broke down regularly on cold nights in the winter, and the friars would suffer chilblain, a malady due to overexposure, which made the skin on their hands raw and swollen. Ritter would try to type his papers with hands cracked and blistered. He'd end up furious about the lack of heat. He'd pound his desk and then pace the hallways to warm up: "This is the twentieth century. My God, how do they live like this?"

Most of the students shared quarters, with more than a dozen sleeping on bunk beds in a single room. But he found a small room of his own on the first floor. It was being used as a storage closet. Ritter cleaned it out and made it his own place. The window faced a courtyard with rows of palmetto trees and trimmed hedges and crushed-stone walkways that intersected to form a cross.

For about a month, he enjoyed the solitude. Then Father Giorgio Eldarov, a general curiat of the order, arrived. The young Bulgarian scholar would eventually become a kind of mentor to the young American students, especially Ritter. But his first lesson was about pulling rank, which he illustrated by immediately kicking the young friar out of the private room.

Eldarov remembered that Ritter "was quite respectful" about it, but "didn't like the idea." He had a way of curling his lip and raising his eyebrow to show his disapproval. And nothing could draw a "Bruce snarl" like the *passagio*, a traditional two-hour walk the seminarians were forced to take every day after the main meal.

There were strict orders to walk in groups of no fewer than three. Everything in the priesthood was done in groups of no fewer than three because, as their superiors professed, to walk alone could cause someone to become depressed or self-absorbed, or, even more dangerous, an individual. To walk in twos was out of the question for the obvious reason that any kind of "particular" friendship could raise too many eyebrows. So it was always at least three seminarians, dressed in their black habits and wide-brimmed hats, tripping along the narrow side streets toward an endless meandering of cathedrals, museums, ancient ruins, and famous monuments. On Sundays, they would take longer day trips along the pilgrimage road from Assisi to Rome, where Saint Francis first lived among the poor, and to the section of caves where Saint Francis is said to have written the Franciscan Rule. For the first few months, the walks were informative, but day after day of mandatory walks began to wear on Ritter.

"This makes absolutely no sense. It is a complete waste of time,"

Brother Bruce would mutter as the superior opened the seminary gate to see the young friars off.

After the first year, the friars got to learn the ropes and would occasionally take a detour from their walks into a favorite bar called the Austrian Café. On hot days, over cold steins of beer and Wiener schnitzel, they'd discuss philosophy and politics, literature and theater. Ritter was a forceful and knowledgeable student, well respected by his peers. He would hold back from conversations and wait for just the right moment to make his points. Then he would make them dramatically and with finality, often destroying his colleagues' arguments with fiery condescension. It was the intellectual equivalent of arm wrestling, and once again he was out to prove that he was the champion.

He had also elevated his skill as the "power broker" to an art, graduating from obtaining simple weekend passes for his fellow friars to drafting official letters for them to the provincial of the order requesting special assignments in foreign countries or continued study. His Italian was not very accomplished, yet he could still go in to the generals of the order and get what he wanted.

"He was always the wise man, the one people went to for advice. It was an intuitive ability of communication," said Eldarov. "They knew Bruce was a force to reckon with, and he usually got what he wanted. . . . He was constantly seeing how far he could bend the rules."

And there were plenty of rules. The Church was still in the dark, stultifying days before the modernization ushered in by the Second Vatican Council. The seminary gates were actually padlocked at 8 P.M., so that anyone who wanted to enter or leave had to make a formal request to the Curia General, who held the keys.

There was a vow of obedience to God and their superiors. But, of course, there were ways to get around the rules without breaking any vows. There were several assistants to the Curia General, or headmaster of the seminary. And Bruce's strategy was to target the ones with weaknesses, or warm up to the ones with good hearts. He would find loopholes or sometimes he would play two associates off each other to get what he wanted. His key connection at the top was Father Sebastian Weber, who was responsible for any special requests made by the American friars. And as Eldarov put it, "Ritter knew how to work this man beautifully.

"Bruce would travel and do whatever he wanted. I was amazed to see him one time in Germany. . . . He was staying at a military base," said Eldarov. "He was supposed to be in a seminary in Wiesbaden and instead he stayed with friends. It shocked me at the time. I mean that was just not done. Even priests were rarely allowed to do that."

This pattern in Ritter's behavior was the beginning of a life of what Eldarov refers to as "false conscience," a concept that the friars studied closely in a course on moral theology. Ritter was passionate in the class during debates on ethics and morality. Eldarov remembers great intellectual arguments between Ritter and his fellow classmates, especially on situational morality. Moral theologian Alturio Iorio's five-volume series on morality and conscience provided the bulk of the reading for the course and the framework for study. Eldarov remembers Iorio's description of "false conscience" and thinking how it applied to the young Ritter.

"It is a complicated theme, but it essentially boils down to a rationalization, convincing oneself that what you are doing is not wrong or immoral when in fact it may be," said Eldarov.

The friars also learned practical skills necessary in the day-to-day life of a priest: how to prepare a homily, how to say mass, how to take confession. They studied the simple and well-laid-out laws governing relationships with parishioners and the vow of celibacy. There were warnings about sexual temptation and how to avoid the inflated sense of ego that can come when parishioners want to deify their parish priests. They were told never to show too much special consideration to one parishioner, man or woman, because it could create the appearance of impropriety.

"Clean as a hound's tooth. You must be clean as a hound's tooth," said one priest over and over again. He would use the same phrase whether he was directing the choir or instructing the friars on the vow of celibacy. "Priests are held to an often inhuman standard. Of course, we are human. But we must understand that our profession is sacred, we are to carry the word of the Lord. Therefore people will expect you to act accordingly. You will be judged instantly for the slightest appearances. Remember that. You must be clean as a hound's tooth."

By the end of the spring semester of 1956, Ritter's preparation for his ordination as a priest was completed. On July 8 of that year at San Apostale Church, he stood among some two hundred other seminarians in the wide marbled nave to celebrate the rite of ordination. His mother and aunt made the long trip from New Jersey to Rome to see "Jack" make his solemn vows to the priesthood. They sat in the mahogany pews marveling at the baroque splendor of the basilica. Frankincense, the smell of Catholicism's ancient traditions, floated through the thick, stale air, which seemed as old as the stones of its foundation. In his pure white vestments, Ritter looked proud, his head held high in reverence and pomp.

Bishop Hector Cunial presented each seminarian with a silver chalice with which to perform the most holy act of the Catholic faith, the Eucharist: the transubstantiation of bread and wine into the body and blood of Christ. Beautifuly enunciated Latin verses echoed among the high arches of the church as the bishop instructed the seminarians in their solemn obligation to perform the Eucharist and the mass properly and respectfully, to uphold the word of the Lord, and to be His faithful messengers of the word.

Ritter bowed his head and turned his palms toward the bishop to be anointed with oil for the "manatergium." The ceremony is a symbolic purification of the ordained priest's hands, which were now responsible for performing the holy sacraments. After the ceremony, Ritter walked slowly in line with the other priests to a table at the side of the altar and washed the oil from his palms with water and lemon. He then waited as the bishop wrapped his hands in a linen cloth.

Following the ordination, the priests joined in saying their first mass. Ritter knelt before the altar's intricately carved marble-and-gilt columns. The eighteenth-century fresco above the altar illustrated with dramatic lighting and swirling rich colors the "glorious martyrdom of Saint Philip." But if he had looked straight up in the center of the dome, high above the altar, there was a more frightening biblical image: "The Blessed and the Fallen image," which depicted the tumultuous and tragic surrender of figures falling into hell while the holy and divine float into heaven.

The figures floating into heaven, oil paintings on the ceiling that seemed to have faded, are harder to see. But "the fallen" are relief sculptures that lurch out of the fresco, their twisted and pained expressions frozen in frightful stares down on the church.

After the ceremony, Ritter folded the manatergium cloth under his arm and gave it to his mother, as is the tradition.

He was now Father Bruce Ritter, O.M.C. (Order Minor Conventual). And his scholarship at the Pontifical Faculty of Saint Bonaventure would become more focused on his doctoral work. He and most of his colleagues moved to slightly better quarters at La Vigna, near the Baths of Caracalla. The newly ordained priests would spend long hours researching and writing their dissertations and preparing for the oral defense of their theses in Latin.

It was during these years that Eldarov and Ritter became close. Eldarov was his dissertation adviser. In the preface of the 202-page work he offered a "special word of gratitude" to Eldarov for his "Job-like patience and unstinting assistance."

Titled "The Primacy and the Council of Florence," it focused on the history of the schism between Eastern and Western Christendom, beginning in the eleventh century. He explored the fifteenth-century Council of Florence, which failed to bring the unity of the Western Church based in Rome and the Eastern Church based on the Greek tradition. Ritter explained the fundamental differences over the *"filioque"*—a significant phrase concerning the relation between the "Father and the Son"—in primarily psychological terms. Ritter also theorized that the "problems of the Council of Florence will be the problems of the new Vatican council."

In hindsight, Ritter's prediction missed the point of the "new Vatican council." In fact, it was an affirmation that he had come of age in a time when it seemed the ancient traditions of the Church would never change, that indeed the Church would continue arguing for centuries over something as esoteric as the *filioque* in a world that had wrought not only Hitler but Hiroshima. There was no way to see it then, but Vatican II would address much more concrete realities. In fact, it would become a historic challenge to the old Church. The Latin liturgy would be replaced by the vernacular and there would be a new ecumenical understanding. In short, the council told Roman Catholics that the modern world was something to be sympathized with rather than condemned.

Ritter and his classmates were among the last seminarians of the pre–Vatican II Church. Their years in the seminary were at a time of crushing conservatism, of ideological resistance to modern philosophy, of an outright rejection of anything that would challenge the precepts of the Church. It was the end of the twenty-year reign of Pope Pius XII—a pale, emaciated, and remote figure, whose physical presence seemed to symbolize the Church itself: rigid, overly moralistic, glorious, ancient, infallible.

The Roman Catholic Church was still a fortress protecting itself against the modern world. Priests even had to swear to something called "the oath against modernism." The Church, with its infamous *Index Librorum Prohibitorum,* was still pressing a stern finger to its lips to silence any books that might incite insurrection. The *Index* had become less effective in the new democracies of postwar Europe. But it was still there, and it could be felt in every library at every parochial school, Catholic college, and seminary. By doctrine, it was still a sin to read any book on that list, including Voltaire, Rousseau, Kant, and especially Darwin. The Church seemed even more rigid, more brittle in clinging to its past, before the inevitable turmoil and change that would be ushered in during the coming decade. Ritter was caught in what is now referred to in Catholic textbooks as "the crisis of modernity."

Then, on October 9, 1958, the word rang through the streets of Rome and all over the world: His Holiness was dead. No one seemed ready for the death of Pius XII, and few were prepared for the profound wellsprings of change that would push to the surface.

On a brisk fall day, Ritter waited in Saint Peter's Square for the announcement of the next pontiff. He and several other Franciscans shifted their feet on the cobblestones among the throng of Catholics at St. Peter's Square and stared out over the Sistine Chapel. The smoke had risen black twice that day. The cardinals were divided, or, rather, there had not yet been a divine intervention. But then, late in the afternoon, a puff of white smoke emerged from the chimney over the chapel. The cardinals were burning their ballots, signaling a decision had been reached: It was John XXIII.

He would be the future of the Church, a man who would begin to breathe life into the flaccid lungs of Roman Catholicism. Within just three months, he announced his intention to convene an Ecumenical Council, which he would call "a new Pentecost" and which several years later, when it was finally under way, would be known as "Vatican II."

It was the beginning of historic change and Ritter was there to see the ephemeral puff of smoke that heralded its arrival.

But he had little time to revel in the excitement and wonder of the new Pope. He was deeply mired in his thesis. Eldarov saw that he seemed to be drifting off on a strange tack and warned him of a fundamental weakness in his argument. Eldarov sensed that the heavily psychological theme of resisting authority was more than just a dry intellectual topic, but perhaps something deep in the core of Ritter's personality.

He advised Ritter not to take the painfully esoteric tangent of trying to explain centuries of Church history through a primarily psychological interpretation of the power struggle between Rome and Greece.

But Ritter arrogantly insisted that this use of modern psychology to understand the ancient conflict would break new ground in scholarship. It did not accomplish anything so grandiose, but it did provide some chilling insight into Ritter's personality—fiercely independent, resistant to authority, and keenly aware of inner conflict.

The direction of the thesis is summed up in these excerpts:

The chief stumbling-block to a union of the Churches today is without question the doctrine of the Roman Primacy. Men will surrender almost anything in their own best interest, for their own good—except their independence. And just as this is true today, so too then, in the Council of Florence; for the Latins and Greeks failed to achieve a lasting union because the Greeks, in the final analysis, refused to submit, refused to surrender their autonomy. . . .

The author suggests that a solution must be sought in the eventual predominance of one aspect of the curious psychological and theological duality, ambivalence, schizophrenia—call it what you will—in the Greek approach to Rome suggested above. . . . For the Greeks entered the fray at odds with themselves, in the very roots of their being divided against themselves, hopelessly schizophrenic in their approach to the Latin Church.

[It was a] . . . personality derived from the ancient traditions which they loved so much and which they held in common with the Latins, the second superimposed and more conscious personality derived from an attempt to rationalize theologically a schism which was not theological in origin but emotional, psychological and culminating in an ecclesiological aberration on the pragmatic level. The Greeks could not wage a successful campaign against the Latins until they had synthesized these warring elements in their own nature. . . .

The council of Florence failed far more through a certain human weakness on the part of these witnesses of the Greek Church. They could not accept submission; they could not finally accept the primacy of Rome—ad humanitatem difficilior.

His fellow students had chosen seemingly more relevant and down-to-earth topics. Fitzgibbons's thesis was titled "The Church in the Experience of 20th Century Converts." Father Juniper Alwell, another close friend who would later work with Ritter at Covenant House, titled his thesis "The Obligation of the Layman." No one has ever had an easy time finishing a doctoral thesis, but the ordeal was particularly difficult for Ritter. He spiraled downward into what some of his fellow friars remember was a deep depression through the spring of 1959.

Ritter turned in his thesis on May 24, 1959, Trinity Sunday. By June 27 he was informed that he had successfully defended his thesis. He scored an 8.51/10, the grade equivalent to a B, making him eligible as a graduate cum laude. But Bruce Ritter never actually obtained his doctorate. In order to do so candidates were required to refine their thesis and have it published in an academic journal. He never did.

It was more than just a technicality. Getting a thesis published in a journal can be a difficult final step, which can require additional research and/or a more focused approach. But these academic formalities never stopped him from using the title when he needed it, whether in press releases or in an official résumé given to the United States Justice Department. Call it "false conscience."

[There are several of Ritter's fellow Franciscan friars—from Rome to New York—who were less than surprised when the sexual allegations surfaced. Most of them opted for anonymity. They wanted to keep any skeletons safely locked in closets to protect what one of them frankly referred to as "the corporate interest," but which others more euphemistically phrased the "family of Franciscans."

However, when the scandal first hit the papers in Italy during Christmas 1989 and the rumors about Bruce Ritter's fall from grace were whispered throughout the Eternal City, Eldarov had a haunting memory of an incident involving Ritter. Eldarov suffered and struggled to understand what happened to his former student and friend. He maintained that he does not judge Ritter and that "only God can do that." But still a memory kept coming back.]

In the summer of 1959, Father Bruce had just finished his thesis and was vacationing in Sabaudia, a seaside town a few hours by train south of Rome. It was a pleasant port with brightly painted fishing boats bobbing in the Mediterranean. There was a long strip of beach within walking distance of the parish rectory and the priests would spend their days off relaxing in the shade of beach umbrellas with a cool breeze blowing off the sea. It was a blessed respite from the sweltering summer heat of Rome.

The luxury of being by the beach was a trade-off for working at the local church and attending to the needs of some ten thousand parishioners. The young priests were responsible for helping to say several daily masses and taking care of parish operations, including the supervision of a dozen altar boys.

That summer, a scandal erupted. Word about an "incident" between Ritter and one of the young altar boys under his care came back to Eldarov and the other Franciscan superiors in Rome.

"Bruce had said that a child aged twelve or thirteen had tried to touch him in a sexual way," Eldarov remembers. "The child was told not to come around anymore. But it was Bruce who made the complaint against the child. At least, that is the way it was brought to us. It was all quite puzzling."

There were priests in Sabaudia who were furious about what happened. Eldarov remembers one fellow Franciscan who was at Sabaudia with Bruce that summer complaining to him that the incident was suspicious and that it should be investigated.

"He was very unhappy about it. He said why would Bruce complain? It does not seem natural that a child would attack a grown-up instead of the opposite unless a child felt that they had been made to do this, to make the adult happy or comply," said Eldarov.

Fitzgibbons was there at Sabaudia that summer as well. When asked about the incident, he remembers a slightly different story. He remembers a young boy, as old as sixteen, hanging out on the beach with several of the priests. The boy wore a tight-fitting bathing suit that was almost indecent compared to the baggy boxer shorts that the priests wore. Ritter told Fitzgibbons that he was filing a complaint against the boy because the teenager had made a sexual pass at him.

"That's the way I remember it," said Fitzgibbons. "It is possible the kid got signals [from Ritter], but my understanding is that Ritter rejected him. He was actually quite angry about it. I remember that. I remember he seemed very uptight about the whole thing. No one understood it."

It is important to remember the time. In the context of the dour, conservative Church in Rome in the 1950s, homosexuality and sexual abuse were not topics readily discussed in Church circles. In fact, they were hardly acknowledged. That is not to say that they were not happening; it was just that there was very little public attention brought to them.

In 1959, the psychological tools to deal with allegations of sexual contact between a priest and a young boy did not exist. The way the Franciscans handled the incident was quite simple and quite common. The boy was told never to come back to the church and given stern warnings about the grave sin of lying and the more grave sin of homosexuality. Ritter headed back to the United States several weeks later. There would be no discussion about it. Case closed.

Having finished his doctoral work, Ritter taught briefly at Saint Hyacinth's Seminary in Granby, Massachusetts, and at Canevin High School in Pittsburgh. He then went on to Saint Anthony-on-Hudson Seminary in Rensselaer, New York, where he taught sociology and philosophy. One of his students there, Julian Zambanini, remem-

62   BROKEN COVENANT

bered Ritter was "frustrated" and "wanted something more exciting
than teaching seminarians on the secluded campus in upstate New
York."

After only two years at Saint Anthony, he went on to Manhattan
College, a respected Catholic liberal-arts school in the Bronx. Times
were changing. It was the fall of 1962. That year two world leaders,
President John F. Kennedy and Pope John XXIII, would do much
to dispel anti-Catholicism, even among the liberals and intellectuals
of the age. They were the new face of Catholicism, exciting and
looking to the future. But within a year both men would also be
buried—Kennedy assassinated on a sunny day in Dallas and John
XXIII passed away over the summer, ending the shortest and perhaps most dramatic papal reign in modern history.

After their sudden deaths came a time of dissent. Walter Cronkite's
voice spoke over grainy black-and-white footage of fire hoses blasting
young black bodies against a wall in Birmingham, Alabama. In Harlem, a man named Malcolm X was speaking out in rage and discontent
in the name of black America. There was a buildup of a few thousand
American military "advisers" in a strange and distant land called
Vietnam. Crazed fans of a group from London named the Beatles
were touching off near riots and the group was planning a tour of
the U.S. There was a stirring in the air, and priests like Ritter, who
had grown up in the strict dogma of pre–Vatican II, would soon
begin a long struggle to cope with the winds of change.

But while the old Church in Rome writhed in turmoil, the American Catholic Church was flexing its muscles. It was young and strong
and coming of age. The *Saturday Evening Post* and *Life* magazine were
filled with cover stories and photo spreads on the momentous changes
sweeping the Catholic Church in America. There were big black-and-
white photos of healthy nuns laughing and playing basketball and of
priests with strong chins in front of the packed pews of newly built
churches. There were 45 million Catholics in America by 1964, nearly
25 percent of the population, and the percentage seemed to be rising
every year. There were 5 cardinals, 30 archbishops, nearly 60,000
priests, and about three times that many nuns, all ministering to
communicants in 22,000 separate parishes and missions. In 285 colleges and universities, in 13,000 elementary and secondary schools,
6 million young Americans were reminded daily that the Incarnation
of Christ was the central fact of human history.

Father Bruce watched this cultural surge of Catholicism in America
from the pulpit at Manhattan College, where he was the campus
chaplain and professor of theology. While some of the staff found

him arrogant and snobbish, the students loved him. He seemed to be a different person around young people. He was exhilarated by their ideas, and eagerly discussed everything from the civil rights movement to the Vietnam War.

By 1967, he was getting involved in the wave of student activism that was crashing down even in remote tributaries like the small, conservative Catholic campus. He organized a program for Manhattan students to work in local community-action projects. He urged them to break out of their sheltered middle-class Catholic upbringings and help renovate burned-out buildings in the neighboring ghettos of the Bronx and Harlem. Over the summer of 1967, Ritter formed the Christian Life Council, which became an official campus organization devoted to social issues and providing educational seminars on the Vietnam War.

One night he sponsored the showing of a controversial film called *The War Game*, which dramatized the horrifying effects of a nuclear war. The film caused a stir on the conservative campus. Ritter was hauled in to answer for it to the dean of students and reprimanded by the head of his department. The following week, he showed it again all day. Later that year, he sponsored another event he dubbed the "Enemies and Brothers Film Festival."

The one-day festival began with a black-and-white U.S. Army training film. The student audience began heckling the military-morale film. They booed when the military spokesman talked about "the need to resist the Communist aggressor in South East Asia" and "the fight for Democracy." In the film, the eager young recruits being indoctrinated just nodded their heads in agreement. The next film began with the same kind of black-and-white image of soldiers in a classroom listening to a sergeant. But this time it was a North Vietnamese military-morale film with English subtitles. It was precisely the same kind of indoctrination about "fighting the capitalist aggressor."

The students nodded their heads with an appreciation for Ritter's cunning statement about the war. On the surface, the administration would not perceive this as an antiwar statement because it presented both sides. Father Bruce would be spared the wrath of his superiors, but clearly with a wink and a nod he was showing he could stand up to the establishment.

As one student remembers, "He was not a flame-throwing liberal, but he knew how to make a statement."

Word of Father Bruce the rebel caught on throughout the campus. A following of students who would come to his apartment on campus to listen to Bob Dylan records and have a beer with the open-minded philosophy professor.

But by 1968 he watched many of his students drop out. They were going on to challenge authority outside the safe walls of the college or just drifting in the confusion of the time. That year, Robert Kennedy would be shot down by an assassin's bullet; more race riots would rip through cities across America; the antiwar protests were turning violent. And on December 10, Thomas Merton died suddenly in a bizarre accident in Bangkok, where he had been invited to attend a meeting of Asian monks. He was electrocuted while trying to plug in a fan. He was fifty-three years old.

Merton's death represented an absurd ending to an absurd year. All of the promise of America in its youth seemed to be changing into a violent and awkward adolescence. Father Bruce was feeling the pull to the streets that so many clergy felt at that time. He wanted to go out and make a difference in a world that was rapidly changing, perhaps even teetering on the edge of chaos. Bruce decided to leave the safety of his campus ministry at Manhattan College. On Holy Thursday, 1968, he headed for the unholy netherworld of New York City's East Village, where he would begin a simple street ministry aimed at helping the poor. Many years later this would become the charitable empire known as Covenant House.

Chapter 5

The Foundation

COVENANT House was built on a myth.

The history of the charity's foundation was so oft repeated that it became a religious incantation of the faithful—easy-reading Christian iconography like the small religious books on saints that were always laid out on long wooden tables or metal book racks in the foyers of Catholic churches. They made the stories seem so simple and so compelling, with their colorful illustrations: Saint Francis among the poor, Saint Paul on the road to Damascus. The truth, of course, was never so simple.

In much the same tone, although the simplicity was masked with an overlay of tough, street-smart language, Ritter recorded his own legend in *Covenant House: Lifeline to the Streets* (1988), a compilation of the monthly newsletters he wrote to his donors and supporters.

"How long will it be before you guys sell out? To money, power, ambition . . . ? Will you sell out by the time you're twenty-five?"

I finished my sermon on that note and turned back to the altar to continue the celebrating of Mass. I was proud that almost 400 students had come to church that brilliant Saturday afternoon in October 1966.

It was a good sermon. I liked that sermon. I had worked hard on it. It was all about zeal and commitment and how the students at Manhattan College should be more involved in the life and work of the Church.

One of the students, Hughie O'Neill, stood up in church and said, "Wait a minute, Bruce." He happened to be the president of the student body and captain of the track team. . . .

"We all think you're a pretty good teacher, Bruce, but we don't like your sermons. We think you should practice what you preach."

That's a pretty heavy shot to take from your students on a Saturday afternoon. (There was a general murmur of agreement from the other kids in the church.)

I thought about it a lot over the next few days and realized, of course, that Hughie O'Neill was correct. The next Sunday, at all the Masses on campus, I apologized to the student body—for not edifying them—and asked my superiors and the archbishop for a new assignment: to live and work among the poor on the Lower East Side of Manhattan.

Hugh O'Neill remembers the day differently.

First of all, O'Neill wasn't captain of the track team, he was a "not very good quarter miler." He was permitted to practice with the team because he was "good at organizing the workouts and my grades were good enough to help inflate the overall average of the team."

There were not four hundred people there. The number was closer to forty. It was not in the church at Manhattan College. It was an informal discussion at Caspar Hall. The students were not sitting up straight in mahogany pews. They were stretched out on couches and leaning back in chairs: "just a bunch of kids talking."

"It was not a day of particular significance," said O'Neill, as he remembered his college days with Father Ritter. "In fact, it wasn't until five years later that Bruce ever said anything about it being a pivotal event in his own thinking."

Five years later. That was about when Ritter began writing and accumulating a small mailing list for his monthly newsletters. It made for a great beginning of his own mythology. For Ritter everything had to be epic. The history he told over and over of the beginning of Covenant House was dramatized into Hollywood-scripted simplicity, bright shining morality. Over the years it evolved into a sweeping tale of one man's fateful vision, as one-dimensional and washed in Technicolor as the Westerns he loved.

Events were not as quickly paced as Ritter wrote. It was not "the next Sunday," but more than several months after the discussion with O'Neill that he made his first request to develop a street ministry in the East Village. It was not until two years later that he actually left Manhattan College.

Before Ritter was able to get approval for such a ministry, he had to employ the skills he had sharpened as a seminary student. He needed approval from the provincial of the order as well as his superiors in Rome. Thousands of priests and nuns tried similar experimental ministries in the streets at that time. Most of them were regarded with suspicion by the pre–Vatican II hierarchy, but the word had come down from Rome. The clergy should no longer be, as they used to say in the seminary, "in this world, but not of it." The message was now for priests to be "in this world and of it." They were being instructed to venture out from behind the dark screens of their confessionals and dimly lit sacristies to the neon-bright reality of the modern world.

Nonetheless, for Ritter to establish a ministry as vague as going to the Lower East Side "to live and work among the poor" was not going to be an easy task. His request had to stand out. He had to let his superiors know that he was one of them, that he was of the old school—the Thomist doctrine, the padlocked seminary gates, and The Rule. He had paid his dues under Pius XII and he needed to communicate that. What better way than to script the request in perfect Latin—beautiful phrasing that would pour off each page like wine from a silver chalice. It worked. Once again Father Bruce manipulated his superiors by playing the rules better than they could themselves.

The provincial of the order, Father David Schultz, approved his request almost immediately. But he told Ritter that there was one catch. As Bruce sat across from his provincial, all the humbling, even emasculating feelings of a young seminarian in the presence of the patriarchy must have come to him. Father Schultz explained to him that he would have to take two other friars with him to help keep the program on the up and up. You know, so there will be no "appearances" and to "assist you in this good work."

There was something about the word "appearances." His superior passed over it quickly, but it was a code word for every priest. It spoke of humanity and sex, of desire and celibacy, of a kind of presumption of guilt that priests carry with them. Everything had to be "clean as a hound's tooth." He was so fiercely independent, that

his superiors must have intuitively sensed a need to make sure the
so-called street ministry was for the glory of God and not the glory
of Bruce Ritter.

There was no getting around the condition. Ritter would have to
comply and later devise a plan that would preserve his independence.
He asked some of his fellow friars to join him, but most weren't
interested in leaving the comfortable environs of the friary to live in
a tenement in the drug-infested Lower East Side. Then he bumped
into Father Seraphin Fitzgibbons, who was teaching at Saint Anthony-
on-Hudson in Rensselaer. Fitzgibbons said he was tired of the safe
and tedious life of teaching seminarians. He felt sheltered, bored,
out of touch. Ritter told Fitzgibbons about his new ministry and asked
Fitzgibbons to join him. It was perfect for Fitzgibbons, but he didn't
think he could get out of his assignment as assistant dean of students.
Before too long, Ritter brokered a deal with Fitzgibbons's superiors
to get him out of his assignment. Ritter talked Father Schultz into
letting him get started with the promise that a third friar would soon
join them. They got their superiors' blessing. In April 1968, on Holy
Thursday, the two Franciscans left for the Lower East Side of Manhattan, a tough neighborhood, which is now more euphemistically
refered to as the East Village. Their ministry had a simple mandate:
"To serve the poor usefully."

They found a rundown apartment on East Seventh Street just off
Tomkins Square Park for $60 a month. It was a railroad flat with
the bathtub in the kitchen and two small bedrooms. It had eighty-
year-old plumbing and the heat and hot water rarely worked.

Greenwich Village in 1968 was a psychedelic Hades, where young
runaways were spinning like fallen leaves in the whirlwind of the late
1960s cultural revolution. Many of them were white kids from mid-
dle- and upper-middle-class families, aging flower children and their
younger imitators all rejecting the age of affluence.

The West Village was sandals and tie-dye. It was awash in fluorescent paint and lava lamps. Soothing incense, sweet golden strands
of pot, and a kind of reckless freedom filled the air. It was bohemia,
and it wasn't menacing.

Cross the Bowery and head east, however, and you were in the
strung-out morning after of the age of Aquarius. The tenements and
brownstones abandoned by generations of factory and dock workers
were dark and sweaty, built too close together. The immigrants had
vanished to the suburbs and the buildings were teeming with junkies,
bikers, leg breakers, numbers runners, and freaks. The cops who
covered the beat were tough and on the take. As the Knapp Com-

mission would soon reveal, police corruption was pervasive on every level. It was standard practice back then for cops to shake down restaurants and to expect "something in return" from anyone—even a priest—who wanted police presence. The cops figured that any priest who lived down there either "needs his head examined" or was "as queer as a three-dollar bill." To them, Bruce Ritter, with his cutoff sweatshirts and jeans, was part of the same "liberal bullshit" that was ruining the neighborhoods where their grandparents first landed as immigrants. To them the city had become an indecent and dangerous place, where the inhabitants needed to be caged, controlled, and patrolled. No idealistic street priest was going to change that. They resented Ritter and everything he stood for. His crime was one of complicity with the decay, the decadence, and the dissent, and many of them were quick to suspect Ritter of the worst of motives.

This animosity between him and the cops simmered for years. But Father Bruce knew a way to get around it. When he really needed something from the local precinct or the courts or an assistant district attorney to help a kid get out of trouble, folklore has it, he would duck into the tenement, throw on his clerical garb, and assume the look and posture of the model priest in the once glorious immigrant Church. For that, even rogue cops were suckers.

The money was always short. To get by, Ritter and Fitzgibbons took part-time jobs driving cabs, working as short-order cooks, and preaching in nearby parishes. It seemed that they were never able to make ends meet, dropping a few dollars for a cab ride for someone who needed drug treatment, $50 bail for a kid busted for stealing, and an endless flow of cash for groceries. They'd pick up cans of soup, a lot of cereal, big boxes of spaghetti, and fat loaves of day-old bread—cheap, starchy foods that expanded in the stomach. Somehow they scraped by in this vague mission to help the poor in any way they could.

Father Ed Murphy, a Jesuit, worked at the Martin Buber House, a storefront on East Sixth Street devoted to organizing opposition to the Vietnam War. He remembers Ritter walking the streets of the Village, but never wanting anything to do with the antiwar movement. He was always too busy talking to the kids hanging out in the street and immersing himself in their problems.

"He was a very private person. He would be very open with the kids, but he closed himself off to most of the other priests and ministers who were working in the Village," said Murphy.

So how was a clear vision to help street kids born out of this vague and open-ended commitment to "serve the poor usefully?" According to the mythology that Ritter has scripted over the years, it came one night when six kids knocked on his door. It was 2 A.M. on a freezing-cold February night in 1969 in the middle of a snowstorm.

What could I do? It was snowing outside and cold. What would you have done? I invited them inside, gave them some food and blankets, and the kids bedded down on my living-room floor. One of the boys looked at me. "We know you're a priest," he said, "and you don't have to worry. We'll be good and stay away from the girls." I thanked him for that courtesy!

The next morning it was still very cold and still snowing very hard. The kids obviously did not want to leave. They had no place to go. The girls got up and cooked my breakfast and burned it; the boys cleaned my apartment and cased it.

One boy went outside for just a few minutes and brought back four more kids. "This is the rest of us," he said, "the rest of our family. They were afraid to come last night. They wanted us to check you out first. I told them that you didn't come on to us last night so that it was probably okay."

These 10 kids had been living down the block in one of the abandoned buildings with a bunch of junkies who were pimping them. The junkies had just forced the kids to make a porn film before they would give them some food. The kids hated that. They really hated that. In disgust and a kind of horror at the direction their lives were taking, they fled the junkies and came down the street to my place.

I tried very hard to find some child-care agency that would take these kids in. I called over twenty-four different agencies.... nobody would touch these kids....

... So I kept them.

I wish I could tell you that my motives were honorable. I wish I could say that I acted out of zeal, compassion, kindness. My motives were not that noble—they were much closer to anger, stubbornness, pride, vanity. I am a very competitive person. I hate to lose....

That's not how Fitzgibbons remembers the early days of the ministry, which had not yet even taken on the name Covenant House. He can't recall any such melodramatic night when a group of six kids knocked on the door, certainly not with the kind of clarity of vision and purpose that Ritter described. To Fitzgibbons, it seemed as if there were endless knocks on the door from an endless flow of down-and-out people at every hour of the day and night. They were alcoholics, drug-addicted kids, strung-out Vietnam War veterans. They were young and old, kids from families in the suburbs, and poor kids who grew up in Lower East Side tenements. They were bound only by their disillusionment and broken lives. It was a messy reality, not anything like the clean drama of the six young kids that Father Bruce would later refer to in his newsletters and his sermons across the country. It is worth noting that Fitzgibbons's name is conspicuously absent in Ritter's writing and talks. Ritter wrote him right out of Covenant House history.

According to Fitzgibbons and others who worked with Ritter in the first year, there was only one incident that resembled the fabled "first six kids." It was a group of six teenage runaways who showed up at the East Seventh Street apartment in the winter of 1970.

Mary Lane and Lee Meyers, two of those first kids to knock on Ritter's door, say their stay with Father Bruce Ritter was not the same story that the feisty Franciscan fashioned into his own legend.

In some ways they are two of the many success stories that could be attributed to the Franciscan's mission. Both of them managed to get off the streets and pull their lives together. They now have good jobs and solid families. To this day, they are appreciative that Ritter provided them with a place to stay and food to eat. But they say Father Bruce was anything but a savior. They survived not because of him, but in spite of him. At least one of the other fabled "first six kids" may not have been so lucky.

In January 1970, Mary and Lee were living in an abandoned building off Delancey Street underneath the Williamsburg Bridge with four other street kids: Julie, Little Bill, Stevie, and one named George, whom everyone knew as Sergeant Pepper. The two boys and four girls, ranging in age from fourteen to seventeen, were like family. They depended on each other. They trusted each other. They looked out for each other.

There was a gradual but significant change in the street scene from the spring of 1968 to the winter of 1970. The flower children were becoming adults and many of them had left the West Village. Slowly the psychedelic scene of the Village was being replaced by a more upscale crowd of writers, artists, and advertising executives, who were paying high rents for apartments. They were just beginning to devour most of the cheap housing. Nonviolent street protests had given way to calls for armed insurrection. The hippies were out, the Weathermen were in. The Tet offensive had shattered any official illusions of winning the war; Nixon was just beginning the illegal bombing of Cambodia. Martin Luther King had been dead two years. Black mil-

itant groups were gunning down police officers in New York City.
That spring, Nixon hailed the American astronauts landing on the
moon as "the greatest week since the Creation." But America was
slipping into a brooding cynicism.

To keep from freezing to death in that winter of 1970, the six kids
warmed their hands on a gas stove in the abandoned apartment.
There was no heat, no running water, no electricity. The single blue
flame from the one working outlet of this old stove was all they had
to keep warm. One cold day, they left the stove on, touching off a
fire that destroyed the apartment and left them with no place to stay.
They ended up crashing in an upstairs apartment where several
junkies were living.

Lee and Mary said the junkies were not "pimping" them and they
were never "forced to make a porn film before they would give them
some food," as Ritter had written in his account.

"That's Ritter's mind working. It had nothing to do with us. Those
people never would have had it together enough to make a film.
They were just junkies, who let us crash on their floor," Lee remembers.

A few nights after the fire, the police raided the junkies' apartment.
Lee was arrested in the roundup, but the rest of the group were let
go. They returned to the burned-out apartment, where one night
they shivered and huddled close together. A blizzard was covering
the city in snow and they had no idea where they could go to get out
of the cold. Little Bill, who was about fifteen years old and a wiry
kid, remembered a priest he had met several weeks before. They
could all go and stay there. The priest's place was clean, he had food,
and you didn't have to worry about cops.

They knew the ropes on the Lower East Side's string of religious
ministries aimed at helping lost kids in the street. There was Judson
House, an alternative ministry affiliated with Judson Church, just off
Tompkins Square Park. There was The Wayword, funded by the
New York Bible Society and run by a Baptist minister. There was
the Living Room, founded by some born-again Christians. Contact
was established by a group of Jewish philanthropists. Odyssey House
was a drug rehabilitation center on East Sixth Street. It was all part
of a sweeping new "religious relevance." The counselors fed the kids
sandwiches and hot coffee. They held rap sessions on everything
from the meaning of life to My Lai. The kids knew how to operate
in this world of alternative ministries, at least enough to be sure that
a Catholic priest would never turn them out in the cold.

They left the apartment, picking their way through the litter-strewn

lot blanketed in clean white snow, and headed out into the icy darkness of the city. They walked on Delancey Street over to Avenue
A and up above Houston to East Seventh Street. The building on
East Seventh was completely dark, but they pushed the door open
and walked up the stairs to a bare wooden door. After several minutes of knocking, the tall, balding priest answered. Ritter said it
was okay for them to sleep in the apartment, but they would have
to find a space on the floor next to a thirty-two-year-old alcoholic
named Billy and two destitute brothers named Bobbie and Eddie.
The older men were snoring, filling the room with the putrid smell
of stale alcohol and sweat. But it was warm inside the apartment and
the five young waifs settled on the floor, sharing two blankets, and
fell asleep.

After the first few days, they found Ritter impatient and sometimes
downright mean, especially to the two girls. He called them "street
sluts" and asked them why they didn't "just go home." The words
showed these kids that he knew nothing about why they were on the
streets. They were only kids, but they could sense a lot of anger
coming from deep inside Father Bruce. And like most teenagers,
they took it personally. When he wasn't putting them down, he was
cold and silent to the girls. But to the boys he was warm and compassionate. Mary figured that as a priest he had to be careful with
young girls; maybe he needed to keep a certain distance so there
wouldn't be any mixed signals or suspicions. They didn't understand
half of it, but something was off about Father Bruce.

They appreciated the fact that he was giving them a roof over their
heads, but Mary couldn't understand his increasingly hostile treatment of the girls. He would kick them out of the apartment early in
the morning to fend for themselves on the street during the day. But
he would allow the boys to stay all morning and afternoon, feeding
them lunch and dinner.

Ritter was spending a lot of time with Little Bill, Stevie, and Sergeant Pepper behind closed doors in one of the rooms in the apartment. He said he was counseling them. Mary and Lee never saw any
sexual abuse with their own eyes, but there was a feeling. They didn't
trust him.

One day, after their first week there, Sergeant Pepper walked out
of the apartment in tears. Mary found him in the street and talked
with him. He was terrified and tormented. He broke down crying.
He said he couldn't talk about it.

"Sergeant Pepper, we're family, man. You gotta tell us what's going
on. Come on, what's wrong?" asked Mary.

Then Sergeant Pepper told her that Father Ritter had made a sexual advance to him.

"I just let it happen, I don't know why. But I just kind of let it happen," Sergeant Pepper told Mary.

"It's not your fault," said Mary. "You didn't do anything."

He was a thin boy with strong Spanish features, about sixteen years old. His blue eyes looked lost through the tears. He kept pushing his long black hair behind his ears as he sobbed.

They were kids, but they'd seen a lot in the street. Not much surprised them. Still, Mary didn't know how to handle her friend's being sexually abused by a priest. She just put her arms around Sergeant Pepper. He cried long and hard, and she cried with him.

Mary was, in the parlance of the times, Lee's "old lady," and was waiting for him to be released from a juvenile center where he was being held on the drug charges he faced for being in the apartment with the junkies. The police never prosecuted the case, and Lee was released after a few weeks. When he got out, Mary told Lee about what had happened with Sergeant Pepper. The group of six kids eyed Ritter with a new air of suspicion and caution. They knew now that his compassion was tempered by an ulterior motive. They were able to accept that he was gay. There were plenty of gay priests in Greenwich Village in the late 1960s and early 1970s, who had dropped out of the ministry. What they couldn't accept was the "power trips" he threw at them.

Father Bruce refused to let Lee stay in his apartment after his drug arrest. He was arrogant and condescending and told Mary to break off the relationship or they would both have to leave. Mary and Lee left Father Ritter's apartment immediately and on bad terms. They talked Sergeant Pepper and Julie into joining them, but Little Bill and Stevie stayed behind, eventually moving into apartments in the same building. No matter how bad Father Bruce was, they didn't want to go back out into the streets in the middle of winter.

Lee was close with Stevie and they ran into each other just about every day on the streets, in the coffee shops, and in the burned-out apartments where they hung out. One day, several weeks after the others had left Bruce's apartment, Stevie told Lee that Father Bruce had made a sexual advance to him as well. Stevie wasn't as upset as Sergeant Pepper. He said he resisted the advance. After two years on the street, Stevie knew the kind of shit that goes down, even with a priest.

"If he tries it again, I'll nut him hard," Stevie told Lee.

Lee and Mary and the others immediately put the word out among their friends that Father Ritter was someone to be leery of. The warning spread through the family of street kids. You could stay with Father Bruce if you needed a place to crash, but you had to be very careful.

Mary and Lee began to hang out in The Wayword on the corner of Mercer and Waverly streets. The Reverend Jim Daniels, a naïve Baptist from a small town in Union County, New Jersey, opened the tiny counseling center with his wife and helped thousands of young people whose lives had fallen into dependence on drugs and who were scrounging to survive. Although they called the streets "freedom," it hardly seemed so to Daniels.

"You have to respect yourself and then other people will respect you," he'd say.

That kind of talk had the reverend pegged as a drag, if not a narc. But after he stuck around for a while and came through for some street kids in crucial times, they knew he was okay. He even traded in his polyester sport shirts and ties for dungarees and a T-shirt. Daniels helped place kids in drug-treatment programs. He helped them find jobs, and lawyers, and medical care. But mostly he just listened to their problems. The word got out on the street that every day at noon the Wayword served about one hundred peanut-butter-and-jelly sandwiches and endless pots of hot coffee to anyone who stopped in. There would be scores of kids lined up on the steps of the brownstone waiting for lunch. Mary and Lee were regulars.

Lee, with his long red hair that stretched to the middle of his back and his purple tie-dye pants, and Mary, who wore wire-rimmed glasses, Indian-print dresses, and construction boots, became very close with Daniels and his wife and were often invited into their home for dinner. They would talk about the war in Vietnam and get furious with Daniels for supporting the American troops there. But he was never arrogant, never condescending.

At The Wayword, brick walls were covered with slogans and psychedelic posters, one with flowers, asked "What if they held a war and nobody came?" One of the first moon shots from NASA read: "We are all passengers on space ship earth." Sitting around the wooden tables was a strange mix of lost street kids, criminals, drug addicts, leering hustlers, and shady men in trenchcoats with money and mixed motives.

One night Mary and Lee were sitting in The Wayword, several weeks after Sergeant Pepper had shocked them with his story about Father Bruce Ritter. As much as they resisted authority in all of its manifestations, Mary and Lee needed someone to confide in. They were hesitant at first, but Mary decided it was as good a time as any to bring it up.

"Jim, you know that priest on Seventh Street who takes kids in?" asked Mary.

Jim nodded. "You mean Father Ritter."

Daniels had met Ritter just several weeks before. He had heard of him and was anxious to meet another minister with a similar mission. But Ritter was not at all welcoming. Daniels was surprised by the rebuff, but had little contact with the priest after that and just figured it was the classic Catholic cold shoulder. Catholics weren't known for their ecumenical spirit.

"What about him?" asked Daniels.

"We know something you wouldn't believe," said Mary. "He is a phony. He's after young boys. Father Bruce made a move on Sergeant Pepper."

Daniels wasn't exactly street smart, but he had been around long enough to know that you take just about everything a street kid says with a hearty measure of skepticism. The allegation was pretty far out, he thought. But then again it was all part of the madness of the East Village at the time. Daniels was shocked, but he was also ambivalent. After all, Father Bruce was doing so much good. He figured the kids had to be exaggerating.

Mary persisted. She was furious and concerned. Daniels remembers the tone of her voice rang true. But he didn't know what to do. Certainly the word of two runaways would not stand up in court against a priest. He just listened to them and nodded his head in sympathy. The more they talked, the more he believed them. Daniels never referred another street kid to Father Bruce.

Several days later, Mary and Lee ran into Sergeant Pepper. He had shifted gears into heavy drug use. Drugs were no longer the boisterous rebellion of a young soldier in the ranks of the counter-culture. At sixteen he was getting strung out. Very confused. More shattered than ever.

On this day he had taken an entire roll of paper-dot acid. He was spinning in the street, with his arms waving recklessly. He had on the blue double-breasted uniform jacket that looked as if it was right off the Beatles album from which he took his name. The coat was unbuttoned and flapping open as he spun in circles. His long hair was falling over his face. He nodded his head with his mouth half open, floating through the hallucinations and the bursts of color in his mind.

Sergeant Pepper grew thinner, eating more acid than food. His eyes grew vacant. After a few years, the bright blue color faded to a kind of glassy gray. The last time Lee saw him was in 1977 on July 4 in Berkeley. He had joined up with the Rainbow People, a commune of unreconstructed hippies, who were there celebrating their annual Rainbow Gathering. Sergeant Pepper had blown his mind.

More than twenty years later Mary Lane is married, with three children, and lives in upstate New York. She has pulled her life together, but has never forgotten about her experiences as a street kid. She is now a counselor at a special school for troubled teenagers. Lee is an engineer in California, also married with children.

They both watched Father Bruce Ritter's meteoric rise to prominence in the 1980s. Mary saw the articles about him in *The New York Times* and watched a profile of him on *60 Minutes*. In 1985, she read an article about his appointment to the Meese Commission on Pornography. She called Lee, and at first they laughed at the irony. But then they fell silent, shaking their heads with disgust.

"He took a group of traumatized kids who were cold and lonely and in need of help and he manipulated them. It can damage a kid forever," said Mary. "Look what it did to Sergeant Pepper. We have no idea where he is now. Only God knows what happened to Stevie. It is a real violation of trust. It is a betrayal, and it began right from the very start."

By the spring of 1970, Ritter was focusing his ministry on runaway kids. This became a source of tension between him and Fitzgibbons. They clashed over their understanding of the original intention of the street ministry. Fitzgibbons argued that it should stick to its stated purpose: a broad-based community service for anyone who needed help. Sure, there were lots of runaways, Fitzgibbons argued, but they were only a percentage of the total population in this poor neighborhood. Some needed alcohol and drug counseling. Many were teenage mothers who needed family counseling. Focusing so intently on teenage runaways struck Fitzgibbons as strange and unproductive. They argued continually. Father Bruce insisted that the young boys and girls on the street had to be the focus. They were the innocent lambs of the mean streets and he was determined to be their savior. With them, Father Bruce felt he could make a difference. He felt a lot of the adults were simply lost causes.

By then Ritter was taking in more than a dozen kids a night and the apartment was getting crowded. He was getting referrals from social-service agencies, cops, and the court system. The streetwise kids were staying away from him, but the fresh runaways from the suburbs were constantly streaming into his apartment. He needed more room. Growing tired of the constant break-ins and vandalism by the drug addicts who lived in the East Seventh Street tenement, Ritter landed on a decidedly Old Testament tactic. He hired some neighborhood thugs with baseball bats and forced the drug dealers out of their neighboring apartments. Ritter has always been proud of that. He even made it part of his mythology, a taste of Errol Flynn to spice up the Bing Crosby image. In his newsletters, he referred to hiring the thugs as "muscular Christianity," or sometimes he defended his action as divine right, saying, "The holy spirit made me do it."

That wasn't the only way that Bruce Ritter played hardball. Fitzgibbons remembers he could be stubborn and self-righteous even about the smallest details of life. The two of them had a white 1965 Pontiac that they were supposed to share. Even if they were living in an East Village flat instead of a monastery, Fitzgibbons believed they were part of a religious community. That meant everything they had was theirs collectively. As Franciscans, they were supposed to forgo any ownership of material possessions. But Ritter would not allow him to use the car.

"He would make me take the subway up to the Bronx for a part-time job I had, even if he wasn't using the car. It was unbelievable. He was really a hard guy to get along with. He was often out for himself," remembers Fitzgibbons.

They had known each other for a long time, and it seemed that all Ritter's arrogance and desire for power were intensifying as he got older. Finally, their differences over the direction of the ministry drove a deep and permanent wedge between them. Without the knowledge of their Franciscan superiors, Fitzgibbons and Ritter parted ways. Fitzgibbons moved into another apartment a few blocks away to continue the ministry as he understood it. And Ritter kept taking in kids at his East Seventh Street apartment. Ritter was probably not sorry to see his fellow Franciscan leave because now he would have the independence that he so much coveted.

It was at that time that Fitzgibbons was questioning his own commitment to the priesthood. He was heading for the great priest exodus of the late 1960s and the early 1970s. Thousands of his generation, those same young men who entered the seminary after World War II, were giving up the sanctuary of the great American Catholic Church. The reform movement in the Church had caused turmoil, and the fallout was that by the end of 1968 an estimated six hundred priests a year were leaving the clergy. By 1970, as many as 20 percent of all priests ordained since 1964 had revoked their priestly vows. They felt suffocated by the Church's rigidity in a world that no longer fit the Thomist rationale on which they were raised. They were getting married, becoming psychologists, coming out of the closet, and simply dropping out.

Fitzgibbons was one of them. He had met a woman at Saint Brigid's Catholic Church, a politically and socially active parish in the East Village. They fell in love, and Fitzgibbons felt he was betraying not only his calling but his own need for a relationship. He knew he had to drop out of the priesthood. Several years later, he left the order and married. He moved back to Hamilton Township, New Jersey, where he is now a family counselor and lives comfortably with his own family.

After that he had little contact with Ritter other than watching his rise to success and constantly wondering why Ritter had written him out of all the glorious history of the street ministry's genesis. Fitzgibbons insists that he does not know if the allegations of sexual abuse against Ritter were founded. He said he never saw any sign that he was violating his vows of celibacy in the beginning years of their ministry in the East Village. For Ritter to have been making sexual advances to the young kids in his care, Fitzgibbons said, would have required "tremendous risk of discovery." It was possible, Fitzgibbons added, but it would not have been easy. He would have been cutting close to the edge of a humiliating and degrading revelation every day.

But every day he got away with it, he must have grown more confident that he'd never get caught.

Chapter 6

The Branches Bow

WALKING along East Seventh Street between Avenues C and D in the summer of 1970, Father Bruce Ritter seemed at home. In the neighborhood of mostly poor Puerto Rican and black families, the inhabitants had come to accept this street priest. For two years, he had committed himself to helping the poor, driving out many of the drug addicts who had tried to gain a foothold in his building. If nothing else, Father Bruce was part of the neighborhood.

One day he heard the sound of an ambulance arriving in front of a vacant lot near his building and he walked along the south side of the street to see what was going on. The ambulance crew was pointing up at a leafless tree. A young boy lay dead, his twisted body sprawled out in the bare branches, which had caught him like some great but indifferent hand after his suicide jump from a six-story building.

That horrifying image stayed with staffers who came out to see it, even though kids died every day on the streets—of heroin overdoses, of senseless murders by fellow junkies, of suicide. It seemed like a forgotten land, where young lives were snuffed out and no one seemed to notice. The Franciscan's mission, his tireless task, was to save the kids before they fell, before they even thought of jumping.

By that summer Ritter had acquired five apartments in his building, expanding his original two-room apartment into a two-floor board-inghouse. He had also taken over a studio apartment in the adjacent building, where he eventually was living. It was here that he developed the idea of the "Covenant" with several close friends and co-workers, including Dave Cullen, Pat Kennedy and her husband, Adrian Gately, and about a half-dozen other social activists from the neighborhood who were involved with the Catholic Church. One night they sat on the floor in Father Bruce's sparsely furnished apartment and wrote out the basic tenets of the covenant, essentially a guarantee of mutual respect and commitment to helping the poor. Over the years the covenant would evolve and become the basis for the charity's name.

In the early years, Ritter relied heavily on volunteers. They were the only staff he could afford. But not all of them agreed with his way of doing things. Jon Eddison, a high school student who came down to help the Franciscan, thought Ritter's focus on street kids was misguided with so many deeper problems in the neighborhood. Stephen Morris, a young medical student who volunteered several days a week, found Ritter's approach to social work chaotic, arbitrary, and at times detrimental to the kids. But Morris also remembers Ritter as a charismatic leader. He made the people who worked for him feel that what they were doing was the most important task in the world. Morris remembers the closeness Ritter engendered with the staff and the kids who stayed there. Several times a week they'd gather in his apartment for group discussions. His voice was always calm but authoritative. He was compassionate and caring.

"He created a sense that we were missionaries," said Morris, who now works in the pathology department at Albert Einstein College of Medicine. "We were out there and he was the shepherd."

But Morris also remembers that there were times when the pedagogy of Ritter's covenant crossed the line into sexuality. On one occasion in 1971, Morris remembers going to talk to Ritter late at night about the problems facing one of the kids in the program. The talk went on late into the night and Morris, who was in his early twenties, felt the conversation was veering off into "a very heavy, latent conversation filled with sexual innuendo."

"At the time it seemed unequivocal to me that Ritter was inviting a sexual advance," said Morris. "It was very circumstantial. I was alone with him and what was classic was that he never asked. He never demanded. He never forced. But he created a situation where it could easily happen."

Nothing did happen between Morris and Ritter, but Morris was not at all surprised when another young male counselor told him several years later that Ritter had made a sexual advance to him as well. And he believed John Melican, one of the street kids in the program in the early 1970s, when he told Morris some ten years later that he had an ongoing sexual relationship with Ritter. He could see how Ritter could cross the line while channeling his sexuality into helping young people.

There was an obsessive quality to Ritter's focus on attracting the young street kids to his apartments. They certainly needed attention and Ritter welcomed them at any time of day. It created a chaotic environment, with people drifting in and out of his life. Some would stay on until Ritter could help them reunite with their families; others would crash there just until they found a job or a new place to live. Others would treat the apartment as a safe haven but continue living on the streets. And there were a handful of kids who ended up living with Ritter for years, adopting the apartments and the safety net he provided as home. Ritter was patient but firm with the kids. He'd give them a place to stay and anything else he could offer as long as they joined in his "covenant."

With Fitzgibbons gone, Ritter was alone and working tirelessly— preaching at local masses and speaking at civic engagements, to raise money to feed and house about fifteen kids a night. He knew he was violating just about every state law there was regarding charitable social-welfare programs. He was not certified by the state agency that monitored charities. None of the apartments he rented would have passed board of health or fire code inspections. He did not have any official licensing or professional training that would qualify him as a state-certified child-care worker.

He was also breaking federal laws. A high-ranking official in the child-welfare system had already warned Ritter that he could be regarded as guilty of "harboring and contributing to the delinquency of a minor" and of "interstate commerce in minors." There were questions about another law Ritter never even knew existed: "the alienation of affection of children." Ritter was so exasperated by this Kafkaesque statute that he wrote about it many years later:

"I had never heard of that one: the alienation of the affection of children—which means that if the kids began to like me enough they wouldn't want to go home again—and that's a crime in New York!"

Ritter never did like rules, and in his antibureaucratic way he seemed proud of breaking them. But as his program expanded, the violations became glaring. The Franciscan's vague street ministry had begun to cross paths with the burgeoning bureaucracy of the city's social-welfare system. He knew if he was going to survive he would have to become registered with the city.

As he walked into the office of the New York State Board of Social Welfare at 270 Broadway in lower Manhattan in the fall of 1971, Father Ritter looked nervous. The drab bureaucratic office represented everything about the social-service bureaucracy that he hated. It was the secular equivalent of the strict rules he rebelled against in the Church hierarchy. There were forms to fill out, procedures to follow, and licenses to be obtained.

Ritter, however, was not there just to come clean about the laws he was breaking. He wanted to tap into the vast reserves of government funding, from which so many rival programs in the city were benefiting. The only way he was going to get to the treasure buried under the sea of bureaucracy was to become an officially licensed charity.

Ritter walked past the gray metal desks, past the brown filing cabinets, the municipal-green furniture, and into the office of Associate Director Robert Walsh. Ritter's case was assigned to Donna Santarsiero, one of the board's evaluators. A young caseworker responsible for the incorporation of all child-care and adult-care services in the state, Santarsiero had kind eyes and was anxious to meet the Franciscan priest.

"Father Ritter?" Santarsiero asked, as all her years of Catholic schooling came back in the form of a humble and deferential gesture to the priest dressed in black clerical garb.

"It's nice to meet you, please sit down," she said.

Ritter was astonished to meet such a warm, intelligent woman in the middle of the maze of the state bureaucracy. He would later tell Santarsiero about the dread he suffered in that office. It was the beginning of a close friendship. Years later, he would persuade Santarsiero to work with him and serve on his board of directors. From his point of view, Santarsiero was a hopeless bureaucrat whom he converted to Covenant House.

That afternoon in 1971, Santarsiero explained to Ritter that she had been assigned to conduct an evaluation of his program. If she felt the program was sufficiently responsive to the needs of the children in its care, she would recommend that the agency become certified. But that would all be pending final approval by the State Attorney General, who had legal jurisdiction over charities, and the Department of Social Services, which had jurisdiction over the fifty-eight social-service districts in the state.

Bruce looked pale, Santarsiero remembers. All the bureaucratic jargon must have sent his mind reeling. He would no longer be the freewheeling Franciscan, carrying out his mission in rags on the back streets of New York City. And Ritter had something else to worry about. Was it possible that the state evaluation could turn up allegations of sexual misconduct? There was some word on the street, or at least suspicion, that Ritter was sexually abusing kids in his care. Stephen Morris had his suspicions at that point. Jim Daniels at The Wayword, which had moved to a new location just a few blocks away from Ritter's program, was no longer advising kids to go there. There were counselors at Judson House and the Living Room, two alternative youth-counseling centers in the Village, who also believed that Ritter's motives were mixed. There was an enormous risk that these allegations would surface, and Ritter must have known that.

One youth counselor who worked on the Lower East Side at the time said, "The problem was that there were rumors with everyone. It comes with the territory in child care. I had heard rumors about Bruce, but I had heard rumors about everybody."

A priest who has since left the Church, but who worked at a group home in the city during that time, said, "There were more than just rumors. There were people on the staff who wanted to confront Bruce on this. But Bruce was the only one in charge. There weren't any real procedures to report it."

Father Pat Molroney, who started another small shelter for runaways on East Ninth Street at about the same time, said, "It's a crowded Irish kitchen down here. Everybody knows what the other is up to, and there were kids coming in who told the other kids to be careful with Bruce. They used to say, 'He's Brucey,' mimicking a lisp and joking about his sexuality. The word was out there. But knowledge was not evidence, so no one did anything."

The threat of revelation *must have* concerned Ritter on a subconscious, if not a conscious level. And one of the most striking things that Santarsiero remembers about the first day she met Ritter is how nervous he was.

Within a few weeks, Santarsiero visited the program, met with the volunteers who helped Ritter, and met with some of the kids. She reviewed the records, which she describes as "a complete mess." The program was loosely structured and unprofessional. It had "nothing even resembling an administration, no established child-care standards in place," remembers Santarsiero. But she still approved their licensing because she felt that once licensed the program would be forced to adhere to the state's standards. Furthermore, Santarsiero felt that she could "relax some of the regulations" because the organization was in its infancy and because it had been formed as "a specialized emergency service to runaways" that "could not completely conform with established, traditional delivery of foster care."

It was an organization with a religious leaning, Santarsiero remembered, "so the state board believed he would become part of the New York Archdiocese child-care system." But the Archdiocese believed he was monitored by the state.

This confusion worked to Ritter's advantage. He was never under the jurisdiction of Catholic Charities, the social-service arm of the archdiocese. In fact, Ritter fought fiercely to protect his ministry from the clutches of the archdiocese.

At the time, Catholic Charities had twenty-two different child-care agencies serving 2,500 kids. The heads of Catholic Charities met monthly with the heads of the certified charities under their auspices. Santarsiero, who in 1972 switched jobs from the state agency to a similar job at Catholic Charities, looked forward to working with Ritter in his developing program. As part of her job, Santarsiero attended the meetings faithfully, and noticed that Ritter attended "very irregularly."

He was cutting a fine line, claiming that he was under the aegis of the Franciscan Order as one way to keep the archdiocese, and Catholic Charities in particular, at bay. Then he would turn around and lead state officials to believe that he was under the supervision of his "Church superiors." It was classic Ritter—finding the perfect way to get around the rules.

The organization finally obtained its charter as a licensed nonprofit child-care agency from the state on November 14, 1972, under the New York Not-for-Profit Corporation Law. It was now officially known as "Covenant House." The new charter stated the organization's purpose was to "identify and attempt to assist in solving the problems of the urban poor and ghetto residents" and "to explore, study, encourage and participate in identifying the social, psychological, and physical problems" of the youths in its care.

On the document, Ritter was listed as one of the three initial directors as well as the executive director and president. The other two directors were, at best, advisers to Ritter.

This original charter was the basis from which Ritter would maintain complete control of the organization for more than twenty years. It would undergo more changes later on that would serve to further entrench a powerful form of patriarchy under Ritter. He would accept no challenges to his authority, not from the Church, not from the state, and not from the people who worked with him. Ritter was

Covenant House. For better or worse, the organization would be completely run and operated by him.

These early years were a struggle. The organization was constantly fighting for financial survival. At the same time, Ritter's child-care program was showing itself to be one of very few in the city that could catch the kids who were falling through the cracks of the established social-service network. The Wayword, Judson House, and the Living Room were not equipped to give shelter to kids, only to serve as drop-in centers. Places like Father Pat's Bonitas House were taking in no more than two or three kids a night. It was glaringly apparent that Ritter provided a unique and valuable service, not just to the kids he took in off the street, but to the city as well.

Covenant House's state certification eventually opened a spigot of hundreds of thousands of dollars in federal, state, and city funding. A $200,000 grant from the City Addiction Services Agency for the 1972–73 fiscal year enabled Covenant House to open a new emergency intake center for boys in the Village at 504 LaGuardia Place. More money from the New York City Bureau of Child Welfare provided funding for a long-term residence for girls at 40 West Eleventh Street, in February of 1973. A few weeks later Covenant House opened its first group home for boys at 207 Wheeler Avenue on Staten Island. Within the next six months, Covenant House would start two more groups homes: at 218 West Fifteenth Street and at 746 East Sixth Street. The street ministry was quickly becoming a professional organization with a full-time staff of caseworkers, a counseling psychologist, and a psychiatrist social worker.

But Father Bruce wasn't relying on the government funding. He was also going out to churches throughout the region, anywhere parish priests would have him, to say mass and take up collections for Covenant House. Someone in power from the archdiocese of New York and New Jersey must have approved of Ritter's program because he was placed on the much-coveted list of organizations for the "propagation of the faith," which entitled him to take up the collections.

Ritter would say two or three masses a Sunday, usually at two different parishes somewhere in the wealthy suburbs of Westchester, the middle-class communities of Queens, small towns upstate, the New Jersey suburbs. His sermons told vivid tales of "urban nomads." It was hard-nosed street talk about prodigal sons and daughters: children, just like the parishioners' own, caught in a world of drugs and prostitution. His voice was somber, sometimes desperate. He looked tired and overworked. The sound of bills rustled in the wicker collection baskets. Ritter got so good at what he did that some priests would not invite him back. Parish priests can get very territorial about their collection baskets, and many of them didn't like the idea of a second collection cutting into their first, the one that goes directly to the parish.

In a single Sunday, Ritter could bring in as much as $4,000 in cash and checks. That multipled by 52 weekends a year could mean as much as $200,000 a year just through his Sunday sermons. At the end of the day, Ritter would collect his money into canvas bags, load it into the trunk of his car, and drive it back to the Covenant House coffers.

S. I. Taubman, Ritter's chief financial consultant at the time, remembers that Covenant House had an operating budget of roughly $450,000 in 1972, about half from government grants and half from Ritter's fund-raising efforts.

He felt "just like a politician" after mass, when he'd stand at the door and shake hands, "building name recognition" and letting the parishioners see his face. Between masses, he'd put envelopes in pews and ask people to write their addresses so he could add them to his mailing lists.

These early mailing lists were a first sign that Ritter had an intuitive ability for fund raising. It was many years before the idea of direct-mail marketing was a thriving industry, yet he was on the cutting edge. In May of 1972, he began writing monthly newsletters. They were simple, direct appeals for help with his mission. They were tales of the street woven with biblical images. Sometimes the letters were upbeat and told about a new program or a kid who had managed to shake his drug habit. Sometimes they were brutally honest about the fatigue and frustration of working with the kids he called his own. But always they were well written, vivid, gripping.

They were also statements on the mission and philosophy of Covenant House. They became his trademark as he slowly developed a more sophisticated and eventually computerized mailing system.

Despite all the cash they brought in, Ritter was never one to save money. He never thought of holding on to funds as an investment and living off the interest as many charities do. The needs for his kids were too urgent. All of the revenues went immediately into expansion.

The shelter was growing rapidly around a core of loyal disciples. Pat Kennedy and her husband, Adrian Gately, lived across the street from Ritter on East Seventh Street. Pat brought her brother, Jim, into the Covenant House fold. He was just out of medical school and a graduate of Manhattan College where he had Father Bruce as a teacher. Kennedy began devoting his skills as a doctor to Covenant House. S. I. Taubman, with his background as an accountant and financial planner, was Ritter's right-hand man on investments and budgets. There was Dave Cullen, a committed counselor and adviser, and nuns, like Sister Gretchen Gilroy of the Franciscan Sisters.

Ed Burns, a lawyer for a prominent Manhattan firm, also began volunteering, handling the legal work on purchases of property and contracts. There were dozens of other prominent and passionate New Yorkers who became part of the inner circle at Covenant House. Most of these loyalists from the early years believed that being around Father Bruce Ritter was the closest they would ever get to a saint. They showed a kind of religious devotion, not just to Covenant House, but to Father Bruce himself. They were fiercely loyal and very protective of the man who founded the mission that changed their lives. They believed in him and they believed that, through him, they were doing God's work.

Taubman was one of his closest confidants. Unlike the others, virtually all of whom were Catholic, Taubman's commitment to Father Ritter's mission had nothing to do with Catholicism or faith in the message of Saint Francis. As Taubman described it, it was his own unique blend of "idealism and Jewish guilt."

"You had to love him," said Taubman. "His commitment to the kids was unending and contagious."

The Jewish accountant and the Irish priest would walk through the Lower East Side, looking for real estate that they could pick up cheap and incorporate into what was becoming a sprawling system of apartments and halfway houses under the mission of Covenant House. Taubman was impressed with Ritter's shrewd sensibilities. He would pull anything he could—guilt, tax breaks, long theological discussions, impassioned pleas, whatever it took to get people to lower their prices.

In late 1972, they bought a beautiful old brownstone on Twelfth Street, with an atrium and a garden, from one of the founding families of a prominent investment firm. They paid roughly half the going rate for the building, convincing the heiress who owned it that she could write off the other half as a donation to charity. It was prime real estate and Ritter eventually made the extravagant apartment on the top floor his private office and residence.

With the expansion of his program, Ritter needed more help. He decided to go back to recruit some of the same students who, years earlier, had challenged him to practice what he preached.

He found Hugh O'Neill, who, as he claimed in his fund-raising literature, came in "sixty to eighty hours a week . . . just because [he] cared about those kids." O'Neill did care about the kids, but the real reason he ended up at Covenant House was that he was sentenced to public service for resisting the draft in the Vietnam War.

He arrived at Covenant House in the fall of 1973 to do his time. At the time, Father Bruce was still battling the state and Church bureaucracies to keep the soul of his institution. It was a kind of paranoid desire to maintain independence that did not always make sense to his staff. But for O'Neill, who would later go into government and become a crucial political ally for Ritter, the avoidance of governmental and Church monitoring was not an indictment of Ritter's character. As far as he could see it was not an attempt to subvert as much as it was a desire to both maintain independence and show compassion for a population that was being written off by bureaucrats and the Church hierarchy.

According to O'Neill, the reason Ritter was insistent about maintaining independence was that Church programs at that time under the archdiocese were excluding homosexuals. Father Bruce would not accept that. There was a philosophy developing that would become an integral part of Ritter's mission. Adopting the jargon of social work, he called it "open intake."

These two simple words—"open intake"—would become the heart and soul of Covenant House's philosophy. It was what made Covenant House an antiestablishment social-service organization. It ran contrary to rules and regulations, and wanted only to have an open door for kids. But it was a philosophy on a constant collision course, not only with the state officials, but even with the Catholic Church.

But there may have been a much darker reason why Bruce was so emphatic on keeping control and resisting Church and/or state regulations. He was living a dual life. And he didn't want to get caught. The man pontificating in church on Sundays about the Dickensian nightmare of street kids was doing precisely what he claimed to be saving them from. He was treading on the edge of discovery at every turn in the early 1970s.

In the spring of 1972, Darryl Bassile wandered into Covenant House, a runaway from a childhood of abuse and neglect. He had grown up with his twin brother and an older brother in a filthy railroad apartment, with bare wood floors and peeling paint, on East Thirty-second Street. They were the sons of an alcoholic mother, he said, who was deeply psychologically disturbed. According to Bassile, her second husband, who worked for a moving company, subjected his stepsons to a life of violent sexual and physical abuse. Almost every week, from the age of nine to twelve, Darryl says, he was taken by his stepfather into a back room off the kitchen and forced to have oral and anal sex while his mother sat in an alcoholic daze at the kitchen table. It was a horrifying childhood, according to Darryl and notes from his therapists.

In 1971, Darryl and his brothers were taken to Catholic Charities, where his mother tried to offer them up for adoption. When she began hitting the boys in the waiting room, the Catholic officials forgot about the paperwork and immediately removed the children from her custody. Darryl ended up in Mount Laureto School for Boys on Staten Island. But he still didn't escape abuse. A gang of three older boys raped him there. When they finished, they strapped the tie from his school uniform around his neck and left him hanging from a tree. Two of them were eventually prosecuted and convicted. Darryl described a horrifying life at the school, of abusive counselors and a menacing atmosphere of violence among the boys. Finally, at the age of fourteen, he ran away with his only friend, John Calvin.

The two boys hopped a bus to Queens, where they slept on the streets and lived off bagels and coffee from a kind-hearted deli owner on Roosevelt Avenue. They eluded the police and either begged or washed a few windows for shopkeepers to have some change in their pockets.

Darryl was a thin ninety-pound waif with a handsome face and shiny blond hair. One day in March, after a few weeks of sleeping on rooftops and under railroad trestles, the two boys wandered into Manhattan. They were hungry and tired and panhandling in the Village when they heard about Covenant House. Some kids told them they could get a hot meal there, a shower, and a bed. No questions asked. Just walk in.

It was late at night when they arrived at the Covenant House intake center on East Seventh Street. They were given some sandwiches and hot chocolate and a place to sleep. The next morning, they were introduced to Father Bruce Ritter.

"He seemed like a very kind, loving man. It seemed like he really cared," Bassile remembers. "He would talk to you and put his arm around you, and I thought, this guy really cares. I still think he honestly did in some ways."

For the first week he was there, Darryl stayed in the residence on LaGuardia Place. He met with Father Ritter and other counselors almost daily while his brothers were being bounced around in the foster-care system. He was given three meals a day, and there were a lot of group discussions. But there wasn't much structure to life at Covenant House, which suited Darryl just fine. Eventually, Father Bruce began calling him at night and telling him to come over to 40 West Twelfth Street, where Ritter was living at the time. Darryl remembers walking through Washington Square Park and then climbing the winding staircase of the West Twelfth Street apartment. They would sit at the kitchen table and talk. At first, there were long discussions about the sexual abuse that Darryl had suffered. Father Bruce told him that he "didn't have to feel bad about that," that it was not his fault. Then they would just spend time together, eating pizza or watching television on the couch.

"My first thought was, oh no, not again. When you get raised with that you know instinctively what they want. But nothing happened and then I started to trust him, I guess. I thought it was just me thinking that way," said Darryl.

But sometime after the first week things changed. They were in Ritter's apartment, sitting on the couch watching television as usual. But as Darryl remembers, Father Bruce lay down on the couch and put his feet up in Darryl's lap. Still staring at the television, Ritter then sat up and moved slowly over toward Darryl. Then he began rubbing his back. It was the only signal a young kid with a history of sexual abuse needed.

"I just knew what to do. I knew exactly what to do," said Bassile. "We had sex. There were no words. There wasn't any discussion about it. It just happened. It was just like with my stepfather. You knew you had to do it. You have to understand that for me love and sex was the same thing. It was the only time my stepfather was ever nice to me. The only time he was nice was when he screwed me. That was my concept of love, as sick as it sounds. . . . When he would go into the back room, we just knew that we had to follow. We knew what it meant. With Father Bruce, it was the same thing. It's like a trained response for a kid who has been abused, and most of the abusers know that. It is just this unspoken thing. I just did what I had to do. It's called surviving."

Each of the roughly six times they had sex it was the same, Darryl said. He would go late at night to watch television, and then the priest would move closer to him or his feet would end up in Darryl's lap. It was the signal, and Darryl would respond the only way he knew how. It was always the same. Silence and sex. No words before or after. The sex was not brutal, as with his stepfather. It was oral sex and mutual masturbation. Never anal sex. With Father Bruce, the sexual abuse was more gentle physically, though just as damaging psychologically to a young kid lost in the world.

Bassile realized there was this special treatment in exchange for sex with the Franciscan priest. He was given full run of Ritter's apartment. Father Bruce would give him a little spending money or take him out for dinner. Ritter would also let him take showers there. Bassile loved the clean, private bathroom after so many years in public institutions, and in the poverty and insanity of the apartment where he grew up.

"I used to turn on the heat lamp in the bathroom. I had never seen one of those before. I thought, wow, this place is fancy. To me, it was like a hotel," he said.

Bassile also remembers that cash was kept in the large oak desk in Father Bruce's office. Small stacks of five- and ten-dollar bills were left in the top left-hand drawer, which usually would be half open. Sometimes there was Canadian currency as well. At the time, Father Bruce was making frequent visits to Canada and would eventually start a program in Toronto. Bassile would wait until the priest went to shower, and then would quietly pull the drawer open.

"I'd steal anywhere from five up to twenty-five dollars. I didn't want to get caught, so I never took a lot. Just enough so that it wouldn't be noticed," said Bassile. Or at least that's what he thought.

One day Ritter was counting the bills and asked him, "You didn't take any money from me, did you?"

Bassile shook his head. At first he was nervous that he was caught, but Ritter never said anything else about it. Later he thought Ritter knew and believed it was the priest's way of keeping him from telling anyone about the sexual abuse. In the confused mind of fourteen-year-old Darryl Bassile, stealing that petty cash was a much more serious crime than the sexual abuse he was suffering at the hands of Ritter.

Besides, Bassile didn't want to do anything to rock the boat. The sexual abuse was still there, but this surrogate father was nice to him most of the time, not just when they were having sex. He craved the attention Ritter provided.

Covenant House exposed Bassile to something else that would become a tremendously destructive force in his life: drugs. Most of the kids who drifted through the program were addicted, and Bassile began to experiment. It started with smoking pot and turned to speed. He and his roommate became close friends and did drugs together. One night, his friend began hinting that he was also involved in a sexual relationship with Father Bruce. That night Bassile confided in his friend about his "counseling nights" with Ritter. A few months later, he was told that his friend had committed suicide.

By the summer of 1973, Bassile's horrible childhood was becoming an adult nightmare. Now he was a high school dropout, addicted to drugs, and haunted by the memory of his friend's death.

That was when Father Bruce Ritter cut the cord, according to Bassile. The counseling stopped. Soon after Bassile was informed that he was being shipped back to Staten Island, this time to a new Covenant House residential facility on Wheeler Avenue off Victory Boulevard. He felt Ritter had used him for sex and then discarded him. Rather than trying to counsel him on his drug problem he simply packed him off to Staten Island.

"That was when I needed counseling more than ever," remembers Bassile. "That's when everything got real bad. But it was like Bruce didn't want to have anything to do with it. At least, it seemed that way."

In 1971, a disturbed and devious kid in his mid-teens named Paul Johnson ended up at Covenant House. He had spent most of his young life bounced between foster homes and child-care agencies. The New York City public school system labeled him "emotionally handicapped" at the age of eleven. He was shipped off to Children's Village, a state-licensed child-care facility in Dobbs Ferry, New York. From there, Johnson went to a foster home in New Jersey and then to another one in the Bronx. In the summer of 1971, a Family Court judge, Justine Polier, asked Father Bruce Ritter to work with Johnson. Polier knew Ritter was developing a reputation as a solid street minister and she felt Johnson was a gifted young man with a very high I.Q. She also knew he was a troubled child with severe emotional problems. Ritter agreed to take the case.

In his first year, Johnson robbed Covenant House blind. He stole everything he could get his hands on. He was a tough kid and Ritter gave him a lot of attention.

"Bruce was the only person I would talk to," remembers Johnson. "He was trying to draw me out of the shell I had constructed around myself. Bruce and I had a relationship that was close. Here was a man who took the time to talk to me, not at me or down to me. And I of course took full advantage of that. Little things, like I'd run over to his apartment and spend a lot of time talking about nothing. We'd talk about me and my hyperactive ways, and what I wanted to do to get my life together. He was into getting-into-your-head type of bullshit. You know, he wanted to 'relate.' Remember, this was the early seventies."

Ritter was close enough to Johnson to write a newsletter about him in June 1973 when he had disappeared after stealing from the staff and other kids. He reappeared a few weeks later and Ritter began counseling him even more intensely. Just as with Bassile, Ritter would call Johnson, who was staying at the East Seventh Street residence, and tell him to come over to his Twelfth Street apartment for "counseling sessions," usually at night, around 8 or 9 P.M. Ritter's form of counseling was casual; there were no rules, no set office hours. They would simply talk in his apartment on the top floor of the brownstone. As Johnson remembers, it had double glass doors that looked out over an atrium and a garden in the back. Ritter was impressed with Johnson's intelligence and was trying to have him placed in a special school for gifted but emotionally disturbed youths. Ritter thought if he could channel all of that mental energy, which was being wasted on stealing, he could make Paul Johnson a brilliant success.

Two years later, when Johnson was seventeen years old, their mentor-and-protégé relationship took a strange turn. They were watching television and talking in Ritter's apartment. It had gotten well past midnight.

"First, I remember he put his feet up across my lap. Then I remember he pulled the two sections together and made it a bed. Don't even ask me what I felt because I didn't think anything. I had no idea what was going to go on. We had a close relationship. This was like, you know, you've seen the pictures of Saint Francis with the kids around him, or, what's his name, Father Flanagan."

In the silence of the night, he felt Ritter's hand moving over his back. Ritter caressed him, but Johnson lay still in fear and did not turn over. He feigned sleep while Ritter's hands moved over his buttocks and his legs. Then the hands stopped. There was no sexual encounter. Ritter turned and went to sleep. Johnson lay in bed staring at the ceiling. He waited for the first light of morning to come through the windows. But when Father Bruce rose before 6 A.M., it was still dark outside. He made coffee and rushed Johnson out of his apartment, about two hours before his staff would begin to arrive.

That day, Johnson locked himself up in his room in the residential dorm on East Seventh Street. The staff did not know what was wrong with him. Father Bruce told them he was worried that Paul was going through a deep depression, that he was acting very erratic and lying. Other counselors, including Steve Torkelsen and Dave Cullen, tried to reach out to Johnson. But they deferred to Ritter on Johnson's case. He was his "mentor," a term Ritter had adopted for senior counselors who worked closely with deeply troubled kids. The way Johnson told it, his reputation for stealing and lying was well known. He says he hinted at his strange predicament to Torkelsen. But he knew no one would ever believe that Bruce Ritter had made a sexual advance to him. Besides, it was only touching, and even Johnson thought maybe he was making too much out of what happened.

After three days in his room, Johnson emerged. He wasn't sure if he was angry or just confused. But he called Ritter from East Seventh Street and said he wanted to talk. Ritter had always told him to be honest about his feelings, so he wanted to be honest about his confusion. Ritter told him to come up to his apartment after 10 P.M. Johnson waited, thinking about what he was going to say.

"I convinced myself I was going to go up there and talk with him about this. . . . I had this big, long-drawn-out speech in my mind. I never got around to it. You have to understand when you get in that man's presence he has an overbearing, intimidating way of keeping you from being honest with yourself, much less anybody else. I never even got around to approaching the conversation at all. I wasn't going to shut the door on him; he was the only friend I had. What do they say? Don't bite the hand that feeds you. Besides, I didn't know anything about what I was feeling. I was a kid, intellectually sound but street stupid. . . . That night we talked a lot and then we went through the same scene all over again."

Again, the night stretched on and Ritter pulled out the sofa bed. He invited Johnson to stay and he did. This time, according to Johnson, the caressing turned to sex. Johnson did not resist Ritter's advances.

"I was just lying there while it happened. There were no words and no discussion; it just happened," Johnson said. "I would say in some way I was a willing participant. But it should also be understood that I was not aware that this was immoral. You have to understand that it was either deal with this or make the mistake of telling someone. Then I was going to lose all the way around. And there was no way I could let that happen."

Johnson again hinted to other counselors that this was taking place. But because he knew that he would never be believed, he kept it to himself.

"Based on my history, I would have been laughed out of the city," said Johnson. "Because they could have thoroughly substantiated that I was a habitual liar, I had been emotionally troubled all my life, and this was just another means of getting some attention. I knew this in my mind. I wasn't going to bother with it."

Johnson had always enjoyed open access to Ritter's apartment, but after they had sex there was an increased amount of license that he felt. He began hanging out at Twelfth Street almost every day. He continued his late-night "counseling sessions" with Ritter. Johnson also noticed that Ritter was keeping cash in the top drawer of his desk. A lot of it was Canadian currency. Johnson was surprised that Ritter would put it out in the open then leave him in the room. Given his history of theft, it was a temptation Johnson could never resist. Unlike Bassile, he was not concerned about getting caught. In Johnson's mind, he was too good to get caught. He would steal up to $100 a week from Ritter's drawer.

One afternoon in the summer of 1975, Johnson pounded up the stairs of Ritter's apartment. Father Bruce was not there, but the door was unlocked. Johnson opened the desk drawer and saw about $300 in Canadian currency. This time he took it all and walked out, the wad of cash bulging in his front pocket. He was stopped in the stairwell by Steve Torkelsen. Torkelsen asked him why he was in the office and then told him to empty his pockets. Johnson knew he was busted and handed over the cash.

"You are really hurting Bruce by doing this," said Torkelsen.

"How am I hurting him?" Johnson asked.

"You stole from him," Torkelsen said.

"So what," he said with the awkward defiance of an adolescent thief. Torkelsen's attempt at a guilt trip made Johnson furious. He felt entitled to that money. Torkelsen knew nothing, or either refused to acknowledge what was the real covenant between Father Bruce and Johnson. Sex for money. Johnson strained to keep his mouth shut. Johnson remembers having the sense that Torkelsen knew what was going on. But Johnson knew if he told now, it would look like he was just trying to save himself by making an unfounded allegation. Instead, this shrewd street kid began to put together an idea for a more lucrative revenge against the priest—psychological blackmail. From now on he vowed to get his money from Ritter up front, with the implied threat of exposing Riter's dirty secret if it wasn't given to him. Johnson wanted to turn the tables of control. The way Johnson saw it, if they were going to have sex, he was going to get paid. Johnson started directly asking Ritter for money. It worked. It was not as lucrative as stealing from the desk drawer, but it was easier. Johnson says he received roughly $60 a week from Ritter while he bounced in and out of the program, until he finally left in 1977.

Johnson claims that he and Ritter had an ongoing sexual relationship until the day he left. He estimated they had sex more than
twenty-five times during those two years. Johnson's relationship with
Ritter did not end when he left Covenant House. Johnson would
reappear through the years, a constant threat to Father Bruce, a
walking time bomb for the organization.

Chapter 7

The Flight

FATHER Bruce Ritter was learning to fly.

At a private airport in Red Hook, New York, he'd slide into the cockpit of a small Cessna and rumble down the runway. Feeling the plane turn against the wind and glide through the sky over the hills and valleys of upstate New York, Ritter would check the altitude and windspeed. The flight lessons were thrilling and dangerous, the way he needed to live: on the edge, pushing the limits. But a more difficult technique than flying in the open air was landing the plane. His instructor was cautious when it came to allowing the priest to take the aircraft down. It was a long time before he trusted him with the landing controls. Eventually Father Bruce got it down, bouncing the plane onto the narrow runway in Red Hook. And eventually he obtained his pilot's license.

It was 1975, and the organization Ritter had founded was poised to soar into the 1980s as one of the largest private charities in the country. But he couldn't see that flight of success. To him, Covenant House had become a stultifying place, just another social-service agency. He felt it was straying from the spiritual and careening into the impoverished realm of bureaucracy.

"... the ... inevitable process of assimilation into the child-welfare system began to occur ..." Ritter later wrote. "... little by little the mission of Covenant House to street kids was gradually being absorbed and colored and finally shaped by the system. . . . . . . [it] was quickly becoming like any other agency, dependent on government funds, subject to government priorities. . . ."

By 1975, Covenant House, with ten residential facilities, was an established "group-home," caring for 120 kids a night. In Ritter's own derisive words, it had become "crisply professional and carefully compassionate." He told his friends he was getting bored and frustrated. He wanted to get out of the social-work business. He didn't see himself as doing God's work. He was a priest, and if this was not going to be a religious mission, he'd say he wanted nothing to do with it.

Behind the scenes, there was another nagging issue. Several members of the staff and board of directors wanted Covenant House to challenge the Church's position on birth control and abortion. It made Ritter furious and he was rapidly getting fed up with the challenges to his authority. He was always a rebel, but he drew the line at violating clear-cut papal edicts. Ritter was contemplating quitting his ministry.

In the late 1960s he had befriended an FBI agent named Alan J. Oumeit, who was doing undercover work in Greenwich Village. He had approached Ritter for "information" on the radical underworld of the Lower East Side. Even though Oumeit insists that Ritter never provided any, they became close friends. When Oumeit began his own charity assisting the network of Catholic missionaries in the impoverished slums of India, he urged Ritter to join him. It had an allure to Ritter, or at least that's what he claimed to his staff. He would tell them about what a great escape it would be to fly himself off to the Far East and start a new ministry. Ritter even went so far as to make appointments with four bishops in India.

At the February 12, 1975, board meeting, Ritter shocked the Covenant House board of directors. According to the minutes he "informed the board that he intended to resign as Executive Director of Covenant House some time during [1976]" and go to India. The announcement left the organization reeling in confusion. It was time for Covenant House to finally set its course—as a state-run, a Church-run, or a Ritter-run agency. There could be no more blurring of the lines, and Ritter's threat of departure made that glaringly clear.

In fact, Ritter was calling the bluff of the entire board. He had decided to play his ace in the hole. From his perspective, Ritter was forcing the board to see that, despite all the rules and regulations, he was Covenant House. It simply could not exist without him.

Just when he had the board of directors—Taubman, Santarsiero, Mark Stroock, and the provincial of the order—panicking about his departure, Ritter went into Phase II of a plan. That May he floated the idea of amending the bylaws of the charity so that he would be able to steer the spiritual direction of the charity, but he kept the details vague.

On June 25, 1975, Father Ritter introduced the amendment. According to the minutes of the meeting, he persuaded the board of directors to "amend the bylaws" of Covenant House to "create members" of the agency, who would ultimately control the organization.

There were few on the board who understood the proposed "membership" structure. Santarsiero and Taubman said they trusted that Father Bruce knew what he was doing and did not question him on the move. The motion was approved. It ended up having a profound and lasting impact, in effect giving Ritter the free rein that he desired.

This was how it worked. The new bylaws provided that the "members" of Covenant House agency would consist of the incorporator, who was Father Ritter, and any person subsequently elected a member by the unanimous vote of the existing members. The bylaws also provided that the members would have the "sole authority to elect and remove, with or without cause at any time, the directors of Covenant House." Through the amendment, the members would also have "the sole power to amend the bylaws." At another meeting a few weeks later, Ritter added another amendment, which provided that the members had "the sole authority to elect and remove, with or without cause, the officers of Covenant House as well."

The trick was that Ritter was the only member. And he never elected any other members. In other words, through the amendments Ritter had created a dictatorship with the euphemism of "sole member." In effect, the changes to the structure of the organization gave Ritter complete legal as well as day-to-day operational control of Covenant House by virtue of his role as sole member, founder, and president.

As sole member, Ritter would never change the bylaws and thus kept complete control of the organization for the next fifteen years. It was a brilliant, almost Napoleonic ploy by a master manipulator.

But none of the rules and amendments took into account a much more significant aspect of Ritter's control: his ferocious will to dominate, the sheer force of his personality, and his exceptional abilities as a leader. Ritter had made himself infallible.

About the alleged scheme to fly to India, Ritter later admitted, "It was not a particularly bright idea. In fact, it was downright crazy. After all, I am not the world's best pilot!"

With his powerbase secure, Bruce Ritter's arrogance went unbridled. After only a few weeks under the new bylaws, he was already executing his papal authority. According to Taubman, the State Department of Youth Services offered Covenant House a $400,000 grant, but along with it would come much closer scrutiny of the program. The state agency would have to investigate Covenant House and establish a set of child-welfare regulations. Father Bruce turned it down. Not bothering to confer with the board or seek Taubman's advice, he flat-out said, "No, thank you," to the agency. Taubman was furious when he heard about it at the next board meeting.

"Bruce, are you crazy? We need that money," said Taubman, clearly illustrating that, unlike the other board members, he carried none of the ingrained deference that comes with growing up Catholic.

"Where on earth are we ever going to get an offer like that again?" he asked.

"Providence," said Father Bruce.

The word was the period at the end of many of Ritter's statements, usually while smiling or flashing his deep blue eyes. Taubman and some of the other board members found Ritter's arrogance infuriating. But he usually proved himself to be right. It was hard to argue with success. The day of Ritter's executive decision not to consult the board or any advisers on the grant was a significant turning point for the organization and for Ritter. It was the point at which he made a full break for independence. He had long resisted the Church hierarchy, and now he had implemented a corporate structure that allowed him to break the grip of the government bureaucracy. Ritter was finally and completely on his own.

Despite his new-found autocracy, Father Bruce was still dissatisfied with Covenant House. The street scene in the East Village had changed dramatically. "The romance is gone," he wrote in 1975. "Middle-class teenagers have learned that New York City is not a good place to run away to. Street life is bitter and hard and the kids are nomads and urban drifters and damaged children. They are not looking for enlightenment, excitement, fulfillment; that quick, beautiful stream of flower children was just a vivid ripple in the history of the late sixties. They are not middle-class kids anymore. They are the children of the poor, and the game they play is survival."

This was the message Ritter was sending out. It was truthful. These were terrible times in New York City. The Great Society had become urban neglect. The once powerful immigrant Church in cities like New York had crumbled. The structure was shaken not only by the exodus of priests but by "white flight" from even the solid neighborhood parishes in the Bronx and Queens. Father Bruce's newsletters were taking a turn to the serious. He was addressing economic imbalances and the "cycle of poverty" that was producing street kids. The gasps he once heard in the pews quickly turned to uncomfortable silences. In his Sunday sermons, the well-off parishioners no longer saw their own children's faces. The faces they saw now were faces of poverty, faces of color, faces they didn't know. The collection baskets didn't fill up the way they used to. Ritter found out the hard way that addressing larger economic problems didn't work in the charity business. He suffered his first—and only—decrease in the budget. It would be the only one in his twenty-one years at the charity. It slipped from $865,110 in 1973 to $795,880 in 1974. With an uncanny ability to understand the direction of the times, he felt the wind was out of his sails. He and his mission were adrift.

It was an era not just of disillusionment, but of betrayal. The Vietnam War lingered between the withdrawal of American forces in 1973 and the fall of Saigon in 1975. That year, pollster Lou Harris showed that political alienation among Americans had steadily risen since 1966 from 29 percent to 55 percent—a "floodtide of disenchantment." The economy was deterioriating and cities bore the brunt of the crisis. New York was on the verge of bankruptcy, social-welfare programs were drying up, and the city was spiraling into ruin. It was the year the *New York Daily News* would scream in its infamous front-page headline: FORD TO CITY: DROP DEAD. And nowhere in the city did it seem more like the end of the world than in Times Square.

It was there, amid the malaise of 1975, that Ritter turned and looked at a growing tide of kids flocking to the Port Authority. The balding Franciscan priest stood amid the filth and the neon and the sin and knew that he had to bring Covenant House there.

> . . . I found myself in Times Square—Eighth Avenue and Forty-second Street—one sultry July night in 1975, about 1:00 in the morning. I became very afraid. I don't remember now why I was there. Perhaps I had gone to the theater with a friend.

The streets were awash with people: drifters, nomads, hustlers, pimps, street people, gawkers from the suburbs. The violence, the foreboding—the air of malevolence—was actually palpable.

Standing on the corner of Eighth Avenue and Forty-second Street I became aware of this very powerful, gut-wrenching conviction that if I remained in child care I was going to wind up in Times Square with these people. I felt as though I had been kicked.

The Times Square Community Planning Board was becoming aware of the problem of teenage prostitution. There seemed to be more young people hanging out on the Great White Way than ever. The once-grand heart of the city had become a haze of neon and strip joints and hustlers. Shrewd businessmen, some with organized-crime ties, had pumped millions of dollars into the sex industry in Times Square. It was boom time in the decade of sleaze—the sexual revolution's reign of terror.

Father Ritter prepared a feasibility study for the community board to see if a Covenant House program should be started in the ungodly place. For several days and several nights, Ritter scoured the area and familiarized himself with the street scene. It was obvious that the need for a shelter was tremendous. Young girls, thirteen and fourteen years old, were brazenly paraded by their pimps on Forty-second Street. There were even younger kids running drugs and handing out fliers for "fantasy escort services." In the dirty back stairwells of the Port Authority Bus Terminal and inside the darkened theaters along Forty-second Street, young boys sold their bodies cheap. Ritter got to know the language of this new reality. The young male prostitutes, fifteen and sixteen, had "seen the elephant," as they referred to servicing older male clients. The older kids, seventeen and eighteen, were "rough trade." They'd been around for a while, maybe too long. The psychedelic drugs and dreams of the runaways of Greenwich Village were gone. Times Square was about survival. It was about what decadence and disillusion could do to a new generation of street kids. Ritter was shocked at the indifference with which the underworld of sexual exploitation was accepted in broad daylight in midtown Manhattan. He was drawn to it and knew that Covenant House had to be there. That was the easy part of the feasibility study. The harder question was where.

Again he walked the neighborhood from Thirty-fourth Street to Fifty-ninth Street, looking for a possible site for the new shelter. Sandwiched between the glitz of Broadway theaters and the sleaze

of Times Square peep shows was a building on Eighth Avenue between Forty-third and Forty-fourth streets. It looked empty. It was
next to a pimp bar and across the street from a porno theater and
a massage parlor.

"You couldn't want a more perfect location," Ritter told the community board members.

Ritter found out the Christian and Missionary Alliance owned the
building. They were a group of Protestant Evangelical missionaries
stationed all over the world. For decades, the building had served as
their headquarters, but they were moving to Nyack, New York. Denizens of the sex industry had approached the alliance with some big
offers to turn their newly renovated chapel into a porno theater and
to convert the residency into peep shows and a sprawling sex empire.
They wanted to put the movie screen on the altar. The alliance refused. But they were also beginning to think they would never unload
the property.

They asked $1 million. It was a good price except Ritter didn't
have anywhere near the finances to close the deal. The total Covenant
House budget for 1975 was $1.2 million, and every cent of it either
was going to programs or was tied up in financing his real-estate
holdings in the Village.

As much as he hated to, Ritter realized that he would have to ask
the archdiocese for help. He arranged to meet with Cardinal Terence
Cooke at the offices of the archdiocese. The twenty-story building at
Fifty-fifth Street and First Avenue was a sturdy rectangle of concrete
and steel, indistinguishable from the other skyscrapers around it.
Above the entrance, there were shiny steel letters that looked more
industrial than spiritual: THE CATHOLIC CENTER.

Ritter took the elevator up past every story of the layered bureaucracy that he so hated. On every floor, a light flashed for each department. Catholic Charities. Immigration Services. Finance.
Personnel. Public Information. And at the top, the executive suite,
the office of the Cardinal. Ritter was running his pitch for the Times
Square crisis center through his head. But he was resigned to the
likelihood that Cardinal Cooke would say no and that would be the
end of it. The Cardinal extended his hand to Ritter with his palm
down. Ritter kissed the ring. Then they talked.

The Cardinal sat behind the polished mahogany desk framed by
a plate-glass window with an expansive view of the Upper East Side
and the East River. He had a simple question: "How much do you
need?"

"Fifty thousand dollars," said Ritter, almost immediately realizing that he had asked for too little and later admitting he wished he'd asked for five times as much.

"Yes," said the Cardinal. "The Church should be there on Eighth Avenue."

"Yes, Your Eminence," said Ritter.

Ritter went to his Franciscan Order in a desperate plea for more financing.

"I think I've just killed myself," he told his superiors. "Will you give me a hundred and twenty-five thousand dollars for a center in Times Square?"

They offered Ritter $25,000 and a $100,000 loan. He was still far short of the money he would need to buy the property, so he turned to the New York–based Culpeper Foundation, which had been a solid supporter of Covenant House, and asked for another $25,000. But they offered to give Ritter $125,000. It was a whirlwind of fund raising that took place in ten days.

Ritter signed the purchase and sales agreement on the property in late July 1976. For the next nine months, he worked alongside several contractors and painters and plumbers, many of whom donated their services. They tore down walls and renovated the building into a crisis center and residential program for the runaways in Times Square. On April 1, 1977, Ritter officially opened the center. Within a month it was clear that Ritter was not going to make the payments on the building.

His director of finances, Steve Torkelsen, put it bluntly: "Listen, Father Bruce, if you cannot come up with a hundred thousand dollars in thirty days, it's all over. We're bankrupt."

Word of Ritter's new crisis center reached Bill Reel, a columnist for the *New York Daily News*. Reel was a powerful writer and the voice of the Irish Catholic working class that was the base of the newspaper's readership. He was sitting at his desk in the *Daily News* cityroom on Forty-second Street and Second Avenue when he picked up on a small item in the archdiocese's weekly newsletter about a priest opening a shelter in Times Square. Seeing a good column in it, he called Ritter immediately.

Ritter listened to Reel and, realizing an opportunity, said, "Why don't you come over right now. I have a story to tell you."

Reel walked across Forty-second Street, drifting into the decay of Times Square. Before his newspaper days, he had worked in an orphanage on Staten Island, learning firsthand how hard it is to care for troubled young kids. He had that in mind as he walked over to see Father Ritter, past the adolescent faces in Times Square full of failure and hopelessness. As he turned the corner at Forty-second Street and Eighth Avenue he remembers being shocked at how bad the place had gotten.

"It was like a sewer over there. There were all kinds of hustlers, bums, derelicts, and slime balls," said Reel. "But I walked into the building and it was clean. It was cheerful. There were kids sitting on throw pillows on the floor. It was like a salvation in all that insanity."

He and Father Ritter sat among the kids while Ritter told him the great legend of Covenant House, spinning his tale like a master. The challenge from his students at Manhattan College, the humble beginning in the East Village, the successes and failures in nearly ten years of saving young lives. It all made for great newspaper copy, and Reel was scribbling madly in his notebook to get it all down—the first of many journalists to take down the legend. Then Ritter turned the direction of the interview to deal with the crisis.

"You know, Bill, I went way out on a limb on this," he said, as he showed off the sprawling building, which was connected by a catwalk to another building that housed a beautiful chapel with mahogany pews and new carpeting. Ritter was just working on having a new altar put in place—simple slabs of stone, where he would deliver his sermons.

"I didn't budget it right, and I may have to close it down," he told Reel, as they walked through the chapel.

That same afternoon Ritter was on his way to the archdiocese to see Bishop O'Keefe, the Vicar General, about getting more funding. Ritter was not optimistic. Reel watched as the Franciscan priest in his best collar jumped into a cab in front of the building and drove off to try to save his newly built shelter.

On the way home, Reel had an idea. He thought he would craft his column as an appeal to save Covenant House, a written plea for the Times Square priest.

Reel wrote a compelling column on May 6 about Ritter's work with the runaways and the beautiful new property he had acquired. Then he wrote, "That's the good news. Now the bad news is that Father Ritter is broke and the whole thing could go under."

A week later Ritter called. "Bill, you won't believe what happened. I am buried under envelopes here," he said, excited with a boyish enthusiasm that Reel was discovering could be contagious.

Reel's readers answered the appeal in the column with $20,000 in donations in just one week and the money was still coming in. It came in envelopes stuffed with five- and ten-dollar bills or checks for $25. But there were thousands of them.

Reel wrote a second column on May 20, which touched off more of an onslaught. By the end of two and a half weeks, Ritter had more then $50,000 in donations from letters responding to Reel's columns. This made Reel part of the legend. In the organization's calendar, where they would list significant dates in the history of Covenant House, under May 6 it always read: "Bill Reel column in *Daily News* saves Covenant House from bankruptcy."

Bill Reel was one of Ritter's earliest and most ardent supporters. He would frequently write about Ritter as the guardian angel of Times Square, carrying out "the corporal works of the Bible." He would tell his wife that helping Covenant House made him feel his newspaper job meant something, that it could still stir people to do some good.

"Father Bruce was the greatest Christian worker in the American Catholic church in my lifetime," said Reel. "He was a great Christian apostle, who mobilized more people, attracted more people, brought out the best instincts in people, taught people to give, motivated them to give. There were tens of thousands of people who were brought in to giving because of Father Bruce. I can't get past the fact that he poured himself out to people in a way that was virtually unique. Mother Teresa is the only other example of it."

Reel would sometimes attend Ritter's services when he was preaching in parishes on Staten Island, where Reel has his home. He remembered seeing Ritter one Sunday after a mass at Saint Anselm's. Ritter was walking by himself in the parking lot before the next mass began. Reel watched the priest pace between the cars and wondered what it was about Ritter that seemed so melancholy and sad. He had a way of keeping his distance. The commitment seemed to consume him. It had taken over his life. Reel had seen a lot of priests pulling scams. He had the skeptical eye of a journalist even about his Church. But, to him, Ritter was genuine.

With the $50,000 raised through Reel and another $10,000 from a New York foundation, Ritter was close to making the payments. The way Ritter told it, a last-minute anonymous donation of $40,000 from a retired woman in New Jersey put him over the top.

Actually, the mythology of thirty days in the spring of 1977 was another Ritter exaggeration. The story behind the real saving of Covenant House from bankruptcy would come later that year.

Nevertheless, Ritter felt he was back to his mission. Kids were flooding into the Eighth Avenue shelter. Ritter was taking in fifty to sixty kids a night. They would sleep on cots and on large pillows thrown on the floor around the altar in the chapel. Ritter's mission had a new urgency.

"Covenant House changed radically back into what it should always have been," he wrote.

The malaise of the mid-1970s was over, and Covenant House seemed to hold an exciting future for Father Bruce Ritter.

"I changed," he wrote. "Times Square changed me."

III

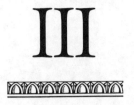

The Temptation

---

*The serpent was the most subtle of all the wild beasts that God
had made.*

Genesis 3:1

Chapter 8

The Deal

IN his colonial-style home on his estate in New Canaan, Connecticut, Bob Macauley, a prominent businessman who moved in powerful Republican circles, was in his pajamas reading the Sunday papers. His wife brought morning coffee to the bedroom on a silver breakfast tray. On it she had placed a newspaper clipping from the *New York Daily News:* another of Bill Reel's columns on the Franciscan and his mission.

It was the spring of 1977. Having already made his millions as the owner of a Virginia-based paper company, Macauley wanted to become a full-time philanthropist. He was a close personal friend of George Bush, then a rising "agency man" in the CIA, who had already made millions on Texas oil before embarking on the presidency. Macauley and Bush had grown up together in Greenwich, Connecticut, graduated in the same class at Phillips Academy in Andover, and become roommates at Yale. Associates and acquaintances privately suspected that Macauley was also an "agency man," although he adamantly denies it.

Macauley had achieved some notoriety during the waning years of the Vietnam War, organizing the Shoeshine Boys Foundation, a philanthropy that provided the poor street kids of Saigon with shoeshine kits so they could "help raise money for their welfare by shining the boots of American GIs." In 1976, in the wake of the fall of Saigon, Macauley even chartered a Pan Am flight with his own money and flew some two hundred injured children out of Vietnam, putting them up for adoption in the United States.

A big man, at least six-foot-two, with a gravelly voice and commanding presence, Macauley relies on instinct. After reading Reel's column, he immediately picked up the phone, called Ritter at his office, and invited him out to New Canaan for dinner. Ritter figured Macauley was just another wealthy businessman who'd donate some money and end up asking him to play golf. Ritter hated golf and all the invitations he got to play it. Wealthy contributors to Covenant House often demanded Ritter's companionship, as if they had paid for it. Father Bruce desperately needed their money, but always tried to create some distance before he accepted it, to spare himself their company. After putting off meeting Macauley for a week or so, Ritter finally made it out to his estate on May 11, 1977.

"I think I could help you," Macauley said, making the dinner-table conversation sound more like a boardroom presentation. "I raised a lot of dough for my own organization and I could help you do the same."

Macauley used the word "dough" a lot. He began talking about "marketing," and about using Ritter's "image" as a "fund-raising tool." He told Ritter he had to build up his "name recognition" and take advantage of a budding new business called "direct-mail solicitation." He batted around the catchphrases of corporate America like golf balls: "bottom line," "cost effective," "more bang for the buck." Macauley also dropped a lot of big names: National Security Adviser Zbigniew Brzezinski; Secretary of the Treasury under Nixon William Simon; and Peter Grace, president of the multinational W. R. Grace & Company. He bantered about his experience in the Republican fund-raising circuit. There was big money in these big circles, he told the Franciscan priest.

Macauley was Mephistopheles tempting Ritter with a Faustian bargain. He could make Covenant House a world-class nonprofit organization and Ritter the head of not just a charity but a sophisticated philanthropic kingdom. There were dreams of Ritter's mission expanded worldwide. For Macauley, it was a venue to apply his business skills to philanthropy. It made him feel good.

"A Svengali in pinstripe" is the way one board member later referred to Macauley.

Ritter was leery but intrigued. Through his ten years with Covenant

House, Ritter had learned how to read the rich and powerful just as he had learned how to read street kids. He knew when to stroke their egos and how to play off their vanity. The street-smart Franciscan knew better than to act too eager.

"I'm not interested," he told Macauley, flatly rejecting the plan over coffee after dinner. "I appreciate what you are trying to do. But where I come from everything is for the glory of God, not the glory of Bruce Ritter. I don't want to be the focal point."

As Macauley continued to explain his idea of getting Covenant House into the sophisticated field of direct-mail marketing, he told Ritter about how they could purchase "mailing lists" and target different sectors of the American populace.

The thought horrified Ritter. He told Macauley that buying mailing lists was immoral, unethical, and inauthentic. To the Franciscan priest, it was a betrayal to turn his religious order's humble history of begging to help the poor into a sophisticated enterprise that could fuel a national charity.

"I am not a fund raiser," Ritter told him. "As a Franciscan, I am a beggar, a mendicant. A mendicant is somebody who goes around and begs for money, not fund raises. There is an enormous difference. Saint Francis commanded us friars to beg. You can only beg for the love of the poor, and for the love of God."

Macauley appreciated Ritter's eloquent theology, but he could also sense that the priest wasn't a sucker.

"Well, you've got to have a spokesman. You have got to have a front man," said Macauley. "You have to become more visible."

As Macauley remembered the evening, they argued for hours. Ritter kept insisting that he was doing just fine running his own organization. Being a charitable Christian, he would appreciate any volunteer work, donations, or even advice that Macauley could offer. But, being a priest who liked things his own way, he added that any kind of involvement by Macauley on an administrative level was out of the question. Ritter thanked Macauley and his wife for the meal and drove back to Times Square.

But Macauley was persistent, calling again the next morning.

"Father Bruce, why don't you come out again? I don't think we finished that conversation. We'd love to have you. Please," said Macauley.

"I can't," said Ritter. "I'm just swamped here. But then again, I guess I have to eat. Can we make it late?"

The next night, Ritter drove again from the netherworld of Times Square to the other world of New Canaan. He wound past the sprawling horse farms with their stately homes lit up in the night, through the dark, winding, tree-canopied roads. He arrived just after 9 P.M. and Macauley was ready for him. With another banquet on the table, Macauley immediately began serving up his business offer.

It was time for Ritter to give a little. The priest still believed he was the one pulling the strings. Like all Faustian bargains, it began with the illusion of control. They talked about what Covenant House had accomplished, and what it could accomplish. They discussed Ritter's philosophy of "open intake." Macauley listened to Father Bruce's impassioned stories of battling to cut the red tape of government bureaucracy and to dance past the rigid rules of the Catholic hierarchy.

"I thought to myself here is a man who feared God," Macauley remembers, "but who was not afraid to challenge the establishment."

This priest was a rebel and Macauley could sense it. He had a "higher purpose," and if he had to bend the rules to carry it out then so be it. Macauley saw in him the same kind of force of will it took to be a good businessman or military commander. He knew Father Bruce was not your average cleric. He had vision. He had, as they say in corporate boardrooms, *cojones.*

Ritter was beginning to see that the kind of advice Macauley was offering could bring in not thousands, but millions of dollars to his charity—numbers that the head of any charity would listen to. They argued and dreamed until 4 A.M.

Father Bruce left with the agreement that he would come out again next week to finish the discussion. By the third night, Ritter recognized how much impact Macauley could have on the growth of the charity, and trusted that his commitment was sincere. There was money and power and influence that came with Macauley's offer, and Ritter believed this paper-mill tycoon and hobnobber with the rich and powerful could deliver. With his own righteous belief in his mission, Ritter convinced himself that the fund-raising plan would not corrupt him, that he understood his vow enough to remain a "mendicant." The deal was done.

"All right," Father Bruce said. "Let's get down to it."

"It's a long-range program," said Macauley.

By the time spring turned to summer, Macauley was working full time in Ritter's Times Square office. The sound of the street was consuming. There were radios blaring, horns honking, and prostitutes fighting with their pimps. Police sirens wailed and heroin dealers peddled their wares like street vendors pushing pretzel carts. There was no air conditioning, and Macauley would watch his sweat drip onto the dog-eared books that Ritter kept in several old, rusted filing cabinets. The records were indecipherable, a businessman's nightmare.

"Bruce, you're broke," said Macauley, after finally converting the crumpled paper and tattered receipts for expenses into a computerized balance sheet. "It's that simple."

Ritter always liked to write about how Reel and a last-minute anonymous donor miraculously saved him from bankruptcy. It was a great part of the mythology, but the charity was actually treading on the edge every week after the purchase of the Times Square property. It was Macauley who saved them from collapse, by directing Ritter on a long-term financial plan.

"How can we be broke?" Ritter would ask Macauley. "We have so much money coming in."

"It's pretty simple, Bruce. Your expenses exceed your income," Macauley would reply.

By the dog days of August, Ritter was spending every working hour with Macauley and then driving out to the Macauleys' comfortable home at night, where they would pore over the pages of their finances. Macauley would put out a basket of fresh rolls and creamy butter, which Ritter loved. Soon Ritter developed quite a paunch. Having fattened his protégé, Ritter's corporate mentor would tease him about it.

"You better thin up," Macauley would joke. "It's not good for the image to have an overweight Franciscan."

The two men would work late into the night, reviewing the charity's property holdings, figuring out how to proceed on selling off the properties in Greenwich Village, and beginning to devise a fundraising plan.

In his blustering tone laced with secrecy, Macauley explained how he helped salvage the charity's finances: by going to "high banking connections."

"We got an executive from Chase Manhattan to come in pro bono. . . . On Labor Day 1978, we hired Keith Brown as the internal financial officer. He was perfect. I hired him on the spot. He really shined. I'd say he was with us for at least five years and was responsible for getting the organization in order," Macauley remembered. "There were other important investors, connections of mine. I won't go into them. Let's just say they were friends."

Macauley's "friends" included Peter Grace, who is right out of central casting for the quintessential American tycoon. A short, abrasive man with a ruddy face, Grace flies around the world in his own private jet, tending to his conglomerate of enterprises in chemicals, energy, and manufacturing spread over forty-five countries. A rabid anti-Communist and adviser to Presidents on cutting bureaucratic waste, Grace is a complex man. He is blunt and caustic, but also regarded as the "most active and dedicated private fund-raiser for the Catholic Church in the world." Mixing his conservative political ideology with his religion, Grace is a master at lobbying people at the pinnacles of power in business and government for a cause if he feels it fits his political interests and his understanding of the Catholic faith. In Covenant House, Grace would find his favorite American charity.

Grace and Macauley were also bound by their allegiance to a secretive, ancient, and international lay order called the Knights of Malta—a kind of old boys' club for some of the world's most wealthy and powerful Catholics. The American Knights, some seventeen hundred members, predominantly corporate CEOs, bankers, and high-ranking members of the political, military, and intelligence community. Membership has included the likes of former CIA director William Casey, Alexander Haig, William F. Buckley, and Lee Iacocca. Athough Macauley is not Roman Catholic, he calls himself a "funny kind of non-Catholic," who attends mass every morning and was made the first honorary member of the Knights. President Reagan was the second. Another of Macauley's friends and fellow Knights is William Simon, a virulent anti-Communist and leader of many conservative political causes. He too would come to see Father Bruce Ritter's Covenant House as something worth investing in. The Knights, shrouded in all their secrecy and conspiratorial air, would become an important base of financial support for Covenant House. For decades, Grace has been president of the Eastern Association of the American Knights.

Macauley did more than just introduce Ritter to these powerful men, he taught him their culture: the rudiments of finance, the importance of planning ahead, and the reality of big money. He showed him how to read a balance sheet and how to strengthen his "portfolio" to allow expansion of the operation. The "God will get us through" attitude made for great fund-raising rhetoric. It could certainly be used in a marketing sense, but it wasn't going to work every time. Ritter caught on quickly.

Macauley was impressed by this humble priest who had picked himself up by his bootstraps. With all the adulation, Ritter was beginning to think if he hadn't become a priest he would have made an excellent corporate CEO himself.

Ritter was soon having lunches at the Plaza, meeting power brokers at country clubs in Westchester, spending winter vacations at Macauley's posh Florida home and weekends at his farm in Millbrook, New York. The power and the pleasures were intoxicating.

Macauley admired Ritter's boyish excitement, which was tempered by "a tremendous ability to assess people from a psychological standpoint." Ritter learned it was a valuable business skill and he grew to rely on it.

But, despite all his intuitive brilliance, there was something happening around Ritter that perhaps he couldn't see. A continental plate was shifting in the American political landscape, and whether he realized it or not, Ritter was moving with it. Macauley was at the vortex of a politically conservative movement that was about to become a new and powerful force in the United States.

In Ritter, this movement would find a surprisingly successful symbol for its ideology. Unlike the gaudy and superficial electronic ministries of the Reverend Jerry Falwell or Pat Robertson, Ritter would become a more subtle and sophisticated icon of the right, cloaked in the garb of a compassionate, streetwise Catholic priest. Ritter was, perhaps unwittingly, soon to become a bit player in a conservative power play with Ronald Reagan starring in the lead role.

For the time being, in the late 1970s, the introductions Ritter was being given to heads of corporations and political ideologues would be a simple means to his end of helping troubled young people. Eventually, however, they would come to own Father Bruce. The corporate influence and the rapid expansion of Covenant House across the country and into foreign lands would forever change the Franciscan's mission. The charity would lose its bearings as it got too big. But that was all hard to see in the heady days of growth that Ritter was planning with his new friend Macauley.

By 1978, Covenant House was just starting to bring in a lot of donations, largely because of the charity's fortuitous entry into the budding industry of direct-mail marketing. Not wanting to abandon the personal appeal that got him started, Ritter was still filling his calendar with appointments in parishes and at college campuses all along the Eastern Seaboard. Between the direct mail and the speaking engagements, the charity's total annual donations had grown to over $3.7 million by the end of fiscal 1978.

Macauley had also introduced Ritter to another source of revenue: corporate donations. Using Macauley's contacts, Covenant House began to open itself up to major corporate financing. Before Macauley arrived, they had had some funding from foundations, mostly the Culpeper Foundation and other smaller institutions. But in 1978, Macauley began lobbying heads of large corporations, many of whom were his friends. In 1979, they received $260,492 in corporate donations. Within three years, there were some 170 corporations, including many of the nation's largest multinational firms, contributing to Covenant House. Within three years, total corporate giving had increased to $395,338, and when combined with foundation and capital-expense grants it totaled more than $2.3 million. By 1980— with Macauley's three years of guidance—Covenant House had more than tripled its annual budget to $9 million.

As Ritter's financial base grew, the charity began to rely less on government grants, which were scant in the wake of the city's financial crisis in the late 1970s and amid a deepening national recession. In 1977, the Bureau of Child Welfare was placed under the Department of Social Services, making it a vastly more layered bureaucracy. Under the new system, most of the oversight of charities and social-work agencies was tied to the amount of government grants they received. In other words, the more money an organization received, the more monitoring they were subjected to.

In addition, the grants Ritter received, mostly municipal funding from Foster Care Prevention and federal funding for meal programs, did not carry the controls that direct grants for child care did. Ritter used his limited government funding for peripheral programs and therefore remained on the margins of their regulations. He was not susceptible to the same audits, guidelines, or reviews as other charities. If Ritter was doing anything wrong—financially, programmatically, or personally—there was no way to detect it. As one administrator with twenty years' experience in the social services put it, he was "simply not part of the machinery."

Father Bruce's itinerant preaching and direct-mail appeals brought in more than just money. He was creating a broad base of support in hundreds of predominantly Catholic communities throughout New York, New Jersey, Connecticut, and Pennsylvania. In parishes, colleges, and business groups, there were tens of thousands of Catholics following Father Bruce's mission and listening to his message. They became a core of "true believers," who watched Ritter's rise to prominence and felt as if they had something to do with his success.

Father Ritter challenged these followers to practice their faith in the real world. Instead of praying every Sunday to a homeless man who was crucified, Father Ritter was urging them to come out and help homeless kids who were being crucified every day on the streets of New York City. Answer phones, serve meals, write a check, or take the bolder step of actually living in the community and devoting a year of your life. "Get involved in saving these kids," Ritter beseeched the parishioners. He wanted Covenant House to sow its care in fields all over the country, all over the world. And he couldn't do that without the help of the hundreds of thousands of people who professed their faith in him.

Ritter's street-tough theology was having a powerful impact on young, idealistic Catholics. In the winter of 1979, when he traveled to a parish in a small northern New Jersey town, called Woodcliff Lake, Father Bruce's words changed Anne Donahue's life. She was a law-school student attending mass with her family. Father Bruce's challenge awakened something in her, a stirring of social and religious commitment.

"I was so mesmerized by what he said I literally wanted to jump in his car and go back to Times Square that day," Donahue remembers. "I knew he was a very gifted leader. I knew I wanted to be a part of his ministry and his vision."

Anne, who was in her mid-twenties, vowed to finish law school at Georgetown University and become a volunteer at Covenant House. She knew a law degree from a prestigious school would afford her the opportunity to make as much as six figures right out of school. But she made a promise to herself to give something back by working with Father Bruce. In the fall of 1982, just after she graduated from Georgetown, Donahue became a live-in volunteer.

John Spanier was a twenty-seven-year-old manager rising through the ranks of a food-services company when Ritter came in 1980 to speak in his family parish, Saint Margaret's in Reading, Pennsylvania. For years his mother had been a faithful donor to Covenant House and she often left its newsletters out on the kitchen table for her family to read. Father Bruce gave a compelling sermon urging people to volunteer. After mass, Spanier's mother said, "If I were in my twenties, that's exactly what I'd do." Spanier remembers he bit his lip, because he had already decided he was going. He quit his job that week and applied to become a volunteer at Covenant House. But by that time the community was so swamped with applications that it actually took Spanier nearly two years to gain acceptance. Spanier and Donahue entered the Faith Community together in 1982 and would go on to fill "leadership roles" within the organization, serving as young but trusted advisers to Ritter.

Father Bruce's corps of volunteers would become known as the Covenant House Faith Community. It began informally with the first

few people coming to Times Square on a daily basis as volunteers in
the mid-1970s and then grew to become one of the largest Catholic
lay communities in the country. Among the pioneers was Marge
Crawford, widow of a prominent New York State politician, who
while in her late fifties began pouring all of her love and devotion
into helping street kids through Ritter's mission. A kind of spiritual
mascot in the Faith Community, she was one of the first of the true
apostles to Father Ritter.

By the winter of 1979 there was an established Faith Community
of twenty-five people, who resided at the charity's Times Square
building. They lived in dorm-style rooms in the main Covenant
House building, facing Eighth Avenue. Every morning before dawn,
they climbed the dark stairs that led to the catwalk connecting the
adjacent chapel. It was cold in the drafty chapel at 6:30 A.M. As the
founder and spiritual leader of the Faith Community, Father Bruce
would pray with them.

The community members worked at the intake center, did outreach on the streets, counseled the young people in their care, or
just answered phones. But their schedules always revolved around
three daily prayer sessions.

On Tuesday mornings, the Faith Community would rise a half
hour earlier for Father Bruce's "theological lesson." Traditional, orthodox theology was combined with a call for social action.

Greg Loken, another early Faith Community member, said, "It
didn't matter to him how you felt about the Catholic hierarchy, or
how you felt about Ronald Reagan, or, to a certain extent, how you
even felt about the kids. He wanted you to love them, but he knew
that wasn't always easy. What was truly important was how many kids
are you taking off the street? How many mouths did you feed today?"

Loken—a talented Harvard Law School graduate practicing corporate law in Colorado—came to the community because he wanted
to do something "in the real world." He was considering the Peace
Corps, but decided against it. Then a friend told him about Covenant
House, which seemed a perfect challenge.

Father Bruce lived with the Faith Community on the fourth and
fifth floors of the Times Square building. Among his followers, he
was often quiet and reserved. He was sparse with praise and rarely
emotional.

One priest who worked with Father Bruce and the Faith Community for many years said, "Bruce was a very private person. He
had his spiel, but he would never get personal even with his closest
friends. He would rarely talk about his family or his past or his

emotions. He would shut himself off. Nobody ever knew anything about Bruce that he didn't want them to know."

Nevertheless, many of the people who worked with him believed they were in the company of a living saint. There were young volunteers in the Faith Community, like Donahue and Loken, and older Ritter apostles, like Peter Grace and Bill Reel, who believed that upon his death there would be a movement for beatification of Father Bruce: the first step in Rome's process of naming saints. But there were others, especially his fellow Franciscan friars, who didn't see him that way at all. One priest who had known Ritter for nearly thirty years said, "He was a competent theologian and a tremendously compassionate man, but I would not describe him as intensely spiritual."

Father Bruce could not only be cold and cutting but he suffered from the sin of pride as well. Although humility filled his fund-raising letters, in daily life arrogance crept beneath the surface, often festering into moods of angry despair that took someone as close as a fellow Franciscan to see. There were also a few "worldly" tastes—like scotch, which Ritter enjoyed after a hard day's work. He smoked nearly a pack a day of cigarettes, until he quit in the early 1980s. Not that a saint can't have a few human habits, but the divine process of canonization requires a kind of perfection of the spirit that fellow priests knew Ritter never had. In 1981, when Macauley used his private plane to fly Mother Teresa in for visits to Covenant House and the White House, Father Bruce confessed the unworthiness he felt around her in a newsletter: "It makes me very nervous to be around holy people. It always seems to me that they can size me up in a wink and nail me for the sinner I am."

But even if Father Bruce did not feel himself to be holy, the Faith Community felt that his humility only made him more so. When Father Bruce turned his attention to one of them, they often described feeling a kind of "glow" or "warm light." In many ways, their religious devotion was not only to God but to Father Bruce—a cult of personality around the man whose mission they carried out.

The development of the Faith Community put Father Bruce once again at the cutting edge of the new developments in the Catholic Church. This Vatican II–inspired street ministry was one of the first to realize the lay community was the future of the Church. After the mass exodus of priests and nuns through the late 1960s and early 1970s, the Church was facing a crucial labor shortage. The idea of communities of lay people carrying out the corporal works of the Church is perhaps the Church's only answer to survival. In purely practical terms, the community provided Ritter with a cheap labor pool of talented young people who were paid $12-a-week stipends and given room and board in exchange for their work.

By the end of the 1970s, the original intent of the charity, to be "of some help to the poor in the East Village," was vanishing into darkness behind the bright neon of Times Square. Father Bruce began closing the original tenements where he had founded his mission. The group homes on Staten Island and West Twelfth Street were being phased out. Most of those programs, which were contracted under the city's Foster Care Agency, brought a fixed amount of aid for each youth, which was no longer applicable in a large shelter that had so many coming and going. The city funding was deemed inadequate, and Father Bruce determined that the group homes were ultimately a "drain on Covenant House." He was breaking away even further from the established social-service network, focusing his efforts primarily on the short-term crisis centers in and around Times Square. By 1979, Covenant House had only two group homes—one for about fifteen boys, aged thirteen to seventeen, on West Fifteenth Street and another for about fifteen to twenty girls, aged thirteen to nineteen, on West Forty-seventh Street. Specifically designed for youths not labeled as "hard-core street kids," the programs were more halfway houses for youths until they could be reunited with families or permanently placed in foster care. Otherwise, Ritter was doing big volume on street kids at the crisis center on Eighth Avenue between Forty-third and Forty-fourth streets. Father Bruce would walk among the kids late at night just before the lights were turned out. He would listen to their stories and tell them he loved them. With about one hundred a night staying there, Father Bruce realized he needed more room.

The horde of young people residing at Covenant House and contributing to the deterioration of Times Square did not go unnoticed by the Community Planning Board, the Broadway theater organizations, and a powerful next-door neighbor called *The New York Times*. They complained about the area's crime and drug trade, to which they felt the location of Covenant House contributed. After all, the community board had approved of a plan for a small program to help street kids, not a full-fledged residential shelter and a revolving door for thousands of not just kids, but young adults between the ages of eighteeen and twenty-one.

Complaints went to City Hall, and soon Ritter's program was being hit with health and fire-code violations. Ritter knew he couldn't fight City Hall. But he did know how to sucker punch the establishment with a threat to set up a soup kitchen in the building, entirely permissible under his charter. He threatened to line up hundreds of derelicts on Wednesday and Saturday, corresponding with the theater district's busy matinee and evening performances. Ritter's neighbors were horrified, and Mayor Ed Koch stepped in with a classic political solution. Promising to find Covenant House a bigger building at a different location, the Mayor pleased the priest and placated the powerful neighbors. Once the crisis quieted, Koch did nothing. So Father Bruce began to look for himself, spotting an abandoned eight-story building that occupied an entire block between Fortieth and Forty-first streets on Tenth Avenue. Owned by the state-run Manhattan Rehabilitation Center, the six-hundred-bed institution was part of a failed state program to build halfway houses for drug addicts. Father Ritter wrote a letter to the state General Services Administration, which handled most of the state's property, and requested the building for a Covenant House shelter. Promptly and flatly denied, Ritter didn't give up. He was going to take it to the top.

Ritter needed to get to Governor Hugh Carey, and he worked some key connections to do so—including Monsignor James Murray, who headed Catholic Charities; Peter Grace, who knew Carey; and Hugh O'Neill, who had gone to work as one of the Governor's advisers.

It was Holy Thursday 1979 when Ritter was finally scheduled to meet with the Governor. An inveterate marker of significant dates, Ritter remembered that it was also on Holy Thursday eleven years before that he first moved to the East Village. "Providence," he whispered to Macauley as they waited for Carey.

Carey explained that the New York City Department of Corrections wanted the building to cure severe overcrowding in its jails. But Carey—either intrigued by Ritter's commitment or intimidated by some of his powerful friends—softened a bit. Staff officials informed Father Bruce and Carey such a complicated transaction could take months, maybe a year. Carey, a devout Catholic, very aware that it was Holy Week, was getting impatient with his staff.

"Get back to me in one hour and tell me why you haven't done it today," he said and slammed down the receiver.

"We'll do what we can, Father," the Governor said.

About a week later, Father Bruce was out at Bob Macauley's estate in New Canaan when a call came from Ritter's secretary. The Governor's office had called and it was urgent. Father Bruce and Macauley moved into the privacy of the wood-paneled library. Good news: The state was ready to offer the building to Ritter on the basis of a five-year lease at $1 a year. Ritter said he'd call back in ten minutes, he just wanted to confer with his board chairman.

"This is great, it's worth millions!" Ritter said to Macauley.

"Yeah, but it's going to cost three to four million dollars to remodel it," said Macauley, bringing the Franciscan down to earth. "There is a way to do it, but it's going to take a lot of planning."

"I am going to pray about it," said Ritter as he slipped away from the library into his upstairs bedroom and prayed for an answer.

He was upstairs for forty minutes and Macauley was growing impatient. Father Bruce had said he would get right back to the Governor's office, and for Christ's sake, Macauley told him, you don't do that in the middle of a deal.

"Bruce, you have to stop praying. What are you going to do?" Macauley asked.

"We have to do it," said Ritter. "It is Providence."

Several days later, Ritter was handed the keys to the three-building complex on Tenth Avenue, near the opening to the Lincoln Tunnel. The rooms were set up in dormitory style; there were libraries, classrooms, a gym, and a large, fully equipped kitchen. But Ritter knew it would take months of work to convert the halfway house for use in the model program he wanted—and some luck to come up with the money.

A fellow Franciscan, the Reverend Giles Van Wormer, came to see the new building and his old friend. Bruce Ritter had become the rising star of the Franciscan community—a trait not always looked upon favorably by his order. To his fellow priests, the eagerness to succeed, the fascination with the spotlight, only made Ritter's intentions suspect. Nevertheless, Ritter's will was so ferocious that most of the friars backed away and called it "the spirit at work."

"How are you going to afford this, Bruce?" Van Wormer asked, as they walked through the halls of the enormous structure.

"Don't you think the God that gave me this building for one dollar will provide the one million we need to renovate it?" Ritter asked.

And, indeed, once again the Lord delivered for Father Bruce. Ritter received a call from Don Wilderman, a Catholic businessman who was impressed by Ritter's mission and wanted to help. Wilderman invited him out to lunch at the Plaza Hotel, where Ritter "almost fell off [his] chair" when Wilderman told him he was the president of NICO, a retrofitting company in New York that specialized in renovating old buildings.

Wilderman's company remodeled the property at a cut rate of $1.2 million, with much of the cost picked up by Peter Grace. Laying down new carpeting, tearing out walls, and repainting the dingy halfway house did a lot to take away the institutional feel of the place. They couldn't get the bars off the windows or the steel gates out of the hallways, but on the surface it looked more like a college dormitory than a prison.

By the summer of 1979, Covenant House was no longer just a small charity in the East Village, not just a shelter in Times Square, but part of the New York City skyline. The main building's massive western façade was emblazoned with a three-story symbol of Covenant House painted in blue. The dove in the hand flew high above the rooftops of the tenements and warehouses on Manhattan's West Side.

It became the headquarters for even further expansion across the country and across the world. By January 1980, Covenant House was taking in over 250 kids a night at the facility. And Father Ritter was being courted by the national media. CBS's *60 Minutes* did a profile of him that year that painted him as a tireless Father Flanagan figure in the seedy underworld of Times Square.

With all the adulation, Ritter's mother came out from her small home in New Jersey to see the new headquarters. The sleaze around Times Square pulsating with neon revolted Mrs. Ritter. And all the commendations her son was getting made her uneasy. With her hair tied neatly in a bun and her stern voice laced with righteousness, the frail old woman still had it in her to ladle out heaping portions of guilt like a thick, hot Irish stew. Shaking her head in disapproval at the Hades of sin in Times Square, she gave her son one of her famous admonitions.

"He who touches pitch," she said, "will be defiled by it."

Chapter 9

The Corporation

BRUCE Ritter was the Donald Trump of Catholicism.

If the 1980s was a decade of greed among ambitious power brokers who financed dizzying growth on paper money, then Father Bruce was a man of the times. Ritter wanted to be not just the best but the biggest. Not just a charity, but *the* charity. The spiritual equivalent of a venture capitalist, Ritter took huge risks bargained on faith. His only collateral: Providence. As well as any rapacious tycoon, Father Bruce understood "the art of the deal," and his entrepreneurial style was about to pay off in huge dividends.

By early 1980, Covenant House was using the eighth floor of the newly renovated building on Forty-first Street and Tenth Avenue as a corporate headquarters. The offices had smoked-glass partitions, polished teak desks, potted ferns, and conference-call-capacity boardrooms. On the walls were oil paintings—pastoral scenes of the Hudson River, watercolors of southwestern landscapes, and a portrait of the East Village tenement where the legend began. There were black-and-white photographs of Ritter with his arms around kids and Ritter out on the streets amid the neon of Times Square.

Father Bruce was so enthralled by his corporate offices that he left his small room in the dingy Faith Community a few blocks away and moved into a large studio apartment on the same floor as his executive suite. Although it is generally not within The Rule of the Franciscan Order for a friar to live outside the religious community, Father Bruce had been on his own for a long time. He was calling his own shots at Covenant House, and his superiors at the provincial house in Union City had little to say about it. He was simply too successful to be bound by the same edicts as his fellow Franciscans. The Rule, Ritter felt, no longer applied to him.

His apartment was functional and comfortable, not at all ostentatious, as was appropriate for a Franciscan priest. It had a fully equipped alcove kitchen, low-pile carpeting with oriental rugs thrown about, oak book shelves cluttered with dusty volumes of theology and history, psychology books on adolescence and sexuality, frayed paperback Westerns, and spy novels. A view of the spires of a nearby Russian Orthodox Church filled the windows. A rowing machine and a set of weights were stashed in one corner, and a Murphy bed was folded up into one of the walls. A plush sectional couch in the middle of the room faced a color television set.

As he slowly became consumed by the increasing executive responsibilities that accompanied the rapid growth of the charity's budget and its programs, Ritter was losing touch with the streets. He had no time to handle a caseload of homeless youths and run a multimillion-dollar charity. He found less and less time to attend daily prayers with the Faith Community.

Plans for expansion to other cities across the country were under way and required all his attention. Ritter's success in New York had brought national acclaim and his direct-mail newsletters were creating a wide base of hundreds of thousands of donors. With all the publicity, requests came pouring in from people begging Ritter to start Covenant House programs in their cities. Macauley was pushing him, making him believe that the expansion was possible, that the financing could be worked out.

Ritter was "cornering the market in child care," as he put it. Spending so much time in the company of such denizens of the corporate world as Macauley and Grace, Ritter was picking up on their language; learning "how to play hardball"; threatening subordinate staffers they'd be "fired on the spot"; and making it clear his orders were "nonnegotiable." But even if he could be ruthless, Ritter's ways were tempered by the compassion his staff believed he had for the kids in his care and by a sense that this was God's work. And no one was better at the business of saving street kids, they believed, than Father Bruce.

But Ritter's success fostered arrogance. Decisions were made without consulting board members. If there was a disagreement with a senior staff member, he dismissed his point of view. Hand-picked by Ritter, the board of directors was a weak administrative body within a power structure that kept Ritter in control as "sole member" of the organization. His authority was absolute. From Ritter's perspective, he and Macauley were running the show, and they liked to call themselves a "cabal."

Sometimes their callousness hurt the faithful, as when Ritter suddenly replaced his long-time supporter S. I. Taubman as the chairman of the board and put Macauley at the helm, barely mentioning the move to the other board members.

Donna Santarsiero, Father Bruce's old friend and a newly appointed board member who had worked in high-powered state- and church-run organizations for years, quickly saw that there was something different about Ritter's Covenant House. Father Bruce and his cohort Macauley were like corporate raiders, ready to move their business of compassion into every available market and crush anyone who stood in their way. There was nothing wrong with effective management or forceful decision making, Santarsiero felt, but there was something being lost in the emphasis on size over content. If Ritter's Covenant House was a company, then the bottom line was "intake figures." Ritter seemed to care more about how many kids he could provide beds for than whether the "warehouses" he wanted to set up were beneficial in keeping the kids off the streets.

In 1982, Macauley and Ritter's big plans were starting to come to fruition. They were simultaneously working on opening new Covenant House chapters in Houston, Boston, Philadelphia, Guatemala, Toronto, London, and Rome. Ritter wanted to see his mission, his philosophy of open intake and his model for the New York Under 21 crisis center, brought to cities all over the United States and all over the world. He was building an empire. Macauley was fulfilling a life-long dream of creating a philanthropical kingdom.

Understanding the importance of having the institutional Church hierarchy behind him, Father Ritter's access to a city began with either an invitation by the archdiocese or methodical lobbying of the archdiocese for its support. Ritter always made it clear that the charity would be under his control, but knew he had to play ball with the powers that be.

The first Covenant House franchise to open was in Toronto. Cardinal Gerald Emmett Carter was impressed with Ritter's work in Times Square. After seeing kids living on the streets of his own city, the Canadian prelate ordered his staff to complete a needs assessment and determine whether Toronto required a shelter like Covenant House. Despite their findings that a small fifteen-room, long-term facility would be more appropriate to meet the needs of Toronto, Carter insisted that Covenant House's Under 21 center be the model. Impressed with Ritter's conviction that his large short-term crisis program was the only way street kids could be reached, Carter allocated a $3 million capital grant to build two facilities in downtown Toronto. A three-story brick Victorian was converted into a thirty-bed residential shelter. Adjacent to that was a modern twenty-four-hour crisis center with a capacity to take seventy-five to one hundred kids a night.

Inside, it was remodeled with unfinished wood paneling, exposed brick, plush carpeting, and comfortable sectional sofas. Bright, clean, and cozy, it looked more like a ski lodge than a homeless shelter. Father Bruce wanted only the best for his kids—an extension of his philosophy that if they were given something decent they were more likely to act decent around it. Ritter also started a satellite Faith Community of some twenty members in Toronto. The new Canadian Covenant House chapter was ready to open its doors in February of 1982.

While he was closing the Toronto deal up north, Father Bruce was busy brokering another down south. The Houston-Galveston Archdiocese offered Ritter substantial funding to build an Under 21 program in Houston to deal with the population of homeless teenagers. This time Father Ritter had a secular advance man—John Kells—who had alerted Houstonians to the harsh reality of young runaways and street prostitution in the city before Ritter even arrived.

Kells, a young assignment editor for local KTRK Channel 13 news, was intrigued by the underworld of teenage male prostitution in the Montrose section of Houston and did a special report called *Boys for Sale*. Ritter, who by that time had become the leading national spokesman on teenage runaways, was one of Kells's main sources in the report. He videotaped Ritter on the streets of Times Square and remembers his "honesty and intensity really came through."

After the show aired, Kells kept in touch with Ritter and urged him to open a Covenant House in Houston. The blond, boyish-looking television reporter impressed the Franciscan, and Ritter accepted Kells's invitation to come and check out Houston's street scene.

Down Montrose—a commerical strip that had become notorious for its drug trade, street prostitution, and dimly lit bars, with names like "The Chicken Coop"—Kells drove slowly while Ritter studied the scene from the car. In the headlights, he could see a half-dozen young runaways waiting for the $20 tricks that bought them drugs. He told Kells to pull over.

"I have to see the kids," the priest said.

Kells watched as Ritter moved among the boys, talking to them, asking them how they ended up on the street, and wondering where they would spend the night.

"He didn't flinch and he didn't panic. He walked right on through, and at the end of the tour he said, 'I've seen enough. I'm going to open a center in Houston,' " remembers Kells.

The Houston Archdiocese helped Ritter acquire some Church-owned property just a block away from the street scene. They also promised to help pull together the financing for the rest of the real estate he would need to construct the program. Kells introduced the tireless Franciscan to the "River Oaks cocktail circuit," a coterie of rich Texas oil and banking families, who live in a high-class section of Houston and who pride themselves on "doing their part for charity." These Houstonians—horrified by Ritter's dark and lurid tales of street prostitution and young boys doing horrible things to survive—welcomed the priest with open arms. Although many of them were Protestant, they saw Ritter as doing Christ's work and that's what counted.

It didn't hurt fund-raising efforts in the conservative Republican circles of the city that Father Ritter was becoming a favorite of the White House. If President Ronald Reagan thought of Ritter as an American "hero," then so did these Texans.

Ritter dazzled them with claims that Houston had the "worst teenage runaway problem in America after New York City." It was a line Ritter would use time and time again while building his empire—in Fort Lauderdale, in Los Angeles, in New Orleans, in Boston. Years later, he would even rattle Anchorage, Alaska, with a slightly modified claim that it had "the nation's highest per capita rate of runaway and homeless youth." Local newspapers were a sucker for that line, and it worked miracles in the charity circuit. Ritter played on what one Houston reporter described as the city's "collective inferiority complex."

"When a slick priest from New York City came in and told these sheltered Texans they had the worst runaway problem in the country, they were horrified," the reporter said. "They believed it right away. So the cash poured in."

Within a year, Ritter had the funding necessary to build a sprawling complex of three buildings, including a state-licensed thirty-day shelter with ninety-eight beds and fifty floor mats, a twenty-four-hour crisis center, and an office building for the administrative staff.

By June of 1983, Covenant House Texas was completed. The symbol of the bird in a hand was etched on the Lone Star State. It was a beautiful complex and Ritter was proud of it. Unlike most struggling social-service agencies in the 1980s, Covenant House seemed to have endless financial resources. In fact, the $3.5 million Ritter spent on Houston renovations was three times the amount of the average annual budget for most medium-sized social-service agencies in cities across the country. And with all that money flying around, some of Ritter's financial dealings were questionable at best.

He hired his niece, Ellen Wallace Lofland, for the "interior decorating" and gave her carte blanche to order only "top-of-the-line" furnishings. She bought everything from carpets to bunk beds to plush sectional couches to mahogany desks—much of it custom made. One former staff member said that Lofland even spent $30,000 just to have furniture coverings redone. Even more money was wasted when the beds she ordered soon fell apart and had to be replaced.

The Houston board of directors was not at first informed that Lofland was Ritter's niece. Ritter never recused himself from awarding the contract, nor were there any competitive bidding procedures, which are standard for charities of that size making such a large financial investment with public money. And Houston was only the beginning of Ritter's nepotism. From 1982 to 1989, Lofland was awarded contracts totaling more than several million dollars to perform interior-decorating services for new Covenant House facilities in Fort Lauderdale, New Orleans, Anchorage, and New York City; she pocketed approximately $170,000. The Houston program was also a cash cow for Lofland's husband, Tandy, who was the construction manager of Intergroup Development, Inc. For Covenant House construction projects in Houston and later in New Orleans, his company was awarded contracts totaling $4 million, including materials and the company's fee of approximately 5 percent—despite the fact that he reportedly had little experience in the field.

Catching on to the conflict of interest several years later, executive director Malcolm Host turned down a high-level staff official's recommendation that Lofland be awarded another contract. "I've been in human services for forty years, and I know you don't use relatives," he said. A conflict-of-interest clause was proposed to be added to the charity's purchasing manual, but it was deleted, staff officials said, because "it would be an insult to Father Ritter."

While the Toronto and Houston programs sprang up quickly, Rit-

ter was meeting some resistance in his more ambitious and controversial plans for expansion into Central America. The idea originated
as early as August of 1980, when Bruce attended an International
Conference on the Family in Guatemala City with Macauley, who
introduced him to a prominent Guatemalan landowner named Ro-
berto Alejos Arzu. Alejos was a shadowy figure, with alleged ties to
the brutal right-wing government. He was also an old associate of
Peter Grace, whose corporate empire stretched throughout Central
America. Alejos begged the Franciscan to come to Guatemala City,
and soon Macauley and Grace were squarely behind the idea. Macauley was already involved in starting another charity there, headed
by his friend from the Shoeshine Boys, a man named John Wetterer
who founded an orphanage called Mi Casa. (Wetterer was the subject
of a *60 Minutes* investigation alleging that he was sexually abusing
his young charges. Wetterer was later investigated by Guatemalan
authorities for allegations that he was a pedophile. He was subsequently cleared.)

Ritter wasn't sure about Alejos's idea, but he claimed that he was
"drawn" into it when he saw the young children of the streets of
Guatemala who survived by begging, stealing, and prostitution. They
suppressed their hunger by burying their faces in paper bags filled
with glue. The children called the taffylike toxic substance that sometimes left them brain-damaged "mother's milk." But if it was these
pathetic orphans who, as Ritter put it in the newsletter, "seduced"
him into starting a Covenant House there, it was Grace and Macauley
who sold him on the idea.

Grace offered a long-term plan to put up hundreds of thousands
of dollars to fund a network of Covenant House facilities in Guatemala, Honduras, Panama, and Mexico City throughout the 1980s.
More importantly, Grace had invaluable contacts throughout the region. His influence as head of one of Central America's most powerful
multinational coporations gave Covenant House clout with the oligarchy, right-wing governments, and the church hierarchy—all of
which he convinced Ritter were essential in establishing the charity's
base there.

From Macauley's point of view the Guatemala program was a smart
investment. Street kids were the commodity of compassion and Covenant House could turn bigger numbers down there.

"You could support a kid for two dollars a day in Guatemala versus
seventy-three a day in New York City," explained Macauley. "So on
average I can support thirty times as many kids. They are all children

of God. So we are doing more down there. . . . We are getting a bigger bang for the buck."

Grace's money was enticing and Macauley's calculus of caring was hard to dispute, but it wasn't enough to placate everyone on the "national board of directors," as the body was now referred to in the dawning of Covenant House's age of philanthropic manifest destiny. Donna Santarsiero questioned the move because most of the donors that gave to Covenant House felt the charity was answering the needs of street kids in inner cities of the United States. There were plenty of charities that focused on international-aid efforts, she said. Covenant House's strength was in focusing on a unique niche of the homeless population in the big U.S. cities. Toronto was far enough astray; Central America seemed exotic.

"Besides," Santarsiero added, "we need to consolidate and professionalize our existing programs."

Santarsiero says Macauley and Ritter treated her resistance as a mere annoyance. They were going to go ahead with the plan anyway and in fact had already come up with the $250,000 for a negotiated purchase of an old hotel in Guatemala City that was a perfect location for what they wanted to call "Casa Alianza." But placating the board was good form, so Ritter persisted.

"Don't you understand?" Father Bruce asked the hesitant board members. "Peter Grace feels like this will save his soul. And frankly, we should take him up on it."

A brutal statement for a Franciscan priest—as if Ritter wanted to show them that even a man of the cloth could stare mixed motives in the face and accept them, if it meant more money for his kids. Father Bruce understood that guilt quite possibly motivated Grace to make his tax-deductible donation from his huge multinational corporation. Maybe it was out of an uneasy conscience for having perpetuated a system of exploitation that let many of the hungry kids whom they would be helping live in abject poverty. "But who cares?" Ritter would ask. Who cared about Grace's politics or his motivations as long as it was helping the kids?

Not everyone saw it that way. There was a sense of hypocrisy and immorality to Ritter's acceptance of Grace's philanthropy that bothered at least Santarsiero and Taubman.

"Bruce, we are not in the business of saving Peter Grace's soul," Santarsiero said.

Nevertherless, there were few challenges from the other board members. Mark Stroock, a senior vice president and director of cor-

porate relations at the powerful advertising firm of Young & Rubicam, whose cousin would later become the U.S. Ambassador to
Guatemala under President Bush, had no problem taking Grace up
on his offer. The Reverend Brian Cullinane, Father Bruce's Franciscan superior, and Marge Crawford, the loyal Faith Community
member, saw no reason not to go ahead. If Father Bruce thought it
was a good idea, they did too. The minority dissenters were overruled.

As the charity ventured into Latin America, some of its dealings
in Guatemala were as shadowy as the jungles where a brutal civil war
had been raging for some twenty years between peasant farmers
defended by guerrillas and wealthy landowners backed by the military. The conduit to Covenant House in Guatemala—Alejos—was a
wealthy sugar and coffee grower with reputed ties to Guatemala's
notorious death squads and the U.S. Central Intelligence Agency.

The building he and Macauley found to house the kids was an old
hotel called Cortijo de las Flores—Inn of the Flowers. Alejos cleared
the path with Guatemalan politicians and the local Church authorities
to open the program in August of 1981.

The hotel was a "tiny paradise," as Ritter described it, with red-
tiled patios, stucco courtyards, and fountains set in the lush sur-
roundings of Guatemala City. The sunlight poured through the
wrought-iron-work on the rounded windows of the building, where
more than 150 orphaned and abandoned boys were provided with
beds and showers and hot meals. Seventy-five social workers, psychologists, school counselors, child-care workers, and medical and
kitchen personnel made up the staff of this long-term shelter.

Many of the children who came to Casa Alianza were orphans from
the government's "counterinsurgency" program, which human-
rights officials had called a permanent war that was among the world's
most brutal. It was these starving, suffering children that Father
Bruce said he cared about, not the politics that put them there. Nevertheless, the mission could not escape the violent history of Guatemala.
When Covenant House was adding a new wing onto one of their
buildings, a construction crew inadvertently unearthed a shallow
grave, where the bodies of nineteen people—allegedly the victims of
death squads—had been dumped. Staff members who saw photographs of the bodies say each skull was pierced by a single bullet
hole. Military troops arrived and blocked off the area, declaring it
an "archeological excavation." Covenant House staffers were told not
to ask any questions about the bodies. Guatemala's bloody past was
literally buried in the ground upon which Covenant House was built.

The military repression and death squads, which had been largely

responsible for the high number of orphans on the street, went unchallenged by Covenant House. With its distinctly nonconfrontational
style, Covenant House flourished in Guatemala, spinning off some
sixty shelters and homes in Antigua and Guatemala City as well as
some of the rural areas where the military had set up "model village"
programs, which displaced thousands of families and put them in
large refugee camps designed to keep them from organizing any
political uprising against landowners.

Part of Covenant House's tremendous success in the region was
that it did not challenge the status quo. Instead it traded off its
connection with Alejos, Macauley, and Grace to gain access and win
acceptance by the Church and the military. All three men were spir-
itually bound by their membership in the Knights of Malta. Grace
was the leader of the U.S.'s Eastern Association of the Knights and
Alejos was the head of the Central American chapter. Bill Simon was
also a member, and this corporate "cabal" later had Ritter inducted.

It was through the Knights of Malta in Guatemala and Honduras
that Alejos opened up the political connections Covenant House
needed to go unchallenged in the region. Any group that was perceived by the military as leftist or that sought to challenge the established order ran the risk of being targeted by the brutal government.
Even human-rights workers, priests, and nuns were being killed in
Guatemala and El Salvador. But Alejos began pouring money from
his plantations into the Casa Alianza in Guatemala and encouraged
his friends from the close-knit families of the oligarchy to do the
same.

At the ceremonial opening in August of 1981—hosted by Ritter
and attended by Alejos's family and other members of the conservative elite—Ritter must have sensed he was in a political bind:

"We are here to care for the children, . . . Homeless and dying
children may not and must not be held hostage to any political ideology, whether of the right, left, or center. . . . the children are the
same," Ritter said in a newsletter that recounted the speech. "Seven-
and-a-half-year-old naked José Francisco . . . has the same parts and
the same needs and the same hungers and the same rights as your
Joeys and Frankies and Davies and Bobbys."

Ritter may have believed that his mission existed in a political vac-
uum, but Grace and Alejos had a long history of alleged links to some
of the most reactionary elements in Latin America. Grace, as head
of his father's empire there through the 1950s and 1960s, was an
adamant anti-Communist linked to many organizations that promoted the interests of American corporations. Alejos had a relation-

ship with the CIA that dated back to at least 1960, when the agency used his plantation to train Cuban troops for the Bay of Pigs invasion. Bill Simon was also active in Central America, and eventually he, Macauley, and Grace reportedly became involved with a private network of aid to the Nicaraguan contras that was just beginning to take root. It was a country where, as one Catholic human-rights worker said, "it's absolutely impossible to stay neutral . . . if you don't speak out you are enabling the violence." Ritter was aligning himself with four men who weren't there just to help orphans.

Alejos owned plantations near the south coast cities of Escuintla and Retalhuleu, an area from which many of the orphans at Covenant House had fled. Staff members claimed that military helicopters would sometimes touch down at the Ciudad Vieja headquarters of Covenant House in Guatemala to drop off kids who had been orphaned by the military's operations in those areas and by the death squads that operated under the direction of prominent landowners. Other times the children would simply be brought to the door in the middle of the night by men in military uniforms, expecting the staff to receive them and ask no questions. Some children at Covenant House told their counselors they saw their parents killed.

"The military did bring kids by, sometimes at night, and the details of their orphanage were always sketchy," said Patrick Atkinson, the Ritter acolyte from the Faith Community who was named executive director of Casa Alianza in Guatemala at the age of twenty-three, even though he didn't speak Spanish. "But that's the nature of the country. You don't have to alienate to do good."

Alejos denied any link to the death squads or the killing of labor leaders who had worked on his land.

"That's a lie," Alejos said. "I don't get involved in that—I'm a practicing Catholic. I don't go into anything violent."

But Jean-Marie Simon, author of *Guatemala: Eternal Spring, Eternal Tyranny,* said of Alejos's relationship with Covenant House, "It's like having Idi Amin on the board of Amnesty International. He's a thug in a business suit."

A Franciscan priest who helped establish Covenant House in Guatemala said, "There was a degree of cooperation with the same people who owned the land or who may have had to do with the violence. But if we weren't there, there wouldn't have been anyone to take care of the kids. Then we would have the parents dead and the kids left abandoned. At least this way, the kids had a future."

It was this apolitical complicity with the establishment that paved a smooth road for Covenant House.

"Ritter was safe because he'd pull in the kids and patch up their clothes," said Dan Jensen, a Catholic priest who worked in Guatemala. "The hierarchy knew he wouldn't ask why the kids were poor."

By 1983, Covenant House had grown into a budding empire with a $20 million annual budget. More than fifteen thousand kids a year flooded into Covenant House's Under 21 programs in New York, Toronto, Houston, and Guatemala. Father Bruce's staff had grown to over five hundred full-time employees, and there were hundreds of volunteers and scores of Faith Community members devoted to his mission. Even the Covenant House vocabulary changed to reflect the growth, sounding more like a conglomerate than a charity. The New York headquarters was now the "national corporate parent," or just "corporate," and the new chapters in other cities were referred to as "subsidiaries," or "subs." Meetings with senior staff officials were held at corporate retreat centers, like Arrowwood in Westchester, with motivational seminars and conferences set amid the golf courses and health clubs.

Across the country, Father Bruce Ritter was traveling to announce his message and carry out his mission. At his office at "corporate," he had begun using a wall-size calendar, where he recorded his speaking engagements and conferences all over the world. The calendar was booked months in advance. From a leather swivel chair with armrests, he orchestrated the building of his empire. His computer kept him constantly up to date on "the numbers" at Covenant House: the number of donors, the number of kids in the program, the number of staff members, the number of donations he'd need to make the projected budget.

Unable to meet the demand of media organizations and community groups and parishes that sought his time, Father Bruce developed a "Speakers Bureau" of about one dozen people—Faith Community members, expert social workers, priests, and others involved with Covenant House—who were sent to carry his message to college campuses, social-work conferences, and anywhere people gathered to hear about the issues affecting homeless youths. Ritter created an Institute for Youth Advocacy, a staff of attorneys and legal assistants committed to promoting legislation and shaping laws that protected troubled youths.

Invitations for Ritter to open Covenant House programs in various cities flooded across his desk. Finally, Ritter used a $150,000 grant from the Charles Culpeper Foundation to form a Covenant House Research and Development Department, referred to as "R&D." This would become the instrument of expansion, Ritter's Trojan horse in building replicas of New York's Under 21 in cities he conquered. And Boston was next.

In early spring 1982, with members of the R&D team in tow, Ritter flew into Logan Airport and took a cab to the Parker House, one of the oldest and most elegant hotels in the city. After checking into the $100-a-night rooms that overlooked the quaint brick buildings of Beacon Hill, Ritter headed immediately for the "Combat Zone," a three-block strip of pornographic bookstores, peep shows, arcades, and raunchy nightclubs. Ritter knew where Covenant House had to be—in the middle of all the sin, where he could do the most saving.

For years Ritter had been frustrated by the fact that his direct-mail marketing strategy did not have substantial returns in Massachusetts. The fact that the Boston Catholics, with a strong network of colleges and charities as well as national political clout, weren't buying into his mission was bothersome. But he was going to change all that.

Ritter's first contacts were two priests—the Reverends Mark Janus and Joseph Bargetta. The chaplains for Boston's Department of Youth Services worked at the Paulist Center on Park Street and for years had seen firsthand the need for a twenty-four-hour crisis center in the Combat Zone. They had alerted the archdiocese, and when Ritter came onto the scene at about the same time, it all seemed providential.

Father Janus worked his contacts in the Archdiocese of Boston to open up the doors for Covenant House. In April, Ritter invited Humberto Cardinal Medeiros, then archbishop of the Archdiocese of Boston, to visit his Times Square shelter and multiservice program. The size, the efficiency, the cleanliness, and the aura of power that surrounded the Franciscan priest's New York City showcase impressed Medeiros. A man of Portuguese descent and a bit of an outsider to the established Irish Catholic power structure of Boston, the cardinal took a liking to Ritter. He liked his entrepreneurial spirit, he liked his business skills, he liked his commitment. His Eminence promised Ritter the full backing of the archdiocese.

During several tours of the city throughout the fall of 1982, Ritter explored the Combat Zone to find a suitable property to house his next franchise. His eyes landed on an eleven-story limestone-and-brick building on the fringes of the city's red-light district. The old Hotel Avery on Washington Street, a dingy 150-room hotel, had been closed for months because of smoke damage from a fire. The owners, Carter Hotel Corporation, were looking for a buyer.

Knowing a good deal when he saw it, Ritter moved fast. He and his R&D staff persuaded the archdiocese to move into phase II: getting Boston's rich and powerful Catholics to put up the money.

In early December, Medeiros invited Ritter to the opulent residence of the Boston Archdiocese for a banquet. The prelate also arranged for thirty-five men and women representing Boston's business and financial leadership to attend the dinner and hear about Ritter's proposal. Medeiros asked for the Boston Brahmins' help in raising approximately $6 million toward rehabilitation of the old hotel and continuing support of the proposed program.

The first "substantial" local offering was made by Thomas Flatley of Braintree, a prominent real-estate developer, who supplied the down payment for the property; others soon followed.

On December 30, Covenant House bought the once grand Avery Hotel for $600,000. A front-page article in the *Boston Globe* heralded Father Ritter's arrival, recounting the mythology of the first six kids and the tireless Franciscan's struggle. And once again Ritter instilled fear with his horrifying image of street kids trapped in a world of prostitution and the "tight grip" of "organized crime" that threatened the city and its youth. Like a traveling theater group, Ritter and his R&D staff trotted out their villains: the Mafia, prostitution rings, and pornographers.

An ecclesiastical Music Man, Ritter was a huckster of sorts. And puritanical Boston greeted this self-professed savior of its youth from vice with open arms—that is, until a nun named Sister Barbara Whelan caught wind of Ritter's arrival.

By accident, Sister Barbara overheard some Church gossip one day about the $6 million that the cardinal had urged private business leaders to give to Ritter. Her jaw dropped. For twelve years, Whelan and her fellow Sisters of Saint Joseph had run Bridge Over Troubled Waters—a multiservice agency that operated a medical van for street kids in the blighted area of the Combat Zone, offering them temporary homes outside the world of drugs and prostitution. They were scraping by at the time on a total budget of about $500,000. So who was this Franciscan friar about to be handed $6 million? Why was the archdiocese so squarely behind his mission? Why hadn't the Bridge been consulted? Sister Barbara was furious.

The more she heard about Covenant House the less she liked it. She disagreed profoundly with Ritter's philosophy of building a large shelter in the center of an area that attracts kids for the wrong reasons. She requested a meeting with the cardinal.

"Our goal is to get the kids with [foster] families who live out of the city. Give a girl of fourteen two weeks in the city and you lose her," Whelan said. "You don't just build a warehouse and stash the kids."

There were other concerns for Whelan. The Bridge had just been hit with a one-two punch. It had been evicted from its former location on Beacon Street because the building was being converted to condominiums. And its budget was dramatically slashed after a belt-tightening move by the archdiocese, which came on top of the Reagan administration's cutting of federal funds that the charity had grown to rely on. The Bridge was in the process of opening a new headquarters facing the Boston Common on Tremont Street, not far fron the proposed site of Covenant House. Whelan worried that the prominence and political clout of Covenant House would swallow up what little was left of diocesan and government funding for her program. "It was like the corner store competing with plans for a shopping mall," she said. She was also concerned that the proximity of the two shelters would lead the youngsters to manipulate the staff by playing them against each other.

With little sympathy from the archdiocese, Whelan launched her own battle. She began by challenging Ritter on his distorted claims, telling reporters he was exaggerating the number of young people on the streets of Boston at least tenfold.

Whelan couldn't understand why Covenant House operated under such secrecy. Ritter's R&D staff never contacted her and refused any cooperation with a close-knit network of adolescent counseling agencies around the state. For a Catholic child-care agency, Covenant House seemed remarkably uncharitable.

Unexpectedly, Ritter called her office one day from his room at the Parker House, which had become his local base of operations during the planning stages. On the phone with the man behind Covenant House, Whelan had an image of a ruthless corporate raider more than the head of a fellow child-care agency. He was curt, telling the nun that he was flying out that afternoon but that he had "about fifteen minutes" to "settle some of these issues."

A few hours later, Ritter walked briskly into the Bridge and Whelan greeted him in her office. The Bridge was clean as a whistle, but modest in its appearance and sparse in its furnishings. She found Ritter a chair and they sat in her one-window office at the round wooden table she uses for a desk. When Ritter's steel-blue eyes locked with Whelan's, she never forgot it.

"They scared me. The power in his eyes was frightening. It gave me a very bad feeling. I know that sounds ridiculous and nunnish. I hate to sound nunnish, but it is the truth," said Whelan, remembering that Ritter had little to say in the meeting and stormed out of her office.

"He treated me like a little girl," she said. "He acted as if he was God and I was to behave. I decided right there I could not let this happen. I was going to risk everything I had to stand up against him, and believe me, we stood alone. There were few people, even in the network of adolescent programs, who would support us."

Whelan, a sturdy woman who wears smart shoes, vowed to dig in her heels. She began attending functions where Ritter would speak— at business luncheons or at city-planning meetings—and she'd raise her voice against the program.

With Whelan leading the way, the battle of Boston against Father Bruce opened on another front—and perhaps a more decisive one. The local business community was catching on to the size and scope of the proposed shelter and was angry that they had not been consulted.

Ritter had shrewdly pushed the purchase and preliminary zoning approvals through by using the considerable clout of the archdiocese and his own legal staff. It was a brilliant maneuver that took most of the businessmen in the area by surprise, especially the leaders of a redevelopment plan in Boston's blighted Combat Zone. As they quickly came to learn, they weren't dealing with just some humble, wide-eyed Franciscan. This was a priest who knew how to play hardball.

The Avery Hotel was part of what was referred to among realtors in Boston as Parcel 30, which planning officials and Mayor Kevin White had been touting as a major redevelopment block. In fact, they had assured investors that the Avery was going to be fully renovated as a hotel that would also include office space and retail shopping. But Ritter had convinced Mayor White and the Boston Redevelopment Authority that the Covenant House program would be temporary. They agreed to a five-year contract to provide services. It was a ploy by Ritter to get his foot in the door, figuring that once Covenant House was set up nobody would be able to tear down a shelter that was helping kids. "Bruce could be very shrewd," said a woman who worked in R&D during the battle for Boston. He knew if they ever actually tried to evict him the press would side with the priest over the developers. But few bothered to ask why a charity would want to invest some $2 million in renovation costs for a program designed to be "temporary." Just about everybody, including the Mayor, was buying what the priest told them.

Ritter's architects were already strolling through the property and planning the renovation when store owners, like Ken Crystal, found out they were going to be evicted. For more than sixty years, Crystal's family shoestore had been in the lobby of the Avery. The store was the family's tradition and livelihood, and Crystal was incensed by the priest's callousness.

The archdiocese began bullying the local business owners, telling them that all of the necessary approvals had been granted and the construction of Covenant House was a done deal. That wasn't exactly true. The proposal required building variances, which meant it had to be brought before the BRA board, which would then make a recommendation. Then the board of appeal would have final say over the variances after a series of public hearings.

Covenant House's R&D team went right to work. The first stop was at the royal palace of Bostonian aristocracy: the Kennedys. The clan was shrewd enough, or at least adequately versed in Church politics, to know to stay away from such a battle. Then Covenant House went after the BRA director, Robert Ryan, and began lobbying him to their cause. Ryan was shown sophisticated proposals based on the existing model in New York. He received letters and telegrams from Covenant House's many prestigious supporters.

Soon Ryan was being quoted in the *Boston Globe* singing Covenant House's praises: "It may not be something that anyone wants in their back yards, but I think developers, landowners and neighbors, once they realize the kind of place it will be and the kind of program the people will run, they will be for it."

Behind the scenes, Ritter and his R&D team had assured Ryan that his wife would be offered a seat on Covenant House's development committee if the project was approved. It was a fact that Ryan never mentioned to his fellow BRA board members while Covenant House's lobbying efforts locked up a positive recommendation from the BRA. But the pressure from the real-estate developers in the area was intensifying and Ritter was running into an all-out war.

He stopped at nothing. Whelan remembers Ritter even brought a street youth from Boston who had landed in the New York program and paraded him before the press corps in Massachusetts. The young man told reporters and testified at commissions that Boston needed more programs for its youth. Sister Whelan said she was later told by a priest who worked with Ritter that the young man in return was given a college scholarship in New York.

"That was unbelievable to me," said Whelan. "He was using kids for his own success."

Marco Ottieri, of Mondev-International, which was building a $130 million Lafayette Mall complex as a cornerstone of the city's redevelopment plan, stepped into the fray. The Montreal-based company's project included a 500-room luxury hotel, a retail shopping center, and a 1,050-car parking garage near the Combat Zone. They had a lot at stake and began threatening legal action against the city.

Cardinal Medeiros didn't like the subtle intimidation by the developer and the real-estate community. He sided with Ritter and was willing to pull the moral high ground in the newspapers if he had to.

"I don't know who would object to caring for young people, those abandoned boys and girls who have the least hope in today's society," Medeiros told the *Boston Globe*. "They deserve a chance, and many are trying to help. . . . We won't be deterred by objections from doing a good work. Otherwise, we would never do anything. . . . This offers freedom to youth from the clutches of vice and crime."

It was the priest and the Boston Archdiocese versus the nun and the businessmen. But history was not on Ritter's side: Mayor White and Governor King, both of whom supported him, were replaced by Raymond Flynn and Michael Dukakis. Then Cardinal Medeiros passed away. The new cardinal, Bernard F. Law, was hardly willing to step into the middle of a dispute between a charity and the real-estate community in his first few months as head of the Boston Archdiocese. He put the entire project on hold.

After a series of hearings before the Greater Boston Chamber of Commerce, Ritter was offered a compromise solution to locate the charity outside of the Combat Zone. But Ritter was not one to compromise. If it was not done his way, then it would not be done at all. He abandoned his plans and put the building up for sale.

Sister Barbara Whelan not only kept her community-based program alive but continued to thrive at a fraction of the cost of Covenant House.

But even in the face of defeat, Ritter had the last laugh. The redevelopment plan ended up a financial boon to Ritter by increasing the area's real-estate values. At the height of the Boston real-estate boom, Ritter waited for the price he wanted on the old Avery Hotel. In December of 1984, real-estate developer Barry Hoffman purchased it for $1.6 million—nearly three times what Ritter had paid. Ritter walked away with his ego intact and capital to fund his next franchise.

Ritter had other setbacks that were tougher to take. After an audience (arranged by Macauley) at the Vatican in 1982, the Pope asked Ritter to build a Covenant House in the Holy City. Ritter did everything in his power to carry out the request of His Holiness. He managed to get a villa donated by a cosmetic-company heiress to house the facility. But even with a pontifical blessing and five years of tireless effort, Ritter couldn't get around the entrenched bureaucracy of the Italian government, which refused the approvals necessary to build a shelter. In the United States, Ritter faced more profound challenges to his empire from rival social-service organizations that questioned his own motives and the effectiveness of the program in Covenant House's national expansion.

In Philadelphia, Ritter's 1982 attempt to open a seventy-five-bed shelter was turned down by the city. Roberta Hacker, then director of Philadelphia's Voyage House, clashed with Ritter on his proposal and discovered she was in a war with an "egomaniac," who, she felt, was more concerned with building a power base than providing solutions to getting poor and troubled teenagers off the streets. The next year, in London, Ritter proposed a large crisis center, and again by disregarding the smaller established shelters around him incurred their wrath. Nicholas Fenton, director of a London youth shelter who was able to marshal enough forces to keep Covenant House out, described Ritter as "very arrogant, very autocratic" and said that he got the impression the priest was "much more concerned with empire building."

In addition to their problems with the priest's personality, the directors of these smaller youth shelters were even more confounded by Ritter's disregard for a decade-long national trend in social services away from large, impersonal institutions. Notorious houses of horror, like New York's Willowbrook and Brentwood, were being phased out. But Ritter was enthusiastically proposing large institutional facilities more akin to "warehouses" than group homes in cities around the country. Hacker, director of a small residential facility that tried to take kids out of the inner city and offer them a stable environment over an extended period of time, said that by the late 1970s most states had in fact already passed legislation limiting the size of youth shelters and institutions to fifteen beds.

The regulations came about through the 1974 Runaway and Homeless Youth Act, which established guidelines and standards that encouraged small, community-based shelters for adolescents who had been forced to leave their homes.

Linda Irwin, executive director of Youth Alternatives, a community-based social-service center in New Orleans that served as a model for the legislation, said, "The idea was to approximate a normal family situation. . . . Our philosophy was that small is better. Kids need to be in an environment that is more homelike. Myself and many others in community-based programs had some strong reservations about Covenant House's approach, whether it helped long term to break the cycle, to get kids off the street. Or whether it was just a big warehouse to put them in while they did what they wanted out in the streets."

In position papers and policy studies throughout the 1970s and into the 1980s, it was an accepted fact that small community-based shelters with intensive counseling and supervision had higher success rates in helping troubled teenagers. By Covenant House's own estimates, about one-third of the kids who came to them didn't return to the street. But small programs, such as those run by High Risk Youth at Children's Hospital in California, had success rates as high as 70 percent.

Father Pat Molroney, who founded his ten-bed shelter for troubled teenagers on East Ninth Street in New York a few years after Ritter started his ministry, said, "We had all realized that small was better; that's why it seemed that Covenant House was more of a product of Ritter's ego than a display of sound social work.

"Covenant House was no different than the other big institutions— it was a monster," said Molroney. "Kids in the New York program were getting beaten up and raped inside there. Ritter was going completely against the tide."

By the mid-1980s, the attack on Covenant House from law-enforcement officials and the established social-work circles had spread from Toronto to Houston and all the way back to his flagship Under 21 program in New York City. Perhaps the most vocal criticism was of Ritter's philosophy of placing large shelters in the hearts of cities' seediest pockets, to which, Ritter believed, teenage runaways were drawn. Ritter's obsession with putting the shelter there was puzzling to social-work service workers as well as law-enforcement officials.

In a 1983 survey conducted by the U.S. Department of Health and Human Services, 83 percent of youth-service administrators from twelve states strongly opposed placing youth shelters in combat zones. A probation officer quoted in the survey said: "Locating a shelter in the combat zone is like holding an AA meeting in a tavern."

Often, locating them there only worsened the situation. In Houston, experts on juvenile delinquency and the social services believed the number of street kids drawn to the Montrose section increased dramatically during the first two years Covenant House was located there. Ritter merely defended his program as fortuitous, setting up shop just before the explosion of kids hit the streets. "Anyone who knows the streets and knows what goes down," said Ritter, "knows that we have to be there, right where the action is."

Houston police officers, like Jeff Shipley, who patrolled the area for three years, and anticrime groups, like the Houston Guardian Angels, reported that the prostitution and drug scene in the area around Covenant House worsened after the charity's arrival.

Chuck Angers, nineteen, who left his home in Corpus Christi after his father died, ended up living on the streets for several years before he drifted to Houston. He said that when he told the police he was homeless he was given the number for Travelers Aid, which then provided a free ride to Covenant House.

"The next day I walked outside and—wow! That was my playground," said Angers. "There was pot, crystal, all kinds of drugs. That was the land of opportunity. . . . Guys could get in if they're not even in the program. They just walk in, take a shower, watch some TV, ask for a late lunch, and then go back out on the strip."

William Raney was kicked out of his home in Houston in 1982 when he was eighteen and stayed with friends for a while until he heard about the newly built Covenant House, where he "moved in" for the next three years.

"Covenant House brought me to the strip. I wanted Covenant House not for the shelter but to get out on the street. That was the start of a fun trip," said Raney, who described a typical day at Covenant House as a twelve-pack of beer, a nickel bag of marijuana, and shoplifting at a nearby Galeria store to finance the drug purchases.

Judy Hay of Harris County Child Protection Services criticized Ritter for intentionally using the misleading term "runaway" to describe such young men. Most of the young men and women flocking to the shelter were over the age of eighteen. In 1985, Covenant House was claiming in its fund-raising rhetoric that there were "up to 5,000 runaways who end up in the streets of Houston each year."

Indeed, there were exactly 5,963 reported runaways in Harris County in 1985. But a full 97 percent of them returned home within two days. Only about 180 kids, or about 3 percent, were what could be considered chronic runaways who would have ended up on the streets and in need of a shelter such as Covenant House. While Covenant House also made liberal use of the term "throwaways," Hay said that in 1985 there were 282 kids who were abandoned by their parents. But approximately half were infants, who were placed in foster care.

The fact was that about 80 percent of Covenant House's clients were young men and women over the age of eighteen. They were typically black and Hispanic, uneducated, and poor, and had little hope of getting a job. They were young people in the earliest stages of an adult cycle of poverty, and providing an overnight shelter was not a solution to their problem.

Similar criticism in Toronto came not only from law-enforcement and rival social-service agencies, but from Covenant House's own executive director, John MacNeil.

"Covenant House had become the McDonald's of child care," said MacNeil, who was the director of a small residential child-care center in Toronto before joining Covenant House in early 1983. "It was a revolving door. The concern was much more over numbers, getting a lot of kids in the program, with less concern for intensive counseling or helping those kids who really needed direction with a way to get off the streets."

The problems the young people faced in Toronto were completely different from those of the homeless kids in New York City or even the older kids drawn to the Montrose section of Houston. Ritter's failure was in insisting that all of the programs be modeled on New York, failing to take into account the different street scenes indigenous to each city. Around Toronto's Yonge Street, the scene was tame—with a string of bars, record stores, and strip joints, and a small amount of informal prostitution. Nothing like Times Square or even Montrose. Teenagers from middle- or upper-middle-class families fractured by divorce or physical abuse or just lack of communication drifted in and out and treated the Toronto Covenant House as a kind of crash pad. Many of the young people would even turn up their noses at the idea of having to sleep on the floor.

While there were at least a dozen young people at any given time in the program who needed serious attention, up to one hundred others were simply using the place as a free motel after they either missed the last bus home or wanted to stay out all night. As a result, MacNeil felt his staff of counselors were pulled in too many directions at once and ultimately unable to help the kids who needed them most.

Under 21 in New York City also had its critics. The New York City Police Department had a simmering antagonism with Ritter in part because of a perception that the charity harbored young criminals who operated in the Times Square area. In the mid-1980s there was an incident in which a young mugger was being chased by police down Forty-second Street and literally turned the corner into Covenant House, where counselors barred the door and prevented the cops from entering the property. It became legend. Although a relatively minor incident, police on the beat exaggerated it over many years. To them, it became a metaphor for what Covenant House was all about.

The Manhattan District Attorney's office also had a broad background of resentment toward Ritter. Their investigators felt if Ritter had as much information about organized crime's involvement in pornography and prostitution as he claimed in newsletters and public-speaking engagements, then he should turn it over to them. If he truly wanted to break up the seedy underworld that he was so eloquent in describing, why didn't he cooperate with the police?

But he did cooperate in another way. According to one former Covenant House staffer, Ritter bought off the police department's ill feeling by offering a dozen local cops moonlighting jobs as security guards at the Covenant House. He paid them what they would have made working overtime for the police department. Some of the cops were later investigated for using different social security numbers on their time cards to avoid paying taxes. When he couldn't buy his way out, Ritter dismissed all the criticism as part of the cross he had to bear for being a nationally known missionary. And he would not be swayed.

In Fort Lauderdale, Father Bruce purchased a beachfront property that was the former Sand Castle Hotel at Vista Mar Street and Breakers Avenue for $2.5 million. As in Boston, Ritter managed to push preliminary approval for his project through the city's boards before any of the nearby business owners knew what hit them. And in the later stages of approval, the fight against Covenant House by Fort Lauderdale's businessmen and motel owners got ugly.

The offices at the proposed site were broken into and ransacked. Filing cabinets and desks were tipped over. The drop ceiling was ripped out. Some $5,000 worth of damage, police theorized, was done by Covenant House's opponents. The business owners, in turn, accused Covenant House staffers of causing the damage themselves for sympathy in the press. After two years of bitter legal wrangling and public finger pointing, the city granted Covenant House the approval and variances needed to begin the renovation. But there were new headaches when Covenant House's contractors discovered structural problems with the three buildings in the thirty-year-old hotel complex. The contractor, Tandy Lofland, the husband of Ritter's niece, ran up a lot of cost overruns.

When construction was finished, the total capital outlay came to

$5 million. At that price, motel owners in Fort Lauderdale said, Covenant House cost more to build than any of the sixteen luxury hotels that were either proposed or under construction at that time in Broward County.

In September of 1985, the twenty-four-hour emergency shelter opened its doors. It had the capacity to house up to 110 kids a night and a staff of 60 employees. A small Faith Community of 6 members was established, as well as a support staff of volunteer tutors, who helped the younger charges with schoolwork and the older ones with job placement. It also provided young mothers with a nursery and classes in nutrition.

Bernie Petreccia, one of the motel owners who led an unsuccessful fight to keep the shelter off the beachfront, said, "Because you're dealing with a priest, no one questions it. It's like fighting motherhood and apple pie."

Through 1985 and 1986, Covenant House ventured deeper into Central America, establishing another Casa Alianza in Panama and completing an expansion of their program in Guatemala to include Refugio Alianza, a twenty-four-hour crisis center in Guatemala City that cared for 50 kids a night. They created 17 group homes in Antigua, which cared for up to 214 children at a time, with an average length of one year, and a network of dozens of other group homes in Guatemala City that cared for an additional 55 youths at a time. The sprawling Guatemalan Casa Alianza became one of the largest child-care agencies in Latin America and the largest of Ritter's satellite programs, rivaled only by New York. There was also an outreach program in Mexico City, with plans to build a crisis shelter and orphanage there as well.

In 1985, Ritter's Research and Development team hit Sin City—New Orleans. At his first meeting at the New Orleans archdiocese in the spring of 1985, Cardinal Philip M. Hannan listened to Ritter's proposal, but told him that because the region was in the midst of an economic crisis he could not count on the diocese for any support. Ritter was told he was on his own.

That's why Hannan was surprised to hear Ritter quoted in the media claiming he was "invited" to come to New Orleans by the archdiocese. Later he found out it was just part of the R&D team's public-relations strategy. The point man for Covenant House in New Orleans was Jim Kelly, a volunteer in the Faith Community who had left a promising corporate career with ITT to help Ritter carry out his mission. Kelly was on a religious quest and pursued it with all of his corporate skills. Combining his contacts in the banking industry with a lobbying campaign of local businesses, Kelly raised millions of dollars.

But the massive fund-raising drive also dried up funding for other area charities, including a small shelter for troubled youths called Greenhouse. A fixture in New Orleans since 1972, Greenhouse was considered a model of intensive, community-based care for adolescents who had been forced to leave their homes. It was struggling to get by on a budget of $360,000. When the Louisiana State Department of Social Services completely cut their funding in 1986, they were left with a nearly $100,000 deficit. They had planned to do an emergency appeal, but Covenant House moved quickly with its promotional campaign on television and direct mail. The national charity's fund-raising budget for its New Orleans venture was an estimated $1 million, more than three times Greenhouse's total annual budget.

After its successful fund drive, Covenant House purchased a building lot on Rampart Street and drew up architectural plans for a residence, a crisis center, and an office building. When the massive project was completed, it was a handsome set of buildings in the French Quarter and won an architectural award for "best institutional adaptation of local architecture." It served as a marked contrast to "Greenhouse"—a big green antebellum structure, which one staff member called "an ugly old thing," and from which the charity got its name. The funky old house, with its porches and spires, was where the small, innovative child-care program had operated for years.

Greenhouse had room for sixteen kids, who were counseled closely by a small staff of psychologists. The emphasis was on intense supervision and long-term counseling. The kids did all their own chores, helped with the cooking, and washed their own clothes. The idea was to empower them and create the independence and responsibility they'd need to get off the streets.

Covenant House, on the other hand, served 115 kids a night as well as 20 mothers with children. There was a cafeteria in which clients were served by kitchen help in uniforms, who prepared their meals through a contract with a food-service company. There were laundry services. There were several large rooms filled with clothes for the taking—most of them new and many of them donated through Covenant House's established network with national clothing manufacturers. There were even designer labels, from Jordache to Jockey. To many of the kids, Covenant House was more like a hotel than a social-service institution. This was Bruce Ritter's trademark

across the country. He wanted his kids to have only the best. He felt
not only that it would improve their self-image but that they deserved
it. The staff at Greenhouse questioned whether the monstrous shelters were good social work.

Its state funds cut and its private funding base swallowed by Covenant House's public-relations machinery, Greenhouse closed its
door a week after Covenant House opened. The counselors left a
handwritten sign on the screen door of the darkened old house for
any youth who came by in need of help. It read, "Please go to Covenant House."

Chapter 10

Letters of Confession

IT was not the angels of God that trumpeted to millions the message of Father Bruce Ritter's mission. It was third-class bulk mail.

Covenant House's sophisticated direct-mail operation began every month with Ritter's legendary newsletter, written in longhand on a legal pad. Those scribbled words—which were worth millions—were programmed into Covenant House's IBM 4300 series computer system and then transmitted via fiber optics to the charity's direct-mail marketing strategists at a Massachusetts firm called Epsilon Data Management on Route 128, "America's Technological Highway."

Epsilon is regarded as the premier direct-mail marketing company in the United States, its vast headquarters housing main-frame computers, libraries of donor lists on circular computer tape, and work stations for software specialists in demographics.

When Ritter's newsletters appeared as a blip on a computer screen at the high-tech firm, Senior Vice President John Groman, who personally handled the Father Ritter account, would review the copy and make occasional recommendations. But even experts like Groman had learned not to question Ritter—his success rate was simply too phenomenal. He was doing something that even the experts couldn't understand.

Once approved by the Epsilon strategists, the newsletter would be interfaced with Covenant House's personalized mailing lists—sophisticated demographic models created by Epsilon and some "ongoing donor bases" that represented Ritter's own faithful followers. Then the software would be sent off to a printer for reproduction of the two-page appeals onto "fully personalized letter text" with "type stock matching stationery" for "all components" and "auto typed carrier envelopes"—all of which was the industry's jargon for a letter that looked as if it came from a friend rather than a large, impersonal nonprofit organization. Enclosed would be postage-paid return envelopes and return slips marked with computer bar codes that would help the computer technicians track how much the donors gave and who they were, and develop a file on their giving patterns.

By December of 1983 up to 300,000 copies of Father Bruce's newsletter were sent out fourteen times a year. Cutting a precise demographic swath across America, the letters would arrive several days later at mailboxes on dusty Texas roads, at California tract houses, at trailer parks in Kansas, and at high-rise apartments in New York City.

Within a few weeks, the returns would come back to Covenant House's headquarters in New York with accompanying checks of anywhere from $5 to $1,000 or more. In one month—December of 1983, for example—the charity brought in an estimated $400,000. That was roughly 20 percent of the annual budget—not an unusual percentage for a Covenant House holiday mailing.

This tidal flow—hundreds of thousands of solicitations sent out monthly and tens of thousands of returns washing back in the ensuing weeks—brought in the hundreds of millions of dollars that built Ritter's empire throughout the 1980s. Nearly every year the number of mailings and revenue returns increased exponentially, until some one million monthly letters mailed out in 1989 brought back a total of $71 million, or about 83 percent of the annual budget.

The Franciscan priest was on the cutting edge of the burgeoning industry as far back as the early 1970s, when he was making his own primitive mailing lists by leaving envelopes in the pews of churches where he preached and asking people to write their addresses on them. This humble approach was professionalized with Macauley's guidance in 1977 and perfected with Epsilon, making Covenant House a blue-chip charity in the 1980s. When many social-service organizations were left reeling by the massive federal cuts under Reagan, the competition grew fierce for any available private funding. Those charities, like Covenant House, Save the Children, and Disabled Veterans of America, that had familiarized themselves with direct mail and invested in the expensive technology not only survived but flourished. The ones that did not suffered and sometimes perished.

"Like anything in history, you have to be at the right place at the right time, and Ritter certainly was," said William Olcott, editor of a monthly trade publication, *Fund Raising Management.* "Ritter's success was a confluence of historical events, like a great ship that rose with the tide in the Reagan years."

There was a faithful donor base at Covenant House that had followed Ritter through thirteen years of hard work. They were 85 percent Catholic, and even though they didn't always give a lot, they gave often. More than 70 percent of Ritter's fund raising came from small donations of between $10 and $100. The core group of donors was housed on a special computer disc that was kept strictly confidential and under lock and key in the basement of the charity's headquarters. While many charities shared their lists or sold them to "list brokers," Father Ritter was obsessively protective of his donor list, not wanting anyone else to tap into the scores of thousands of people who had grown loyal to his charity and to him personally. Despite offers of up to $1 million for the list, Ritter never sold it.

This core group of donors was courted and preserved by Covenant House's donor communications department. Although Ritter was emphatic about writing his own monthly newletters, the department had a staff of roughly thirty people—mostly Faith Community members and volunteers—assigned as "writers" to handle personalized responses to the faithful donors. The writers crafted return letters to the core group with Ritter's signature, creating the illusion that the priest sat down at a desk and typed a reply to each person who contributed regularly or who stuffed a sizable check in an envelope. In the return letters, writers would respond directly to what the donor had written. For example, if a donor mentioned that her "Uncle Joe" was sick, the writer would respond with "I am saying a prayer for your Uncle Joe." No way to mistake these missives for form letters. The donor communications department used special bar codes to keep files on each donor as well as which writer had handled the response. Then the stacks of letters would be taken to the basement of the corporate headquarters, where a bank of a dozen pen machines mechanically duplicated Ritter's signature in blue ink. By the end of the 1980s, the donor communications department was operating twenty-four hours a day.

Old ladies from Illinois and Catholic families from Connecticut began looking to Ritter as a personal pastor, an image that the letters fostered. They would ask Father Bruce to pray for their husbands with cancer or to say a mass in honor of their young prodigal sons and daughters. Cash offerings for masses were deposited in what was known as the "Mass Account," which investigators later alleged was a revolving slush fund of untraceable petty cash for Ritter. Staffers couldn't remember Ritter saying any of the masses. A Faith Community member who helped write the correspondence found the process manipulative and misleading.

"He made it seem as if he was directly involved in these people's lives," she said. "He didn't have any idea who they were. Sometimes they would come to visit and expect to see Father Bruce. They had an image of him in a small parish in the city. We'd get these people showing up from Indiana who were tourists in New York. When they saw the corporate headquarters a lot of them were pretty surprised."

The sophisticated marketing strategy done in conjunction with Epsilon produced one of the highest rates of return on direct mail in the United States. Ritter was the talk of the industry.

"He was a phenomenon," said Stan Woodruff, who has been in the business since it first began and is now chairman of the board of the Third Class Mail Association. "The way the direct-mail marketing industry viewed him was close to canonization."

Jerry Huntsinger, the "dean" of the industry, proclaimed Father Ritter "the best writer of direct mail alive."

The directors of most nonprofit organizations couldn't write "worth a damn," as Woodruff put it, and relied on experts to write their letters for them. The result was that they were often bland appeals, the passion getting lost in the translation. Ritter, on the other hand, threw in his own personality, his own message, and his own words. One personal touch was at the top of each letter, where Ritter would state the exact time in the evening that he was writing. Usually it was quite late at night or just before dawn, giving readers an image of a tireless priest burning the midnight oil just to get the letters out.

Between 1979 and 1983, Covenant House's direct-mail fund-raising tripled from $7 million to $22 million. By industry standards, the five-year growth was "unprecedented" and "remarkable." The rate of increase slowed somewhat from 1984 to 1986, but from 1987 to 1990 the annual donations again tripled, from roughly $30 million to more than $90 million.

Ritter's involvement with direct mail and his ties with some of America's most powerful political conservatives were not purely coincidental. Direct mail was the power base of the new right and the brainchild of Richard Viguerie, a conservative ideologue and author of the 1980 paperback *The New Right: We're Ready to Lead.* Early on, Viguerie saw the value of mail solicitation as a way for the right to get out its message despite what he perceived as a "liberal bias" in the media.

Viguerie accumulated a library of mailing lists that contained vast numbers of prospective conservative donors, which in the hands of leaders of the new right's political and social causes became a war chest to carry out their political agenda. And there was big money out there in America's mailboxes. Charitable giving through direct-mail solicitation was a 1980s growth industry—rocketing from $22 billion a year in 1970 to $50 billion by 1980 and up to $114 billion by 1989. With just less than half of that total charitable giving going to religious ministries, Ritter was riding the church charity gravy train in its heyday. Even the series of sex and money scandals that rocked televangelists Jim Bakker and Jimmy Swaggart during this gold rush of giving served only to help Ritter's ministry, as hundreds of thousands of people who wanted to give their tax-deductible dollars to God turned toward more established church-oriented charities such as Covenant House.

Viguerie courted a reluctant corporate staff at Covenant House. They didn't give the prince of direct mail their account, but they did buy some important lists that contained millions of addresses of households in the conservative heartland of Reagan America, rapidly expanding the charity's donor base. But this didn't come cheap.

The organization spent $4.4 million on fund-raising costs in fiscal 1982–83, or about 24 percent of its total budget. More than half of that was spent on targeting the "ongoing donor base"—which gave $14.1 million. In other words, Covenant House was receiving $5.42 for every $1 spent on the "ongoing donor base"—an outstanding rate of return.

In a search for new donors, which included more explanatory information on the organization, Covenant House spent $1.8 million. The new donors provided $3 million, which amounted to a $1.68 return on every $1 spent—an equally phenomenal rate of return for new donors, when compared to other charities.

Similar charities, such as Boys Town and St. Jude's Children's Hospital, typically raise about $3 for every $1 in the ongoing donor base, and usually consider their new donor drives successful if they break even.

To write the newsletters, Father Bruce often retreated to Macauley's farm in upstate New York, where he could find the time to concentrate. At times torturous to finish, the letters were always made compelling by Ritter's strong voice as a writer. Some of the more compelling newsletters were later compiled in a thin paperback mass-mailed to millions and titled *Sometimes God Has a Kid's Face*.

At their best, the newsletters served as an ongoing dialogue with the donors, acknowledging their ownership of the program, their "right to know" what was happening and how their donations were being spent.

But at their worst they were misleading, manipulative, and prurient. Ritter seemed fixated in his writing on what he called the "X-rated children"—the innocents of Times Square up against a monstrous sex industry that was trying to steal their dignity and their youth. Thematically, the "kids vs. sex" provided "an easily identifiable villain," something that direct-mail marketing experts had concluded was effective. But in a deeper, psychosexual sense, the newsletters seemed to indicate a "complex chemistry at work," as one staff member who occasionally proofread the newsletters put it. Within the lines of the prose were "darkly fascinating images of young bodies and neon lights." And between the lines were subtle but revealing confessionals. As Ritter wrote in the introduction to another compilation of the letters: "If you think it at all important to know who I am, read these newsletters. Who and what I am, for better or worse, is smeared all over these pages."

Perhaps the most recurrent characters in the newsletters were young white males caught in prostitution. Ritter described many of them as "good-looking" and "blond," and went into obsessive detail about their physical features, from the size of their feet to the shape of their bodies. His choice of words, his use of imagery seemed to have a sexual undertone running just beneath the surface. Rosanne Haggerty Redmond, a writer in the donor communications department, said that donors occasionally saw through the newsletters' prurient side and that many complaints were registered.

She felt that those donors who picked up on the lurid language were "absolutely right," that it was "more like eroticism than fund raising."

This is an excerpt from the newsletter of September 1977:

> "I'm a hustler," he said, and watched me carefully with a total awareness that made me afraid.
> I liked him a lot. I mean I really liked him. I felt the electricity, the chemistry operating between us. He knew it before I did.

The next newsletter extract, from 1978, was about a kid who had just come into Covenant House. Ritter was "counseling" the youth at the crisis center late one night and making him dinner.

> I stepped on his foot just a little and said I was really glad he was here, and walked over to the stove to stir the mashed potatoes.
> The boy [tall, blond, and mildly retarded] got up, walked over to the stove, and bumped into me, except that he didn't move away. We stood there, his right side to my left side, foot, calf, thigh, hip, shoulder pressed together. I stirred the carrots and peas, said I hoped he was hungry, and moved over to the broiler to check out the hamburgers.
> The boy walked around the table and into me, bumping me, and did not move away, his left side to my right side, foot, calf, thigh, hip, shoulder pressed together. I stuck a fork in the hamburgers, pronounced them ready. It was great having him around.

Sometimes the newsletters seemed to be a kind of public penitence in which Ritter dwelt on his kinship with many of the sinners. For example, in his August 1977 letter he wrote about a man who owned a "raunchy brothel," which provided peep shows and young kids to johns at a cut rate. The man came to Ritter with a donation to the charity. The way Ritter related the story, the pimp handed the money to him, saying, "This is for your kids. We like what you are doing. I'm in a bad business, but I don't like the kids getting hurt. God bless you." Ritter refused the money and meditated on the street scene as a biblical allegory.

> There's a mystery here, in this story, of grace and sin. I wish I understood it better than I do. . . . The more I thought about it, the more . . . [it] oppressed and obsessed me. I think he tried to do a good thing, yet what he does across the street is clearly evil. . . .
> . . . I can't get that "God bless you" out of my mind. . . . my mind reels, and I can't understand it.
> I know a lot about mixed motives. I'm the world's expert on mixed motives—my own—trying to disentangle the good from the evil, to unravel the knotted skein of my better self . . . the weeds growing with the wheat . . . and suddenly I am overwhelmed by my kinship with this man, for we are both sinners hoping in the mercy of God and His forgiveness.

Through his writing, Father Ritter also developed a theology on the sin that was around him, establishing his own Dantean levels of hell for the sinners in Times Square. First came the kids, who he felt weren't really sinners at all. He wrote that he found it "very easy to love a kid who's into 'the life' because he or she doesn't really have any choice and is looking for love in all the wrong places." Worse were the pimps. He wrote: "Where pimps are concerned my ability to forgive flies out the window. I loathe and despise them. I hate what they do to kids. . . . Even worse are the pornographers. I despise the greedy hearted businessmen who publish and distribute the vicious and violent and degrading pornography that floods this country."

But with johns—mostly older men who pay for sex with the youths—Ritter didn't have much trouble. For these lonely men Ritter showed a great degree of forgiveness; providing for them a special place just above purgatory. Although he said he had trouble with what they did he could "usually manage pretty well" to forgive them.

Most johns are sad and lonely guys trying to buy some friendly company for a few minutes at a time. I mean sometimes the commodity being exchanged is not only just sex, whether it's the kid selling or the john buying. Sometimes it's a lonely desolate kind of love, two needs meeting in a quick, anonymous encounter.

In fact, Ritter understood so intimately the johns, or "chicken-hawks," as they're called on the street, that in his August 1980 newsletter he actually used the first person plural, implying that he was guilty of the same sin:

You see the word on the street is, johns prefer chickens—kids. Because of greed and lust, and our sloth and fear.

Ritter's word imagery became more lurid as the years went on. Perhaps because he received such a positive response from the letters, or perhaps because, as his mother warned, the "pitch" that surrounded his work had "defiled" him, he took more chances on the edge of self-revelation. A classic example was his August 1983 newsletter, set in Fort Lauderdale, when Ritter was trying to open the shelter there. While building his empire, Ritter often cruised the streets of the cities where he proposed his franchises. He became intimate with the details of the prostitution scene. More than a fascination, it seemed to be an obsession. The young male prostitutes were the muse for much of his writing.

My blue Mustang was instantly anonymous. So was its balding, fiftyish driver in slacks and T-shirt. Just another john cruising. . . . From midnight to 4:30 A.M., I cruised the Strip. . . . It was a quiet night but there were still dozens of kids working. Some would just stand provocatively—the hustler's stance. Others would make those minute, secret hand signals. The bolder ones just beckoned or whistled or called. My stopping for red lights gave still other striplings the opportunity to wander over and wonder if I was looking for some action. No thanks, I said.

It was getting on toward 3 A.M., and I was pretty tired and had decided to pack it in. One more trip, I thought. The streets were rapidly emptying and the girls and the boy hustlers stood out now even more obviously.

Heading north, I stopped for a red light on Ocean Boulevard and looked over the now deserted beach. I didn't see the kid approach my car and was startled when he spoke to me.

"Do you want to give me a ride?" he said.

He was a nice-looking kid, sixteen, maybe seventeen, I thought. Nice eyes, nice hair. A little scared maybe.

"Sure," I said, and laughed—mostly to put the kid at ease. . . .

"My name is Bruce."

"My name is Dan," he said.

"Where're you from?" I said.

"Minnesota," he said. . . .

I drove south on Birch Road and made a decision to continue the conversation.

"How are you surviving?" I said. "How are you making it?"

"Hustling," he said.

"Are you hustling now?" I said.

"Yes," he said.

"How much do you go for?" I said.

"Eighty dollars," he said, and hastily added, "but I do everything for that. I can go for less." . . .

And then my eyes began to burn and they began to glisten and blurred oncoming headlights and I was glad it was dark in the car and he couldn't see the tears forming.

Another newsletter was about a remarkably similar scene in Hollywood, where Ritter was cruising the streets. He was there with some free tickets to the opening of the Olympics. The newsletter was a first plea to his donors for their help to start an Under 21 shelter there. Instead of focusing on an explanation of the program or the need for it, Ritter told a lurid tale of another anonymous encounter with a young boy, also blond, also handsome. A curious way to promote the need for a shelter.

I drove up and down Santa Monica Boulevard—the most *notorious* meat rack in the country—half a dozen times. It was as I had remembered it. I could have picked up at least fifty kids. . . .
I stopped for a red light on the corner of La Brea and Santa Monica. A kid was sprawled on a bench there, facing the oncoming traffic. His left leg was thrown casually over the back of the bench, the other stretched straight out along the seat. His right thumb pointed somewhere in the direction of the Pacific Ocean, in the Hollywood hitchhikers' gesture. It meant he was available.
He seemed to be about sixteen. An average everyday kind of kid. A nice kid.
The light took a long time. We looked at each other. I didn't say anything. He didn't either. . . .
I wondered what he saw in my face. Did he see the dismay and sadness and misunderstand? Did he think I was condemning him for trying to pick me up? Or maybe something else? Did he see concern? Did he suspect that I cared? Did he know that I liked him?

Ritter also reflected on the importance of his writing in understanding who he is. He conceded that the letters were "inescapably autobiographical."
"The only way I knew how to write about the kids was to describe the way they involved themselves in my own life, how they finally came to live in my own heart and mind and to own me. And, in a few case, let me own them," Ritter wrote. "Quite often, I have skirted that risky edge of self-revelation, and each time just as consciously drawn back from that inviting precipice."
Father John McNeil, a psychotherapist and one of the founding fathers of the Catholic gay-rights movement, believes Ritter was often caught off balance at the edge of the "precipice," tumbling into the hole of sublimated desire. McNeil, who has known Ritter for many years, said he had always felt that Ritter was homosexual. But he said he never had any evidence that Ritter was actively gay and, prior to the allegations being made public in the press, never suspected him of breaking his vow of celibacy.
McNeil's 1985 book, *The Church and the Homosexual,* is a rational and compassionate reevaluation of homosexuality based on scripture and current psychological research. The former Jesuit was the first member of the Catholic clergy to publicly challenge the Church on

its position against homosexuality. An important and controversial voice in the Church, McNeil sees a lesson in Ritter's life story as told through the newsletters.

"I've always suspected that Bruce was gay because of the intensity of his commitment, which takes on a kind of pedagogical eros," said McNeil. "But a lot of great teachers of children sublimate their desires—just as a lot of heart surgeons put their sadistic impulses to good use in cutting open chests."

But the newsletters were not just conflicted confessionals; they were exploitive. Bill Treanor, a long-time youth-program lobbyist and former staff member of the Senate Judiciary Committee on Juvenile Justice, had been a critic of Ritter's programs since the early 1980s. Treanor felt Ritter's newsletters perpetuated a dangerous misconception about homeless youths—painting the majority of them as prostitutes or caught up in sophisticated pornography rings. Statistically, Treanor said, Ritter's portrayal was a gross exaggeration. In fact, a 1983 survey conducted by the U.S. Department of Health and Human Services estimated that only 12 percent of homeless youth were involved in prostitution. Treanor and other professional youth counselors estimated that less than 2 percent were actually involved in pornography.

Nevertheless, Ritter continued to use inflated figures to capture the attention of a society that otherwise seemed indifferent about the plight of these young people.

"He did that because it was the best way to appeal to his donors. Hey, send me twenty bucks and I'll fight the porn industy," said Treanor. "It's easier to be dramatic than to say that sexual and physical abuse of kids happens primarily in the family, before they run away. That won't work in direct mail."

The misconception was also an "incredible burden" to put on the kids, said Marilyn Rocky, a former Covenant House spokeswoman, who was always critical of Ritter on the point and eventually resigned from the charity. The newsletters and slick promotional packets that Covenant House printed were also filled with white faces. The photographs were predominantly of fifteen- to eighteen-year-old boys and girls—many of them carrying backpacks and standing in the neon of Times Square.

"The real story with 90 percent of the kids was that they were black or Hispanic, poor, with little or no education and almost no opportunity for employment. But poverty doesn't sell," said a former Covenant House director of program development. "Sex and prostitution sells. People see that and want to save the kids. Why Father Bruce was obsessed is a different question, but the fact that it worked was all the organization cared about."

As the direct-mail program and the titillating newsletters fueled the multimillion-dollar fund-raising machinery, it became more and more difficult to dispel the prefabricated myths. Directors became increasingly intolerant of anyone who objected to the portrayal of the youths in the propaganda as young white victims of prostitution and pornography. The fact was that most of the youths were the victims of a more "complex set of evils": an unbreakable cycle of poverty, drugs, and physical and sexual abuse perpetrated by the family and failing education and health-care systems. They were undereducated, untrained, and unemployable. The letters, therefore, seemed only to perpetuate the status quo with uncomfortable images, rather than challenge it by exposing these more unsettling truths.

And there were other dangers in the fund-raising machinery that Covenant House had built around Father Ritter's newsletters. *Fund Raising Management's* Olcott followed Ritter's rapid rise to prominence. He wrote many glowing articles and profiles about Ritter, but kept a critical eye on his dizzying success. Olcott felt that the charity's identity was too intimately linked with its founder—leaving it in a precarious position if he should die or, as the euphemism goes, become "controversial." The corporate staff at Covenant House were aware enough of those dangers and cautious enough with their most valued asset to take out a $10 million "key-man life insurance" policy on Ritter.

"Father Bruce was the great rallying point for Covenant House's fund raising. He was the icon. In the process, he created a tremendous illusion about who he was and how he started the organization. That can be very dangerous," said Olcott. "When you center all of your fund raising around one man, you can run into trouble. If it crumbles and falls apart, it can be disastrous for the organization."

IV

The Fall

The serpent said . . . "On the day you eat it your eyes will be opened and you will be like gods, knowing good and evil."

The Jerusalem Bible, Genesis 3:5

Chapter 11

True Believers

THE windows of the Faith Community looked out on Times Square's tawdry crossroads of the rich and the poor, the powerful and the powerless. From the brick building on Eighth Avenue and Forty-fourth Street, the religious volunteers could see the glittering marquees of the Broadway theater district, where men and women arrived in limousines to see $100-a-seat musicals. Just across the street, beneath the raunchy neon of peep shows and hourly-rate motels, homeless people begged with paper cups and street kids hustled drugs or their bodies.

Faith Community member Mark Redmond would lean against the frame of the large kitchen window after dinner and watch the city—confident that he was on the right side of the street, helping the poor.

Redmond was in his early twenties and finishing up a management training program at Metropolitan Life when he decided to volunteer to help Father Ritter carry out his mission. He was proud of his decision, proud that he had rechanneled his life against the careerist current of the 1980s.

Like many of the people who went through the Faith Community, Redmond believed it changed his life. Close friendships were formed among its staffers and many couples who met in the community married. Redmond and his wife, Rosanne Haggerty, met during their two-year service as volunteers. Ritter had become a powerful force in their spiritual lives.

Ritter was preparing these talented young people, like Redmond, Anne Donahue, Greg Loken, and John Spanier, for positions of great responsibility. Within a year of joining the Faith Community, Redmond was appointed director of one hundred religious volunteers— one of the largest lay Catholic groups in the country. Loken emerged from the community to start Covenant House's Institute for Youth Advocacy. At the age of twenty-three, Patrick Atkinson headed Covenant House's Latin America program, one of the largest child-care agencies in the region. Anne Donahue would years later become the executive director of the Los Angeles program.

These faithful followers would become spiritual buffers to stave off what Ritter called the "social-service types" who worked in the organization. Ritter wanted a core of loyalists who understood the religious nature of his mission. He knew the sprawling organization was in danger of losing its spiritual bearings, and these young people were to be the moorings that kept it from going adrift. He called them the "keepers of the Covenant." The certified social workers who joined the staff as it became more professional cynically referred to them as "true believers," or simply "the cult."

Father Bruce systematically moved the best and brightest of his followers into key positions as "ombudsmen." The ombudsmen had complete veto power over the administrative staff in New York and at each of the satellite programs when it came to decisions on whether or not a kid would be admitted or removed from the program. It was a way for Bruce to ensure that open intake was a confirmed policy. The administrative staff, many of whom had social-work degrees or were trained youth counselors, resented the fact that their power was undercut by these untrained Ritter acolytes. The Faith Community volunteers felt they were missionaries on a religious quest, not just social workers. This created a constant tension within the day-to-day operations of the charity.

Anne Donahue tells this story. It was New Year's Eve, 1982, a raw evening, and she was avoiding Father Ritter. She couldn't let him know what she was about to do. Debbie, a sixteen-year-old mother of two, had arrived at Covenant House several months earlier with her newborn daughter, Crystal, and told the intake center that an abusive boyfriend was holding her one-year-old son, Bobby, hostage until she returned. It was another confusing tale of poverty and violence in New York City. Many of the professional counselors at

Covenant House had little patience for Debbie, who was described as "volatile and demanding," and on the verge of being abusive herself to Crystal.

But Donahue felt that Debbie's "temper tantrums" were understandable given the fact that she was desperate to get Bobby back. The professional counselors wanted to refer her out to the State Department of Social Services, where she ran the risk of being separated from Crystal, since she was technically classified as homeless. For several months Donahue kept Debbie in hiding and waited for something to happen. Finally Debbie heard through friends that her boyfriend had disappeared, leaving Bobby at his apartment with his sister. It was Debbie's only chance to get her son back. She begged Donahue and a Covenant House ombudsman named Jim to help her.

Even though the executive director of Covenant House told Jim and Donahue that it was a "police matter," they believed it was the right thing to do. Jim's role as ombudsman technically gave him the authority to overrule the administration, so, despite his lack of experience in social work, he intervened in the case.

Jim, Donahue, and Debbie drove the blue Covenant House van to the Bedford-Stuyvesant section of Brooklyn, one of New York's most dangerous neighborhoods. They climbed a dimly lit stairwell in a drug-infested tenement, grabbed the baby and left.

From Donahue's perspective, "this was the embodiment of the covenant" in Covenant House—protecting young people, as the place itself got bigger and more institutional, from being "swallowed up in the pressures of agency guidelines instead of the young people's needs."

Debbie and her two children were sent off to a residence for mothers and children several states away. Donahue says she doesn't know where Debbie is today. But she is proud of the risks she took and proud of the fact that she never told Father Bruce, although she believes in her heart that he would have agreed with her actions. This was the kind of fierce dedication that Ritter had instilled in his faithful core. They were willing to go above the law.

But to Covenant House's professional managers, like Under 21 program director Linda Glassman, the volunteers' missionary flame often burned out of control. The Faith Community, she said, was predominantly young, white college graduates from wealthy backgrounds, who were often manipulated by the street kids. The custody battle that Donahue cites is a classic example, Glassman said, of the kind of shoddy casework and impetuous decision making within an agency that she felt strayed too far from even the most basic child-care agency guidelines. Custody battles are always confusing and take time to sort out. The "Rambo approach" can be very dangerous and complicate the problem.

Before joining Covenant House, Glassman had been the head of a statewide coalition of runaway programs in California. In that position she had expressed reservations about Covenant House's policies. But at a conference she met Ritter, who convinced her that she could bring her knowledge to Covenant House and help him make it more professional. Ritter lured her, saying that his fast-growing charity could provide a full medical and legal staff to help kids, something that the smaller community-based shelters she worked with could not. She knew that the vast wealth of Covenant House would allow her more resources to help young people. She took Ritter up on his offer, but later learned that he had no intention of changing policies. There was a stubborn resistance to long-term casework, and much of the charity's money was squandered on a never-ending expansion of subsidiary programs, renovations of existing facilities, and high salaries for an inner circle that had nothing to do with providing direct care.

Those who tried to reform the program were seen as infidels. Some of Ritter's inner circle became like undercover agents within the charity, ensuring that Father Bruce's vision of the covenant and his sacred policy of open intake were carried out. Any hints of betrayal were reported back to Ritter. John MacNeil, executive director of Covenant House's Toronto program, was one of the few senior staff members who dared to challenge Ritter on his policies. One night, the Toronto Under 21 center was packed with more than 120 kids. Seeing the pressure that the overcrowding had placed on his staff and determining that the kids could not be safely administered to, MacNeil did what no other executive director had dared to do. He broke the covenant of open intake and turned away several kids, confident that they had homes and enough money to pay for bus fare.

This was when MacNeil learned about what he called Ritter's "network of spies." The Toronto Faith Community's ombudsman, Dorn Checkley, had not been consulted on the decision to violate the policy and immediately notified Ritter. MacNeil said one of Ritter's key senior staff members, Sister Gretchen, called and told him that it was a "serious digression" and that he would "pay dearly for it." According to MacNeil, the "true believers" began monitoring him; staffers from the New York office even made surprise visits to "check on his work."

This was part of Ritter's bizarre management style. Steve Torkelsen, one of Ritter's chief confidants, would instruct staffers to use code names in meeting notes so that no one, except them, would know to whom they were referring.

"It was a lot like working for a big corporation. Things were done in secrecy," said MacNeil. "There was a lot of dishonesty from the top that filtered down."

To senior staff officials at rival social-service agencies the secret power circle and the religious righteousness of the Faith Community was a destructive energy within the charity and one that affected other community-based charities.

"The Covenant House people believed they had a light for these kids, and the only thing they were accountable to was that light," said one executive director of a New Orleans program that worked closely with Covenant House. "They were responsible to God as God had revealed himself to Bruce Ritter."

This religious crusade aggravated the nagging antagonism between Covenant House and law-enforcement agencies, especially the Manhattan District Attorney's office, which felt that the religious zealots often skirted the law and naïvely harbored young male criminals. This hostility between Ritter and the Manhattan D.A. heightened around a 1985 incident.

A fifteen-year-old male prostitute was found severely beaten and half naked on the streets of Greenwich Village, and Covenant House was called in to help him. He claimed he was abused by a pornographer and assaulted for not cooperating with a film. He also had a chilling allegation that he had engaged in many illicit sexual relationships through a pedophile-priest sex ring on the East Coast. The allegations were never confirmed. But a detective in the New York City Police Department's Public Morals Division, who was knowledgeable about the case, said that his investigation was thwarted because Covenant House officials discouraged the youth from cooperating.

The investigators felt that Ritter was trying to cover for his fellow priests, and, according to Anne Donahue, the incident became the stress crack that fractured the relationship between the charity and law enforcement. The Public Morals Division considered filing obstruction-of-justice charges against Ritter, but foresaw the public-relations disaster it could be and abandoned the idea.

Donahue, who was also directly involved in the case, said, "The bottom line was that if he continued as a witness he was in far greater danger for his life and safety than if he just clammed up and disappeared. . . . The police were out to get Bruce ever since."

Ritter's faithful followers caused friction with another group—the gay community. The religious volunteers often brought a confused message on homosexuality to the kids on the street in the form of a Catholic creed: Love the sinner, hate the sin. For the young street kids who were gay or for those, like many of the male prostitutes, who were confused about their sexuality, the message was unproductive and sometimes damaging. Many in the social services believed Covenant House had an institutional insensitivity to gay teenagers. They claimed that it often treated homosexuality as a disease that kids "caught in the streets" rather than a sexual orientation. The religious beliefs of the staff led to subtle and not-so-subtle messages of a rejection of their homosexuality.

Heightening the conflict between Covenant House and the gay community, Father Ritter took a controversial stand in the early 1980s on New York City legislation that sought to bar discrimination in hiring homosexuals at city-funded agencies, even Catholic ones. Ritter supported Cardinal John O'Connor's bitter opposition and eventual lawsuit against Mayor Koch's Executive Order 50, as the proposed law was called. O'Connor felt the legislation violated Catholic doctrine against homosexuality.

There was a great deal of debate within Covenant House, which had many openly gay as well as closeted staffers. Father Ritter appeared once again to be doing the work of conservative elements in the Church by adding Covenant House's name to the controversial lawsuit.

Public stands, such as the one Ritter took on Executive Order 50, served to deflect any outward suspicions the public might have had about his sexual orientation. His perceived enemies—the "gay underground," the social-service establishment, law-enforcement agencies, Mayor Koch, even the Mafia—became a faceless group of villains who were out to get him. He told congregations and wrote in newsletters that someday "they" would try to do him in.

Ritter seemed to be at war within himself, an unsettling sense of internal conflict that those who were close to him felt manifested itself every day—through his obsession with his enemies, the confessional and lurid tone of his newsletters, and a compulsive need for control and order.

At his charitable headquarters Ritter was constantly ripping up the carpeting and tearing down walls to remodel the interior. He was incessantly ordering his niece's firm to refinish furniture and reorganize the corporate offices. On one occasion, Glassman remembers, she saw Ritter arguing bitterly with interior designers about where and in what sequence to place a stack of donated gray and green carpet squares.

Ritter, never happy with his accomplishments, brought a perfectionist streak into his management style. His authority could never be challenged and, the few times Glassman or other female staffers tried, his language was often defensive and sexist.

"All you women are just the same," he muttered on one occasion when Glassman approached him about making changes in the program to provide more services to the female prostitutes, who outnumbered the males but seemed to get much less staff attention.

Father Ritter was not always the compassionate priest portrayed in the fund-raising literature. He often showed his staff a side that was filled with contempt and rage, although he would usually catch himself when it pushed its way to the surface.

"He could be the meanest, most sarcastic, cruelest man you'd ever meet," said Glassman. "But in public he could be masterfully self-deprecating, and very open about his own faults. He knew how to separate his inner life from his public persona."

In the Faith Community lounge, copies of *National Catholic Reporter* and *Commonweal*, the two leading liberal Catholic publications in the U.S., would pass from hand to hand. Without television or radio or much money to go out, the volunteers would read and discuss current issues in the Church. Many considered themselves among the ranks of a re-emerging peace and economic-justice movement within the Catholic Church.

If Father Ritter's Covenant House was caught between the twilight of the legacy of the Great Society and the dawning of the Reagan era, it was also caught between two strong currents within the Catholic Church at a time when the aftershock of Vatican II was still reverberating throughout its institutions. One current was from the new breed of Catholics, like many members of the Faith Community, who used the sixteen documents of Vatican II as ammunition to bring about social and economic change as well as to supply fresh ideas and new theology. The cross-current was the resurgence of conservatives, like Grace and Simon, who devoted their time and money to bolstering the rigid and unbending doctrines of the ancient Church, as a reaction against the disarray that Vatican II had created.

These two forces were set on a collision course within Covenant House. The largely conservative and wealthy men who made up the clear majority on the Covenant House board of directors were steering the ship. But the Faith Community members charted the spiritual direction of the mission on the street.

For Mark Redmond, this tension within the charity touched off a slow process of disillusionment. When he first volunteered, Covenant House was in its last days as a community-based charity. It had not yet been consumed by the expansionist vision of Macauley, Grace, and Simon. But he could see the corruption of Ritter happening before his eyes. He remembers Ritter coming into the Faith Community breathless with excitement after flying from a Florida vacation with Peter Grace in his private jet.

"Peter Grace says we can be a forty-million-dollar charity someday!" he told Redmond.

Ritter's growing allegiance with the new right was also noticed by fellow priests who worked within the charity. One evening Father Bruce was returning from a dinner at a midtown restaurant with Grace, Simon, and Macauley. He walked the men through his building, showing off some new improvements.

Father Edward Murphy, a Jesuit who had just joined the staff at Covenant House, was working the late shift that night and Father Bruce made the introductions. Murphy's mind flashed back to Greenwich Village in the late 1960s, when he used to run an antiwar education project at the Martin Buber House on East Sixth Street. Murphy realized that it wasn't that long ago that he had been protesting in front of the White House while Nixon and then Treasury Secretary Bill Simon were probably sitting in some boardroom in the inner sanctum of power. He remembered the time, about fifteen years earlier, that he had picketed the front entrance to Grace's chemical empire in midtown Manhattan, protesting the corporation's imperialist policies in Central America. And now here these men were with Father Bruce in Covenant House, providing not just more money but a new direction for the charity.

As Covenant House expanded into Central America, there were many members of the Faith Community eager to help out down there. It was during the time that the government of the Guatemalan general José Efrain Rios Montt was massacring leftist Catholics and El Salvador's right-wing death squads gunned down San Salvador's Archbishop Oscar Romero on the altar. Yet the same conservative Central American oligarchy—the military, the Church, and business leaders who slaughtered leftist Catholic workers—was opening wide its doors to the balding Franciscan and his Casa Alianza. It raised questions among religious communities like the Maryknolls in the region and ultimately filtered back to the Covenant House Faith Community in New York.

A Jesuit in the Bronx, Father Jim Joyce, told Redmond, "The people supporting Covenant House are the same people killing the Jesuits down there. Can't you see that?"

There were some, including Joyce, who went further, suggesting a "contra connection" in Covenant House. Persistent rumors circulated among the staff that Covenant House's operations in Central America were becoming outposts for the Reagan administration's covert network of private aid to the contras. The rumors were strong enough for Redmond to ask Father Bruce about them and about his ties to some allegedly unsavory characters in the region, especially Alejos. Ritter dismissed his dealings with Alejos and other shadowy figures as "necessary connections."

"You get nowhere without them," Ritter would say.

The overall expansion of Covenant House in Guatemala and Honduras, and eventually Panama and Mexico, was brokered by Grace, who ultimately established a complicated network of charities and Church groups to generate "humanitarian aid" for the contras.

Through the early to late 1980s, Grace used his position as the head of the New York chapter of the Knights of Malta to establish a new partnership with AmeriCares, the Connecticut-based charity founded by Macauley. The Knights used their local representatives in the region, especially Alejos, to handle the distribution of aid provided by AmeriCares. Because the Knights of Malta are an ancient order, with the status of a sovereign state, they are afforded diplomatic immunity, which means shipments sent directly to them did not pass through customs. Therefore, it is not known what precisely was contained in the hundreds of thousands of metric tons of aid that AmeriCares sent into Central America. But Macauley insists all of it was "humanitarian," mostly surplus medicines and expired vaccines donated by American pharmaceutical companies, which received tax breaks in return.

Ritter's connection to the AmeriCares pipeline was direct. From 1983, he was listed as vice president of the nonprofit organization. Grace and Simon also served on AmeriCares' advisory board. Zbigniew Brzezinski was listed as the honorary chairman, and other members of the advisory board included retired U.S. Army general Richard Stilwell and Prescott Bush, Jr., George Bush's brother, who also grew up with Macauley.

It is reported in Penny Lernoux's *People of God* as well as in a 1985 report on a fact-finding mission by Reed Brody, former New York

State Assistant Attorney General, that AmeriCares was a conduit in the network of private aid to the contras, although Macauley has denied the link.

In 1988, it was reported that AmeriCares' 1983 tax returns show that the nonprofit organization distributed $291,383 in food and medicine and $5,750 in cash to Mario Calero, who was the brother of the top contra leader Adolfo Calero and who was establishing aid to contra camps in Honduras along the border with Nicaragua.

Macauley's charity later flew two hundred tons of newsprint to the Nicaraguan opposition newspaper *La Prensa* in 1986. The paper, whose editor, Violeta Chamorro, defeated Sandinista President Daniel Ortega in the 1990 election, was used by the Reagan administration as a litmus test for Nicaragua's intentions to carry through with promises to allow freedom of the press. In 1988, Macauley tried again to fly fifteen tons of paper to *La Prensa*. But this time his flight was blocked by the Nicaraguan government, which accused AmeriCares of being a "CIA front" and "part of the secret network of private groups used by Lieutenant Colonel Oliver North to deliver aid to the contras."

The Sandinistas claimed "humanitarian" aid had to come from a "neutral" party, which they claimed AmeriCares was not. Since the State Department and Colonel Sam Watson, a national security adviser to Vice President George Bush, paved the way for the shipment, it seems the Nicaraguan government had a point. Macauley claimed at the time that he had no prior knowledge that the U.S. government had tried to intervene on his behalf. But given his personal relationship with Bush and an investigative report on AmeriCares by Russell W. Baker in the *Village Voice* that cited a 1985 memo from Oliver North that mentioned Macauley by last name, it is hard to believe Macauley's assertions that he was not involved with the private effort to fund the contras. But Macauley continues to deny any involvement in the covert effort:

"We never funded the contras. . . . I'll take an oath on the Bible. I'll tell you the exact truth, I am not connected with the CIA. AmeriCares is not connected with the CIA. I make that very clear when I meet with the president. He agreed. He said, 'No you are doing humanitarian aid.' . . . The president is the commander in chief and I would do anything in that service. . . . But there has never been a connection with the CIA. . . . The whole thing they have tried to drum up is not true."

It was an elaborate web of intrigue, in which Ritter seemed the most unlikely of players. What was a medieval theologian who worked with street kids doing as vice president of an organization with alleged links to the CIA?

Macauley and Grace's friend William Simon didn't miss out on the excitement in Central America. He was a board member of the Nicaraguan Freedom Fund, which also allegedly used the Knights of Malta and a connection with AmeriCares to provide supplies to contra camps along the border of Honduras.

A host of other conservative funds and charities also funneled aid through the Knights of Malta to the Guatemalan highlands around Nabaj, a region where a brutal military regime had established its "model village" program to forcibly relocate Indian peasants. These controlled settlements were described by human-rights groups as "little more than concentration camps."

[Covenant House's bizarre and little-known connections to the secretive world of Central American dictators and the U.S. intelligence community would reach the height of absurdity several years later, in April 1989. Lieutenant Colonel Oliver North telephoned Father Ritter to see if he could perform his community service sentence for his involvement in Iran-contra at Covenant House. Although Ritter was "flattered that North asked," the public-relations team advised him not to get involved with the colonel because he could alienate some donors.]

Covenant House's strange dealings in Central America—difficult to document, impossible to pin down—were unsettling to Redmond and other members of the Faith Community. But nothing left Redmond more disillusioned and bitter about his time at Covenant House than another set of allegations that surfaced in the fall of 1983. Several members of the Faith Community told him that Father Bruce had made sexual advances on them. The questionable ties to shady Central American governments passed as bad irony, but the sexual allegations were a glaring violation of Ritter's religious vows, and an abuse of his power. One member of the Faith Community, who was a close friend of Redmond, told him that he was going to report the allegations to the Franciscans.

Redmond knew he had to leave the Faith Community. His vision of Covenant House and his respect for Father Bruce were shattered. Redmond said that when he left he was "more than disillusioned." He was "broken."

But for those who stayed on, more disturbing paradoxes surfaced as the agency expanded. While child-care counselors either were volunteers or were paid annual salaries that ranged between $13,000 and $15,000, Ritter had a select inner circle of senior staff members who were paid top salaries. There was a glaring hypocrisy in a child-care organization illustrating its priorities by paying public-relations and program-development experts professional salaries and its front-line staff of child-care counselors poverty-level wages that were low even compared to those of small, community-based charities.

Ritter could be tyrannical, sometimes arbitrarily threatening to fire low-level child-care workers for the smallest infractions. He would stalk the building with a radio scanner in his hand and listen in on the communications of the security staff. When he saw something he didn't like, Ritter or a member of his inner circle would appear out of nowhere, often to undermine decisions being made by the staff.

Rick Agcuili, a floor supervisor in the Under 21 program, who had been with the charity off and on for eleven years, points out that he admired Ritter's desire to remain a hands-on leader, but that ultimately his need for control was at odds with his desire to build a far-flung empire.

It was during 1983 and 1984, at a time when Ritter was spreading himself thin and under tremendous stress, that Agcuili and others grew suspicious of Ritter's frequent late-night "counseling sessions" and mysterious visitors, most of them young men.

Agcuili, who then worked as a counselor at the drop-in center on the ground floor of the building at Forty-fourth Street and Eighth Avenue, said that he had been ordered to notify Ritter "immediately" any time a youth was admitted who was involved in organized prostitution or pornography. His preoccupation with the issue seemed strange to Agcuili. From the fearful victims of pimps and pornographers, who Agcuili says were few in number, Ritter would select a certain client profile that he followed closely—young males who were white or light-skinned minorities and who were often intelligent and articulate. The others were usually handed back to Agcuili.

"Why didn't he immediately want to know about the kids who were having a hard time finding a job, or the kids who were hooked on drugs, or the kids who felt they had to do drug running to survive in the streets? It didn't make any sense," said Agcuili.

It struck Agcuili as strange given the fact that, during those two years, he and other staff workers on the night shift would see a steady stream of young men go up to Ritter's eighth-floor office, often late at night. They were referred to as "summer guests" or "visiting volunteers." Senior staff members, like John Spanier, would post memos at the security booth at the entrance to Covenant House informing the guards that the select young men were to be given access to Ritter's office.

"It raised a lot of eyebrows," Agcuili said. "Father Bruce opened himself up to questions about his sexuality and questions about his conduct. There was a lot of discussion about it within the staff. People believed that he was gay. I don't think people thought he would abuse the kids."

Ritter employed only a small inner circle of executive staff members, including Loken, Atkinson, Torkelsen, and Kells. They were referred to by lower-level staff members as the "golden boys" because most of them were handsome young white males. Ritter's clear favoritism toward them raised more questions among staff members.

No one personified the "golden boys" more than John Kells. Ritter had successfully lured Kells away from his job as an assignment editor at the Houston ABC-TV affiliate in 1985 with an offer to become vice president of public relations for Covenant House.

"I believed that I was doing something that mattered. It fed into my entire sense of justice," said Kells. "I was doing great work, and yet I hadn't sold out to a corporation. I was working for a living saint. It was like being in the Peace Corps, but winning every time you went out. . . . You could have all this compassion, and still get paid well."

Indeed, Kells was paid very well. His starting salary was close to $90,000. He was also given a $100,000 loan to purchase a home and a car. When other staffers asked why Kells received so much, Ritter told them that Kells had received a comparable salary at the Houston television station. In fact, Kells earned closer to $35,000 as an assignment editor in Houston. The salary was puzzling at a charity constantly making urgent appeals to donors and paying its child-care workers only subsistence wages. But Ritter always defended Kells.

The two seemed to share an intense commitment to saving young lives. One of Kell's first moves when he came to the organization was to make highly produced "public service announcements," using the images of the young kids, mostly white models who played the part of street kids, in the natural setting of Times Square. The PSAs were slick and gripping, and they aired for free all over the country. They carried the message of Covenant House and brought attention to the plight of homeless youths before millions of TV viewers every night. Kells estimated that the PSAs were the equivalent of "$40 million worth of free advertising."

Kells's success as a public-relations man was that he found gimmicks that not only appeared on the surface to be useful to the kids but became vehicles to increase Covenant House's exposure in the media and ultimately raised more money. His critics in the administration felt that his emphasis was on the latter. For example, Kells was the mastermind behind the "Nineline," a toll-free hotline for youths in distress. The number was easy to remember, 1-800-999-9999, and was flashed into the subconscious of kids and parents on television and billboards nationwide. But the real value of the Nineline was the increased publicity it gave Covenant House and the new donors it attracted. Some nights, the Nineline had nearly as many potential donors calling as it did kids in crisis.

Before Kells created the Nineline there were several different national hotlines for troubled youths already established, although none of them was as highly publicized. Despite the duplication of effort, Covenant House pumped $3 million a year into the hotline. The agency took up to five thousand calls a day, although it never published any breakdown of how many of the callers were donors and how many were troubled young people. It had a database of more than twenty thousand agencies, which allowed counselors to locate immediate help for any caller in need. There was an enormous investment in technology to establish the sophisticated phone system, but Kells justified the cost because the phone lines were also used in fund-raising.

Kells claimed that the amount of money raised through the Nineline was "minimal at best." But by 1989, the projected annual income from telemarketing via the Nineline phone system was $4 million, or about 5 percent of the annual budget. There were 150 volunteers who answered phones and a full-time staff of 56 operators, or "phone crisis workers." Although the standards of the National Charities Information Bureau clearly state that costs attributed to fund raising should be documented in a separate category, the Nineline was always budgeted as a "counseling service." That allowed Covenant House to hide a considerable portion of the amount of donor dollars spent on fund raising and may have misled donors as to exactly how much of the money went directly to services for the kids.

The Nineline also achieved a very specific and calculated goal for Covenant House: recognition by the Ad Council, a highly respected national organization made up of the country's top advertising firms and major media outlets. Campaigns by the Ad Council are often considered among the best in the country and are done on a pro bono basis for major national charities. The media outlets agree in turn to offer free access to the airwaves or large spreads in newspapers and magazines for the advertisements. Recognition by the Ad Council is a coveted prize in the nonprofit field. Despite its massive expansion, Covenant House had been denied acceptance in the mid-1980s because it was not considered a full-fledged nationally syndicated charity. The Nineline put them "over the top on that," said Mark Stroock, a board member and vice president of Young & Rubicam, which is a member of the Ad Council. It brought in millions of dollars a year for the charity.

Kells's energy seemed endless. It was he who got Ritter a contract with Doubleday to write a book that was based on a collection of his essays. It was he who negotiated with Walt Disney to sell Ritter's life story as a feature-length film. It was he who persuaded Ritter to take advantage of the explosion of broadcast ministries in the mid-1980s and start a nationally syndicated radio show called *The Family Hour,* produced by Covenant House staff and modeled on a similar talk show called *Focus on the Family,* hosted by Dr. James Dobson, regarded as "the Dr. Spock of the far right."

The "outreach van" was also the brainchild of the young Kells. Again, it was a "marriage," as Kells puts it, of two concerns. On the one hand, it was a solid tool for child-care counselors to get out in the community. On the other hand, it was jokingly referred to by some staff members as the "news van" because Kells drove so many media people around in it. He would convince the reporters that they were being offered a rare look inside the world of street kids: an exclusive. It usually worked and got Covenant House prominent play in features on homeless youths or teenagers with AIDS or young lives lost to crack or whatever was the news fad of the moment.

"It was intrusive for the kids. They didn't want their faces filmed. And sometimes they were pressured, subtly pressured, to cooperate. It was often manipulative," said one Covenant House counselor who worked with the van.

Kells has always claimed that Ritter was simply offering the media what they wanted: a sexy story. But even Kells concedes that Ritter's fascination with the young bodies for sale on Forty-second Street made him suspicious about Ritter's motives. Years before the scandal broke, he told several New York journalists, as well as Anne Donahue, a close friend at the time, that he believed Father Ritter was gay and that he would not be surprised if he had acted that out with young street people. In fact, Kells claims that he lodged a formal complaint of misconduct against Ritter in the winter of 1988 to an executive in the Toronto program. The complaint, Kells said, grew out of an incident in Toronto, to which he had accompanied Father Ritter for a speaking engagement.

After Ritter gave his sermon he spent time talking to a young male resident of the Covenant House facility there—with blond hair and blue eyes—and then invited the young man back to his hotel. Kells claims he followed Ritter and the young man to the hotel and saw him take the young man into his room.

"I waited outside. I don't believe anything happened," said Kells. "But I do believe it was inappropriate. It was the only time I ever saw anything untoward and, from my perspective, it was reported according to policy."

But Kells's complaint, like those made by other staff members, was simply met with a denial by Ritter and went no further.

There were others among the inner circle of talented young men who surrounded Ritter who found out about the complicated chemistry that was at work in Ritter's life. It was the dark side of reality at Covenant House, and it shattered their faith, not only in Ritter but in the organization as well.

One of them was a member of the Faith Community who was invited to work in the executive offices. Confident, articulate, and naïve, Bill had just graduated from college when he joined the Faith Community in 1982. By the fall of 1983, Father Bruce was working closely with Bill, encouraging him with promises that he would do well in a "leadership role" within the organization. It was the height of the expansion phase and Bill was on the inside of an exciting time in the "corporate" office. Ritter would often select young staff members to join him for late-night talks in his office or dinners at nearby restaurants when he was in New York. One evening, Ritter invited Bill out to dinner. During the meal, Father Bruce removed his shoes and began rubbing his foot against Bill's foot under the table. The young man moved his foot and passed it off.

After dinner Ritter invited him back to his apartment. As they talked on the couch, he moved closer and began rubbing Bill's back and his legs. To Bill these were clear sexual advances. Furious, he quickly stood up, but no words were said. There was an awkward goodbye and he left the apartment.

There was no one for the young volunteer to confide in. He felt he couldn't inform any of the senior staff, not Loken or Torkelsen or Sister Gretchen. He believed they were so loyal to Father Bruce that they would not only report the allegation directly back to him but believe his denial. The board of directors was a remote entity—having little to do with day-to-day operations. No system of accountability existed.

In early November, John MacNeil came to New York to visit "corporate" for a special meeting of senior staff officials at the Arrowwood retreat center in Westchester County. While working in the executive offices, Bill had learned about MacNeil's reputation as one of the few in "corporate" who had ever challenged Father Bruce. He recognized that MacNeil was perhaps the only person in the organization to whom he could report such an allegation.

After being introduced to MacNeil at the executive offices, Bill volunteered to show him to his hotel in Times Square. He knew the short walk could be his only chance to get the complaint off his chest.

"What do you do when you're disillusioned with someone? It's pretty crushing when you realize that somebody is interested in you not for your spiritual value but for some other reason. Has this sort of thing ever happened to you?" Bill asked MacNeil, amid a ramble of disjointed and awkwardly phrased questions.

MacNeil had no idea what this young man—whom he had just met—was talking about. He only knew that it was a very strange course for a conversation to take on a crowded street in New York City. Then Bill got a little bit more specific.

"There is just something bad that has happened. Has anybody ever touched you? Put a hand on you? It's pretty startling," said Bill.

MacNeil noticed that Bill was constantly looking over his shoulder as he talked. He seemed frightened, distraught. The conversation was so strange and the circumstances surrounding MacNeil's relationship with the corporate staff in New York were so strained that MacNeil actually believed Bill was setting him up. He figured that somehow Bill was trying to put him in a compromising position that could eventually backfire on him.

MacNeil understood that it was a "completely irrational and paranoid thing to think," but that was the environment of Covenant House. There was "so little honesty in the place that people had to float rumors or feelings. No one could be honest with each other."

Bill was choking on the words. MacNeil calmed him down and they talked for hours, walking around Times Square and stopped at a diner for a cup of coffee. Bill finally told MacNeil about the sexual advance Ritter had made.

It didn't surprise MacNeil. For over a year he had suspected Ritter of mixed motives. While he never believed that Ritter would take advantage of the kids in his care, there were things that had always been disturbing to MacNeil, especially the lurid content of the newsletters and the occasions when Father Bruce would insist on talking in graphic detail about the life of the young male prostitutes.

MacNeil, like just about everyone else, had heard the rumors about the "golden boys" in Ritter's executive offices, but he dismissed it as gossip. More disturbing to MacNeil were the several occasions when street kids had told him that they didn't trust Father Bruce. One youth several months earlier had told him, "I don't like the way that man looks at me," when Father Bruce had stopped in Toronto to visit the program. As an experienced social worker, MacNeil knew counselors had to be very wary of such a vague allegation by a problem teenager. But he also knew young people said things for a reason. Statistically, it was an aberration for kids to make up an allegation against an adult. And oftentimes they came in the most veiled references.

This was moving through MacNeil's mind as he listened to the shaken Faith Community member breaking down. MacNeil knew that Bill was young and naïve and he could see that the experience had shattered his faith in a man for whom he had had great respect. He figured that the only place such a complaint could be taken was to Ritter's Franciscan superiors. He recommended that Bill call them, which he did. Eventually questions were asked of Father Bruce by his superiors at the provincial house in Union City, New Jersey, but the allegation was only of a "sexual advance." Although Ritter, as president of Covenant House, clearly stood in a superior/subordinate relationship with the youth, the Franciscans felt there was little ground for any action to be taken because the young man was not technically in the care of Covenant House. The case was dropped. Even with their knowledge of such an allegation Ritter was permitted to continue living in his apartment behind his eighth-floor office, rather than in the more traditional and disciplined setting of a Franciscan residence.

MacNeil tried to muffle his anger after hearing Bill's allegation, but his disillusion with Ritter kept boiling to the surface.

At one meeting in a conference room at the corporate retreat, about a dozen of the top staff members—including vice president Joe Donnelly; finance director Robert Cardanay; executive director of New York Ron Williams; vice president of program development Sandy Hagan; and vice president of human resources Pat Connors— sat around a circular table discussing the management structure of the charity. Father Bruce had his back to the window. The curtains were open and the sun came in over the sloping hills of the surrounding golf course, creating a silhouette of Ritter's face. MacNeil remembers he couldn't see Father Bruce's eyes as he talked.

Father Bruce was discussing a plan to do away with several administrative positions, such as those of executive vice president and vice president of administration. The administrative decisions were already being made by Father Bruce without consulting the staff that was present. MacNeil raised an objection and brought up the fact that the covenant that Ritter philosophized about with the kids did not exist between the staff. He challenged Ritter to bring the immediacy and honesty of the covenant into the administrative structure.

Ritter listened and then began a wandering discourse on the meaning of the covenant and its origin from a passage in Ezekiel. From there, Ritter began talking about the kids in the street, and how the covenant extended to them in a different way than to the staff. His prurient language and fascination with explicit detail about the sexual lives of young male prostitutes crept into the soliloquy. It seemed remarkably off the track to MacNeil. With the recent allegations from the Faith Community member fresh in his mind, MacNeil launched into an ill-timed and not-so-subtle attack on Ritter.

"Father Bruce, how do you know so much about this?" MacNeil asked. "How could you possibly know all of this in such detail?"

"Because I have been in the business since 1968," Ritter said indignantly, sensing that the question carried a profound undertone of distrust. "I talk to the kids and they talk to me. I think I understand them very well. It may sound vain and it probably is, but I think I understand them better than anyone in this country."

"But how could you know? I mean, why is it important to know so many details? It seems lurid to me," MacNeil said.

Knowing that Ritter had not directly counseled kids for several years, MacNeil continued, "I think it is very difficult for these kids to be honest about their experiences. It takes a great deal of time and trust to break through to the other side."

It was not a direct confrontation, but it was as direct a challenge to Ritter's authority as any senior staff member had ever made in public. There was a hush over the small group of staffers. Father Bruce leaned forward and emerged out of the sunlight that was beaming in. The shadows that covered his face disappeared. Suddenly Ritter's cobalt-blue eyes were locked on MacNeil in fury. Father Bruce said nothing, but walked out of the conference room, furious and indignant.

"I think he always wanted to get caught," said MacNeil, who several months after his dramatic challenge to Ritter handed in his resignation. "I think he always knew there would be a sense of relief when it finally happened. Think of what it must have been like to keep all that inside."

Chapter 12

The Payback

"AND then there are the unsung heroes . . . their hearts carry without complaint the pains of family and community problems. . . . A person like Father Bruce Ritter is always there."

—President Ronald Reagan's 1984 State of the Union address

THROUGH THE EARLY 1980s many people lost patience with the inefficacy of U.S. government–run agencies and with throwing their dollars at social-service organizations that did little to solve the problems of poverty and human suffering. It was easy to see that millions of Americans were worse off even after two decades of vastly increased social spending by the government. The Great Society, it seemed, had done less to create opportunities for the disadvantaged than it had to create a new permanent underclass.

This collective despair gave wide berth to the Reagan administration as it gutted social-welfare programs. In New York City alone from

1981 to 1991, the percentage of federal funding in the city's overall budget dropped from 19 percent to about 11 percent for a total loss of $2.4 billion in funding. In cities across the country, hundreds of millions of dollars to finance public housing as well as job training, health care, and social services evaporated. Conservatives defended the cuts, convincing the American electorate that the solution to its problems existed somewhere beyond government programs, somewhere in the entrepreneurial ethos of America, somewhere in the hearts of good Americans and the free-market system.

By 1984, the Reagan administration's massive and historic transfer of social responsibility to the private sector was well under way. One new symbol for this shift was Father Bruce Ritter's Covenant House, which was fast emerging as the paradigm of what a social-service program could accomplish in the age of privatization. It tallied the biggest numbers of any charity in the country dealing with troubled youths, and it did so with only 5 percent of its budget coming from the federal government. A full 95 percent of its annual income was raised through private donations and corporate contributions.

This seemingly magical mix of social welfare and free enterprise embodied in Covenant House was being widely heralded by a matrix of conservative businessmen. Macauley, Grace, and Simon were at the center of a new era in charitable giving in America, in which the traditional Democratic-liberal basis of most social-service charities would be challenged by conservatives with their own agenda, their own way of showing compassion. In the national charity circuit, they were referred to as the "charity mafia." They were rich, they were Republican, and they were Catholic. Their pursuits were blessed by Cardinal John O'Connor, archbishop of New York and Grand Protector of the Knights of Malta. The political backbone of the Catholic right was provided by former Secretary of State Alexander Haig, Jeane Kirkpatrick, Jack Kemp, and Republican Senator Jeremiah Denton, the "new right's Catholic stars."

Among them, Macauley, Grace, and Simon knew personally the CEOs or top board members of just about all of the Fortune 50 companies. They told this sphere of friends—corporate chiefs, bank presidents, Wall Street tycoons, and prominent politicians—the legend of Father Bruce Ritter. They influenced the influential to hold fund raisers, to make corporate contributions as well as personal donations to Covenant House. Covenant House's annual black-tie dinner at the Waldorf-Astoria raised more than $1 million in a single night. Macauley would call up his friend, then Vice President George Bush, and recount tales of the work of the Franciscan priest who represented a new kind of American folk hero. They made Ritter the toast of the Republican charity circuit.

In 1984, Reagan named Father Ritter in his State of the Union address while tens of millions of people listened. It brought a national spotlight onto Ritter and helped sustain an already phenomenal growth rate that took the annual budget from $24 million in 1984 to about $90 million by June 1989.

Covenant House seemed to offer a dynamic approach to the complex set of social and economic factors that were displacing families and resulting in so many young people living on the street. They saw it as a solution—perhaps not a perfect one, but at least a step in the right direction at a time when America wanted to see results.

To many experts in the field of social welfare, however, Covenant House embodied the kind of quick-and-easy answers that ultimately did more harm than good. A short-term "crisis-oriented" program, Covenant House was less successful than community-based projects with highly trained staff that targeted early intervention for families in crisis in order to prevent children from hitting the street. Programs such as Homebuilders in the Bronx, Home Away from Homes, and Flowers with Care were community-based programs with intensive counseling and guidance for the young people in their care. Although they handled far fewer numbers, these smaller youth-care agencies had much higher success rates than Covenant House.

Large crisis-oriented programs, such as Covenant House, "appeal to our yearning for simplicity and easy answers," wrote Lisbeth B. Schorr in *Within Our Reach: Breaking the Cycle of Disadvantage,* "because simple programs and narrowly defined interventions aimed at precisely defined problems make for easy measurement, assessment, and replication. . . . So we are left with a myriad of halfway programs which fail to ameliorate some of our most profound social problems."

But for all the attention that Ritter received as a darling of the Reagan era, there was, of course, a payback. The new right's agenda permeated Covenant House. The Children's Defense Fund and most other social-service charities involved with youth care were screaming about the Reagan administration's federal budget cuts to women and children, about the homeless, and about the lack of affordable housing. But Father Bruce was silently cultivating his close relationship with the Catholic leaders of the new right.

Soon they came to own him.

Simon and Grace were busy making their millions, but not too busy for well-orchestrated attacks on the American bishops' pastoral letters on nuclear war and the economy. Covenant House was the cloak of sanctity worn in their crusade against the liberal Church. The two tycoons led a vitriolic campaign against the bishops' treatises, branding the letters dangerous intrusions by the Church on matters it had no business looking into: war and greed. From their perspective, it was fine for the Catholic Church to raise its moral voice against abortion and pornography, but capitalism and the military-industrial complex were not areas where they felt the tenets of Catholicism applied. Too damned much money was at stake.

Simon formed a twenty-seven-member Lay Commission under the aegis of the American Catholic Committee, which included Grace and Alexander Haig among its members, to attack the 1986 Catholic bishops' pastoral letter—claiming that the bishops were "economically illiterate" and "whiny."

Titled "Economic Justice for All: Catholic Social Teaching and the U.S. Economy," the bishops' letter reiterated the Church's social teachings on Christ's "preference for the poor." Among the specific recommendations were an increase in the minimum wage and more vigorous action to provide full and equal employment for women and minorities. "That so many people are poor in a nation as rich as ours is a social and moral scandal that we cannot ignore," the bishops wrote.

Having seen firsthand the cycle of poverty in America's inner cities for more than twenty years and having come of age during the Depression himself, it would seem that Ritter would have enthusiastically supported the bishops' letter. It would seem that the board of directors at a charity that provided services for youths who were predominantly members of a permanent underclass would embrace a Catholic message based on the ecclesiastically sound doctrines of Christian social teaching, to break the status quo that had left so many young people a legacy of complicated social ills. How could a Franciscan possibly disagree with the bishops' point?

However, the letter was met not just with indifference but with disdain by Ritter and the majority of Covenant House's prominent board members, who by the late 1980s were a blue-chip crowd of bankers, bond lawyers, and corporate CEOs. There was only one board member who had a professional background in child care: Donna Santarsiero. Fifteen out of the eighteen were white males, and twelve of them were either CEOs or senior vice presidents of corporations. They included: Ralph Pfeiffer, chairman of the board of IBM World Trade; Denis Coleman, executive vice president of Bear, Stearns & Company; Richard Schmeelk, president and CEO of Salomon Brothers; and Edward L. Shaw, Jr., executive vice president and general counsel of Chase Manhattan Corporation.

Grace summed up his own point of view on the issue of poverty in America:

> There has always been the poor and there has always been the middle class, and so on. If you go way back in history, you'll find the poor. You can't get rid of the poor. . . . If you have a second home on Long Island, you should not worry about that. . . . I have three or four homes. . . . I don't feel at all guilty about this. . . . The Bishops don't realize that if I, or a thousand people like me, really felt that they could live only with what they needed, they probably wouldn't work very hard. You know, people are selfish; we're born that way; and we have to fight it within ourselves. But born selfish as we are, if everybody followed the Bishops' suggestions, no one would bother working.

It was a time when the denizens of Wall Street, like Simon, cashed in on LBOs, hostile takeovers, and junk bonds. The moral ambiguity and greed that characterized the 1980s was a contagion to which even Ritter was not immune—despite his vow of Franciscan poverty. Ritter was paying himself a steadily increasing salary that went from $43,000 a year in 1980 to $64,000 in 1983 and then jumped to $98,000 in 1985—putting him in the top fifth percentile of salaried employees in the U.S.

Ritter even played the stock market. He put his money in a paper products company called Greif Brothers Corporation, of which Macauley was a director. The stock did well, and by the end of 1984 Ritter had 15,302 shares, worth $250,275, which when combined with his salary gave him more than $300,000, which he stashed in a special account called the Franciscan Charitable Trust. Ritter had created the trust with the assistance of his counsel Edmund Burns in 1983 because, Burns said, Ritter wanted to keep his Greif Brothers stock "out of the control of the Franciscans."

It was a private slush fund that Ritter kept hidden from his tax records, from most of the board members, and from his religious order, despite the fact that it was created in their name. To put Ritter's financial finagling in some context, most diocesan priests earn a stipend of about $6,000 a year in addition to room and board. Orders like the Franciscans, which have a strict vow of poverty, typically receive even smaller stipends. Ritter didn't flaunt his wealth. But like the patrician financiers who had become his mentors, he was comfortable with the power it gave him.

Through the Roaring '80s, the rich got richer and the poor got poorer. The number of people living below the poverty line in the U.S. was rapidly increasing. By 1988, the federal government's own statistics showed that more than 33 million people, nearly one in seven, were poor—an increase of 33 percent from 1980, the year Reagan was elected. More than one-fifth of all children in the United States lived in poverty—a fact attributable to a dramatic increase in the number of families headed by women. In the same period, statistics from the Internal Revenue Service show that one-half of one percent of U.S. households possessed 35 percent of the nation's wealth. Two percent of all families held 54 percent of the country's net financial assets. It was a concentration of wealth that had not been seen since the Great Depression.

The point of Reagan's privatization policies and his eagerly endorsed spirit of "volunteerism" was to steer the government away from taking an active role in trying to change the conditions that create poverty. The goal was a system in which wealthy people gave their money when they wanted and to whom they wanted, with as much as possible being given in the form of tax shelters. Covenant House was very sophisticated in explaining the tax benefits that were available to donors under new tax codes that favored the rich. They hired "planned giving" experts, some of whom had actually found ways in which the tax code made some forms of donation profitable. "Deferred giving plans," for example, gave a donor not only a deduction but relief from capital gains as well. In some instances it turned donors into investors.

Voluntary giving by the rich to the poor, as opposed to government taxation, had other advantages. It came with all of the attendant glory of awards dinners, in which the biggest donors were made "man of the year." Some were bestowed with the highest national honor of all—the White House Volunteer Action Award, of which Macauley and Ritter were both recipients. Macauley, Grace, and Simon were each made Covenant House Man of the Year at the charity's annual black-tie benefit at the Waldorf-Astoria ballroom.

In 1985, when Grace was awarded the honor, John Kells claims he couldn't bring himself to shake Grace's hand because of his infamous business partnership with a Nazi scientist named Otto Ambros, which was disclosed in an investigative report by the *Village Voice*. But in a classic illustration of the moral ambiguity of the Covenant House staff, Kells had no problem putting together a multimedia slide show and boasts about how it incorporated twenty-eight different projectors, which bombarded the screen with glorified images of Grace's life history and the many Covenant House programs he had funded. It ended with the words: "Thank you and God bless you, Peter." When Macauley received the award in 1983, there was an enormous video screen with a videotape message from Ronald Reagan to Covenant House. After Simon was named Covenant House Man of the Year in 1986, board member Mark Stroock walked out of the glittering Waldorf ballroom with Father Bruce.

"What do you think of our Man of the Year?" asked Ritter.

"Bruce, you know what I think of Bill Simon," said Stroock. "I don't see how a guy who comes to the shelter once a year to hand out turkey at Thanksgiving while his Cadillac idles outside can be given the award. He doesn't make time for the board meetings, never mind show any sincere compassion for the kids."

Ritter replied, "Well, I guess we have to give the devil his due."

"As long as you put it that way, we have an understanding," Stroock replied.

Ritter was not naïve about his "covenant" with these conservative tycoons and the new right. Many of the board members said that Ritter knew exactly what he was getting into.

"He used them as much as they used him," said Greg Loken, who dismisses Ritter's ties to the new right as a "political melodrama." It had become an article of faith among the "liberal" critics of Covenant House, Loken said, to trash Reagan, and because Ritter refused to do that he was attacked as a Republican tool. But Loken maintains that Ritter did it all "in the interest of the kids," covenant of necessity.

To most of the social-service people in the field, however, it was an unforgivable form of complicity. Father Bruce was not only buying into their agenda, he was hurting the hundreds of other agencies that provided services poor youths needed. Father Bruce was in effect using expedient alliances to build his own empire while encouraging a status quo that was putting more and more homeless youths on the street.

But even those who criticized Ritter for such relationships understood that he had done something valuable, something that few had been able to do before. He had managed to bring together a diverse community—rich and poor, Republicans and Democrats—to support a growing population of deprived kids, and to cast a national spotlight on their needs. His genius was that he was able to put it on a "common ground where everyone could reach it," said Anne Donahue.

Ritter *(lower left)* with his mother and siblings at their home on the outskirts of Trenton, New Jersey.

By age thirteen, young "Jackie" Ritter was doing odd jobs to help his family pay the bills during the Depression.

3

Ritter in his Navy blues.

4

Brother Ritter as a young seminarian in the Franciscan order.

5

Father Bruce Ritter wearing his Franciscan robes just after being ordained in Rome.

Mary Lane and Lee Meyers, two of the "first six kids."

Reverend Jim Daniels in front of his East Village coffee house.

8

9

Darryl Bassile at age fifteen when he first wandered into Covenant House after fleeing a childhood of sexual abuse.

Bassile just after the scandal broke.

10

Ritter cruising the streets in front of the Times Square porno theaters in 1978.

At his Times Square shelter on Eighth Avenue and Fourty-fourth Street, where an overflow of street kids slept on rubber mats in the chapel.

Ritter, his wealthy benefactor Robert Macauley, and Pope John Paul at the Vatican in 1982.

Ritter testifies before the Meese Commission on Pornography.

Ritter counsels some street youths at his flagship "Under 21" program in New York City's Times Square.

A Covenant House van cruises the streets of Times Square, with 'outreach' counselors handing out food and giving advice to young people in need.

Though suffering through chemotherapy treatments, Ritter continues to write his newsletters.

With Ed Koch in 1987 after defeating the New York City mayor in a bitter battle over the purchase of the former Maritime Union Building.

Ritter celebrates his victory in front of the Maritime Building, which some staffers call "the ark."

Ritter and former President Ronald Reagan, who called the priest America's "unsung hero" in his 1984 state of the union address.

Kevin Kite, Ritter's accuser, stands in front of Covenant House's flagship shelter and national headquarters in Times Square.

Mid-November 1989. Ritter with Kite, who is wearing a concealed tape recorder for the Manhattan District Attorney's office.

Kevin with his father, Alton Kite, at home in Texas for Christmas.

Father Ritter faces the biggest press conference of his life, three days after the news broke that he was being investigated by the Manhattan D.A.'s office for his relationship with Kite.

Covenant
MORE PROGRAMS
FOR
HOMELESS YOUTHS
NEGLECTING IS NOT
THE
ANSWER

Residents of Covenant House in New York City protest cuts in funding and the loss of donations in the wake of the scandal.

The fallen priest just days before he announced that he would step down as head of the charity he founded.

The grip the conservative board members held over Ritter was not well known, and was certainly not the public perception of Covenant House. The reason was that Covenant House's support existed on two levels: the major donor list, which was made up largely of wealthy and conservative friends of Grace, Simon, and Macauley; and a diverse base of millions of people who contributed between $10 and $100 each. Targeting these two vastly different groups for fund raising required differing approaches.

Among the higher-level donors, it was well known that Covenant House catered to their political agenda—focusing on the right to life, privatization, and antipornography, and emphasizing the fact that Covenant House did not use government funds. The staff in the donors bureau played up the conservative themes in their telemarketing and donor communications. But the smaller donors, the "great unwashed masses," as one member of the development staff called them, were a tapestry made up of traditional conservatives, East Coast liberals, blue-collar Catholics, yuppies with some extra money, and religious fundamentalists from the Deep South, or as the staff liked to refer to them, "mom and pop front porch."

The great unity of that broad base of donors, however, raised a complicated set of questions for the staff: Was Covenant House, through its manipulative fund raising, distracting the good people that made up its donor base from the real issues that created the complex socioeconomic problems that put the young kids on the street in the first place? Was focusing on pornography and prostitution as the two great demons that stole the lives of these young people blurring the real issues of poverty, drugs, housing, and health care? By making it appear that their clients were predominantly young white boys and girls from outside the inner city, was Covenant House deliberately sustaining the same racist attitudes that perpetuated the disenfranchisement of the youths in the program?

With his eminent status among the new right, Ritter was often invited to Washington to speak before select committees and special-interest groups on issues ranging from moral disintegration of the family to modification of the tax code.

His prepared remarks before the Senate Caucus on the Family, delivered on Capitol Hill January 26, 1984, illustrated the politically inoffensive posture of his agenda and how it captured the themes embraced by the new right. The fifteen-page speech addressed what Ritter felt were the major problems facing poor and homeless youths, whom he called "runaways." The majority of the statement focused on pornography, prostitution, and the disintegration of the family. All of the issues were imbued with a "moral component," a buzzword for right-wing legislative causes in the Reagan era.

Ritter cited an increase in the divorce rate, the rising number of children born "out of wedlock," and the fact that "45 percent of Americans changed their residence from 1975 to 1980." He bemoaned the ills of society, criticizing "distinguished advertising firms" that "cynically turn around to use children in seductive, sexually suggestive ad campaigns to sell products to adults."

But Ritter never stated the fact that there also were more poor young children in America than at any time in its history. He did not state that federal budget cuts had decimated a social-support system for those young people. He didn't say that in the Reagan era those children had only limited access to health care or affordable housing, or that the infant mortality rate was as high in some poor areas as it was in the Third World. Instead, Ritter focused on "being fair to American families" by offering them "tax breaks."

He also promoted "tax credits to businesses" as a solution to the homeless problem among young people. "Provisions of accelerated depreciation and tax credits for investments in property used by programs benefiting children and families could attract substantial private capital," said Ritter, sounding more like a convert to Reaganomics than a priest trained in medieval theology.

In a letter to Jack Kemp, the Bush-appointed Secretary of the Department of Housing and Urban Development, dated March 10, 1989, Ritter gave one of his clearest statements in favor of the political ideology behind privatization. In the letter, Ritter also registered his "strong endorsement of 'Enterprise Zones,'" an idea originated by Kemp to give tax breaks to businesses that invest in distressed areas, a pillar of Reagan's trickle-down theory. He offered other proposals on possible changes to the tax laws that would benefit charities like Covenant House and also dovetail with the administration's efforts to put the burdens of social service on the private sector rather than government.

The letter was timed ten days prior to a meeting between Ritter and Kemp and during a year when Covenant House was applying for a $500,000 grant from HUD for an expansion of the New Orleans program. Ritter's political ideas expressed in the letter obviously impressed Kemp, who described himself as a "big fan" of Father Ritter.

This was the political covenant in the making. Ritter was pushing the right buttons for the Reagan and Bush administrations' special interests. But there were other more innovative ways in which Ritter was carrying out the conservative agenda back home at his head-quarters in New York. The clearest example: the Institute for Youth Advocacy.

The institute's legislative agenda focused its energy on issues that they felt were "morally imperative," but that were also politically inoffensive. Roughly two-thirds of the institute's publications dealt with pornography and prostitution. The steady stream of local, state, and national leaders who visited Covenant House were told—and left believing—that "the greatest needs of disenfranchised youth were for more shelters like Covenant House and stronger anti-pornog-raphy legislation."

The director of the institute, Greg Loken, conceded that other than his volunteer work in the Faith Community he had no expe-rience in the social services. He had formerly been a corporate lawyer and had to become a "quick study" on the issues of child care and the broad range of social and economic issues affecting the lives of poor young people. With Ritter as his mentor, Loken focused on the problems of child pornography and juvenile prostitution. He worked tirelessly on *New York* v. *Ferber,* a 1982 case before the Supreme Court, which upheld New York State's obscenity laws regarding child por-nography. According to the institute's bibliography, Loken filed two amicus curiae briefs used in the court's opinion. It was good work. Who could argue that upholding laws that stopped such heinous exploiters of children was anything but good?

The criticism, as board member Santarsiero put it, was that it "tre-mendously overrepresented a very small segment of the population in Covenant House's care and underrepresented a very large segment of the population."

Loken also developed a close working relationship with the Justice Department's Office of Juvenile Justice and Delinquency Prevention (OJJDP). The office, dubbed by *The New Republic* the "biggest policy pork barrel the right wing has ever seen," was a favorite of Attorney General Ed Meese and was headed by Meese's close friend Al Reg-nere.

Loken was an ardent supporter of an OJJDP-funded group called the National Center for Missing and Exploited Children, which was created in 1984. Loken served on the advisory committee to the public-interest group, which used a $3.3 million OJJDP grant to whip up a hysteria of news stories, public-service announcements, and milk-carton photographs announcing that over 1.5 million children "disappear" every year. The grossly exaggerated figures were fre-quently used in Covenant House fund-raising material, and the charity benefited from the attention the center raised. But investigative newspaper reports exposed the figures as false and manipulative. In fact, there were no more than a few thousand missing children in the entire country, and most of the calls they got involved custody battles by parents, not kidnapping or some faceless evil underground. After two years, the center managed to track down only 120 children.

Loken also coauthored a report "prepared under cooperative agreement" with OJJDP in 1987 which went into nearly obsessive detail on the history of juvenile prostitution and child pornography, tracing both evils back to ancient civilizations and describing later development in the nineteenth century.

This kind of work put Covenant House in good standing with the leaders of the new right's antipornography crusade, especially Regnere and his OJJDP. The institute even lent Regnere its support in his efforts to push for a federal policy that sought to diminish programs that rehabilitated juvenile offenders and substitute for them a punishment-oriented system resembling that for adult offenders. It was repudiated by the National Council of Juvenile and Family Court Judges and was later described as "an embarrassment" by the Justice Department.

Ironically, despite his moral pronouncements, Regnere was involved in a bizarre incident in which police found a cache of pornographic magazines at his home. When asked about it, Regnere told *The New Republic,* "I probably had a little around the house, like I bet lots of people do. . . . [But] I don't use and I don't enjoy it." The magazine also cited a bumper sticker on the back of Regnere's family station wagon that read HAVE YOU SLUGGED YOUR KID TODAY?

These were the people Covenant House was dealing with in its new alliances—but the relationships always facilitated a payback to Covenant House for its work.

Covenant House received a $1.7 million grant from the Justice Department's Office of Juvenile Justice in 1983. The money was distributed over a four-year period, from 1983 to 1987, to maintain its shelters in Houston and Fort Lauderdale.

The grant was only one facet of a goldmine of federal funding that Covenant House received at a time when other charities saw their funding slashed, leaving many struggling just to stay in operation. Although Covenant House always touted the fact that only 5 percent of its funding came from government sources, the percentage hid the tremendous increase in the total budget and therefore the overall increase in government funding that Covenant House received through the 1980s. In other words, as Covenant House's private base grew rapidly, the government funding kept pace. Covenant House increased its government dollars by more than 100 percent in the 1980s, receiving $1.6 million in government grants and contracts in 1980 and $3.6 million by 1989.

The grants and contracts were awarded by an array of federal agencies, including the Labor Department, Justice, Housing and Urban Development, and Health and Human Services.

In 1985, Covenant House won a grant from the Adolescent and Family Life Demonstration Program under the auspices of the Department of Health and Human Services. It was one of only thirty-two grants awarded, out of a pool of three hundred applicants. Over a five-year period, Covenant House received $1.5 million, an average of $300,00 a year. Covenant House did not meet the grant's guidelines—such as a maximum of $250,000 a year and use by charities caring for adolescents primarily under the age of seventeen. (More than 70 percent of Covenant House's clients are eighteen years old or older.) Nevertheless, Covenant House was awarded the highly competitive grant largely because it complied with the not-so-subtle political mandate to "encourage abstinence" and to "promote adoption." The phrases were considered buzzwords in the right-to-life movement, allowing such agencies to make sure funding went to the right places. Critics claimed that they were circumventing the constitutional separation of Church and state.

There were other hidden pockets of federal money at agencies that appeared to bend over backward to support Covenant House. For example, several grants were made to Covenant House through the Federal Emergency Management Agency, a strange source for a child-care agency's budget.

"These guys were working the entire federal trough," said Treanor. "I've never in my life heard of a youth-service agency getting money from FEMA. . . . Somebody very close to the administration was pointing them in all the right directions."

Ritter's institutional obsession with the issue of prostitution and pornography had made him a favorite not just of Reagan and Bush but of Attorney General Edwin Meese. And with all the federal money doled out to the Franciscan's charitable empire, Meese made Ritter an offer he couldn't refuse.

On May 20, 1985, Meese announced the formation of his Commission on Pornography and invited Father Bruce Ritter to be one of its eleven distinguished panelists.

He instructed his commissioners to "determine the nature, extent, and impact on society of pornography in the United States and to make specific recommendations to the Attorney General concerning more effective ways in which the spread of pornography could be contained, consistent with constitutional guarantees."

Born of political pressure by the new right's antipornography crusaders—including Jerry Falwell of the Moral Majority and Charles Keating, Jr., who had founded a group called Citizens for Decency Through Law—the commission was given $400,000 and one year to come up with its conclusions.

But before the commission got under way, Ritter had to file a full financial disclosure form and undergo a review process by the Attorney General as part of the confirmation. By that time, Ritter's salary was more than $98,000 a year. A Franciscan priest earning nearly six figures was sure to raise eyebrows. It was not just that Father Bruce had forgotten his sacred vow of poverty, but by earning that much money he was betraying the soul of the saint from whom his order took its name. Three knots on the rope belt that accompanied the Franciscans' traditional black robes and sandals were there as constant reminder to the friars of their three solemn vows. But Ritter had long ago given up on wearing his vestments. Even when he attended ceremonial functions, he would wear the more common black clerical garb and collar—a subtle but not unnoticed slight to his fellow friars. Most of the time, Ritter chose a wardrobe of jeans, preppy sweaters, and expensive running shoes.

This disregard for his vows—especially his impressive salary— would not look good on his financial statement to the commission. Ritter was entering the political fray and didn't want to furnish the press or his enemies with ammunition. So he came up with a way to hide his compensation from the charity's public records.

Ritter gave Burns the power of attorney over the Franciscan Charitable Trust, and then Cardonay and Ritter set Ritter's salary at $38,000, with the remaining $60,000 transferred to Ritter's secret trust fund. From that point on, it became Ritter's standard formula for receiving his salary. With his money matters in order, the Franciscan priest was ready to hit the road with the Meese Commission.

The Justice Department scheduled six hearings over eight months in various regions of the country. They heard testimony from a series of porn stars, male and female prostitutes, rape victims, rapists, wife beaters, lawyers, experts, and vice cops. They watched hundreds of hours of films on sadomasochistic sex, bestiality, orgies, and every fetish in the book. Father Ritter sat in the darkness of a government office through hours and hours of films with titles like *Cumming of Age*, *Gym Coach Bondage*, and *Street Heat Orgy*.

The commission was considered a joke by the press. Dubbed "The F-Troop of the Erogenous Zones," it was perceived as a thinly veiled attack on the First Amendment, financed by taxpayers' money, and a manifestation of the far right's obsession with pornography. In a *Time* magazine cover story titled "Sex Busters," the reporter sneered that the commission was part of "a new moral militancy." *The New York Times* in an editorial concluded that "The Meese commission's connection of pornography and crime outruns its own evidence."

The commission comprised four conservatives, four liberals, and three "middle-of-the-roaders." Ritter was considered among the last. With his Franciscan prudishness, Ritter disagreed with the majority of commissioners, who felt that mere nudity was not pornography. Ritter obsessed about possible abuses, such as closeups of the genitalia of Michelangelo's *David*. He condemned Dr. Ruth Westheimer for extolling orgasms in premarital sex. He declared that even love manuals should only include couples who were married. But Ritter took at least one liberal stand—asking the commission to back a national curriculum on sex education in schools, which was strongly opposed by the conservatives. Dr. James Dobson, a member of the National Advisory Committee of the OJJDP, was shocked at Ritter's stance, believing he had a loyal follower of the new-right crusade in Ritter.

Ellen Levine, then editor of *Woman's Day* magazine and the commission's token representative of the media, endorsed Ritter's suggestion. Ritter and Levine, although frequently at odds on the commission, formed an alliance over the national curriculum and grew to become friends. Although Ritter's point of view was more closely aligned with that of the conservatives, Levine appreciated Ritter's sophistication on the issues and respect for intellectual discipline. Later, Ritter would invite her to serve on Covenant House's national board of directors.

But Ritter quickly learned the danger of falling out of line with the new right's agenda. Although it was his only clear break from conservative ranks, Ritter began receiving threatening letters from members of the Moral Majority and other special-interest groups, criticizing him for his "liberal" position on sex education. He told Levine that he had received a letter from Russell Kirk, the ultraconservative intellectual and author of *The Conservative Mind*, a 1953 book regarded as the "Magna Carta of the New Right." Greg Loken—who served as Ritter's legal assistant throughout the hearings and who was constantly at his side—had also gotten some complaints from Senator Jesse Helms's staff about Ritter's stance. Ritter was consumed with worry and "fraught with anxiety" about what the new right could do to him, Levine remembers.

"This is terrible. This is terrible. My God, I am going to lose my funding," Ritter told her after receiving the letter from Kirk. "I don't think you realize the kind of problems that are associated with my votes here. If I go anywhere into the liberal area, they could move their funding out of the program."

During a break in the commission's scheduled hearings, Ritter stopped off in New Orleans to visit the newest site of Covenant House, which was still under construction. The sultry air in the twilight of the French Quarter was miles away from the dusty government buildings and high school auditoriums where the puritanical commission met. The strip joints and barkers, the transvestites and drunks, the tourists and the sounds of zydeco were all there on Bourbon Street.

And it was here that John Melican, a drifter from New York City who had stayed with Ritter on the Lower East Side as a young runaway in the early to mid-1970s, somehow ended up.

Melican was "scratching and clawing and hustling and driving cabs and dishwashing and doing everything just to keep abreast." One night, he saw Ritter on television while the Meese Commission hearings were starting in Washington and heard that he was going to be in New Orleans to start a new program. So Melican arranged to meet with him. He was close to turning thirty and felt that he was in a "revolving door going nowhere." As a teenager in Greenwich Village, Melican was a "very bright, very handsome kid," according to Stephen Morris, a staff counselor at the time. But he was also a hustler, and after Ritter took a special interest in him, Melican says, their late-night "counseling sessions" turned into a sexual relationship similar to Ritter's encounter with Bassile and Johnson. It started as late-night discussions in Ritter's apartment, usually with the television on, evolved into hugging, and ended by becoming another one of Ritter's awkward and silent sexual relationships.

The difference, Melican says, was that for him the sex was a straight-up deal. He got cash and a place to stay when he needed it, and Ritter got what he wanted in bed. As Melican got older, he kept up the relationship. Ritter continued to help him financially through the years, giving him a part-time job in 1980, paying for his treatment for alcoholism at the Sacred Heart Rehabilitation Center in the fall of 1983, and doling out cash anytime he saw him. Melican appreciated Ritter's efforts and believes his heart was in the right place, even if his motives were conflicted. Melican believes Ritter tried hard to help him turn his miserable life around.

But that night Melican laughed to himself at the hypocrisy of Ritter's stand on the Meese Commission. Here was Ritter expressing his moral outrage over the genitalia of Michelangelo's *David* during the day, and sleeping with young men at night. But Melican saw more than just hypocrisy, he saw an opportunity. He needed at least half a grand to pay back his ex-wife, and he knew he could hit Ritter up for it.

He met his Franciscan mentor for dinner at Mama Rose's, a restaurant near the Covenant House property. Ritter brought two other Covenant House workers with him and showed his dinner guests the architectural plans for the new building. He was brimming with excitement about Covenant House's plans for the Big Easy.

After dinner, Melican and Ritter walked back to the Maison DuPree Hotel, where Ritter was staying. There was no invitation up to Ritter's private room, just more of the same unspoken understanding of what was going to happen. They went into the hotel room and Melican took a shower while Ritter took off his collar and turned on the television. Before the blue glow of the television, Melican slid into bed with the priest. There were no words exchanged, Melican claims, just silence and sex. The next morning Ritter wrote a check for $500 to Melican on his personal Chemical Bank checking account, dated July 7, 1985.

After summer turned to fall, in the windowless basement of the white adobe Scottsdale, Arizona, city hall, the commission gathered for another in its series of work sessions on pornography. Fellow commissioners Dr. James Dobson, the conservative Christian broadcaster, and Dr. Judith Becker, a nationally recognized expert on the treatment of sex offenders, were debating the "tendency toward promiscuity in teenagers."

Suddenly, Ritter came out of nowhere with a point that he seemed to feel was very important. "So much of the available pornography is homosexual pornography," said Ritter, surprising many of the commissioners with the sudden deviation from the topic. "Is this commission obliged to say that . . . heterosexual activity is no more normative for the good of society than homosexual activity?"

Ritter was desperate for the panel to include homosexuality in its examination of "antisocial behavior." He was emphatic that homosexuality was "less than normative." After his diatribe on the abnormality of homosexuality, the commission put it to a vote. Ritter lost eight to two. The Franciscan was a sore loser, continuing throughout the proceedings to interrupt with his insistence that the commission had to take a stand on what was proper and improper sexual behavior.

The medieval scholar had to have a hierarchy of sin and wanted to be clear where homosexuality fit in.

The commission's sexual McCarthyism was catching on across the country, and Jerry Falwell himself organized a boycott of the 7-Eleven chain and other convenience stores that carried pornography amid the beer and cigarettes. Enough legitimacy was being brought to the antipornography crusade that *Penthouse* hired Harvard professor and star defense attorney Alan Dershowitz to debate the panel in New York. Dershowitz, as if he had a sonar to the epicenter of hypocrisy on this panel, aimed much of his cutting polemic directly at Father Bruce Ritter. He pointed his finger at the priest, accusing him and his fellow commissioners of trampling on the Constitution.

"It is as American as apple pie to be sexually aroused," said Dershowitz, staring at Ritter, "and it is equally proper for a writer or photographer to design expression to be sexually arousing."

Ritter's face flushed with anger and his blue eyes gazed at Dershowitz, but the legal pit bull kept coming. Noting Ritter's remarks from an earlier session that because pornography condones extramarital and premarital sex it represents a direct attack on the family, Dershowitz boomed:

"Yes, yes, Father Ritter, it is a direct attack on your beliefs, and I have the right to make that direct attack. Whether it is by getting a soapbox and standing on the corner and saying, 'I disagree with you, I think adultery is a good thing, and I think your view of sexuality is a bad thing.' I would have the right to say that, and I would have the right to advocate it through the use of pictures, words, devices, or any other form of expression. . . . Let's debate it, let's argue it. . . . Let's see who wins. You will probably win, but you have no right to shut down the marketplace and the stall from which dissenting ideas come."

Philip Nobile, who was then an editor of *Penthouse's Forum* and was coauthoring a book on the commission titled *United States of America vs. Sex: How the Meese Commission Lied About Pornography,* covered the proceedings from start to finish. Nobile, who is fond of telling people he's "more Catholic than Bing Crosby," trained in a seminary, went to Holy Cross College, and did doctoral work in theology and philosophy at the Catholic University of Urbane in Belgium. He considers himself part of the "rise of the Catholic left," having written for *Commonweal* and *National Catholic Reporter.* He was also a staff writer for *Esquire* and *New York Magazine.* But he concedes that when he became editor of *Forum* his career fell into a "black hole."

In Ritter's eyes, Nobile was not just a pornographer, but one who betrayed his faith. Nobile could sense the cold, silent righteousness of the stern Franciscan. Nobile says he had no indication that Ritter was gay and never suspected it until a call came to him from a pay phone in New Orleans while he was putting the finishing touches on his book as the Meese Commission was just completing its work.

It was John Melican—more desperate for money than ever. He had decided to cash in on his dirty secrets about Ritter. Nobile met with Melican and could see that his best hustling days were long gone. The years of alcohol and drugs had taken their toll. His teeth were broken; he was thin and strung out. But he was "smart, quick-tongued, and engaging," Nobile remembers. Melican told Nobile that he had had a sexual relationship with Ritter on and off for nearly fourteen years since he was a seventeen-year-old kid staying at Covenant House. Melican had been bounced between juvenile jails and foster homes before ending up in Ritter's care at Covenant House. Melican told Nobile about the sex he and Ritter had during the Meese Commission meetings and about another encounter as recently as July 4, 1986, while watching the centennial celebration of the Statue of Liberty on television. Nobile took notes. Melican was given a lie-detector test, which indicated that he was being truthful about the sexual relationship. Nobile then tape-recorded his allegations.

While Nobile spent several weeks trying to investigate the story, Melican ran up a large hotel bill in New York. Nobile's editors told him to cut the informant loose. For more than three years, Nobile would sit on the information. It was impossible to prove and there were no other accusers with whom he could corroborate or disprove the details of Melican's allegations.

In the final report of the Meese Commission hearings, released on July 9, 1986, was Ritter's long-winded personal statement:

The message of pornography is unmistakably and undeniably clear: sex bears no relationship to love and commitment, to fidelity in marriage, that sex has nothing to do with privacy and modesty and any necessary and essential ordering toward procreation. The powerful and provocative images proclaim universally—and most of all to the youth of our country—that pleasure—not love and commitment—is what sex is all about.

In the end, Ritter had challenged the conservative agenda on two votes, but on the rest he kept in line. He understood his covenant with the new right, even if he exerted just enough independence to save his self-respect. He played his cards right. Ritter could not afford to alienate the new right, certainly not people like Kirk or Helms, who could turn his increasingly conservative donor base against him. He would be a fool to alienate Grace or Simon, both of whom would continue to help finance his empire at home and abroad.

Perhaps the most important supporter Ritter could not have afforded to lose was the man most adamant about the issue of pornography: Charles Keating. Lincoln Savings & Loan—which was still in its heyday before the political-influence scandal and violation of banking regulations brought it to its knees—was a cash cow for Covenant House. By the end of the 1980s, Keating would loan Ritter an estimated $40 million. He also held several fund-raisers, including one in Scottsdale, his hometown, while the Meese Commission was there for a work session. It was after Keating heard Ritter rail against the ills of our society, especially pornography and homosexuality, that the priest was given the first annual Charles Keating Award of $100,000. Later there was also a $1,000-a-plate ball sponsored by his organization, Citizens for Decency Through Law. The Registry Resort hotel in Scottsdale was decorated with maypoles and a two-hundred-foot floral arrangement. The Artie Shaw Orchestra and the Phoenix Boys Choir performed. Senator Dennis DeConcini showed up, and Ritter gave the benediction at the gala, which raised $800,000 for Covenant House—the largest fund-raiser in the state's history.

Keating came to New York on several occasions to visit his Franciscan friend and comrade-in-arms against pornography. The two men were symbols of the time in their own different ways—a ruthless banker in the wild days of deregulation and a revered priest cashing in on privatization. Neither man knew they would also be among the first of the fallen in the age of reckoning—the 1990s.

Keating loved Le Cirque, an exclusive Manhattan eatery for the rich and powerful that became synonymous with the fast money of the decade, and that's usually where they met for dinner.

One evening at Le Cirque, seated at a round table were Ritter, Keating, a few members of his large family, and Robert Macauley and his wife. The group held hands as first Ritter and then Keating said a prayer before the French cuisine and fine wine were brought to the table.

"God bless Covenant House and this important mission that you have given to Father Bruce," Keating prayed over the din of the restaurant, his eyes closed and his head bowed, "and, God, please help Father Bruce to do his good work. . . . Amen."

Chapter 13

Cancer

CLIMBING a steep mountain trail in the northern reaches of the Adirondacks, Father Bruce Ritter was having a hard time breathing. He pushed his legs in front of him and kept hiking the narrow trail, until finally he asked his long-time friend Dr. Jim Kennedy to slow down a bit.

"Let's get a breather," said Ritter, trying not to look at Kennedy, who by that time was studying Ritter's shortness of breath with the eye of a physician.

"I want you to come in when we get back," said Kennedy in that doctor's tone of voice—flat and clinical.

"Don't be ridiculous," said Ritter, still fighting to catch his breath. "Just a cold."

"I'll set up the appointment," said Kennedy, as they turned back up the hill. It was the summer of 1986.

The week-long camping trip in upstate New York was tradition for Kennedy and Ritter—close friends and coworkers who had struggled through many hard years together at Covenant House. Kennedy, a man admired by the staff for his tireless commitment to the charity, had been the medical director since the 1970s. They fished and hiked and got away from the tremendous stress of day-to-day operations at the charity.

When the two men got back, Kennedy was insistent about Ritter's coming in for a checkup. Kennedy spotted a tumor in Ritter's chest and he was diagnosed with Hodgkin's disease.

Tests showed the cancer hadn't spread, but Ritter was concerned with the impact he felt his illness could have on the future of Covenant House. Until he and Kennedy could come up with a plan on how to release the information without doing harm to the charity, he told very few staff members about his condition. He canceled trips to Guatemala and Panama so he could immediately begin treatment. Ritter decided to call his old friend Bill Reel at the *Daily News,* and ask him to break the sad news publicly. Reel wrote a touching column about the man whom he had often described as "a true, living saint."

"Bruce was terribly afraid of dying," said one priest who knew Ritter for more than thirty years. "He was not at all willing to come to any acceptance of it. He decided instead to fight it every step of the way."

Through months of painful chemotherapy treatments, one of the people who helped nurse him was Monica Kaiser, a young member of the Faith Community who had a wide-eyed midwestern charm and a beaming smile. Kaiser, in her early twenties, had left her job as a former loan officer in the credit union at Ohio Bell Telephone to volunteer at Covenant House.

She saw Father Bruce as a man of courage and strength, and she worked tirelessly with the other members of the executive staff to help him through the cancer treatments and keep him up to date on what was happening. The treatments made Father Bruce look gaunt, his pale skin taking on an almost ashen color. He suffered from nausea and deep fatigue, but his steel blue eyes never lost their intensity.

With a sharp Irish wit in the face of death, Ritter joked with his friends that the cancer wasn't that bad because he could use it as a "sympathy vote" in their next fund-raising campaign. In private, however, the cancer brought on somber reflections for Ritter and the charity that he believed would be his legacy. He decided to address some of the long-standing criticisms of his programs: that they were too crisis oriented and that they did not offer long-term solutions to the youths in their care. He created an experimental program in New York called Rights of Passage, which offered a handful of kids an opportunity to attend a community college, high-school-equivalency classes, or intensive job training. He wanted eventually to expand the program and make it a model that would be incorporated into the subsidiary sites as well.

By 1987, however, the problems of the young men and women coming to Covenant House were increasingly more complex. The previous year marked the advent of a new and highly addictive drug called "crack" cocaine and the rising epidemic of AIDS. Crack and AIDS had changed forever the landscape of social, psychological, and health problems faced by inner-city youths.

Suddenly Covenant House's stand on sexuality and its Catholic view that condoms were a sin was becoming a part of a charged debate and a desperate matter of life and death to kids on the street. It is hard enough to teach a kid that abstinence is a viable way to prevent contracting AIDS, but for those who turned tricks to stay alive it was useless. Child-care counselors were lining up against the Church's established doctrines. Ray Deeton, executive director of the Toronto program, referred to the clash as "condomgate." Catechism was being met head on with a public-health crisis. There was a desperate need for condoms to be distributed among the youths and especially the hustlers, who were contracting the deadly disease at a frightening pace.

Fed up with the Church's strict doctrine, Covenant House child-care workers in Toronto began handing out condoms, arguing that if they were going to save kids' lives from AIDS, they would have to go above the Church's law. The local press caught on to Covenant House's unofficial position, and there was public outcry against it by prominent Catholics. The Toronto cardinal ordered Ritter to see that "the policy be discontinued," but a movement to challenge the established Catholic doctrine was spreading among the ranks of Covenant House's child-care workers. Ritter was panicking about what was shaping up as another confrontation between his staff and the larger conservative Catholic establishment.

In an eight-page letter to the Reverend John May, chairman of the administrative board of the U.S. Catholic Conference, Ritter expressed his concern in cautious words.

"Because Covenant House is so prominent in the public eye, and because the threat of AIDS to street kids is becoming a major public issue, the position we take here may inevitably be held by the public to reflect on the general viewpoint of the Church," wrote Ritter. "There is simply too much danger of causing an increase in premarital sex, while only a remote, highly diffuse effect on the prevention of disease."

Ritter knew when not to be a maverick. But there were dozens of

senior staff officials, including Greg Loken, who disagreed with the
charity's position. Loken challenged Father Bruce on his stance, but
Ritter begged him to understand how explosive a direct challenge to
Church teaching on such a controversial topic could be.

"You have to understand, I have to do it," said Ritter. "They will
kill me on this issue. I will be crushed."

The condom issue was closely watched in the gay community, and
Covenant House was targeted as a new enemy by some militant
groups that were increasing their ranks amid the onslaught of AIDS.
But the AIDS epidemic and the increasingly high rate of drug-
addicted youths gave Ritter renewed determination to make Covenant House an even larger and more important institution. Ritter
built an expanded medical ward to deal with the health problems
wrought by both.

He started plans for an AIDS floor at the Forty-first Street facility
in New York, to be completed within the following year. He did
studies on the AIDS rate in the Covenant House population—finding
that a startling 10 percent of the youths in its care were likely to test
positive for the HIV virus by age twenty. Once again, Ritter wanted
to go into an expansion phase. He couldn't hand out condoms, but
that didn't mean he couldn't help the AIDS victims. (In the small
circle that suspected Ritter of sexual improprieties, there were rumors
that Ritter had AIDS, not cancer. But they were later dismissed by
senior staffers and board members who knew him well. One medical
expert affiliated with Covenant House told a board member that
Ritter showed none of the physical symptoms of an AIDS sufferer.)
Through the fall and winter of 1987, Ritter battled against his cancer
and continued to work hard. It was taking its physical toll, but he
barely lost his stride.

When Ritter heard that the National Maritime Union Building in
Chelsea was up for sale, he moved quickly. The monstrous, eleven-
story building, which looked vaguely like a ship with its mock-port-
hole windows, had a capacity for some eight hundred beds, a full
gymnasium, a professionally equipped kitchen, a well-stocked library,
and office space—the perfect place for an expansion of the Rights
of Passage program, which would create more room at the Forty-
first Street site for a state-of-the-art AIDS ward.

Ritter discovered that Mayor Koch had already proposed purchase
of the building, a "verbal agreement" of $30 million to convert the
facility into a work-release program. In a ruthless bid for the property, Ritter offered the Maritime Union $5 million more than the

city and cinched the deal. When Koch heard about it, he was furious and told the press that Ritter was playing "dirty pool."

The city sent a team of inspectors to one of Covenant House's Times Square buildings, where they issued a list of violation notices. Koch wasn't afraid of intimidating anyone, even a Catholic priest. He cared as much about what he called "my city" as Ritter did about what he called "my kids."

Under the land-use review procedure, Koch claimed that the city had to wait six months before an agreement could be signed, but a private charity like Covenant House did not.

"He took advantage of that," Koch complained to reporters, adding that he would petition the Board of Estimate to condemn the property, thus turning it over to the city. "He stole my jail."

Koch tried to offer Ritter several other properties for his program in exchange, but Ritter wasn't interested. Two of the sites were small vacant lots, and one was "an abandoned coffin factory that I wouldn't put my dead cat in," Ritter said.

The battle for the Maritime Union building was on. Ritter prepared for what he thought might be the last great fight of his career. It was a classic New York City tale, with a Jewish mayor known for his mouth against an Irish priest regarded as a living saint.

"We bought that building fair and square," said Ritter, rebutting Koch's charges. "Quite frankly I feel intimidated, pushed around, threatened."

Koch shot back, "If anybody's intimidated, it's me. I have a job to do and I can't allow myself to be intimidated. So I am going to trust in God."

But Ritter put his trust in politics. He personally lobbied the Board of Estimate and gathered a majority of supporters who would block Koch's move. On October 26, 1987, Koch surrendered, conceding one of very few political defeats. He told the press he was "infuriated" and asked, "How can you beat a priest with cancer?"

"I think Ritter has abused his position," Koch said. "As a priest, he has great credibility. As a priest who has cancer he has great sympathy and has a cause which everybody loves and endorses—including myself. But he violated the golden rule: Do unto others as thou would have others do unto you."

Ritter, the papers said, had no comment. He was going to University Hospital that day to begin nine weeks of outpatient radiation treatment. Ritter had the building of his dreams.

To expand the Rights of Passage program and to prove to the city that he could make the hulking Maritime Building a beautiful new facility, Ritter summoned what many feared would be his last burst of energy. He was frail from the cancer, but he was determined to die with his boots on. He knew he needed to raise more money—a lot of money—if he was going to make it work. Back in September, at the height of the battle with Koch, Ritter had called Chris Walton, Covenant House's senior vice president for funding and development, into his office.

"Can we raise an additional ten million dollars this year?" Ritter asked Walton.

It was an extraordinary request. Already Covenant House had one of the highest growth rates of any charity in the country. This was asking Covenant House's fund-raising machine to do what no charity had done before.

"I need an answer in fifteen minutes," said Ritter.

That conversation launched what *Fund Raising Management* magazine called a "landmark effort in charitable giving," a case study in how effective a marketing enterprise Covenant House had become. At first, Walton's strategy was to use the war with Koch as a rallying point for a mass appeal to donors. The media coverage "almost unanimously favored Father Ritter and Covenant House," Walton's team determined. They figured they would set up Koch as the bad guy and send out a message to donors that poor Father Bruce Ritter needed their help to save the kids from the cold city bureaucracy's desire to build another dingy prison. It was a sophisticated marketing plan, pitting the saintly priest against the cynical politician.

But all that planning went out the window when Koch gave in. They had to start all over. The wording in the letters to donors was modified: "We need to beat the mayor . . ." became " . . . we had this big battle with City Hall. But that's over now."

The strategy was for Ritter to send a personal letter to 20,000 of Covenant House's best donors out of an active donor group of 600,000. The letter thanked each donor for his or her high level of past commitment to Covenant House and provided details of the Rights of Passage program, the need for the building, and the establishment of a $1 million "Challenge Fund," which the donors would subsequently be asked to "match" dollar for dollar.

The mailings included the cream of the crop in direct-mail packaging and special awards or "recognition levels," such as "Book of Honor" ($500) or "Wall of Honor" ($5,000).

The appeal raised $1 million in three days—and did so only a few weeks after the Black Monday stock market crash. And it didn't stop there. Covenant House sent out 45,000 more Challenge Fund letters and raised $7 million more. The "Matching Fund" phase began with telephone follow-up calls. The Nineline, which was promoted as a tool to help kids in crisis, was quickly turned into a facet of the fund-raising machine. The phone lines were tied up with calls to the first group of donors, thanking them for their support and encouraging them to meet the Matching Fund. Calls went out to 11,878 of the top 20,529 donors. The goal was to raise $1.1 million, but it brought in $2.7 million, more than twice the targeted amount. About 40 percent of those called made additional pledges of an average of about $600 each.

After that, Covenant House's direct-mail machinery went into high gear. The mailing lists stored on circular cartridges for computer tapes spit out the mother lode of all mailings. More than 700,000 "match" mailings to prior active and inactive donors were rushed to the postal service. Within twenty weeks of the mail date, 150,000 Americans had contributed $16 million more to Covenant House. The total amount raised was $24 million, which was only slightly less than the entire federal government's allocation that year for support of runaway and homeless youth programs across the country. It was among the highest dollar returns for a single philanthropic direct-mail appeal in history, according to *Fund Raising Management,* and covered three-fourths of the Rights of Passage building's total cost of $33 million.

The following year, Covenant House was awarded the nonprofit industry's prestigious Gold Echo Award for successful direct-mail marketing. But the stunning successes of the campaign were actually offset by significant losses. The bidding war, combined with his frozen investment in a Times Square property he bought several years earlier, meant Ritter was carrying nearly $50 million of debt. The building was the Times Square Hotel, which he had hoped to turn into a profitable hotel to finance the charity. But the investment had become a severe strain and a public-relations problem for Ritter, who was having trouble evicting the hotel's previous tenants.

By the end of 1987, Ritter was strapped with such heavy debt service that he was forced to make belt-tightening decisions in other areas of the budget. Rather than scale back his expansion plans, or limit spending on the corporate side, Ritter decided to cancel the health benefits of his child-care workers, most of whom were already paid less than $15,000 a year. The total savings from the decision was $80,000 out of a budget of $75 million. One child-care worker said that he knew of colleagues who were actually admitting their own children to Covenant House's emergency health-care clinics when they were sick because they lacked their own health plan. A handful of other staffers also used Covenant House as a kind of day care or to provide their children hot meals and supervision, two necessities they couldn't afford on their own meager salaries. All this while people like John Kells continued to make nearly $90,000 a year. Dr. Jim Kennedy was reimbursed roughly $80,000 for his part-time work. Executive director Ron Williams made $75,000. Ritter himself made more than $90,000, when the secret deposits into his Franciscan Charitable Trust were taken into account. Ritter also felt he had enough money available that year to offer his sister, Cassie Wallace, a bridge loan of approximately $131,000 to enable her to purchase a house.

The stringent fiscal policies led to the shutting down of the program that housed older males who were working or trying to find work and living at the Eighth Avenue center as well as the ICU, or Intensive Counseling Unit.

"A lot of the staff felt these were among the most valuable programs at Covenant House. They were the front line of counseling," said Rick Agcuili, who had worked in both areas.

The hotel, once thought of as the future cornerstone of the charity's endowment, had become a weight around its neck. The rundown building was accumulating hundreds of citations from the city's Department of Buildings, Health Department, and Fire Department. There were unlit fire exit signs, exposed electrical wiring, dysfunctional elevators, inadequate ventilation, and a substandard sprinkler system, which, when replaced, cost Covenant House $2 million. Just several months after he purchased the hotel, however, the City Council passed legislation calling for a moratorium on the conversion of single-room-occupancy buildings. Scores of greedy landlords had been buying up SROs and rapidly transforming them from affordable housing for the poor into luxury condos for yuppies, and the city was moving to put an end to it, which drastically reduced the property value of the Times Square Hotel, the largest SRO in the city.

For the tenants who lived there, Ritter's ownership of the building was their worst nightmare. An October 1987 article in *City Limits,* a small but respected New York–based monthly magazine, published a scathing exposé of a Catholic priest turning his back on the poor and evicting tenants from his SRO. But the story went nowhere in the mainstream media. The newspapers and television preferred not to tarnish the image of a living saint. The other side of Bruce Ritter would go largely ignored, but not by those who had to live in his building.

One of the people interviewed by *City Limits* was a seventy-seven-year-old man who said he was evicted for nonpayment of rent after he lost a part-time job and was no longer able to meet his $450-per-month rent on Social Security alone. The hotel refused the man's request to move to a smaller room that he could afford and proceeded with the eviction. Another tenant, Dennis Katz, a disabled veteran, faced an eviction because his government check was late. Rather than fight it, he moved out.

"Don't let that collar fool you," Katz said. "Father Ritter should be in a gray suit."

Joe Vickery, a wheelchair-bound tenant activist, claimed that the hotel management was intimidating residents and allowing junkies into the building to make it a more dangerous and unlivable environment. After he filed a complaint with the housing court, Vickery claimed that he started getting harassing phone calls at three and four in the morning. Just after Covenant House bought the property, Vickery remembered meeting Jim Harnett, who told him that he would soon be asking people to move out because of "Church business."

The contempt the Covenant House management reportedly showed for its tenants, almost all of them poor and elderly, was strangely reminiscent of Ritter hiring "friends for $50" to force out the junkies in his apartment house in the East Village to create more room for his kids. In 1987, Ritter had little to say on the matter, referring it instead to his public-relations man, John Kells, who said, "Our desire was to build a safety net under those kids."

In June 1987, the Columbia Tenants Union was brought into the hotel by angry tenants. Covenant House had a rent strike on its hands. In a letter to Ritter dated August 17, tenant leader Jerry Ferber wrote, "Harassment and deceit are polluting the premises. A church-owned operation should adhere to the commandments of the good Lord above."

When Covenant House did evict tenants, it often failed to notify the Crisis Intervention Services and other support services, as is the custom among the city's contracted social-service organizations. Covenant House's hotel management also began refusing to take referrals from several social-service agencies that had been placing clients at the hotel for many years. There were more rooms available because of the increase in evictions, but the staff told the social-service workers that there were none. On several occasions, they used other excuses, such as "the boiler is broken" and later that "the pipes are leaking."

Ritter was also having problems with employees. Evelyn Garcia, the hotel's front-desk manager, filed a complaint with the State Division of Human Rights, alleging that two Covenant House executives running the hotel had told her "not [to] hire blacks for the front desk [but to] hire pretty whites." Another employee, Darlene Williams, also charged that the hotel's managers were racist. According to several other staff members, there was a memo that read: "When Darlene goes on maternity leave next month, let's see if we can't replace her, preferably with someone who is white and good-looking."

With the headaches mounting and the building falling deeper into disrepair, Ritter tried to get rid of it. The situation was desperate enough that Ritter appealed to the city to send him homeless families with children in order to charge the city the same astronomical fees—up to $1,800 a month—that other hotel operators were paid for housing homeless families. All this from a charity whose motto was "Times Square—No Place for a Child." Even his loyalists told Ritter that the venture had become a tremendous embarrassment. Harnett was close to resigning over the issue. But, as Ritter said in *The New York Times*, "I'm trapped. Who wants to buy the largest SRO in New York?"

The only available buyer was the city. But Koch wasn't about to do Ritter any favors. The last resort was a man named Ronald Mitchell, who wanted to buy the hotel and turn it into a youth hostel. He offered $21 million. Covenant House accepted. But Mitchell could only put up $500,000, so Ritter called upon his old friend and fellow antipornography crusader Charles Keating, Jr. Once again, Keating saved Ritter. Keating put up the financial backing for Covenant House to loan Mitchell $4 million in the form of a mortgage.

It was that kind of real-estate speculation that makes it easy to understand why Keating's Lincoln Savings and Loan went belly up years later, costing taxpayers an estimated $2.5 billion to bail it out. How did they think Mitchell's idea for a youth hostel would stay solvent charging college students $8 a night in Times Square? Mitchell went bankrupt in less than six months. Ritter was left still holding the bag.

Tran Dinh Truong, dubbed one of the worst landlords of the city by the *Village Voice*, watched all of this from across the street, where he owned the Carter Hotel, one of the city's most notorious SROs.

When Covenant House was forced to put up the hotel for auction, Tran showed up at bankruptcy court and made an offer. Despite motions from the city, the Legal Aid Society, and several tenants' rights groups, Covenant House went into negotiations with Tran at the orders of the banking officials who had granted the loans to Mitchell.

In effect, Covenant House, as one of the secured creditors, handed the building over to a man who forced scores more of the tenants out on the street. Ritter's good intentions, in the end, only perpetuated a nightmare for the poor tenants of the Times Square Hotel. Adding insult to injury, when Covenant House moved out of the hotel they took a beautiful old grandfather clock that had been in the lobby since the 1930s. The clock became a symbol of the ruthlessness with which many of the clients felt they were treated by Covenant House, and for years after they pursued an unsuccessful legal battle to get the clock back.

Ritter moved on. And his next victory was the most important one of his life. He beat cancer. After a year of intensive chemotherapy, Father Bruce had turned the corner on Hodgkin's disease. For those who knew him well, Ritter was a changed person as he slowly convalesced. He seemed to have a new strength. He had already been courted by presidents and created an empire; now he had conquered his cancer. He felt not only blessed to be alive but invincible.

A priest who had known Ritter for many years said that he seemed to have a new desire for intimacy, a new desire to work closely with the kids once again. "The cancer scared him. It made him look at his life and reevaluate some things," said the priest. He was tired of fund-raising and corporate management; he wanted to get back to his roots.

As Anne Donahue put it, "I think there was always something in him that wanted to get back to the days in the [East] Village, when he just wore jeans and a sweatshirt and had the kids sleeping on the floor."

And it was with all of this sense of victory and power and desire for intimacy that Ritter traveled to New Orleans in February of 1989. He was at the pinnacle of his success, proud of his newest Covenant House franchise in the seedy underworld of transvestites, pickpockets, pimps, and prostitutes on the fringes of the French Quarter. The beautiful Covenant House building, a replica of an old New Orleans hotel, sits in the middle of the sometimes surreal underworld of New Orleans.

In the gay bars on the back streets not far from Covenant House, Kevin Lee Kite was crashing from life in the fast lane. For a few years the twenty-five-year-old college dropout had been on a binge of alcohol and cocaine financed largely by his work for a male escort service called Texcourt, which was run out of Dallas.

Kite made up to $100 an hour with a three-hour minimum. After he had "worked his way up," he kept 60 percent of the profits, plus tips. And he was in demand; a young-looking strawberry blond, in good shape, with "very little body hair," which he describes as an oft-requested attribute from his clientele of mostly older men. Though he had just turned twenty-five, he looked about eighteen. He was intelligent and sophisticated and says he often had felt a kind of warmth for many of his clients, who he says often treated him "like a son." He says he worked out of some of the finest hotels in Dallas, including the Adolfis and the Anatole, as well as the Hyatt in Houston.

But he wanted to party in New Orleans during Mardi Gras, so he rented a convertible on a credit card he had stolen from his father, a conservative Baptist accounting professor from Gainesville, Texas. Alton Kite, a tall Texan with a long, slow drawl, never accepted his only child's "homosexual lifestyle," as he always called it. When Kevin was younger, his father was known to go out into the gay bars in Dallas and even all the way to New Orleans to look for his son and drag him out of what he saw as a world of sin. He would bring Kite back to redemption at their modest three-bedroom home hidden behind rose bushes on a street called One Horse Lane. Gainesville, population thirteen thousand, has twenty-one churches. And Mr. and Mrs. Alton Kite faithfully attended Sunday services at the First Baptist Church of Gainesville. Life in the Kite home consisted of church, trips to the shopping mall, afternoons at the country club, and twice-weekly games of bridge with their neighbors. Kite was a good student in high school, and his father even bought him a new car. Within a year he totaled it in an accident.

His father's righteous condemnation of his sexuality did a number on Kite's self-esteem. To Kite, stealing the credit card and renting the convertible was a fitting form of rebellion. It was a scene right out of his favorite book, *Less Than Zero*—decadent and dangerous. He related most to the reckless male character, whose self-destructive ways became the catalyst for close friends to discover how much they cared for each other. In real life, however, Kite didn't have those kinds of friends. He was alone. He was getting older. His beard was a little thicker, his voice deeper, and the money was drying up in the escort service. Besides, he had grown tired of the compromises. He wanted to get his life under control. He wasn't a kid anymore.

After a wild night of partying on Fat Tuesday, Kite claims, his wallet was stolen. It's the same line just about everyone on the street uses, which raises questions as to what exactly Kite's true story was. Nevertheless, according to him, the next morning he was broke and had no one to turn to. He covered his eyes against the bright sunshine of the February afternoon and stumbled into the police station. They referred him to Covenant House. Some kids in front of the building gave him the lowdown on how to get in. First, lie about your age. Say you're under twenty-one, they told him. Second, make up a fake name. And third, look desperate.

Kite listened to their advice and wandered into Covenant House like a poster child right out of their marketing campaigns. Clean cut. Blue eyes. Strawberry-blond hair. He was articulate and engaging. He also came up with a story that seemed to be taken right from the pages of Ritter's most lurid newsletter. He told the counselors at the intake center about his involvement in a prostitution ring run by organized crime, and about their pushing him to become a mule in the drug trade. Kite was immediately informed by counselors that his life was in danger. It seemed strange to Kite that they were taking him so seriously without looking into his past, but he decided to go with the story and see what happened. He stayed at Covenant House for several days, during which he occasionally slipped out to stay with a man he had met in the French Quarter.

After his first week at Covenant House, Father Bruce Ritter came to visit his subsidiary in Sin City. His arrival was treated with a great deal of fanfare. Kite watched as the staff toiled away, cleaning the facility and putting out fresh flowers for their founder. Kite claims he didn't know who Ritter was, but quickly sensed that he was a "very important man."

That afternoon Father Bruce made his way through the intake center and the courtyard, talking with the kids in the program. He wore a collar. Kite wore a blue silk shirt, tight jeans, and cowboy boots. Ritter was introduced to Kite, who was using the assumed name of "Greg Hutcherson" at the time. Hutcherson was actually a twenty-year-old next-door neighbor in Gainesville. Ritter studied him before he walked over. Kite felt that Ritter was immediately drawn to him. They struck up a conversation and Father Bruce spent a good hour with Kite, and then quickly finished up with the other kids, most of whom were black and Hispanic and poor.

Ritter immediately told his staff that Kite was someone who needed special attention and that he was considering taking him back to the New York program. He said he also believed that Kite would make a perfect candidate for a special scholarship at Manhattan College that he was arranging for several gifted residents of Covenant House. Ritter talked Kite into flying back to New York with him by promising to help him turn his life around.

Ritter and Kite boarded a direct first-class flight on Continental Airlines at 7:10 A.M. from New Orleans to Newark airport. Ritter took with him Kite's intake file, in which there were notes from a physical, stating that Kite was healthy: He was not addicted to drugs, he was not HIV positive.

They talked on the plane about Italy and especially Assisi, which Kite had visited on a high school trip. They talked about books, Ritter mentioning a recent favorite, *The Hunt for Red October,* and Kite saying he loved mysteries, especially Agatha Christie. After about an hour of casual conversation, Ritter began asking pointed questions about Kite's involvement with prostitution, about what he did for his clients, and about how much he charged. Kite was surprised at the priest's interest in the details, but figured that it was his business and that he had to ask those kinds of questions as a counselor of troubled youths. Kite gave him all the details he wanted.

Kite claims that he opened up to the priest and told him his real name, his actual age, even that he had taken some college courses. He says that Ritter told him he was "the boss," that his age was not important and that he could still help him redirect his life. Ritter told Kite about the New York City center of Covenant House and said that he usually went out to a house in the country on weekends.

"Maybe we'll go out there this weekend," he said to Kite. "It will give us a chance to get to know each other."

They landed in Newark and hopped in a taxi to New York City.

"Oh, by the way," Father Bruce said in the cab, "just to make things easier, use the name Jim Wallace. That's my nephew. It will make it easier to explain why I am bringing someone back with me."

Kite thought that it was strange for a priest to be so secretive. But Ritter told him that it was because he was afraid that the escort service could trace him back to New York if too many people found out about his true identity.

When they arrived at Covenant House, Ritter told Kite to wait in the lobby. He stared out on Forty-first Street, dirty and packed with traffic. He watched two teenager mothers, who were speaking in Spanish, push baby carriages into the entranceway to Covenant House. He saw the faces around him of poor black and Hispanic teenagers. Their voices were loud and their language was of the streets. There was an air of danger, not much different, Kite thought, from what it would be like at a homeless shelter. It was nothing like what he had expected. He had thought it was a small ministry for troubled street kids, not a warehouse for poor minorities. He had no idea how he was going to fit in at such a place.

Fifteen minutes later, Ritter arrived carrying a small overnight bag. He had changed out of his collar and into a pair of jeans, a gray flannel shirt, sneakers, and a down vest. The two of them hopped into Ritter's gray 1990 Toyota. They cruised out of the city and wound their way up the Taconic State Parkway toward Rhinebeck.

Kite stared out the window at the New York skyline, fading into the distance behind the rolling hills of Westchester as they headed north. Kite had never been to New York and was already convinced that stumbling into New Orleans's Covenant House was one of the best things he had ever done. A first-class flight, and now a vacation in the country. Not bad. On the trip up, Kite mentioned that he loved new clothes, and Ritter pulled into a shopping mall off the highway in Dutchess County. Kite picked out several pairs of pants, a few shirts, and a $110 pair of sneakers. The total tab came to just over $300 and Ritter put it on his credit card.

They arrived in the quaint town of Rhinebeck near sunset and drove down a long driveway. Pine trees that lined the entrance were still decorated with faded red Christmas bows. They pulled up to a secluded cottage nestled among the pines on the banks of the Hudson River, on the grounds of the former Astor mansion, which was owned by Mary and James Maguire, both of whom had been active supporters of Covenant House for years and who offered the small cottage on their property to Ritter to get away from the city. She was a bank executive who had offered financial advice and helped facilitate several loans to Covenant House. He was a prestigious New York attorney with Hall, McNicol, Hamilton & Clark and on the charity's board of directors.

The main room of the cottage was roughly twenty by twenty-five feet, with windows that looked out over the trees and the banks of the Hudson. A couch in the middle of the room was before a large fireplace. To the right of the main room was a small kitchen with a breakfast table and a bathroom. On the other side was a small room with a sofa bed, a television, and another, smaller fireplace. They dropped off their bags, turned on the heat, and went up to the Maguires' sprawling white mansion on the hill, where Ritter briefly introduced Kite to them as his nephew.

Then Ritter and Kite went out to get pizza and rent a few movies: *Agnes of God, Murder by Death,* and *Becket.*

Ritter pushed *Agnes of God* into the VCR. Kevin lay on the floor, Ritter on the couch. About an hour into the movie, Ritter pulled out the sofabed and put sheets and a blanket on it. He stripped down to his underwear and climbed in bed. There was an awkward silence when Kite realized it was the only bed in the cottage. Ritter broke the silence by inviting him to sleep in it. Ritter turned and fell asleep, while Kite watched the rest of the movie and eventually fell asleep. Morning came fast and Bruce was up early reading the papers and making coffee. They went out to breakfast and talked about Kite's life, about school, about Covenant House. Ritter showed him the countryside around Rhinebeck and talked casually, occasionally tapping the steering wheel to a Carly Simon CD on his car stereo. He was "hipper than you'd expect from a priest," says Kite. He used the word man a lot, and kept saying, 'Shit, you gotta get it together.' "

By late afternoon the sun was setting behind the bare trees and the evergreens on the banks of the Hudson. They went back to the cottage, put on another movie and took their same positions, Kite lying on the floor and Ritter sitting on the couch. This time Ritter put his foot on Kite's back and began slowly rubbing from Kite's shoulders to his lower back.

"I said to myself, well, this is weird," Kite remembers. "But I figured he was just trying to be nice. I kept telling myself not to act stupid. The night before it hit me that it was strange, but nothing had happened. So I just passed it off. I figured he was just very physical and that it was my own problem that I was even thinking anything was strange."

Ritter again pulled out the sofabed and put the sheets and blanket on it. He got undressed and told Kite that it was "time for bed." But on the second night, Ritter began rubbing Kite's shoulder in bed and then slowly moved his hand farther down Kite's body to the top of his underwear. Kite says Ritter began fondling his genitalia and then stopped. There were no words. Kite did not move. He had had sex with scores of older men; it was certainly not anything new to him. But he didn't know how to handle the sexual advances from a priest.

"The whole thing freaked me out. I guess I shouldn't have been surprised, but I really thought he was sincere about wanting to help me out, and in a lot of ways he did," says Kite. "It was just all pretty confusing. I started reviewing my whole life, thinking about how strange it was, and then I fell asleep too."

Kite woke up to the sound of Ritter making coffee in the kitchen.

"Let's go to breakfast," Ritter said.

Kite was surprised that there were no words about what had happened. There was complete avoidance. Kite began to think that perhaps he had made too much of Ritter's advances. After all, he figured, nothing had actually happened, just a little touching.

They drove back to Covenant House that Sunday night and Ritter

ordered a staff person to set up the VIP room on the eighth floor
for Kite. It was just down the hall from Ritter's apartment. In the
room were two single beds with floral-patterned quilts, antique furnishings, and a large color television set. He stared at the framed
photographs—one of President Reagan standing before an American
flag and another of Reagan shaking hands with Ritter in the White
House. He was beginning to realize from the size of the charity and
Ritter's aura of importance that he was a national figure.

Kite thrived on the special attention he received from Ritter. He
relished the idea that he was placed in the private rooms with clean
sheets and meals anytime he wanted. He was several floors above the
masses of poor young people thrown together in large residential
dormitories or sleeping on rubber mats on the floor of the intake
center.

Over the next few days, Ritter was very busy. Kite sat in the VIP
room mostly watching television. He and Ritter would see each other
at breakfast in Ritter's apartment, and then Ritter got tied up in
meetings and paperwork. On the third night, just after midnight,
Father Bruce knocked on Kite's door.

"Come on, I'll show you New York City," said Ritter, as Kite quickly
put on his shoes and the down coat that Ritter had given him.

They walked out of the building and headed east on Forty-first
Street, through the Port Authority and into Times Square. In silence,
they strode past the drug dealers, the prostitutes, the peep shows,
the porno theaters, and the adult bookstores. Some of the people on
the street said hello to Bruce. Kite couldn't tell if they were undercover cops or Covenant House staff or male prostitutes. Out there,
everyone started looking the same. Father Bruce stopped before the
pulsating neon and pointed to the theaters like a tour guide.

"These are the arcades where you can watch straight sex; over
there is gay sex," he said in a tone as hardened as the street they
were on, and as if none of it fazed him. It was a strange way to show
someone the city, Kite thought.

"He was giving a kind of matter-of-fact Gray Line tour of Times
Square," Kite remembers. "I had never been there, but I knew there
was more to the city than that."

After four days in the VIP room, one of Ritter's top staff members,
John Spanier, brought Kite to an apartment building on Forty-sixth
Street, where he was given his own one-bedroom apartment. Other
volunteers and nuns associated with Covenant House also lived in
the building.

On Friday afternoon they packed up and headed for the secluded cottage in Rhinebeck again. It was the same scenario. They watched television. Kite lay on the floor and Ritter sat on the couch. Again, Ritter caressed Kite's back with his foot. Ritter pulled out the sofabed and prepared for bed. Later, Kevin got into bed as well.

"I was still watching TV and he started fondling me, and he rolled closer. I just kept watching TV. . . . I was allowing it. I didn't know what else to do," Kite remembers. "He pulled my hand over to him. I rolled over. There was mutual masturbation."

There were no words. There was no eye contact. Just slow, silent sex before they turned and fell asleep. The next night, they again engaged in mutual masturbation. For Kite, his relationship with Ritter became a "business experience."

"I just started thinking, okay, if this is the way life is going to be this is the way it is going to be," said Kite. "There was no way I was going home to my parents. I just wanted to get into college and get on with my life. There was no way I was going back to Gainesville."

Sex for Ritter and Kite became a ritual, Kite says, that began in Rhinebeck and stretched on for months in Ritter's apartment. As his workload and the tensions of the day-to-day operations increased, the sex slowed down to about once a week, usually on Sunday nights. Ritter was almost always busy with paperwork and meetings during the week, but would call Kite on Sunday afternoons and tell him to come to his office at 6 P.M. for dinner and an "appointment" for counseling.

They would usually eat at Kraft's Diner on Forty-second Street, not far from the Covenant House corporate offices, or occasionally at the pricier West Bank Café in the theater district off Broadway. After dinner, they'd go to Ritter's apartment and watch *Star Trek: The Next Generation* or a TV movie. Usually the sex would begin, Kite says, with Ritter caressing him while they watched television. Then Ritter would pull out the Murphy bed, where they would engage in mutual masturbation. Later on they advanced to oral sex. They never had anal sex, Kite said. They took occasional trips to Rhinebeck, but most of the sexual activity took place in Ritter's eighth-floor apartment on their Sunday-night "appointments," as Ritter always called them.

Kite has kind words for Ritter as a man who legitimately helped him through a hard time. He believes the Franciscan's kindness and compassion were sincere. He believes that Ritter honestly cared about him and wanted to help him get his life together. They became very close. Ritter would often say to Kite, "I see myself in you more than anyone else I've ever met."

During his first few months there, Kite was introduced to lower staff workers as "Father Ritter's nephew, Jim Wallace." Members of the "inner circle," including John Spanier, say they knew it was not the young man's real name and many suspected that he was considerably older than the nineteen years he professed to be. None of them, however, asked any questions. Father Bruce was handling the case and that meant no one should interfere.

Kite was given a job in Loken's Institute for Youth Advocacy, where he filed documents, answered phones, and clipped newspaper articles. Monica Kaiser, then a full-time staff member of the institute, says that at first no one questioned why Ritter would take the young man away for weekends in Rhinebeck because they all assumed that he actually was Ritter's nephew. However, many of the staff, especially she, were annoyed with Kite's behavior. He was demanding and obnoxious, and most of his demands were met or ordered to be met by Father Bruce. But everyone figured it was because he was family.

"He looked like Bruce. There was something about them that was very similar," said Kaiser. "When he came in with the same fair skin and the blue eyes, it just all seemed to fit. He even had the same expressions as Bruce and his niece, Ellen Lofland. So we didn't say anything."

But in early June, when Lofland, the sister of the real Jim Wallace, came to visit Covenant House and several of the staff asked her about her brother, and why he had been staying with Father Bruce, Lofland had no idea what they were talking about. Suddenly Kite's identity was in question. Ritter had never bothered to tell his niece that he was using her brother's name as a cover for the male prostitute with whom he had become sexually involved. Lofland went straight to Kite and demanded to know why he was using her brother's name. Kite told her that Father Bruce had instructed him to do so. The few senior staff officials who knew reluctantly told her it was the truth. She was furious.

The ploy had blown up in Ritter's face. He apologized to his niece and then devised a plan to get Kite a new identity. Although Kite says that he never felt his life was threatened and that he told Ritter that he did not mind using his real name, he claims Ritter insisted on creating a new identity for him. Ritter said he wanted to be sure to protect Kite from the evil pimps of the escort service. He saw himself as the great protector of his kids against any threat, whether real or perceived.

Ritter called in Greg Loken and began the process, which senior

Covenant House employees had used before on at least a half-dozen other young people who needed protection. They had secretly devised a way to steal an identity from a deceased young person by appropriating the deceased's birth certificate and Social Security number. This was how it worked. Loken made a call to a priest he knew in Jamestown near Lake Erie. The priest, Father Duval, thirty-one, was a former director of Covenant House's Casa Alianza in Guatemala, who was then working as a parochial vicar of Saint James Roman Catholic Church in Jamestown.

Loken made the situation seem desperate and Duval was soon in action. Duval discovered that a ten-year-old boy had died of leukemia in 1980, which at the time would have made him nineteen years old, just about the perfect age for Kite's new identity. Using the boy's name, Timothy Michael Warner, and the names of his parents, Terry and Betty, Duval provided a fake baptismal certificate backdated to December 27, 1970. The certificate bore the forged signature of Patrick X. Crotty, a priest who did not arrive at Saint James until 1972 and who had since left the priesthood to marry. Father Duval also obtained a certified copy of the dead boy's birth certificate. It is unclear how he managed to do that, since the law dictates no one is allowed to obtain such a document of a deceased person except family members or their representatives. The Jamestown city clerk's office has no record of having issued such a certificate, and exactly how it was obtained remains a mystery. But Duval handed both the forged baptismal certificate and the stolen birth certificate over to Loken who then gave them to Kite in a manila envelope, which also contained an application for a Social Security card and a passport. Kite later discovered that Warner already had a Social Security number, and he simply used the old number rather than apply for a new one.

Kite had a new identity. He was Timothy Michael Warner. Ritter never consulted the parents of the dead boy; he never considered the ramifications if the parents found out that their dead son's name was being used by a former male prostitute. He did it all in the name of helping his kids.

The first day Kite began publicly using the name "Tim Warner" was when he and Ritter went to the June wedding of staff member John Spanier in Reading, Pennsylvania. Ritter and Kite stayed in the same hotel room, and late in the evening after the rehearsal dinner, they were lying on the same bed together. Kevin smoked cigarettes and watched television, while Father Bruce marked the readings in the Bible for the service and prepared some notes for the homily. He closed up the Bible and then moved his hand over to Kite, caressing him. There was a knock on the door. Ritter jumped up, threw on his T-shirt, and quickly pulled down the sheets on the second bed. Observing the priest's quick thinking, Kite thought to himself he must have been through the drill before.

"I didn't know you smoked," Kite heard a young member of the Faith Community say in the doorway as he spoke to Ritter.

"I don't. I have someone here with me," said Ritter.

Ritter and the Faith Community member talked for a few minutes in the doorway and Ritter came back in the room. The risk of discovery was something that didn't seem to faze him. He never said a word about what would happen if he was discovered. About a half hour later, Kite and Ritter were lying in the same bed in their underwear when the telephone rang. It was Monica Kaiser. She was looking for Kite, whom she had promised to take shopping before the Saturday-afternoon wedding.

"He's right here. Hold on," said Ritter, handing the phone to Kite.

Kaiser could not understand why Kite would be in the room that late. She noticed that Kite's voice sounded strained, as if he couldn't really talk. He sounded "upset." This was the first time that Kaiser began to strongly suspect that something was going on between the two of them.

At the wedding, Kaiser tried to sit down and talk with Kite, but it was "one of those social hours from hell," as she put it. She knew it was also not the best place in the world to get a reading on the situation. She just watched the way the two interacted.

Immediately after the wedding Ritter had to get back to Covenant House. A scheduled visit to the New York crisis center by President Bush on June 22 had Ritter in the middle of some $300,000 in renovations to make the place look good. The visit would bring a lot of media attention, and Ritter worked tirelessly to make sure it all went off as planned. The Secret Service requested a full architectural plan of the building. The President's advance men arrived a few days before the scheduled visit and began scouring the building.

Ritter told Kite not to go to his job in the Institute for Youth Advocacy for several days, and not to attend the presidential visit. There would be too many television cameras there, he explained.

"The whole country will be watching that. Your identity could easily be revealed," Ritter told Kite.

On the afternoon of June 22, network television crews began setting up in Covenant House's flagship crisis center. Big vans and trucks emblazoned with the networks' symbols idled in front of the building, which was crawling with reporters and photographers and Secret

Service men. President and Barbara Bush arrived and were given a tour of the facility. Afterward, they sat with a group of about ten residents of Covenant House to talk about the problems faced by street kids.

For just the right touch, Ritter had four young white youths flown in from the New Orleans, Fort Lauderdale, and Houston programs. It would be a "better racial mix," he told the Covenant House staffers who arranged for their flights and lodging in New York. He needed to keep the myth he was marketing perpetuated on network television.

"Do you normally have this many cameras?" asked Bush, as he sat down, forcing a round of laughter from the kids, who seemed a little uneasy at the idea of having a rap session with the President and his wife.

"Yeah, this is about normal," said one of the young males in the group, causing the laughter to continue.

Barbara Bush held the child of a teenage mother in her arms and the cameras flashed wildly; the image appeared on every network news show and the front pages of newspapers across the country. The message of Covenant House was being beamed out to millions. Bush also used the Covenant House visit as a platform to announce his elaborate "Thousand Points of Light" initiative. And on that day none of those lights burned as brightly as Father Bruce Ritter.

"Now this is the man, this is the President of the United States, so I think you should tell him what he really needs to hear about street kids," said Ritter, starting the conversation while Bush smiled and readjusted his tie. "What do you think is the most important thing for him to know about life on the streets?"

A young man with a white T-shirt and a wide smile said, "I'm eighteen going on nineteen and all I know how to do is sell drugs. . . . I can make a hundred dollars a day in drugs, what do you think I'm going to do, work at McDonald's? That ain't no money."

Bush didn't respond.

"My brother got shot in his heart with a forty-four Magnum because a drug dealer said he shortchanged him," said a young girl with a baby. She showed no emotion when she said it. Barbara Bush listened intently and shook her head. Bush at the time was still pushing for the NRA-backed legislation that refused to put a ban on automatic rifles.

"You need to give a kid a chance," said a young man, who admitted he was struggling to break an addiction to crack. "We need rehabs. You go to them and they want all this money. At Fair Oaks, they want fifteen to twenty thousand dollars and you don't have a dime."

Bush moved around uncomfortably in his chair, and when it was appropriate he nodded his head with understanding and asked, "So is there no hope? Is that what you are saying?"

To these young people, these were the prevailing issues that needed to be brought to the attention of the President: an economic system that afforded them little opportunity but to sell drugs; the violent world of New York City's streets; and a criminal justice system that focused on incarceration for young drug addicts instead of rehabilitation.

Not one of them mentioned pornography, and only one young man, a twenty-year-old self-admitted hustler flown in from Fort Lauderdale by Ritter, mentioned prostitution. He had soft blue eyes, long black hair, and a thin goatee. Ritter interrupted the conversation to direct the questioning away from the issues of drugs and a lack of economic opportunity and back to the long-haired hustler.

"I'm very interested in what you have to say. It really disturbed me. You said there are young kids on the street?" asked Ritter.

"Yeah, I'm in Fort Lauderdale, but I'm from Chicago. Kids are selling themselves on the streets. . . . They're like twelve years old, you know," said the young man.

Kite sat in his apartment and watched the nightly newscasts carrying Father Bruce Ritter's public image as the savior of young lives.

"I thought, this is a hoot," said Kite. "There was the President of the United States sitting next to a chickenhawk. They were patting him on the back for all the good work and I just kept thinking, what a hypocrite."

Throughout the summer of 1989, Kite was left alone to drift in and out of corporate headquarters. He had a card key that gave him access to any office. And he had a seemingly endless flow of cash from Ritter, which he used to tour the bars of Greenwich Village. He was a regular at The Monster, a popular gay bar, and also hung out at some of the pickup bars on the East Side of Manhattan, where younger men hustled an older clientele.

Although she didn't especially like Kite, Monica Kaiser was angry that no one was counseling him. Working in the corporate offices, she often ran into Kite. She found him manipulative and arrogant. But she sensed that he was troubled and that he needed a lot of supervision. Ritter claimed to be his "mentor," the word he used for the "close and intensive counseling" of what he called "high-risk cases." But the fact was that Ritter didn't have time.

Then, one day, Kite claimed he was violently raped by a male whom he had invited back to his apartment. He confided in Kaiser what had happened. Ritter dismissed it as "probably rough sex" from one of his "johns" and suspected that Kite was back to his "rotten street habits." It was a fairly insensitive position for a counselor to take without any exploration of the facts, Kaiser thought, so she tried to help by talking with him and encouraging him. They became friends. She became his surrogate mentor and alerted Ritter that she thought he needed psychological counseling.

"He has to get used to this new lifestyle. I think counseling would open up too many wounds and would be emotionally too much to deal with," Ritter told her. "He's getting ready for school. Let's let him get started and then we'll see about counseling."

Kaiser, like most of the staff, was not professionally trained to counsel troubled youths. But she could see that Kite was getting anything he wanted and nothing he needed. She questioned Ritter's judgment in preparing to send such a flamboyant and openly gay young man to a conservative Catholic institution like Manhattan College. When she brought it up with her fellow staff members, they'd say, "You shouldn't question Father Bruce. He knows what he is doing."

The weekly stipend and the free flow of petty cash that went out to Kite troubled her. She was conscientious enough to write a series of memos questioning the checks that were given to him. By September, the checks included: nearly $3,000 in the form of "stipends"; $1,303 that was listed as "school supplies" but actually went for apartment furnishings, including a color television set; $2,997 for room and board at Manhattan College; a $2,198 personal computer; nearly $300 for Kite's private telephone bill; about $500 for clothing, including a designer jogging suit; and hundreds of dollars more for items listed only as "miscellaneous."

The checks came out of the office of the president, but it was not clear what line item they should have been filed under. In one memo to Ritter as well as the finance department, Kaiser wrote, "Again I would like to bring the issue of checks released to Tim Warner [Kite] to your attention. It is an issue that needs to be resolved."

"He could get anything he wanted," Kaiser remembers. "He would go upstairs and just come down with money. He would come into the office counting bills. I would be so mad. There was one time that Kevin was going to go back to school, and we gave him money for the subway and he said, 'No, I am going to get Bruce to have you drive me up there.' "

A few minutes later, he came back down to the office with Father

Bruce's keys, a note telling Monica to drive him there, and more money in his hand.

"I was furious," said Kaiser. "It was like he owned the place. I returned the keys to Bruce and I asked him about it. He laughed it off, saying, 'Well, keep him away from me. He's got a cold.'"

As Kaiser put it, "There were all these pieces that we didn't even know formed a puzzle." But she and other staff members knew something was "not quite right." At least one other official on the eighth floor wondered about the special attention that Father Bruce afforded to Kite. He was constantly hanging out in Ritter's office, and it seemed strange that he was up there late at night on Sundays. It was assumed that Father Bruce was counseling him, but the official wondered, "Why didn't it take place during the day?" She brought to the attention of the chief operating officer, James Harnett, that the situation created at least an appearance of impropriety.

"There were people who would sit around and see the kind of access that he [Warner/Kite] had," said the woman, who no longer works with the organization. "I think the inner circle of his staff knew what was going on, or at least strongly suspected it. In fact, I know they did. But no one wanted to believe it. No one wanted to face it. I know I didn't."

Kite began his courses at Manhattan College in September. He did very well the first few weeks—scoring an A on an English paper and a B on his first Art History exam. He felt for the first time that he was on the right track and doing it on his own. But there was a lot of pressure that came with school, pressure that Kite found difficult to manage. Rather than focus on the school work and channel his intelligence into learning, Kite began obsessing about the relationship with Ritter that had landed him there. He felt it was built on the same shoddy rock of compromise that was the rest of his life. He was still prostituting himself in a way, just for less money and a slightly different payment plan. He also grew angry with Ritter because he had so little time to deal with him and the problems he was having in school. Every time he met with Ritter, he says, it would evolve into the same pattern of sex and silence. Kite craved attention and he wasn't getting it.

The sex wasn't good and it wasn't lucrative, so Kite claims he told Ritter that he wanted to stop it. He tried to confront Ritter about it on several occasions. Each time Ritter listened and said he understood, but then they would continue. Another troubling aspect for Kite, who was openly gay, was the closeted silence of the relationship, which he found not only awkward but also degrading.

"Let's back off of this for a while," Kite claims he told Ritter after one of their Sunday-night trysts. "I am in school now. Let's just see how things go."

"I'm sorry. I'm sorry," said Ritter. "It will never happen again. In fact, we'll make an agreement. We'll see each other ten times, and I promise you it won't happen in that time."

Kite saw Ritter two times over the next week. On the third night, he walked into Ritter's office and Father Bruce was holding up three fingers and grinning.

"That's three," he said softly, just out of range of several staff members who stood in the room. The following Sunday, Kite and Ritter again went out to dinner and had sex.

Kite brought up the issue several days later and Ritter again apologized. But he added, "You know, if you ever did anything to hurt Covenant House, things wouldn't go well for you. You know that, don't you?"

It was the first time Kite had felt a direct threat related to their sexual relationship. It changed the understanding between them and made Kite furious. Ritter had also cut Kite's weekly stipend back by $50 a week. That made him even madder. It left him with little money to cruise the bars that he had gotten to know in the Village. Understanding firsthand how powerful Ritter was, Kite felt the sexual relationship was getting out of control. He began to look for a way out.

In mid-October a rumor was circulating in Covenant House that a young male hustler named Sean Russell had been killed and that somehow Covenant House staff officials were involved. Russell, a blond, blue-eyed waif from Florida, who had been pictured on the cover of the charity's annual report that year, was stabbed to death in a bizarre murder-suicide by a transvestite in midtown Manhattan. The police considered the case closed within a week after it occurred. Nevertheless, another former Covenant House client said that Russell had bragged shortly before his death that he had been having sex with senior staff members. The word of Russell's death spread quickly among a group of kids who did "the Covenant House thing," which was lying about their age when they were actually over twenty-one, and staying at Covenant House for shelter while they hustled as male prostitutes in a higher-class area called "The Loop," between Second and Madison avenues near Fifty-third Street. The young hustlers were plugged in to a lot of information about Covenant House, and Kite knew a few of them. They spread rumors that Russell's murder was connected to his affairs with Covenant House staffers.

Kite grew paranoid when he heard the tale of what had happened to a young hustler who, as he heard it, had turned on a Covenant House staffer with whom he was having an affair. It made him wonder what someone as powerful as Ritter would do if he ever felt someone was going to disclose the nature of their relationship.

In the middle of the anger and the confusion and the difficulty he was having with rebuilding his life, Kevin Kite was watching talk-show host Sally Jessy Raphael. A woman caller said she was in a sexual relationship with a very powerful public figure in her town and wanted to get out of it. But the man insisted that she couldn't and threatened to ruin her life if she did. The female caller said she didn't know what to do because she was afraid if she went to the police they wouldn't believe her and would cover up for the man, a leading local politician. Sally told the woman to go to a newspaper and tell them everything. Then go to the authorities. The newspaper would act as a "safety" in case anything happened and would put pressure on the law-enforcement authorities to investigate the case, Sally added. Kevin Kite listened to the talk show and nervously began hatching an idea.

V

The Flood

God saw that the wickedness of man was great on the earth. . . . "I mean to bring a flood and send the waters over the earth, to destroy all. . . ."

Genesis 6:5, 17

Chapter 14

God, No. It's Not True

"PICK UP on six," an editor shouted across the clicking of computer terminals and the chatter of reporters in the newsroom of the *New York Post.*

Every day at the newspapers in New York City, a half-dozen people call to drop an anonymous dime on a public figure or tell reporters about a "major scandal." They are politicians furnishing reporters with ammunition on their enemies; collect calls from correctional facilities with convicts proclaiming innocence; and drunk cops ready to expose corrupt captains. Just about none of these telephone calls from nowhere pan out. But once in a great while, a story comes across the line that actually goes somewhere.

Kevin Kite called the *Post,* having decided to go forward with his story. Taking his cue from Sally Jessy Raphael, he started the process by planting the information at the paper for "security." It was late October when Kite asked to speak with a "high editor." After being put on hold and ignored by several different clerks, his persistence eventually got him transferred to the metropolitan editor, John Cotter. Through years of bouncing around on New York City's nightside with pub owners, priests, cops and criminals, and those who write about them, Cotter had heard some rumors about Ritter. But he

didn't let on about that until months later. He just told me to pick
up the line "on six" and "check it out."

Figuring Kite was just some sick street kid pulling a scam, I dutifully
took notes but didn't believe a word he said. Kite told the whole story
about meeting in New Orleans, the trips to Rhinebeck, and the Sunday night trysts with the priest. I asked if he had any way of docu-
menting his claims. He said he worked in the executive offices and
could get receipts of the expenditures on him. I figured he'd never
show up, but set up a meeting for later in the week at a diner next
door to the *Post* building in lower Manhattan. But Kite did arrive,
ten minutes early, looking clean-cut, his reddish hair short-cropped,
wearing glasses, and a yellow sweater and jeans. He smoked an endless chain of Marlboro 100s. He was articulate and worried, convincing and manipulative.

He spread the documents out across the green Formica table at
the diner. They looked real, and the expenditures were strange for
a charity that always complained it was strapped for cash. (I had no
idea at the time that the actual annual budget was some $90 million.)
Why would a street kid be given a private apartment and a private
dorm room? Why would they buy him a computer? Why would there
be expenditures on clothes and furnishings for his apartment? At a
bare minimum, the story seemed to be shaping up as a charity that
was fast and loose with its money.

Kite's allegation of sex with Ritter was another story. A newspaper
would never take the word of an acknowledged former male prostitute against a legendary Catholic priest. But there was something
in Kite's voice and his demeanor that made it seem as though he was
worried about his future. He hinted at just "disappearing," rather
than going forward with the allegations. I advised him to talk to a
counselor he trusted within Covenant House, to let that person know
what was going on, and to keep me informed. The notes were filed
in a cluttered desk drawer, where over the next two weeks they slowly
sifted toward the bottom.

Kite went straight to Monica Kaiser, the only person he felt he
could trust, and told her his real name and his real identity, and
about the sexual relationship he was having with Ritter. For days they
agonized over how best to proceed. On one occasion, Kite secretly
tape-recorded their phone conversation, using a cheap device he
bought for $25. He was starting to build his case and was going about
it quite methodically.

Monica Kaiser, who always felt she had found a deeper faith in
God through Father Bruce Ritter and his mission, was about to go

through a slow and shattering process of disillusionment. She was caught between Ritter, a man who always felt she had changed her life, and Kite, a confused former hustler whom she had befriended and wanted to help.

Through Ritter's battle with cancer, Monica and Father Bruce had grown very close. Although she recognized that at times Ritter could be aloof, she admired his leadership. He made his staff feel that they were on a mission blessed by God. Father Ritter was the most important force in her young life. And this powerful man, this compassionate pastor, had big plans for her. After her first two years as a volunteer, Father Bruce had made her director of the Faith Community. After that, she was given a senior staff position in the Institute for Youth Advocacy. But throughout the fall, she had also grown close to Kite while serving as his surrogate mentor in the absence of Ritter, who was always wrapped up in plans for presidential visits and press conferences or traveling around the country to raise money.

Although she found Kite's allegation deeply disillusioning, she knew she had to report it, not only because it was a serious charge but because she sensed that Kite was telling the truth. It was not the first time Kaiser had been told about Ritter's mixed motives. She had also heard from other Faith Community members that Ritter had approached them sexually as well. She had always dismissed those allegations as a misunderstanding, but now things were beginning to add up. Growing up in a devout Catholic family and attending parochial schools all her life, Kaiser had been taught to tell the truth and trust her heart. She had no idea what she was in for.

She quickly discovered how difficult it was to report such an accusation within an organization that had become so faithful to its founder and president. Not only would she be branded a fallen angel who had betrayed Father Bruce but she was afraid his inner circle would tell him and provide a way to cover it up. With no adequate system of accountability at Covenant House, she decided to go straight to the New York Archdiocese. Unwilling to discuss the nature of her call with a secretary, she couldn't get an appointment with anyone on the cardinal's staff, and no one returned her calls. She decided to go to a Franciscan priest who she thought could help her. He was out of town. So Kaiser waited. Kite, however, did not.

He first called Dr. Andrew Vachss, a writer and lawyer who specializes in sexual abuse cases, on November 7, after hearing his name in passing from another Covenant House counselor. Vachss was out of town, but his secretary provided Kite with an 800-number hotline for victims of sexual abuse or assault. The operator on the hotline referred Kite to the Crime Victims Unit at St. Luke's Hospital in Manhattan, which had a history of advocacy and counseling for gay men. Kite had talked with Crime Victims Unit counselor Jane Seskin and was already in touch with the Manhattan District Attorney's office. His allegations against Ritter were gaining momentum.

By November 10, Kite had called me back at the *Post* and began informing me of each stage of the investigation. After his first meeting with the D.A.'s office, he called the *Post* again. He told me he had met with the "police," but he didn't know exactly who.

"I've been talking to Linda. Uh, I don't remember her last name," he said.

"Do you mean Linda Fairstein?" I asked.

"Yes, that's it. Fairstein," Kite said.

For Linda Fairstein, head of the Manhattan District Attorney's office Sex Crimes Unit, to be involved in the case meant the scandal was gaining speed. It seemed hard to believe that the District Attorney would take the case seriously. One could easily speculate that Kite was just a manipulative, disturbed kid who hadn't gotten what he wanted from Ritter emotionally or even financially and had fabricated a charge of sexual misconduct in response.

But why would a prosecutor, especially a powerhouse like Fairstein, who hated to lose cases, take Kite's charges so seriously?

In the early stages of the investigation, Fairstein met with Kite regularly. They were becoming friends, or at least allies, and Kite was on a first-name basis with Linda and her husband, Justin. After listening to Kite's first concealed recording of his conversation with Ritter on the afternoon of November 15, Fairstein quipped to Kite: "It's not bad, I'd give it a six. But you can't dance to it."

Although the dialogue on the tape implied a sexual relationship between Ritter and Kite, there was in fact nothing specific that would confirm it in a court of law, and certainly there was nothing illegal, per se, about the sex. What Kite needed to establish on tape was a quid pro quo of sex for money. That would be considered fraudulent use of the charity's funds. Kite told Fairstein that he had another "appointment" with Ritter scheduled for Sunday night, November 19. Again, the wire team was brought in, this time to hide the small Nagra SN tape recorder in the pocket of the green down jacket that Ritter had given him. As scheduled, they met at Ritter's apartment at 6:30 P.M. The tape was rolling.

Sitting on the couch with his briefcase opened, Father Bruce was finishing up some paperwork. He didn't raise his head, but glanced quickly at Kevin over his reading glasses as he entered.

"I'll be with you in a second," he said. "Do you mind if we go to Kraft's and just get something quick?"

"Sure," said Kite.

Ritter closed his briefcase and put on a new hat, a Russian-style cap with fur lining. They headed for Kraft's Diner on Forty-second Street, just around the corner from Covenant House. As they walked in, Ritter studied his hat self-consciously in the reflection of the glass door.

"What do you think of the hat?" he asked Kite with a boyish smile.

"It looks fine," said Kite in a dry, uninterested voice. He smiled to himself that he could still have the ability to knock the wind out of Ritter's arrogance with something as simple as a "bitchy" comment about a hat. Ritter took it off as they walked in the door.

Ritter ordered soup and some pasta, and then began devouring the rolls in the breadbasket. They talked about President Reagan's visit the week before and the girl in the audience who had asked Reagan why he spent so much money on the military.

"I'll always be polite to him in my house," said Ritter, while he buttered his bread. "No matter how you look at it, it's good publicity. And that's what pays the bills."

Then Ritter got down to the business of mentoring.

"Let's rehash the whole thing. Tell me why you're not happy at school," he said.

Talking over dinner, Kite said he was skipping class because he was depressed with his life. Ritter responded that he was confused and disappointed by Kite's sudden disappearance, which was why he had turned off Kite's weekly stipend. Ritter suggested that perhaps Kite was not ready for the responsibility of college and that he should get a job.

With Covenant House staff workers coming in and out of the diner for coffee and sandwiches, it wasn't a good place for Kite to bring up anything controversial. After dinner, he and Father Bruce walked back up to Ritter's apartment for what was shaping up as their usual Sunday-night ritual.

Inside the apartment, Kite carefully placed his jacket over the arm of the couch, with the concealed microphone pointing out. Ritter turned on the television.

The movie *Klute* was on. Kite almost laughed out loud at the irony as Jane Fonda, playing a prostitute, talked to a john while the film kept shifting to a scene of an investigator secretly tape-recording their conversations.

Then Kite stood up. He knew he had work to do. Quid pro quo, he thought to himself.

"I'm going to get a beer," he said as he went into the kitchen.

Kite came back and Ritter moved closer to him on the couch, rubbing his chest and remarking, "You are getting thin, aren't you?"

"I don't know," said Kite. "This movie is really bothering me."

Kite stood up again. There was no sense getting a sexual encounter on tape since it wouldn't help the case. Besides, the tape was running out. He went straight for the jugular, trying to link their personal relationship to money.

"You said if I came to visit you I'd get my money back. Now I want my money. I didn't get my check because you turned it off," said Kite, his words sounding a little bit stiff but trying to make sure he phrased things properly. "I came to see you the other night and tonight and now I want my money."

"Okay, I'll make sure that John Spanier turns your check back on," said Ritter.

Kevin grabbed his coat, said goodbye, and closed the door behind him. It was the last time he would see Bruce Ritter. Walking directly home, he took the tape recorder out of his pocket and placed it on the kitchen table. He lit up a cigarette and called Linda Fairstein at her Upper East Side apartment.

"Just a minute, Justin and I are watching *Klute*," said Fairstein. "Let me turn it down."

"I can't believe it—you're watching it while I was out living it," said Kite, laughing nervously.

The next day, Kite returned to Fairstein's office with the tape recorder, which was again shipped off for duplication and a transcript. While Kite was in her office, District Attorney Robert Morgenthau came by.

"I'd like you to meet our star witness," said Fairstein, as Morgenthau shook Kevin Kite's hand.

The week of November 20, on the eighth floor of the Manhattan District Attorney's office, the distinguished lawman Robert Morgenthau was smoking a cigar in a high-back blue leather chair framed by a wall of photographs that included a black-and-white shot of Robert Kennedy. Investigations Bureau Chief Michael Cherkasky, Assistant D.A. in the Rackets Bureau Dan Castleman, and Fairstein were sitting at a long polished mahogany table. They listened to words of caution from Morgenthau, who saw such a highly controversial case as one that needed direction. If they proceeded, they were targeting a Catholic icon, and they'd damned well better be right about it.

Discussions in the early part of the investigation centered on what, if any, crime had been committed by the revered Franciscan priest in his relationship with Kevin Kite. The sexual aspect, if true, was indeed a violation of the Church's strict doctrine on celibacy and a horrible violation of the trust placed in a child-care worker, but it was in no way illegal. Ritter and Kite were consenting adults. There was no evidence of rape or sexual harassment. Kite admitted that the sex was of his own free will, even if he did feel it was a misuse of trust and a manipulative exercise of Ritter's power.

The only criminal act, it seemed, was that Ritter was using Covenant House funds to pay for a "private affair" with a client of the organization. A quid pro quo of sex for money could be legal grounds for a case of fraudulent use of charitable funds. The shady expenditures on Kite also raised some broader questions about the fiscal integrity of Covenant House. Certainly it was worth poking around in the nonprofit organization's books. The investigators had already had a hint of "irregularity" at Covenant House just one month prior to Kite's arrival, when they had arrested four people in connection with an unrelated petty fraud at the charity.

After the briefing, Morgenthau transferred the case out of the Sex Crimes Unit and into the Investigation Bureau. It seemed obvious that if the investigation was going to go anywhere it was going to go in the direction of charity fraud. Cherkasky was busy with the high-profile racketeering trial of Mafia boss John Gotti, reputed head of the Gambino crime family in New York City.

Therefore, the case was largely the responsibility of Castleman, a cagey, methodical prosecutor. After the Thanksgiving holiday, Castleman started pushing ahead with the case and setting up interviews. One of the first on the list was Monica Kaiser. When she walked in the side door of the D.A.'s office at 1 Hogan Place, she knew she was walking away not from just a job but from a spiritual mission that was a large part of her life. She was about to turn evidence on a man she had once believed should be canonized.

Walking down the long corridors of the D.A.'s office, past cops in uniform, undercover detectives, attorneys with briefcases, and prosecutors with bulging case files tucked under their arms, Kaiser was frightened. She wanted guarantees of confidentiality, promises that the media would not get hold of her name. Through hours of in-

terviews with Castleman she spelled out her questions about the relationship between Kite and Ritter, about the money made available
to Kite, about the night at the hotel, about the rumors, and about
her suspicions that something was very wrong. She had no direct
proof of sexual misconduct, but she believed Kevin Kite was telling
the truth.

On December 2, a white van from the Manhattan District Attorney's office pulled up in front of the Forty-sixth Street apartment
building where Ritter had provided Kite with his own one-bedroom
apartment. Two plainclothes employees of the D.A.'s office quickly
loaded Kite's possessions into boxes and carried them out to the van.
They drove up to Kite's private dorm room at Manhattan College in
the Bronx and seized the computer, the furnishings, and just about
everything else Ritter had bought for Kite, as evidence in the developing case.

Kite was placed in the Witness Aid Program and put up in the
Mayflower Hotel on the West Side. He was given a $15-a-day stipend
for food—a lot less than he had got from Covenant House. Kite was
told not to talk to reporters, but the first thing he did when he got
there was call the *Post*.

Confirmation that Kite had been placed in the Witness Aid Program moved the investigation beyond the preliminary stages. The
Manhattan D.A. had now completed two wires and several weeks of
interviews; he had seized evidence and was now using taxpayers'
dollars to protect the witness. Through the next week, law-enforcement sources confirmed the details of the investigation. Things were
beginning to move fast.

On December 6, I telephoned Ritter in New Orleans for what
would be my only extensive one-on-one interview with him on Kite's
allegations and the D.A.'s investigation. Trying to resist the learned
deference to priests that comes with a Catholic upbringing, I went
straight to the point, asking questions about his sexuality, about Kite's
claims, and about all the sordid details that had surfaced. Ritter was
sitting in the shadows of a small office that doubled as the sacristy at
the Covenant House chapel in New Orleans, preparing to say mass.
My questions caught him off guard.

"God, no. It's not true," Ritter said. "I'm so careful. I'm so careful,"
he added, as if talking to himself. "God, why is he doing this?"

Right away the words struck me as strange. What does he mean,
"careful"? Careful about what? There was a long pause. I said nothing. Then Father Ritter launched into a rambling discourse.

"I think one possibility here is that I am being set up by organized crime. I fought them on pornography, on prostitution rings. I've even named names in talks across the country, names like Matty The Horse Ianniello, the people who run Show World [a strip joint in Times Square]. . . . I think it is deadly serious. I think Timmy is trying to save himself from the mob. . . . Before you make any moves you have to realize that this is life or death for Covenant House, if not me personally. I'm not going to be able to recover from this even when the grand jury says there is no evidence. I've got to have a chance before you break a story like this to respond to it."

His tone was one of desperation rather than indignation. I had expected the latter. His wall of alibis seemed almost rehearsed, as if some horrible premonition had suddenly become reality. And any reporter who hears a public figure first defend his actions by saying it was the "Mafia" grows immediately more suspicious. Such a predictable defense only ratchets up the level of cynicism.

"He [Kite] was involved in a male escort service run by the Mafia," Ritter continued, still groping for an explanation, "and as he became older and less attractive as a prostitute, the Mafia was making him do drug running. He was trying to escape from organized crime because he was a mule. We believed he was in great danger of being killed."

"Why do you think the District Attorney, a responsible law-enforcement agency, would be investigating these allegations so thoroughly then?" I asked.

"I don't know. There can't be any evidence," he quickly responded.

Then Father Ritter abruptly turned his tactics, suggesting in a more subtle way that perhaps the District Attorney had reason to want to hurt his reputation.

"There has always been a certain antagonism there," Ritter said.

"Are you saying that the District Attorney may be out to get you?"

"No, no, not at all. I don't know. I don't understand this."

Father Ritter knew better than to badmouth the investigators who were after him. He backed off that tactic quickly. He began to sound more and more like any other public figure caught in a scandal, foraging for alibis. We had not even gone through the details of the accusations and he was constructing elaborate defenses.

I needed to know some facts. So I asked straight questions about his relationship with "Tim Warner," as Kite was being referred to.

"He came to the program here in New Orleans, claiming that he was in danger from a prostitution ring. He was brought back to New York to keep him safe. That's not his real name," said Ritter.

"But why was he given a private apartment in midtown, a private dorm room and scholarship to Manhattan College, over a thousand dollars in furnishings, his own personal computer, and weekly checks for spending money? I have copies of the receipts. What are all these expenses? Is that normal for a youth at Covenant House?" I asked.

"Tim was a very flamboyant youth. He needed the privacy, he needed to get away from the school environment. . . . We were helping him. All of those checks were for food and so he could get started again. . . . The whole thing is crazy. We thought we were helping him. He started out doing very well in school, like a house on fire. But he couldn't handle the pressure. . . . Covenant House tried to set up job interviews for him. He wouldn't show up. He had fallen back into rotten street habits: lying, borrowing money, saying it was for food and buying clothes and things with it. We tried so hard to help that kid. Why is he doing this?"

"Have you ever gone away on a weekend with him or done anything that could give someone the appearance that perhaps you were having an intimate or sexual relationship with him?" I asked.

Ritter paused.

"On one occasion we went away to upstate New York. It was his first weekend in the city," said Ritter.

"Were there any other occasions?" I asked.

"No."

"You never went away with him anywhere else?"

"Oh, yes. There was a funeral in New Jersey. So we drove down to the wake and drove back."

This was critical. That car ride was after his accuser had been wired by the Manhattan District Attorney, and a *Post* photographer and I had even staked out their departure. We had photographs of Ritter in the car with Kite. I knew Ritter had lied about the number of weekends they spent together at the mansion in upstate New York. He also didn't mention that he had stayed in the same hotel room with Kite one night the previous summer. For the time being, I was just letting the line run. The key was the conversation in the car on the way to the funeral.

"What did you and Tim talk about in the car?"

"I don't remember. His school work. Why he wasn't going to school. How he was doing in general. That's about it."

"Did he ask you about any sexual relationship that he believed you were having?" I asked.

Ritter paused again. He seemed to be thinking a lot before he spoke. That was understandable.

"He did mention something. I couldn't really hear what he was saying in the car. It was raining very hard. I think I asked him what he meant and we didn't really talk about any sexual relationship. Why? What is this? Did he say that was what we talked about?" asked Ritter. "You know, when you work this closely with kids you always run the risk of being accused of something like that."

During the thirty-minute phone interview, Ritter started to unravel. He told me he had to get off the phone to say the 5:30 P.M. mass. I hung up, trying to imagine Father Ritter sitting in the sacristy preparing to celebrate the most sacred communion—the holy Eucharist—with a congregation of people who believed in his mission.

Before he went out to the altar, Ritter quickly called Kells and his assistant, George Wirt, at Covenant House in New York. Wirt picked up the phone. Their conversation was short, but Wirt could hear the quivering in Ritter's voice and it worried him. Then Kells came to the phone.

"I want you to be available, there is something happening. The *Post* has a story about an investigation by the District Attorney. I'll have to call you back," said Ritter.

Kells said he would wait for Ritter to call back, but asked Ritter for a quick rundown of what it was all about.

"It's complicated. It's about Tim Warner and it sounds pretty serious," said Ritter. "He's accusing me of spending a lot of money on him and something about misusing funds. There was some mention of a sexual relationship."

Kells sank into his chair. He demanded to know more. Mass would have to wait.

"What is this all about?" asked Kells.

"I don't know the details," said Ritter.

Wirt and Kells were worried. They had never heard Ritter so shaken. He was always confident and quick on the phone. Now he sounded as if he were on the verge of tears.

"You didn't say anything to the reporter, did you?" asked Kells.

"Yes," said Ritter.

"What?" asked Kells. He was fearing the worst. He knew all too well how reckless Ritter could be with the press.

"Well, I told him that it was absolutely not true and that we need some time to respond. And I told him that I thought maybe it was the Mafia who was setting me up," replied Ritter.

"Don't say another word if he calls back," said Kells, already picturing the garish blockletter headlines in the *New York Post*. Kells knew how bad it was that Ritter had brought up the Mafia. He knew a reporter could make such a defense look ridiculous in print. He knew he had a crisis on his hands.

"John, I have to go," said Ritter, hanging up the phone. "I'll call back."

In the shadows of the sacristy, Ritter donned his vestments. Then he walked out into the fading light across the courtyard. The mass would be held in the auditorium because the chapel was too small for the two hundred staff members, donors, and runaways who had gathered to hear Father Ritter. Before he arrived, he was stopped in the courtyard by Alex Comfort, the head of fund raising at the New Orleans chapter. Alex was with a wealthy Louisiana woman who had decided to donate $40,000 a year to the charity for the next three years. She wanted to meet the priest whose newsletters and mission she so admired. She wanted to hand him the check in person. Comfort figured the mass could wait for a $120,000 commitment. It was a terrible moment. Ritter's mind must have been reeling with visions of a national scandal. Nevertheless, he stopped in the courtyard. He took a deep breath and summoned his concentration while the elderly woman showered him with praise for his work and his compassionate writing about the children he saved. It was the kind of flattery and admiration that Ritter had learned to accept graciously.

"Thank you very much," said Father Bruce, keeping his practiced tone of appreciation without pandering. "Your donation will do so much to help my kids. There are just so many of them."

Ritter stepped out into the auditorium of the New Orleans chapter of Covenant House and genuflected before a table that served as the altar. He bowed his head and began the mass before a reverent congregation. In his homily, he discussed "life at Covenant House after Bruce Ritter."

His voice, as always, was somber. It droned like a church organ—lyrical but heavy with meaning. It commanded attention. He talked about what would happen to Covenant House in the coming years. He talked about the importance of making sure it remained an organization faithful to his Franciscan Order. He said that when it came time for him to "leave with my gold watch off into the sunset" he had faith that his staff would carry on the mission he had started twenty years ago.

Father Bruce had talked before about how Covenant House would carry on without him, mostly around the time he discovered he had cancer. But that talk had quieted down considerably since he had beaten Hodgkin's disease and was in solidly good health. No one realized the homily was a veiled acknowledgment that his time might be up. The telephone call was like the cock crowing for the second time in the Garden, a sign that Bruce and his mission would soon be betrayed. The homily struck a note of finality, a recognition that things would never be the same.

According to the liturgical calendar, the readings Ritter would have marked in his lectionary for that day—the eve of the Feast of St. Ambrose—were from the Book of Isaiah and the Gospel According to Matthew. The second reading from Matthew was titled "The True Disciple" and dealt with the importance of carrying out the good works of the Lord to enter the Kingdom of Heaven:

"Everyone who listens to these words of mine and acts on them will be like a sensible man who built his house on rock. Rain came down, floods rose, gales blew and hurled themselves against that house, and it did not fall: it was founded on rock. But everyone who listens to these words of mine and does not act on them will be like a stupid man who built his house on sand. Rain came down, floods rose, gales blew and struck that house, and it fell; and what a fall it had!"

Ritter left abruptly that night, having canceled his address to the annual board meeting to catch the next flight back to New York.

Within minutes of getting off the phone with Ritter, Kells called me at the *Post*, panicking and groping for information. We arranged to meet at 9 A.M. the next day to go through the allegations. Throughout the eight-hour meeting, Kells did his public-relations voodoo dance, throwing skeletons across the story's path. He talked about how he once had made a "horrible mistake" in the "blind pursuit of a story." It was a report on teenage prostitution, he said, and he had failed to conceal the identity of a young male hustler, only to find out later that he had been "beaten severely" by his pimp.

"That's why I took this job. It just made me rethink everything," said Kells. "I know what it's like to have your priorities in the wrong place. I mean, for me, this is a kind of journalistic penance. I do it for almost nothing."

(It wasn't until weeks later, when I had had more time to pore over the records, that I discovered Kells's actual salary was over $100,000. Kells had also just completed the paperwork on a loan from Covenant House for $100,000 as an incentive to stay in the organization. His last job, as a midlevel editor at a Houston television station, had paid only about $38,000. Some penance.

(Anne Donahue, who was a close friend of Kells, later suggested that the tone of dishonesty that Kells established in the early stages of the scandal contributed to an escalation of media attacks on the organization.)

During the interview, Kells called in Covenant House's attorney Ed Burns, and the two of them played a lot of games. When all documentation on the safe-house program was requested, they at first said it would take a while to dig it up. Later they said that the program was so secretive that no documentation existed. When confronted with the financial documents showing elaborate expenditures on Kite, they conceded that the documents were authentic, but disputed the allegation that they were excessive.

Greg Loken was then trotted out and stated that there were only two youths out of the twenty thousand they cared for each year who were involved in this safe-house program. He said that the other youth was currently living with him in his home in the Bronx and was also attending Manhattan College. Although the other youth did not have a private apartment or a personal computer, or as many expenditures on clothing and petty cash as Kite, Loken claimed they were at least comparable.

"It's very difficult to protect them, it is also very expensive, but that's what we do," said Loken.

I asked for all documentation on "Tim Warner," but was told that the request was out of the question because all information on clients at Covenant House was "strictly confidential."

"We just don't do it, no matter what happens. We are in the business of advocacy. That is our priority," said Loken righteously. He also added that the organization—by maintaining its policy of absolute confidentiality—had in the past incurred the wrath of several law-enforcement agencies seeking information about Covenant House clients.

Kells and Loken disappeared out of the office for long stretches of time; at one point I walked down the hall to see where they were and was quickly escorted back to the conference room. They also told me Ritter wasn't in the building, although I later learned he was. I asked to speak to Monica Kaiser and was told she was "out sick." In fact, she was under a kind of house arrest. Her phone was monitored and her messages were pored over by the Covenant House faith police.

A source in the D.A.'s office had said there was something illegal going on with the "Mass Account," which was money contributed to Father Ritter by donors who wanted him to say masses in honor of their loved ones. The books were reluctantly brought out—with whiteout over many of the entries. I took notes on everything and photocopied what I was allowed to. There was a feeling of panic in the air, which fueled more suspicion. Despite all the deceptive and aggressive tactics, no one simply said the allegations weren't true. No one bothered to calmly ask that we not run the story until they could speak with the D.A. and clear up what could have simply been a horrible misunderstanding.

I left Covenant House knowing that there was a lot that didn't make sense. But there was one thing that was particularly troubling— Ritter's claims that he had fallen into the hands of what he still perceived as two of his worst enemies: the Manhattan D.A.'s office and the gay community. It was easy to dismiss the Mafia as a paranoid excuse from a man who was caught, but any grudge by law enforcement or the gay community had to be explored.

One lead suggested that Kite might have been involved in a conspiracy by one of the militant gay groups. David Wertheimer, a city Human Rights Commissioner and a founder of the Gay and Lesbian Anti-Violence Project, had been called in as an adviser to St. Luke's staff members on Kite's case before it was presented to the Manhattan D.A.'s office. Wertheimer told the staff at St. Luke's that allegations of Ritter's homosexuality had been surfacing for years and he recommended that Seskin contact the Sex Crimes Unit of the Manhattan District Attorney's Office.

The case's connection in the early stages to such a prominent member of the gay-rights community lent some credence to Ritter's claims. Wertheimer, however, realized that he could contaminate the case by creating the perception that it was a "gay conspiracy" rather than a valid criminal investigation. He backed off as soon as the allegation became a criminal investigation and refused to be quoted in the press. He was at times deceptive with reporters, telling them that he did not even know Kite, when in fact Kite claims the two had actually met to discuss the case. But Wertheimer seemed to have legitimately distanced himself from the entire affair. Throughout my extensive interviews with scores of Covenant House staff members, senior staff officials, and members of the board of directors, not one of them suggested with any plausibility that Father Ritter's downfall was the result of a conspiracy within the gay community or an "outing" of the Franciscan priest.

It was late Friday afternoon and the *Post* decided to hold the story over the weekend. The Covenant House board members were already working behind the scenes, calling each other back and forth. Ellen Levine even called her fellow board member Dr. Jim Kennedy with a question she broached delicately. Wasn't it impossible for a man at the age of sixty-two who had suffered through heavy doses of chemotherapy to have sex?

Ritter's long-time friend was embarrassed by the question, but offered his medical opinion. "No," Kennedy said, an erection for Father Bruce was "not a physical impossibility."

Anne Donahue was in Los Angeles at the time with Harnett, who rushed back to handle the crisis. When he arrived in New York, Harnett began calling the board members to inform them that there would be an emergency meeting on Monday. A telephone tag game was played within the inner circle of Covenant House with the few facts they had. Everything was distorted and disjointed, and the board members were in a panic. But when Harnett called Levine, she responded somewhat differently from the rest of the board. She wasn't afraid to ask the obvious but difficult questions.

"Could this be true, Jim?" she wanted to know.

"I don't think so," Harnett replied.

Ritter told Harnett not to call Macauley. He wanted to make that call himself.

"Bob, there have been some allegations made against me that are coming out in the paper and I wanted you to know about them," said Ritter, going on to explain in vague terms that they involved a sexual allegation. Ritter assured Macauley that they were ridiculous. With his corporate mentor, it was important that Ritter maintain his composure, just as a CEO would in the face of a brewing scandal in his company.

They talked briefly and Macauley "got on the horn right away" to Bill Simon and Peter Grace. To defend their protégé and patron saint, the corporate trilogy came up with plans of their own. They had the advertising firm of Young & Rubicam put together full-page ads for the *Washington Post* and *The New York Times,* which they wanted to run the following Sunday to counteract the anticipated bad publicity.

"Y & R had it back to me by fax in one hour. They were to be paid for and signed by me, Peter, and Bill. I knew we had to go on the offensive. You don't just sit around, for God's sake. It was time to defend the man," said Macauley.

Over the weekend, Levine's reporting instincts had her reaching out to friends for a more objective analysis of the situation.

Levine talked about what she calls her "homosexual sonar."

"I was doing my litmus test. Women often think they can tell if someone is gay. I never got any vibes from Bruce Ritter. I just didn't think it was possible that Bruce Ritter was sleeping with that young man."

She also began lining up heavy artillery in the defense of her friend Father Ritter. She called John Scanlon, a public-relations expert, who had represented everyone from mobsters to politicians to greedy corporations. Scanlon was regarded as one of the most effective spin doctors in the country.

When Levine told him about the story that was to break in the *Post,* the first thing that struck him was a memory from the previous summer when Ritter had been awarded $200,000 at the home of the leveraged-buyout king and Covenant House board member Ted Forstmann. After the dinner, Scanlon's wife, a psychologist, had told him she was convinced Ritter was gay because of his intense commitment as well as his obsession with young male prostitutes. Scanlon knew firsthand from his years in the seminary, before he dropped out of a "vocation in the priesthood" for a more lucrative vocation in public relations, that homosexuality was part of the "fabric" of seminary life and the priesthood. Scanlon is a brutally candid man. It was not that he was shocked by the charge that a priest would be gay or break his vows, it was that he didn't believe Ritter was capable of such a betrayal of trust.

"I had seen a fair amount of homosexuality [in the seminary]," says Scanlon. "I mean in fact a couple of times was involved in it myself as a kid. You know, the kind of affairs of the heart. You are in the seminary and the only thing that fucking looks good is the freshman when you are a senior. There was a lot of wrestling and so on and so forth and massaging of genitalia. (laughter) You know but that is a fairly common thing. (laughter) I mean I never [did anything]. But there was a lot of wrestling."

"It's one thing for a priest to be homosexual, even to have homosexual relationships. But this was just such an affront to any kind of moral sense that we have. This was a guy who was in the business of finding these kids, caring for them. And a large number of these kids were probably where they were because of the sexually abhorrent things that had been done to them. The notion was just so stunning and shocking that I couldn't believe it. I didn't believe it."

Scanlon insists that the work he did for Covenant House in the preliminary stages of the scandal was minimal and pro bono. His immediate advice to Levine was to move forward with a libel suit against the *New York Post* as quickly as possible. He advised the board to retain Cravath, Swaine, & Moore, the large and powerful New

York law firm that represented both defendants in two of the most explosive libel trials in recent history: *CBS* v. *General William Westmoreland* and *Ariel Sharon* v. *Time*. Cravath is known as much for its thoroughness as its aggressiveness. The firm has been described as a "pack of Dobermans clamoring to be unleashed."

After speaking with Levine, Scanlon met with the Covenant House attorney Ed Burns.

"I had a long talk with Burns and recommended that they hire Cravath and begin to plot the potential strategy for a libel suit," says Scanlon. "I am a big believer in planning."

Scanlon concedes that it was obvious there were no apparent grounds for a successful libel action if the *Post* was reporting that the Manhattan District Attorney was investigating Ritter. Instead, the strategy of threatening a libel suit was part of a national trend, as both the CBS and *Time* trials illustrated. Highly publicized libel attacks could be used as tools of vindication by the powerful and as a means to drain resources from any recalcitrant media that might threaten their power. Such suits are called "nuisance suits" in bars where lawyers hang out, and had chilled newsrooms across the country not with just caution, but with fear.

The plans to bring legal action against the *Post* were never executed, although Cravath was retained by Covenant House, and bullying language and veiled threats were volleyed at the *Post* by Kells before and during the stories. Having Cravath's "Doberman" attorneys on a leash was part of a broader strategy of killing the messenger. The plan was to make the *Post*'s coverage of the story the focus of reporters' attention rather than the allegations against Ritter.

"I was doing everything I could to piss on the story," says Scanlon. "The *Post* had a real credibility problem. So the plan was to go for blood. . . . The story read like it was from the school of journalism where you just march a guy into the D.A.'s office and then say this is a story. That's why I thought the story was bullshit. No one knew what [the *Post*] had gone through in the reporting on this."

Levine would take all of Scanlon's advice back to the board in a series of crucial meetings and phone calls over the weekend. But there was one more phone call Levine had to make: to Ritter himself. She'd developed a tremendous respect for Ritter as a man of compassion. But, understanding a "boyish quality about him," she also knew he was very vulnerable. They were very close friends. In fact, Ritter used to joke publicly about his affection for Levine.

"If I weren't a priest, I'd marry you," Ritter would often say to her at board meetings or fund raisers.

It was Sunday night and an emergency meeting of the board was scheduled for the next day. Levine was at home in New Jersey, where she lives with her husband and two sons. She personifies what one would expect of the editor-in-chief of a leading woman's magazine— glamorous, intelligent, confident, and someone who has "no problem talking about sex." Levine felt an urgent need to talk with Ritter in person about the allegation. It was late when she called his apartment.

"Bruce, what was the nature of your relationship?" she asked.

When Ritter paused, she broke the silence and rephrased the question.

"Is it true?" she asked, one of Ritter's few confidantes with the candor to put the question to him directly.

"Oh, God, no," said Ritter. "It is not true. I mean, what can I say? How do you defend yourself against that?"

She remembers that Ritter's voice sounded "deep and troubled."

Levine was not reassured by the course of the conversation. To her, perhaps the most worrisome piece of information she had been able to gather was that the District Attorney had wired Ritter's accuser. She asked Ritter to try as best he could to reconstruct the conversation. Ritter sounded frantic, worried.

"I don't know. . . . I don't know," he said. "I cannot remember. It was raining very hard, that's all I remember."

Levine believed that Ritter's accuser was a "complete sleazoid," as she still refers to him. She thought the *Post* was a "rag" and that the story was "the worst kind of trash." Nonetheless, she was consumed with questions. Why was Father Bruce so evasive on the conversation in the car? Why was there so much worry at Covenant House, and not more anger at such a ridiculous charge? There was no reason to be worried, she thought. If nothing had happened, the truth would eventually come out. Why was a man of so much faith so paranoid about the attack on his character? It's not true, she assured herself. She didn't sleep at all that night.

Chapter 15

The Story Is About S.E.X.

THE windows in the newsroom at the *New York Post* framed a December sky washed in gray, the piers of the South Street Seaport, and the dark, swirling waters of the East River. In the background, the spires and cables of the Brooklyn Bridge arched out over the river, carving an elegant silhouette before it all seemed to disappear into the fog over Brooklyn. It was Monday, December 11, 1989. A hard rain was falling.

Inside the sprawling newsroom, fluorescent lights glared off grimy gray walls and a mud-tracked carpet. Police radios crackled with crime codes and reporters clicked away on banks of big, old computers—secondhand clunkers picked up cheap. Phones rang and editors shouted orders for Chinese food.

Metropolitan editor John Cotter and managing editor Lou Cola-suonno were standing around the layout desk trying to come up with one of the bold headlines that made the *Post* famous.

It was just after 3 P.M., and they were having a hard time getting just the right words to fit the headline on the Father Ritter exclusive that would run in the next day's editions. In just a few hours, the presses would be rolling; the bundles would be loaded into fleets of trucks and delivered to newsstands across the city, serving up scandal to some 500,000 construction workers, Wall Street traders, taxi drivers, housewives, drug dealers, sports fans, mobsters, New Yorkers.

At the *Post*, they still call the front page "The Wood"—an anachronism from the days of lead-line type, when the large, garish letters in the headlines were carved out of wooden blocks. Even in the age of computer graphics, the oldest daily newspaper in the country held on to the language of its tradition. That tradition was perhaps the only thing sacred at the *Post*. Everything else was fair game.

Taking a stark file photo of Father Ritter in his priest's collar and moving it around on the layout paper, Colasuonno used a thick red grease pencil to jot down a few working headlines. Ritter's name was recognizable enough to use in the headline. But he didn't like the way it looked to abbreviate priest. "Fr." and "Rev." didn't fit well on the page. He wanted something simple that jumped out at the reader, that had just the right tone, that, above all, would sell papers.

Cotter and Colasuonno started laughing. The front-page layout desk is also where the best jokes of the day come from in a newsroom known for its black humor. The ethics of running the Ritter story had been debated for over a week at a newspaper that had not become famous for debates about ethics. The tension fueled a kind of fiendish mischievousness, making the soon-to-fall priest a goldmine of one-liners for the newsroom's most impious wags.

"How about 'Kingdom Cum'?" said Colasuonno, running his hands across the blank layout sheet to show where the two lines of block letters could fit neatly beside the picture of Father Ritter. Bawdy laughter broke out, which Charlie Carillo heard from his desk across the newsroom. Carillo's running monologue of one-liners and practical jokes were well known at the *Post*. He walked through the newsroom and approached the front-page layout desk as if greeting an audience. Mimicking a thick Brooklyn accent, Carillo belted out his idea for the perfect headline.

"Turn the Other Cheek," said Carillo.

Colasuonno and Cotter were laughing harder, and it was spilling into other parts of the newsroom. Carillo's timing is perfect. He waited for the moment the laughter died down to come up with another: "Our Father Who Art in Kevin."

There was a small group of people in the newsroom laughing fitfully and shaking their heads. As it faded Cotter walked into his office, unconsciously massaging a small tan patch of nitroglycerin that was taped to his chest. The glycerin patch was there to open the arteries and shock life into a heart that had already endured a full cardiac arrest. Cotter's heart was known as much for its weakness as for its warmth.

A red-faced Irish newspaperman of another era, he thrived on instinct and adrenalin for more than a quarter of a century in the business, and was one of the most respected editors in the city's tabloid wars. An intellectual posing as a profane practitioner of print journalism, Cotter was as well versed in Graham Greene and James Joyce as he was in John Gotti and Al Sharpton. The loyal commander of the *Post*'s troops rarely sat at his desk. He alternately paced in the small office and stood with one leg up on a radiator and stared out a window at the rain. Cotter knew how big this story was. He was annoyed at me for being too cautious in my reporting. This was a newspaper war and he didn't want to get beat. In one conversation I questioned the ethics of reporting an admitted male prostitute's allegations against a legendary priest, especially since the D.A. was focusing on fraud, not sex. To Cotter, the question was tabloid blasphemy.

"This is not fucking morality, it's the *New York Post,* pal. The story is about sex. S.E.X.," he said, punching the air with each letter for emphasis.

"This isn't some fucking course in ethics, this is a newspaper. You're going soft on this story. Let's get it in the paper. I'll kill you if we get our ass kicked."

Then Cotter broke the tension by laughing—a kind of slow cackle—under his breath. Snapping between his teeth one of the cigar-size pretzel sticks that he kept in a plastic container on his desk, he added, "Besides, you're insubordinate."

This was the kind of story that Cotter described as "rockin', " and, once it got rolling, it could set him off on silent Keith Richards–inspired choruses of air guitar in the middle of the newsroom or at Maguire's bar when the early editions came up just before midnight.

In a larger office next to Cotter's, the editor of the *Post,* Jerry Nachman, was devouring a roast-beef sandwich and gulping cherry soda out of a one-liter bottle. Nachman's office looked like a Natural Museum of History exhibit titled: "Newsman." There was a well-preserved Royal typewriter from circa 1930 and a baseball bat with Nachman's name carved in it. The walls were covered with reporting awards and an enormous poster for the play *The Front Page*. Scattered around the edges were half-empty packs of cigarettes, half-filled ash trays, and stacks of newspapers. Nachman wanted an update on the investigation of Ritter.

"Talk to me. What have you got?" he asked.

After listening to the facts I had gathered over a month and a half of reporting, he agreed that the paper needed to be cautious. That year the paper was salvaging its reputation from the days of hype and "Wingo" circulation games under Rupert Murdoch, the Australian-born tabloid king who had owned the paper for ten years until he sold it, in 1988, to New York real-estate developer Peter Kalikow. Under Kalikow, the *Post* had broken several major investigative stories and was conscious of improving its image. With twenty years of experience in radio and television at CBS and NBC, and having begun as a street reporter, Nachman's journalistic background is orthodox, or as he likes to put it, "I'm Jesuit trained." The Ritter story was radioactive—and no one wanted a meltdown.

"Res ipsa loquitur," Nachman blurted out. "You know what that means? It's Latin. 'The thing speaks for itself.' In other words, stick to the facts. This isn't one to fuck around on. We don't need to dress it up."

Nachman never contemplated backing off from the story. Cotter would never have let him do it. But there was a series of events the day before it ran that reassured him.

Early that afternoon, he called veteran reporter Mike Pearl, known as "The King" at Manhattan Criminal Court, where for more than twenty years he has covered every major story in the city and become a tabloid legend. Pearl had spent the morning putting feelers out to top sources in the Manhattan District Attorney's office about the Ritter investigation. He came in smiling.

"What do you think, Mike?" Nachman asked Pearl.

"I think it's a hell of a story," said Pearl. "It's solid as a rock."

"What happens if the kid is a psychopath? What happens if they drop the case?" Nachman asked.

"Then that's the next story," said Pearl, without blinking. D.A. COVERS UP PRIEST PROBE.

Pearl was kidding, but only half kidding. He was from the old school and that meant winging it. Get what you can. Run it. Let the chips fall where they will.

There was something else that struck Nachman as critical. He called it the "body language of the District Attorney's office."

The D.A. had wired Kite twice and placed him in the Witness Aid program. These were two key points that indicated the D.A. was deep into the investigation. There was no backing out. Morgenthau was taking this one seriously.

Nachman and Cotter gave the green light to write the story for the next day's editions. The angle would be that the Manhattan District Attorney's office was conducting a "fraud investigation" into whether the legendary street priest misused funds to maintain a "personal relationship" with a former male prostitute. We decided to stick to the facts of the investigation rather than rely on the young male prostitute's word. We wanted to stick solely to what our sources in the District Attorney's office were telling us. The story did include the fact that the investigation was spearheaded by the Sex Crimes Unit, which implied that there was an allegation of sex involved. It was a fine line to cut, but it's the way we played it. *Res ipsa loquitur.*

Close to deadline, Nachman got a call from Stanley Arkin, the attorney that Covenant House had hired for Ritter. Arkin had developed a specialty in criminal law, defending high-profile executives and public officials caught in sex scandals. The fact that Covenant House hired Arkin to represent Ritter showed that they were taking the D.A.'s investigation seriously. Arkin was furious and playing hardball: "This is sleazy and seamy. You better be damned careful if you print that, that's all I can say."

Nachman interrupted Arkin's rant.

"Counselor, I don't know what you are talking about. We are running a story about a defalcation," said Nachman, flaunting the kind of legalese that only attorneys listen to.

It is a vague word, but one that carries a specific legal ramification. The primary definition is "embezzlement," but it has a secondary meaning of "failure to meet an expectation or a promise." The word was meant to scare the hell out of Arkin, leaving him wondering exactly how much we knew about the Covenant House funds and Bruce Ritter's financial and sexual indiscretions. Nachman remembers that Arkin "made a strange noise on the phone," which he took to mean "Oh, shit, they know more than I thought they knew."

Upstairs on the top floor of the *Post* building, the phone was ringing in Peter Kalikow's office. The *Post*'s publisher was a relatively new player in the power game of New York City journalism. But he knew it was a game he liked. Calls came from the Covenant House board members, Church officials, politicians, and even members of the *Post*'s own staff who thought trashing a saint was a bad idea. Prominent Catholic board members, like Peter Grace and Bill Simon, had put the word out, and the high-pressure calls were aimed at blocking the story before it got to print. There was even a call from Jack Kennedy, the powerful head of the Pressmen's Union, who also happened to be the brother of Ritter's personal physician and Covenant House board member, Dr. Jim Kennedy.

Kalikow, sensing that a storm was brewing, called Nachman up to his office and asked a very simple question: "Are you sure we're right?"

Nachman had a simple answer, "Yes," and went back downstairs.

By the time he got there, there were more phone messages. Geraldine Ferraro, whose son had worked at Covenant House as a volunteer for part of his public service from a drug conviction, had gotten wind of the story. She called to tell Nachman that what he was doing was insane. She knew Bruce Ritter and knew this couldn't be true. The Governor's staff was calling and wanted to know what was going on. The archdiocese was putting out its feelers to any reporters and editors with whom it had contacts.

Valerie Salambier, the president of the *New York Post*, was also feeling the heat. A glamorous, high-powered executive, she brought aboard in the post-Murdoch era to regain the confidence of advertisers. The famous line from a Bloomingdale's executive to the *Post*— "Your readers are our shoplifters"—was tough to live down, and Salambier was doing everything she could to impress her new accounts. She had been the publisher of *TV Guide* and a senior vice president for advertising at *USA Today*. The night before, she had received a late-night phone call from Ellen Levine, whom she knew from years in the magazine business. Levine was livid.

"Valerie, what the hell is going on? Is the *Post* working on a story on Father Bruce?" she asked.

Salambier had heard the story come up in several meetings, but did not know the full details. Levine told her that Covenant House had hastily scheduled a board meeting and that it was a full-blown crisis at the charity. She told Salambier that the story, even if it turned out to be false, would destroy the largest charity in the world providing care and counseling to troubled teenagers.

At work the next day, Salambier suffered "fleeting moments of terror." She had been working hard to build up several crucial ad accounts. In a fierce battle to win advertisers, Salambier knew that a story like this could ruin not just Ritter's reputation but the advertising accounts she had carefully cultivated. She believed the story was powerful enough that if it was wrong it could conceivably kill the paper. John Cotter told her not to worry. She never interfered.

The day the story ran, Robin Farkas, chairman of Alexander's department stores, a leading retail chain, was on the phone. Alexander's was what ad execs called a "continuity advertiser," with long-term commitments. The nearly four hundred pages a year they purchased for ads were necessary for future planning of the paper's layout and pulled in more than $1 million a year in revenues.

"It was not the kind of client you want upset with a story of this magnitude," said Salambier. "There were no direct threats. It is not good form. But there were certainly points of view expressed about what a story like this would do to the 'image of the paper' and the 'demographic base' if it was not true."

Farkas, who was a supporter of Covenant House, just called to say that he was "very concerned about the story" and "a real believer in Bruce."

Salambier understood the message. Farkas' was only one of such calls of "concern" that she received that afternoon. But for a tabloid struggling to survive the newspaper war in a shrinking retail advertising market, they might as well have been holding a gun to her head. Nevertheless, the paper remained unbowed. Cotter just kept telling me to "relax" and keep working on the story.

It was 8 P.M. and the story was written, edited, and laid out. The paper was on its way from the fifth-floor cutting room to the ground-floor pressroom for the first run.

Meanwhile, at Covenant House headquarters, the emergency meeting was getting under way. The board members had had the weekend to swallow the details of what was going on but none of them were able to digest their shock and outrage, which most of them directed at the *Post*.

The focus of the meeting was "strategies of damage control." It was not a full board meeting, but the key players were there: Father Bruce, Kells, Harnett, Levine, Stroock, Burns, Macauley, Denis Coleman, Taubman, Ralph Pfeiffer, Santarsiero, and Jim Kennedy. They pulled up to the Chelsea building in their cabs and chauffeured Lincoln town cars. The "great ship" was taking on water. The full sense of panic hadn't set in yet, but alarms were going off and clearly the board members were eyeing the lifeboats. They filed into the boardroom and took their seats.

The first order of business was for Harnett to give a complete rundown on the charity's history with the youth. Reading from an intake file, Harnett gave the facts: A twenty-year-old former male prostitute was introduced to Father Ritter at Covenant House in New Orleans in mid-February. He told staff that he was a male prostitute who wanted to get out of a prostitution ring run by organized crime, but that he feared for his life. Ritter flew with the youth to New York and told him to use the name of Jim Wallace, Ritter's nephew. Later a new identity was provided for him with the name of Tim Warner. (The Covenant House board members were not told how the identity had been created and were not informed until a week later that the young man's real name was Kevin Kite, age twenty-five.) Father Ritter placed the young man in a special program and took him into a "mentor relationship." Harnett folded up the file and the meeting began.

Harnett was worried that the *Post* story would reveal a secret program that he said "a few of you may never have been informed of": the safe-house program. Actually, none of the Covenant House trustees—except Ritter, Macauley, Kells, and Harnett—had ever heard of such a program. It was explained to them as something that was developed to protect youths who were "the most high risk of all"— those caught in the world of organized crime and prostitution.

They were assured that there were minutes that documented the formation of the secret program. When board members asked for the minutes to be produced, they were told they were not available. They were never produced.

The board members were told that a youth who was part of this vague program called "safe house" was living with the head of the Legal Advocacy Department, Greg Loken. They learned about another youth who had been sent to live on a farm owned by Bob Macauley in upstate New York. There were others sent to live in a "vacation home" and in a "rectory." Altogether, there had been approximately twelve youths in the program over the last five years.

How was it possible, the board wanted to know, that they had never been informed of such a controversial program? It violated every basic standard of child care. From Ritter's point of view, that was precisely why they weren't informed.

Board member Donna Santarsiero, with more than twenty years' experience in both state- and diocesan-run social-service programs, was furious. She had seen Ritter do this kind of thing before: go ahead with whatever program he liked without bothering to seek the advice of the board or even any experts on the staff. It was part of the swashbuckling side of the great risk taker. But Santarsiero was offended and outraged that she had not been consulted on such a questionable undertaking.

She disapproved of the program immediately. There were no guidelines, no criteria for who would be admitted to the program, no accounting of it in the budget. She stated all this on the record at the meeting. Still, she restrained herself.

"It wasn't a time to be jumping down Bruce's throat," she said. "This was a time to worry about the consequences of such an allegation to the organization, an agonizing time to be sensitive to Bruce's pain."

Then it was Mark Stroock's turn. Stroock was a senior board member, vice president of one of the best advertising firms on Madison Avenue, and one of the fiercest of the Ritter loyalists. The board was relying on Stroock for direction on crisis management. He had come up with a clear game plan and a presentation. The strategy was simple: kill the messenger. Scanlon's tactics had now become the Catholic charity's policy.

"Bruce, we can get through all this. We can counteract it all because it is the *Post*," said Stroock. "We can make it look salacious. We have perfectly respectable people in the press who will write favorable things. We are going to have to call in every favor we can."

Ellen Levine's experience as a journalist told her that the story was going to explode and that the charity's initial reaction was critical. She agreed with Stroock about his "kill the messenger" tactic. She added that the board needed to prepare a press release to distribute to the media immediately after the news broke. Levine was emphatic that the board go over the language of the release and reach a consensus. It touched off another brushfire among the board members.

Kells and Stroock had a working document, which they introduced to the board. There was a reference to the youth who was making the allegation as a "highly disturbed young man" and a "sick individual."

Santarsiero had some questions. "Have we done a psychiatric test on this young man? Do we have any records?" she asked.

Then she added, "Even if he is a disturbed man, which I don't know if he is or is not, we cannot say that. It would be a complete breach of confidentiality."

Santarsiero's sensitivity was perceived as disloyalty.

"Well, what do you want to say, Donna? Should we say he is a great guy? What do you want to propose?" one of the board members retorted.

"I am just saying that we need to be careful. We are in the business of counseling troubled youths. You don't then come out and call them 'sick kids,' " Santarsiero said, realizing that a deep rift between blind loyalty to Ritter and professional standards of social work was opening up between the board members.

There were other issues that Ritter brought forward. He had been the youth's mentor and he said his way of counseling could be "misconstrued" or "misinterpreted" by the media.

Ritter told his loyalists that he had taken the youth to John Spanier's wedding in Reading, Pennsylvania. They had stayed in the same room at the hotel because he had "forgotten to mention that [he] was bringing the boy." Fearing that the media would get hold of that, Covenant House had already called the Reading Inn and warned them that if they released their records they would be violating the privacy of a guest and that it could be grounds for a lawsuit. When I called them for that information, a manager said, "We have been informed by the organization that those records should not be given out." Ritter also told them that he had taken the youth to Rhinebeck on "one or possibly two" occasions for the weekend.

Even with the scant bit of information they had, Santarsiero was appalled at the violation of all standards of propriety. The same hotel room? A private cottage? She understood that Ritter wanted to work closely and directly with the kids, but it was clearly a grave violation of any standards of social work to take a troubled young prostitute away for a weekend to a secluded cottage. That, she thought from her experience with the archdiocese, was even a violation of the guidelines set for priests in dealing with parishioners. It was not just poor judgment: It was outrageous.

She stared at Ritter and watched him provide his explanations in his solemn voice. Then her mind flashed back to the day Ritter first walked into her office, seeking to have the organization chartered. She remembered how nervous he was. She realized his face had the same expression of worry and fear on it. She thought back on all the years of power and arrogance, compassion and kindness. And she fought back a feeling that the allegations were true. She hated it; the gnawing suspicion seemed like such a betrayal. After all, this was a disturbed street youth trying to destroy a good man in a trashy newspaper. She kept setting up the facts that way to push the suspicion out of her mind.

The other board members were not suffering that kind of crisis of faith. Not yet. Ellen Levine wanted to hear more about how the board could move to file the libel suit. When would Cravath be retained?

After the presentation, Stroock did something he didn't want to do, but knew he had to do. He looked Ritter in the eye and said, "Bruce, you have to tell me if there are any more allegations that could be brought against you. Are there any kids who have ever threatened this before who might come forward? Are there any other funny-money charges that could be brought against you? You have to think back if there is anything. If there are, we must know them now. It is imperative that we don't get blindsided."

There was a pause. The other board members turned to look at Ritter, and then sensed that even looking at him while he answered could be perceived as betrayal. They bowed their heads and stared at their notepads. Ritter looked Stroock in the eye.

"Mark, there are none," he said, breaking the silence with a stern voice.

That was good enough for everyone there. Santarsiero felt some of her suspicion fading. That was all they needed to hear. Now Stroock and company were ready to declare holy war against the *Post*. Phase II of the strategy would be a full-blown press conference. But they wanted to wait and see how the story looked in the paper, to gauge the initial reaction by the other media, and see if the D.A. would drop the investigation purely from public pressure in favor of Father Bruce.

With the official order of business over, Ritter and his loyalists continued to talk informally. Ritter rumbled that he must be the target of a setup by someone—maybe in the District Attorney's office. They were all aware of what was generally perceived in Covenant House as "bad blood" between them and the D.A. Stroock and Kells and some other board members were shrewd enough to realize that attacking the D.A. was an insane course. They warned the other board members to be careful. The last thing that Ritter needed was Morgenthau mad at him. It would do nothing but hurt their chances of having the case dropped sooner rather than later.

Ritter also stated it was possible that certain "enemies of the Church" might be trying to ruin him for his controversial stand against the gay-rights legislation, or perhaps because the organization had refused to hand out condoms. Macauley was convinced that one of these "anti-Catholic groups" was behind the scandalous accusations. He was all for hiring private detectives "to bust the case wide open." The names of ACT UP, a militant gay-rights group, and Dignity, a Catholic gay-rights group, were both mentioned. There was a seething resentment in what they were saying, an implied fury that the liberal social-service groups would certainly take advantage of the scandal. It was agreed that they would have to investigate "Warner's" past to "get to the bottom of this."

It was getting late, past 10 P.M. At the *New York Post* building on South Street the ancient presses were now rolling at full speed. The first copies were bundled and loaded onto a fleet of maroon trucks emblazoned with the image of the *Post*'s founder, Alexander Hamilton.

The trucks pulled out from the loading stations and disappeared into the darkness, bound for newsstands and bodegas from every corner of Queens to every block in Brooklyn, from Manhattan all the way out to Massapequa.

TIMES SQUARE PRIEST PROBED, was the headline in two-inch block letters. "Former Male Prostitute Cites 'Gifts'—D.A. Eyes Father Ritter," read the subhead in smaller print. A red bar angled across the corner of the front-page read "Post Exclusive."

The board members picked up the early editions as they hit the stands. The story was not as bad as they thought. It was carefully constructed to chronicle the investigation by the D.A. It did not go into detail on the alleged sexual relationship. It was straight and simple.

"Well, that's it," said Stroock in a telephone conversation with Kells late that night. "Cut the *Post* off. They've shown their cards."

Kells was using words like "kick their heads in" and "time to bash back."

They hung up, unable to sleep, but prepared for the war that would begin the next morning. By 9:30 A.M., reporters were storming the Manhattan District Attorney's office for information on the investigation. They were able to get some confirmation that the story was accurate, but little more than that.

At Covenant House, television satellite trucks had pulled up in front of the building. Before the cameras, Covenant House officials stuck to terse denials: "The *Post* is chasing headlines, not the truth. . . . There will be a swarm of libel lawyers all over them. . . . We won't even merit the accusation with a response."

In his anger, Harnett forgot about the warnings not to attack the District Attorney. In an interview with the Associated Press he said, "I think it was outrageous and disgusting for the District Attorney to outfit this kid with a wire to try to entrap Father Ritter. I can tell you Father Ritter is a lot calmer about this than I am."

Showing his experience in serviceable sound bites, Arkin told reporters, "There is no criminal case, there never was a criminal case, and there never will be a criminal case. He is a victim of a wrongful accusation."

Largely owing to a crush of media, Manhattan District Attorney Robert Morgenthau made an extraordinary move on the morning of December 13. He commented on a case under investigation. Reporters like the *Post*'s Mike Pearl, who had covered the courthouse for more than twenty years, had seen that happen only once or twice before. The pressure on the District Attorney was mounting. He had to do something to give his detectives time to work.

"The investigation is in its earliest stages," said Morgenthau. "No determination has been made as to the truth of the allegations, nor can such a determination be made until the investigation has been concluded. We expect Covenant House officials to cooperate fully."

The same day Cardinal O'Connor also jumped into the fray, standing by Ritter in a statement issued to the press.

"In all my personal associations with Father Ritter and those who work with him, I have seen nothing but self-sacrifice and commitment to the most abandoned in our society. As Archbishop of New York, I have held Father Ritter's work in highest esteem."

A Church official who works in the archdiocese later remarked on the statement, pointing out the significance of the fact that O'Connor had begun referring to Ritter in the present perfect tense.

"It sounds ridiculous," he said. "But that kind of usage is agonized over. It was a way of getting distance from Ritter."

Behind the scenes, the battle was on: the Church, the law, and the press.

Covenant House was on the attack. "Spin doctor" Scanlon was working hard on his old friends and cronies. It was time to call in favors, cut shrewd deals, and use any pressure he could to change the course of the story, to redirect rivers of ink away from Ritter and send them rushing toward the *Post*. The general idea was to schmooze on the phone with the power brokers of the news world to downplay the significance of the story or, if need be, to all-out bash the *Post*.

"The *Post* is on a fucking insane course with this thing," Scanlon told one senior editor at a prominent publication. "You should blow them out of the water on this. I mean really kick their ass."

Kells called to officially inform the *Post* that we were being cut off. It was the first veiled threat of a lawsuit.

"The only communication Covenant House will have with the *Post* on this matter will be a letter from our attorneys, which you should expect shortly," said Kells, banging down the receiver after he read the statement.

But at Covenant House there was little time for anything as time-consuming as a libel suit. The public-relations machine was working until all hours, assessing damage to the organization and trying to come up with strategies to minimize it. The damage-control team was busy getting a loyal following of reporters into its corner, and handling a flood of phone calls from angry donors who wanted to know what was going on. The story could not have come at a worse time. It was the height of the fund-raising season. The two weeks before Christmas are the most important time of the year, when up to 20 percent of the annual budget is brought in. All of the plans for "positive media exposure" were drying up amid the burgeoning scandal. The networks were canceling their scheduled live shots for Christmas Day, and the magazine profiles and newspaper articles would all be swinging their attention to the priest accused of sin.

On day two of the scandal, Kells and Stroock decided it was imperative to move on to a full-blown press conference. The organization needed to try to bring the controversy under control and see what they could salvage of the Christmas fund drive. They began arrangements to hold the press conference the following morning.

They were also developing a list of columnists they could "count on." Bill Reel, of course, was at the top. They had already fed Reel some "inside information" that they believed this accusation was a conspiracy against the Church, or at least a vendetta by the D.A. They couldn't provide any facts as of yet, but they were working on it. Reel was preparing a column for the next day to blast the D.A. and the *Post*. It fiercely defended Ritter and raised questions about a conspiracy.

Newsday columnist Dennis Duggan was also on the attack. In an article with the headline "A Good Man Smeared with Rumor's Mud" Duggan took shots at the *Post* for publishing the story.

"It is one thing to drive a president from the White House," Duggan wrote. "It is quite another, and far more self-hating task we set for ourselves, when we apply whips and scorn to those among us with the courage to go where most of the rest of us dare not." One journalist would later describe this quagmire of defending Ritter as "the Irish writer's Vietnam."

Stroock read the Reel and Duggan columns in Ritter's office. Now he was confident that things were going as well as could be expected. That afternoon Stroock and Kells prepped Ritter for the press conference. They ran questions by him and used video cameras to analyze his responses. It was important that he adopt just the right tone, compassionate but forceful, concerned but not worried. He had to listen to questions and try to confront them head on.

"And don't feel like you need to answer too long," Kells added. "Just answer the questions and stop."

Kells knew how Ritter could get going and take off on a tangent. Given the current atmosphere, that could be very dangerous. This was no time for Ritter to get mystical about his "love for the kids" or about how he "owns these children" or about how he felt a certain "kinship" with the johns who pick up young hustlers. They were confident that Ritter could do it. He was a masterful public speaker, and they knew how well he could do under pressure. They coached him but they knew Ritter was better at it than either of them.

Late that afternoon Stroock and newly appointed chairman of the board Ralph Pfeiffer were in Ritter's office finishing up the details for the next day's press conference. Stroock knew public relations and he knew how important it was for the client to be completely honest, to come forward with anything, no matter how small, that could later be construed as part of the scandal. He knew he was risking his relationship with Father Bruce to do it, but he asked the question one more time.

"Bruce, things are going well. We can survive this. But you have to tell me now if there are any other allegations that could surface. Anything you can think of? As absurd as they might be, you have to tell me if any other kids ever tried to make any allegations, or threaten you, or blackmail you. If there are any questionable financial transactions, tell us," said Stroock.

He waited and then continued, "If the press finds them before we do, it's over. I cannot defend you unless I know I am not going to be hit from the blind side. If we are, we are all going down the tubes."

This time Ritter waited longer to answer. He looked hurt. The pause from Stroock's point of view seemed like pain rather than guilt. He felt bad for asking. Pfeiffer looked at him coldly. But he knew he had to do it.

"There is nothing," said Bruce.

He did not follow up with any efforts to be convincing. He just left it as a cold, stated fact.

"I believed him," said Stroock. "I believed with all my heart that he was telling the truth."

On the way out of the office, Pfeiffer put his arm around Stroock. As the former chairman of the board of IBM World Trade he knew how to manage people. It was no time to criticize anyone aboard a ship taking in that much water. It was a time to stick together. He voiced his disapproval as gently as he could.

"You've got to stop asking him that," said Pfeiffer. "You're unnerving him."

Chapter 16

▗▚▟▚▟▚▟▚▟▚▖

The Press at the Altar

IN a fourth-floor office at Covenant House's Rights of Passage building in Manhattan, Father Ritter sat in a straight-back chair with a white towel draped around his shoulders and tucked under his collar. A makeup artist dabbed rouge on his pale cheeks to prepare him for the television cameras that awaited him. It was December 14—Ritter's day of reckoning before the press.

Stan Ford, a Vietnam veteran and a kind of personal bodyguard, stood silent, almost at attention, silhouetted by the morning light through one of the round, mock porthole windows of the old Maritime building. Ford and Ritter had grown close over the years, and it was painful for Ford to watch his commander-and-chief suffer the humiliation of scandal.

Downstairs in a large auditorium, the television crews were lugging in heavy metal cases packed with sound equipment, tripods, and lighting. Bulky men in baseball jackets were there early to establish position and to plug into a hundred-unit sound system called a "mult box" for what promised to be a packed press conference. The reporters straggled in, drinking the free coffee and picking up the glossy packets of Covenant House literature that were stretched out on a long table. Each reporter was given a copy of Ritter's book

Covenant House: Lifeline to the Streets, with significant pages of the legend marked in yellow highlighter. This was micro-management of the media at its best. There was even a Christmas tree decorated with blue bulbs and white doves, which the public-relations team recommended as a "good spot for stand-ups."

Two long days had passed since the story broke. Ritter had spent most of them trying to get a handle on the press's reaction to the scandal and being prepared and briefed by his staff. There were more than one hundred reporters, photographers, and television crew members herded into the auditorium.

The press conference was a production hosted by John Kells but directed from the wings by Stroock, Los Angeles's Al Tortorella, and John Scanlon, three of the best damage-control experts in the country. Their style was to keep a very low profile, working not so much with reporters as with the powerful editors and publishers who can shape the direction of a story. They would let Kells be the front man for the press conference, cannon fodder against the army of reporters bristling with questions.

The stage was overflowing with more than thirty poinsettias in full bloom. And on a three-sided backdrop to the podium were Christmas wreaths strategically placed, giving the impression of a halo of holly around Ritter's head from just about every conceivable camera angle.

Ritter was dressed in his white collar and formal black clerical garb. He walked briskly toward the dais and squinted as he surveyed the reporters. One thing was for damn sure: This was no friendly parish. There would be no gasps from the pews at his riveting tales of life in the streets. Ritter lifted his glasses out of his left chest pocket and placed them low on the bridge of his nose. He stared down at the notes he had prepared. A thicket of microphones was taped and mounted to the dais. Every television network and major newspapers all over the country, including the *Washington Post,* the *Boston Globe,* and the *Los Angeles Times,* were represented. Ritter began:

"First of all let me deal very directly with the allegation that there has been some financial impropriety at Covenant House and most directly attributed to me by a newspaper here in New York. It has been stated in this newspaper that Covenant House and I specifically spent $25,000 on this man with whom I had a special relationship. We have just completed a full audit of the organization and they have found our books in perfect order," he said.

The reporters scribbled their notes. No one would ever bother to ask how an $85 million organization could possibly carry out a complete audit in two days. But before they could even think of that, Ritter launched into a list of numbers and expenditures. It was a public-relations ploy intended to distract from the real issue with a smoke screen of numbers.

"Every penny is accounted for. The sum expended on this young man is not $25,000. It is $9,800. Furthermore, $3,500 of that was directly given to Manhattan College, another $1,300 was spent on books and other supplies. . . . This young man was employed as a clerk in our Youth Advocacy Institute and received for a full week's worth of work $120, not $200 as was stated in the newspaper. He was also provided with a $2,220 computer for his school work, something that the college requested that he have," said Ritter.

"I am absolutely certain that the allegations of financial impropriety against Covenant House are simply not true," he continued, and then gave a dramatic pause. "The other and more painful allegations about my personal conduct are deeply offensive to me. This has been without doubt the most difficult week of my entire life. By innuendo, by allegation, by misstatements and inaccurate information, the impression has been given that I have been guilty of sexual misconduct. I categorically deny those statements. I categorically deny them."

Ritter repeated the second phrase while removing his glasses in a theatrical gesture, as if to say, "Okay, now this is from the heart, not just notes."

Donna Santarsiero heard the words as she sat in a chair off to the side of the dais. Barely able to see through the forest of television-camera tripods, she managed to get a direct view of Ritter's face, of his mouth moving, of his eyes shifting. The words echoed through her mind. "I categorically deny those statements. I categorically deny them."

She felt sick to her stomach, suddenly realizing that she didn't believe Ritter.

"It sent chills down my spine," Santarsiero remembers. "It was the most disturbing thing I've ever felt. I hated that I felt that way."

Ritter went back to his notes.

"This year 25,000 kids will come to Covenant House. . . . They, many, most actually, have been forced to exchange sex for money, for shelter, for food, for comfort. There is no mystery about what happens to a kid who lives on the streets. They are what is called in our profession simply 'high-risk kids.' They are many of them extremely damaged young people."

Ritter's somber, church-organ tone was warming up. The speech was beginning to sound like the lurid newsletters and fund-raising pitches he made every day. The broken pacing, the dramatic pauses, were actually doing their magic on the press corps.

"If I am proud of anything at Covenant House it is that we practice open intake. That means we never turn a kid away. No matter how troubled. No matter how damaged. For many of our kids, it is already too late. The damage they have suffered in their families, the distortion of their personalities is so massive, the erosion of their character so complete that for all practical purposes it is irreversible. They are above all else what we call high-risk kids. There is a special program here in Covenant House for the most high-risk kids of all. They are kids who are fleeing involvement with organized crime. Generally kids that have been involved in organized prostitution rings, the escort services, they are in danger of their lives. They know too much. They come to us for help and sanctuary. There is no other organization that can help them, or as far as I know tries to.

"We began to organize a specific safe-house program for these kids almost 10 years ago. I wrote a newsletter then with a remarkable, an incredible, similarity to the young man who brought these allegations. He was from a Southwestern city, the same city the young man in question came from. He was with an escort service and fled for his life with me to New York. I would like to read the ending of that newsletter.

"He was gone the next morning. Nobody knows where or why. Probably because he just couldn't trust anybody that much, that soon. I never got a chance to use any God talk on him. I pray a lot for Mark. I don't think he will come back. Programs like Under 21 can't help the Marks of this world. People like Bruce can, if he weren't running programs like Under 21 and had the time for that total investment of caring that can reach out to a kid like Mark."

Ritter looked out at the crowd of reporters over the top of his reading glasses. The cadence of his speech was halting, and full of emotion. No fire and brimstone. He slowly closed the book he had written, as if it were a sacred tome, and continued the defense of his name.

"About five years ago, we began to organize a special safe-house program because so many kids were coming to us. You can't put them in the regular residence. It is too dangerous for them. We have used as a safe house private homes, a rectory, a farm, a vacation home. There are currently four of these kids. Their needs are enormous. They are almost always boys, they are bereft of family and friends. They are terrified. They are incapable of trust. After being rented out for years, they find it impossible to trust anyone. Treatment programs cannot help these kids, only people can. A young man came to our New Orleans program early this year. He convinced our staff there totally that he was such a young man. My staff and this kid also convinced me that this was true. I brought this boy to New York. He stayed in a guest room on the eighth floor for three weeks before he was moved to an apartment. . . . I want you to know that I am not a romantic about the work that we do. I think, and it may sound arrogant, and it probably is, but I think I know more about these kids than anyone in the United States. I know what they need and I know what we have to do in order to help them.

"For the first five years of Covenant House, I was Covenant House. I had no staff. I had no one to help me. More than a thousand kids lived there with me in that apartment. They simply lived with me. I had very direct and personal relationships with hundreds and hundreds of these high-risk kids. The plan we had for the young man who came to our safe house in New York was to put him in that program. He needed a human net, a human social net to support him, and he needed an education. I chose to become his mentor, quite frankly because there was no one in Covenant House who had more experience than I. Hundreds of Covenant House kids today each have personal mentors. I made a covenant with this young man that we would speak the truth with each other. My staff helped him in incredible ways. . . . My staff took him home to visit their families, to share holidays, family celebrations, weddings, and funerals. We introduced him to our friends and families and were proud to do that. I gave him clothes. I gave him some sweaters that I didn't need. I gave him a jacket because it was cold. We tried so very hard and we failed.

"It is probably better to say that I failed. If I had to give a reason for my own personal failure it is probably hubris. I thought I knew more than I did. I misread his agony. I was too busy to listen. I could not reach out to him. There were miscommunications between me and my staff. If he came back today we would welcome him back to Covenant House. What happens to me, ladies and gentlemen, is not really very important. I decided long ago that I did not care about that. What happens to the kids is very important. The work here that we do is of extraordinary importance. And I think that what I feel most distressed about and what has caused me the greatest pain of all is that the millions and millions of people in this country who have loved these kids and supported them have had their faith in me shattered and perhaps their willingness to continue to support our

kids and care for them. And I ask for your prayers for them and for
me and for this young man for whom we really cared very much.
That is the end of my formal statement and I will be glad to take
questions."

The speech was mesmerizing. It took a moment for the reporters
to get their journalistic guard back up. Kells stepped to the dais. He
put his hand on Father Ritter's back, a reassuring sign to his boss
that he had done a good job.

"We are going to go left to right and you will be allowed one follow-
up question," said Kells. "Please be polite to your colleagues."

The hands flew up. Reporters jockeyed for position. But this crowd
of journalists was surprisingly reverent to the priest. There were
polite questions about the budget. There was some confusion on the
amount he spent on the youth and on the history of Covenant House.
What year was it that the first group of kids knocked on your door?
Now, you said the computer was $2,220, right? At first, no reporter
could look the Franciscan in the eye and ask, "Did you have sex with
the youth in question?" In his prepared statement, Ritter never directly addressed that issue. He said, "The impression has been given
that I am guilty of sexual misconduct. I categorically deny those
statements." Perhaps in his mind the sex was not a professional misconduct, but an agreement between consenting adults.

But then Mary Civiello, a reporter for WNBC–Channel 4 who had
covered Ritter for years, asked the most direct question of the day.

Q. "Father, can you tell us if you ever had sexual relations with
this youth in question or any other youth in Covenant House?"

As she asked the question, Father Ritter's Adam's apple bobbed
up and down. He looked to make sure he was in front of the microphone before he answered. And then he stared directly at her, almost
through her.

A. "Never. Never . . ."

Kells interrupted on the last "never," slightly cutting off the word
as it was spoken. "Next question," said Kells. "Let's go over here."

"Wait a minute, I have a follow-up," said Civiello.

"I'm sorry, I thought you had already asked two," said Kells.

"No," said Civiello, as she then fell into the numbers trap.

Q. "You said you spent $9,500 on other kids you have had in the
program. Is that for the same time period?"

A. "Yes."

Q. "Father Ritter, you said you misread his agony. What do you
mean?"

A. "The problem was I am on the road too much. I travel incessantly. While I was away, there was miscommunication with my staff.
For example, the boy began to fall back into his old lifestyle. He
began to pick up johns. He told one of our staff members that he
had been raped by one of his johns. When I asked him about it, he
told me that it happened and that it happened in the apartment of
his john. I think he was afraid to tell me it had actually occurred in
his own apartment. My staff assumed that I knew and I did not.
Quite frankly, I did not believe the boy that he had been raped. He
had been a professional prostitute for many years, with hundreds
and hundreds of customers. I simply assumed, wrongly, that he had
picked up a john and had engaged in what they call on the street
'rough sex.' "

Q. "Father, this young man taped a conversation with you in the
car. Did you have any knowledge that it was being taped?"

A. "Absolutely not."

Q. "Did it seem a suspicious conversation to you at all, Father?"

A. "Toward the end it did. It got a little weird. It got a little
inconsistent. I was confronting the boy on the fact that he was dropping out of college. I had demanded that he . . . Demand is too strong
a word. I was urging him strongly as gently as I could that he should
stay in college and maintain his initiative there. The boy was very
distressed. He was tired of trying so hard, of trying to change. Sometimes we cannot change and we do not change. We are what we are.
Sometimes God simply has to accept that. We become God's problem."

Ritter's chest heaved. He seemed to be on the edge of a deeper
explanation. But Kells, perhaps sensing this, quickly interrupted.
"Let's come over here to the right," he said as Ritter exhaled.

"Hold it. Hold it," said the reporter. "I get a follow-up."

Q. "Do you have any idea what his motivation might have been?"

A. "I didn't know it was happening."

Q. "Thinking back on it?"

A. "The only reason was one that I did not suspect but that my
staff told me about. When the boy dealt with me he often put on, as
he said, 'a happy face.' I was completely unaware that he was often
not happy with me because I could not go to Manhattan College as
a kind of surrogate father. And because I . . . because he thought I
was criticizing him for not getting grades as good as I thought he
was capable of. . . . and, I . . ."

Kells: "Coming over here to the right. Next question."

Q. "Father Ritter, it may come down to his word against your word. You have told us that you thought D.A. Morgenthau was going to drop this investigation . . ."

A. "I have not met with the D.A. That was a miscommunication somehow between yourselves and wherever you got that information. . . . I have the greatest respect and admiration for Bob Morgenthau. He is doing exactly the kind of job he has to do. We are cooperating fully with all of his requests, anxiously with all of his requests. We are totally confident that he will find absolutely no fiscal irregularities with Covenant House, which seems to be the brunt of the investigation."

Q. "Does Mr. Morgenthau share your concern that the investigation needs to be completed quickly in order not to hurt your donor base?"

A. "I am sure he will move as quickly as he can. He must complete a thorough investigation. He has to do his job."

Q. "You have been quoted as saying you were being set up by organized crime, do you still believe that was the case?"

A. "I thought about that. It's a possibility. I have many enemies. But I do not believe that it is an effort of organized crime. I do believe quite strongly that other groups are using the allegations not only to embarrass me but to embarrass the Church."

Q. "What other groups, Father?"

A. "I do not wish to say."

Ritter's eyes darted around at the reporters jotting down their notes. He took a deep breath while he could.

Q. "What do you do to overcome the questions? How do you restore the faith?"

A. "I wish I knew."

Q. "Is there some kind of strategy? A plan of action?"

A. "Well, we must certainly begin . . . You know, I was thinking this morning about that quote from Shakespeare: 'He who steals my purse steals trash. But he who robs me of my good name takes that what enriches him not, but leaves me poor indeed.' And I am very poor indeed."

Q. "Father Ritter, are there regulations established for counselors? And do you think that you violated those in taking the kid away?"

A. "There are guidelines in our crisis program that are very strict. There are no personal relationships whatsoever. None. However, in our long-term programs, those guidelines do not, emphatically do not, apply. They are mentor relationships. They are deep and personal and caring. Mentors are invited to bring them into their lives.

It is a totally different kind of supporting, trusting, nurturing relationship."

Q. "Father Ritter, are there any other kids who got tuition paid for? And you've estimated that you spend $15,000 to $18,000 a year on the average kid. What are those expenses for?"

A. "There are well over two hundred kids in our long-term educational/vocational program. Dozens of them receive scholarships. Dozens. Jim Harnett will answer the second question."

Harnett: "Expenditures are all quite similar in our programs. They pay to feed the youth, to clothe and house them. We provide counseling services and security."

No one bothered to ask if the $9,800 they said they spent on Kite was above and beyond that average of more than $15,000. Were we supposed to believe that all of the kids got $100-a-week stipends, private apartments, expensive jogging suits, Reebok sneakers, frequent dinners at high-priced restaurants, and weekends in the country at a private cottage?

Q. "Father Ritter, you said that what happens to you is not important. Only what happens to the kids is important. That being the case, why not step aside?"

A. "Because I am so closely identified with Covenant House. I think that without me presently in this leadership role the work we do would suffer very much."

Q. "Under what conditions would you consider resigning?"

A. "I honestly see no reason to resign. I am guilty of no crime. I am guilty of no crime."

Kells: "Okay, we'll have two more questions and that's it."

Q. "You said you have mentored others and that this was a special relationship. What exactly made the relationship special? How do you choose?"

A. "It wasn't. It is special only in the sense that a mentoring relationship is special. In no way is it different from other mentoring relationships."

Q. "Father Ritter, what do you think of the *New York Post*'s role in this?"

A. "I suspect that the *New York Post* was manipulated by this young man and those that used him."

"Thank you very much," said Kells, as he escorted Ritter away from the dais.

The reporters rushed back to their newsrooms, ready to write the story that would run on every front page in the city. *Daily News:* RITTER: SAYS IT AIN'T SO. *Newsday:* RITTER DENIES MISCONDUCT. *Times:*

RITTER DENIES SEX ALLEGATION. *Post:* RITTER CONCEDES ERROR IN JUDG-
MENT.

After the press conference, the staff waited nervously in Kells's
second-floor office for the 6 P.M. newscasts for a reading on how the
story would be played. Kells's small office had been dubbed the "nerve
center" for the crisis-management team. Clustered there were Ritter;
Kells; his assistant, George Wirt; Stroock; Harnett; chairman of the
board Ralph Pfeiffer; board member Denis Coleman; and attorney
Ed Burns. The coverage on all three of the networks' local affiliates
looked "very positive."

"You did a fine job," said Stroock. "You've reestablished your credibility. I think we are through the worst part of this thing."

Ritter looked tired and drawn. They patted him on the back; a few
of them even gave some mock applause, which seemed inappropriate.
But the consensus was that Ritter had been humble but not apologetic,
forceful but not arrogant.

When the adulation subsided, Father Bruce was quiet. Then he
addressed his cabinet of loyalists in a very "matter-of-fact" tone.

"There is something else you should know," said Ritter, pausing
for about the amount of time it takes to pull a pin out of a grenade.

"There are probably going to be some copycat allegations," he
added.

"What? Well, I mean, how many?" Kells asked.

"I don't know. There could be several others," Ritter replied.

Over the next few minutes Ritter calmly expounded on the "other
kids" who he felt could come forward. One member of the inner
circle who was present at the meeting remembers Ritter mentioned
three or four names, including Paul Johnson and Darryl Bassile.
Ritter explained that Johnson had asked him for money at one point
and that he had given it. "I kept him off my back," Ritter said.

But Ritter provided few details and dismissed the threat of "copycat" allegations, treating them as minor problems that would need
to be worked out. But if he knew of more accusers who would come
forward, it was not a minor problem.

"We've lost it," one of his loyalists thought to himself, as he quietly
watched Ritter from across the room. "He is doing as much of a con
job on us as he is on everyone else."

It was a decisive moment. Ritter had lost the confidence of key
members of his inner circle.

Stroock hadn't lost his faith, though he couldn't understand why
Ritter hadn't told them before the press conference.

"Bruce, we talked about that. I told you if there was anything else you should have brought it forward right away so we could deal with it," Stroock said, trying to control his sometimes hot temper.

Ritter had no answer. Nonetheless, Stroock still didn't believe that Ritter was guilty of any sexual misconduct. He felt he knew Ritter too well and he knew how manipulative the street kids could be. Besides, Stroock, like every other board member and senior staff official under Ritter, had his own pride and his own ego on the line. More than that, they had their faith on the line. This Franciscan had changed Stroock's life, deepened his commitment to God, and made him feel good about helping other people.

"I guess it went past me," Stroock later said. "I guess I didn't want to believe it."

After Ritter mentioned the "other copycats," there was a long uncomfortable silence. His staff felt the weight of the scandal sink in. George Wirt was silent and felt his heart drop.

"I thought we were through the gauntlet," said Wirt. "But we were headed for the iceberg."

"It was Oz," said Kells. "We didn't know what to believe."

Despite the crisis of confidence inside the palace, the press coverage was extremely favorable. Kells and Stroock began to believe they could make it through the storm.

After all the other reporters had left the press conference, *Newsday*'s Dennis Duggan was granted a private interview with Ritter that afternoon. Duggan was among the most passionate writers in defense of Ritter. And they owed him the exclusive in order to keep him among the faithful.

Duggan is a strong voice in the city, with a long and distinguished history in the world of New York newspapers. He, like Ritter, grew up in an Irish Catholic family during the Depression. He rejected his Catholic upbringing and came of age as a member of the Socialist Workers Party, slamming the conservative politics of the Catholic Church in his college newspaper. But he nonetheless felt a certain kinship with Ritter.

During the interview, Ritter broke down. Duggan began his column with the pitiful image of Ritter crying in a third-floor office of the charity's headquarters.

" 'It's something I'll have to live with the rest of my life,' said the Reverend Bruce Ritter, wiping at his eyes," Duggan wrote.

He went on to refer to Kite as "Judas." He poetically lamented the possible loss of funding that the scandal could cause and the harm it could ultimately cause the street kids who relied on the charity. They were the "potential victims of a sorry, shabby game played by cynical adults who ought this morning to feel ashamed of themselves."

The newspapers were beginning to shift their pressure away from Ritter and direct it not only at the *Post* but at the District Attorney's office. There were appeals in the editorial pages of *The New York Times* and the *Daily News* for Morgenthau to proceed with the investigation promptly to save the charity from financial ruin.

Meanwhile, there was another kind of pressure mounting on the District Attorney. Calls were lighting up the switchboard with complaints from Catholics about the D.A. crucifying a saint. There was a kind of implicit anti-Semitism to many of the phone calls, with people asking why prosecutors with last names like Morgenthau, Fairstein, and Castleman were investigating a Catholic icon. Former Governor Hugh Carey was also furious about the investigation. At Christmas parties in the city, Carey was privately threatening to bring Manhattan District Attorney Robert Morgenthau before the Catholic Lawyers Guild of New York. Later he would make the threat publicly. At other Christmas parties, Morgenthau was telling some of the big names in New York City journalism that the investigation was only "the tip of the iceberg."

Inside the archdiocese, Cardinal O'Connor was monitoring the events daily with his public-relations team and two of his monsignors, James Murray and William Toohy, both heads of administration in Catholic Charities. The question was to what extent, if any, the archdiocese was responsible for the overseeing of Covenant House. Was there any way in which the archdiocese could get caught in the scandal? His Eminence was assured that the overseeing of Ritter's conduct was purely the province of the Franciscan Order and that any Church investigation of alleged misconduct would have to be undertaken by the Franciscans. That point was clearly made to Father Connal McHugh, a Covenant House board member and the provincial of the Franciscan Order based in Union City. Ritter had fought to keep diocesan hands off his charity, and now as far as they were concerned they were in no way going to be dragged into what even the cardinal referred to as an "awful mess," unless it was as a savior coming to the rescue of the embattled Franciscan and his troubled charity. They wanted official distance from the scandal, but they would never turn down an offer to get their hands on the financial empire that Ritter had created.

On December 15, another emergency meeting of the Covenant House board was called. Santarsiero again voiced her "outrage" at the safe-house program. This time Ritter was not present. She wanted to make sure that the program was immediately disposed of, or, if board members supported it, that it was voted on as soon as possible. She demanded that it be brought to Ritter's attention. She was assured by Kells and Harnett that it would be.

At the meeting Kells insisted that Covenant House needed to do its own private investigation to uncover what he was convinced was an "anti-Catholic conspiracy." The sentiment was in the air. That week ACT UP held a demonstration in Saint Patrick's Cathedral. One of the demonstrators threw the Eucharist onto the ground, leaving Cardinal O'Connor in tears. It was a horrible desecration of the cathedral, and it had New York's Catholic community justifiably furious.

Macauley continued in his insistence that there were enemies of the Church trying to do Ritter in. Stroock wasn't vocal about it, but believed the conspiracy theories were "horseshit" and a "paranoid distraction."

"I think it crossed everyone's mind in the beginning," said Levine. "But I don't believe that now, not if you look at it rationally."

It wasn't conspiracy that the board members needed to worry about. A gear in the cosmic machinery was shifting and it was about to crush Bruce Ritter. The past was finally catching up with the aging Franciscan. Ritter couldn't see it. Like the protagonist in an ancient Greek tragedy, Ritter was blind to the events unfolding around him.

On December 14, hundreds of miles away in Ithaca, New York, while Ritter was holding his press conference, Darryl Bassile was on his way from a part-time job to an afternoon appointment with his psychotherapist.

Bassile had ended up in Ithaca in the spring of 1975, after he left the drug-treatment center in which Ritter had placed him. Bassile says that the sexual abuse that he had suffered at the hands of his stepfather and then with Ritter had left him "just really confused."

For nearly fifteen years, Bassile moved from one apartment to another in a haze of drug abuse, dead-end jobs, and two broken marriages. But in 1988 Bassile had finally shaken his addiction to cocaine, given up smoking pot, and gone into therapy. In October of 1989, a therapist gave him *Victims No Longer* by Mike Lew, a recovery book for survivors of child sexual abuse.

The book gave Darryl a "compass" to begin to chart his own recovery. He was finally able to hold two jobs, delivering pizzas and working part time at a center for mentally disabled adults. He accepted the fact that his mother was probably mental disabled, which gave him an explanation for the horrifying pattern of neglect to which she had subjected him and his brothers. Although he was shelling out nearly half his salary to pay for his $80-a-week counseling sessions, he didn't care. He felt that he was finally conquering his past as a victim.

Bassile had no idea that a storm of controversy was brewing around Ritter. A half year before the story first broke in the *Post*, he had told his psychotherapist, Daniel Matusiewicz, about the abuse he had suffered as a child, from his stepfather and from Father Ritter. He told Matusiewicz that he never tried to inform the staff about what was going on because they would never have believed him, a common fear among abused youths.

On December 14, when Bassile sat down in his therapist's office for his normal forty-five-minute session, Matusiewicz dropped a *New York Post* article in his lap.

Bassile couldn't believe what he read. The article detailed allegations of sexual misconduct against Ritter. Surprisingly, Bassile didn't feel as much anger as he did relief. Now he could prove that he was telling the truth. He felt it was a kind of vindication. What did anger him was Ritter's denials, but he saw no point in coming forward. At least, not yet.

On December 15 in Washington, D.C., Paul Johnson, who had changed his name since leaving Covenant House, was in his third marriage and still scheming, although it had become a little more sophisticated. He had started what he called "a financial consulting business" in the city. On his way to work, he picked up the *Washington Post*. As he turned the pages, a tiny picture of Ritter's face caught his eye in a story buried inside the paper. At first glance, he figured it was just another presidential award or another glowing profile. Then he read the headline and his jaw dropped. Someone had finally caught up with Ritter. He couldn't believe it. He called Ritter and left a message.

He loved the image of Ritter reading his message. He could imagine the kind of panic that would set in when he saw the name on the notepad. Johnson knew what his story could do to Ritter. Late that night, after four or five scotches, he picked up the phone and dialed Bruce Ritter again. He still couldn't get through, and he knew Ritter was trying to avoid him.

He had read in the *Washington Post* that the story was first published in the *New York Post*. On the following day, in the late afternoon, he called the *New York Post* newsroom and asked to speak to the reporter on the Ritter story. Johnson told me the full details of his history with Ritter. He explained that he had trusted Ritter and still believed that he truly cares about the kids. But he also made disturbing allegations about his sexual relationship with Ritter. He told about what he called "psychological blackmail" through forged credit cards. He explained that in 1986 he had set up corporate accounts in the name of Covenant House on Avis and Holiday Inn credit cards, which listed him and Ritter as the cardholders. He said, he went on a spending spree in 1986 and Ritter picked up the bill knowing that Johnson would go public if he didn't. Johnson was willing to tell the whole story on tape and to testify to the District Attorney. He agreed to come to New York for an in-person interview.

There were inconsistencies in Johnson's stories, but the bulk of his story held up. He had names of staff members, descriptions of the inside of Ritter's apartment, and statements that appeared to be easy to corroborate. Many of them, including the detailed description of the sex, provided a kind of forensic match to the allegations that Kite had made, even though none of those details had been published. It was clear Ritter had an M.O.

Johnson was up front about a history of lying and a string of criminal convictions, ranging from auto theft to larceny. He even had an outstanding warrant in Los Angeles for a fraud case. He was certainly not the most reputable witness.

Johnson's life after Covenant House had become a ruin of alcoholism, money scams, and paranoia. He could be articulate and at times convincing, but then would fall silent. For nearly two months, I researched his allegations. Just about everything Johnson claimed checked out—the credit cards were under his name and Covenant House's; he had charged some $10,000 to them, and several staff members said they remembered him and that he did have a close relationship with Ritter.

Johnson agreed to take a lie-detector test and passed.

On December 12, John Melican was working as a house painter in Seattle. Still drinking, he was about to be evicted from his apartment for failure to pay the rent. He had his own problems and had no idea that Ritter's past was catching up with him. But when freelance writer Philip Nobile read that the district attorney was investigating Ritter's relationship with a male prostitute, he ran to his old files from the days of the Meese Commission to find the interview he had done with Melican more than five years earlier. The story had been in the back of his mind as he watched Ritter's meteoric rise to fame in recent years. Nobile found the slightly yellowing, twenty-four-page typed transcription of his taped interview with Melican buried in a cardboard box in the back of a closet.

He made some calls and heard that Melican was living on the West Coast. Nobile knew he had a dynamite story and called his editors at the *Village Voice*.

The Greek chorus shouted its warnings. Trapped in his own tragedy, Ritter couldn't hear it. But in the wings, three of his accusers—Bassile, Johnson, and Melican—were just about to make their entrances.

VI

The New Covenant

*God spoke to Noah: I establish my Covenant with you, and with
your descendants. . . . There shall be no flood to destroy the earth
again. . . . I give you everything, with this exception: I will
demand an account of every man's life from his fellow men.*

Genesis 9:8–9, 3–5

Chapter 17

Runaway Superstar

CHRISTMAS in New York, 1989. Fifth Avenue sparkled with blinking lights and tinseled bells. Cheerful crowds gathered around the holiday displays in shop windows and Rockefeller Center's towering Christmas tree.

Covenant House, usually brimming with activity during its busiest time of year for fund raising, was cast in a deep darkness. Between December and January, Covenant House, like many charities, raises up to 40 percent of its annual donations. The staff was fearful that the money would simply dry up, that the scandal would cripple what was once the fastest-growing charity in the United States.

Of Father Bruce Ritter's fourteen newsletters a year, the mid-December correspondence with donors was traditionally a special holiday appeal—a time when the founder trumpeted the successes and heralded future plans. It was one of the largest mass mailings of the year, reaching nearly one million donors across the country. But the newsletter of December 18, 1989, one week after the scandal broke in the newspapers, sounded more like a dirge.

Hello, my friends,
It's been the worst week of my life. . . . I don't think anybody

could have missed the sensational coverage in the New York Post, and then in the newspapers and on all the radio and TV stations for the past week. It's why I am writing to you today. . . . [A] young man has accused me and Covenant House of financial improprieties in providing care to him, in order to have a sexual relationship with him. I categorically deny both allegations. They are not true. I will be totally and completely exonerated and vindicated when Manhattan District Attorney, Robert Morgenthau, completes his investigation. . . . It has been a time of extraordinary pain and grief for me. I have said many times that I do not really care what happens to me. . . .

Peace,
Fr. Bruce

The staff was reeling from the scandal, desperately trying to find a way not only to salvage the fund-raising season but to keep the charity from descending into an uncontrollable downward spiral of bad publicity. Kells, Harnett, and the rest of the crisis managers decided that the charity needed to get more information on Kite. Everyone who had worked with him, from John Spanier to Monica Kaiser, knew he was older than the nineteen years he had professed to be. Clearly, the preliminary casework was a disaster, but no one had criticized it, for Kite had been Father Ritter's responsibility. The crisis team checked Kite's original intake file and found the name "Greg Hutcherson," which was the first false name he used in New Orleans. They traced the name back to Gainesville, Texas, and dispatched Malcolm Host, the executive director of Covenant House in Houston, to the home of the Hutcherson family with a photograph of Kite. It was not Greg Hutcherson, Host was told, but another young man from Gainesville named Kevin Kite.

The trail led Host down One Horse Lane to the modern three-bedroom home of Alton Kite. Host knocked on the door and was greeted by the solid, straight-backed frame of the senior Kite. Host told Kite that his son had made a "horrendous accusation" against "a priest who was helping kids." Host explained that his son had nearly destroyed their charity and asked the senior Kite to come to New York to straighten out the mess. Alton Kite did not know who Father Ritter was and told Host that he had not seen his son in more than a year, but agreed to go to help "undo some of the damage." Kite explained to Host that he was not surprised his son was "lying again" and that he believed his only child had a "personality disorder." It was a "pattern of lying," Alton Kite said, brought on largely by his "gay lifestyle."

Host called John Kells and Jim Harnett and told them the details. Within a few hours, they had Alton Kite on a plane headed for New York City.

The Kites' family life had been a long and bitter tragedy of misunderstanding. Kite had stolen checks, committed fraud, and even stolen his mother's jewelry. He could be "very convincing," said Alton Kite, and "had a history of hurting anyone who tried to help him." But this broken bond between a father and son seemed like a goldmine to the Covenant House public-relations machinery, with Kells at the switch. That Kite's own father had called him a liar was the perfect comeback in Ritter's defense.

There was, however, a catch. Father Bruce was always adamant about not breaking the covenant of confidentiality with the young people in his care, not even to law-enforcement officials when they threatened to charge him with obstruction of justice.

Kells, Macauley, and Stroock told Ritter he was "insane to even think about not using the information." Kite was an adult, they rationalized, who was about to destroy the charity, not a young man who needed its care. Reluctantly, Ritter agreed to break the code of confidentiality to save himself and the charity.

Alton Kite sensed that the Covenant House officials were overjoyed to have found him. He says they even discussed helping him pay off some of the debts his son had incurred, but the only thing they ever bought him was an answering machine to handle the deluge of calls from the media.

"I knew they had a vested interest. I wasn't completely naïve about what they were doing," said Alton Kite. "But I felt responsible for my son. I wanted to set the record straight."

When Alton Kite met Father Ritter in his office, Ritter was on the verge of tears. But there wasn't a lot of time to talk; Kells was anxious to get Alton Kite out in front of the press conference he had called. Neither Kells nor Ritter, nor even the reporters, ever informed Kite that his son was cooperating with a full-fledged investigation by the Manhattan District Attorney. Kite took Covenant House's word that his son's allegations were lies. The press conference was held for a small group of hand-picked reporters, who later reported his claim that his son was a "habitual liar." Once again Kells had reporters jumping through Covenant House's hoops.

Persuading Kite's father to come forward had staff members furious. How could they break the covenant of confidentiality? The organization always preached that the young people who came there would be protected, that they would not be turned over to abusive parents or to law-enforcement officials against their will.

"Behind any troubled kid is a bad relationship with a parent," said one child-care worker at Covenant House. "That they used that to save Father Bruce's image was despicable. It was the worst kind of violation of trust."

"It's where they broke the covenant," said Donna Santarsiero.

Father Bruce and some of his inner circle were also getting ruthless with the staff, drawing a clear line between the loyalists and the infidels. In a panicky atmosphere, in which staff members were told to choose sides, anyone who dared to question what seemed at least to be gross errors of judgment by the founder and president was immediately alienated and deemed disloyal.

Donna Santarsiero was shocked at the "ruthlessness" of the board and the senior staff in its defense of Ritter. They seemed to be betraying everything the organization was supposed to be about to protect the man who created it. Even Ritter began saying particularly uncharitable things, calling Kite a "sick kid," and a "drug runner." Santarsiero felt the cold corporate mentality that had taken over Covenant House during the last ten years was about to destroy its soul in defense of the legend of Father Bruce and the mythology that fueled its growth.

On December 20 at 10 P.M., Kevin Kite was sitting in the hotel room eating fast food on his $15-a-day allowance from the Manhattan D.A.'s office, and flipping through the television channels when he landed on Channel 5's *Fox News*.

The introduction to the lead story of the night horrified him: "Bob O'Brien rips the mask off the secret identity of the former male prostitute and accuser in the Covenant House scandal. . . ."

Kite watched as his father's long, leathery face filled the screen. It was his worst nightmare. In the Texas drawl he knew so well, Alton Kite publicly condemned his wayward son, calling him a young man with a "history of lying" and asking forgiveness from the television viewing audience for "any harm he may have caused." Kevin Kite had known that taking on Bruce Ritter would be a long and ugly battle. Fairstein had prepared him for that. But he had never thought his family would be drawn into it.

He fell apart. He stumbled straight out of the hotel and into the darkness of New York City, down into the string of Greenwich Village bars where he used to hang out. He threw back as much alcohol as he could get his hands on, and blacked out within a few hours. According to Kite, the next two days are gone from his memory. The next thing he said he could remember was being admitted to the emergency room at the Payne Whitney Psychiatric Clinic in Manhattan. He had tried to cut his wrists.

Kite called Linda Fairstein, but she was on vacation. He tried Kaiser, but she was home with her family in the Midwest. From the fourth-floor windows of the psychiatric ward, he looked out on the shoppers hurrying home for Christmas. He stared at the paper ornaments taped to the metal doors in the ward, chain-smoked Marlboro 100s, and read *The Bridge Over the River Kwai*.

That night, Darryl Bassile was in his apartment in Buffalo, New York, waiting up for the eleven o'clock news to get the latest developments in the Covenant House scandal. He watched Kite's father stare into the camera and call his son a liar. It made Bassile furious. He knew what it was like to be manipulated and abused by Ritter's power. He knew what his parents would have said if he had ever told them that he was being abused by a priest. He saw straight through Covenant House in their attempt to discredit Kevin Kite. That night, Bassile decided to go forward with his story. No longer opting to stay out of the fray, Bassile wanted to see Ritter prosecuted. He wanted Kite to know he was not the only one.

The next morning, he called the New York Archdiocese but was passed off to a secretary, who told him that he would have to speak with the "order with which the priest in question is affiliated." He was given the number of the Franciscan Friars in Union City. Bassile called and detailed his allegation, leaving his full name and phone number. No one returned the call.

On December 22, he called Covenant House and asked for Father Bruce Ritter. He left a message, which was listed on Ritter's phone log and later seized by investigators. Ritter never returned the call.

As Bassile was fighting his way through the resistant bureaucracy of the Church and the walls around Covenant House, Kite remained under surveillance and on medication for severe depression, and protesters were gathering at the *Post* building with placards that read: ANTI CATHOLIC and APOLOGIZE TO FATHER RITTER. But on December 24 the man at the center of the storm calmly prepared to say his traditional midnight mass in the Faith Community chapel.

Just before midnight on Christmas Eve, the chapel's doors on Forty-fourth Street off Eighth Avenue were opened to the cold night air. Some two hundred of Father Bruce's faithful staff, loyal donors, and true believers filed into the same old building where Ritter's odyssey through the underworld of Times Square first began. The altar was adorned with one hundred red poinsettia plants, scores of potted evergreens, and a Christmas tree decorated with white doves and blue bulbs. Father Ritter and Anne Donahue, as was their Christmas ritual, set up a string of lights that glimmered among the plants and evergreens, making it look like a small forest at twilight. Father Bruce loved Christmas. He understood it as an especially difficult time for the kids in the program. He often reflected on his own loneliness and feeling of neglect as a child at Christmastime, and wanted to make the holiday a special time for the kids in his care— even if he was in the middle of a tawdry scandal.

Anne Donahue sat in one of the front pews and stared at the enormous artwork behind the altar as Father Bruce said mass. She'd seen the dramatic relief sculpture thousands of times before. When she lived in the Faith Community, she prayed before it three times a day, and through her years on staff she frequently attended masses there. But the irony of it was suddenly glaringly apparent. The roughly thirty-five-by-thirty-foot sculpture of hammered copper depicts a modern interpretation of the crucifixion of Christ in Times Square, entitled *Passion on 8th Avenue*. Ritter had commissioned it from Charles Bukovich in the late 1970s.

In the center of the enormous artwork, a Christlike figure—though slightly balding, with an anguished face and no beard—is being raised for crucifixion on a fire escape over a scene of Times Square. The image on the cross looks vaguely like Ritter himself. In the background are buildings, billboards, and two marquees that read RUN-AWAY SUPERSTAR.

There are two figures raising the body onto the fire escape; on the left-hand side is a street kid in jeans and on the right is a pimp dressed in high-heeled boots, a long coat, and a cap, jabbing a broken bottle at the Christlike figure's throat.

The action at the center is surrounded by a series of street scenes tinged with biblical metaphors and allusions to Father Bruce's legend: a mobster threatening youths with a gangland-style execution; two people in a knife-and-razor fight; a police car; a priest saying mass; a politician padlocking a porn shop; a young boy and girl being approached by a pimp in front of the Port Authority Bus Terminal; a young girl in pain being treated by a man resembling Saint Francis in blue jeans; a dove hovering overhead in the form of a street pigeon; four figures fighting and gambling over ripped clothes; and a television reporter and his crew capturing the scene from the street. Above it all are three images framed in the ladder of the fire escape— a blindfolded politician, City Hall, and a judge.

It was against this mosaic of metaphor that Ritter said his last public mass at Covenant House. He did not address the scandal but gave a theologically sound sermon on the "true meaning of the birth of Christ." It was a rather complicated homily, with an analysis of the liturgy, befitting the medieval theologian that he was. This time there was no discussion of his kids, no prurient appeal about young prostitutes; just a priest saying mass.

Ritter moved among the crowd and greeted the people who came to show their support: Macauley, Loken, Spanier, members of the Faith Community, many of his fellow Franciscans, families who had contributed to Covenant House, and scores of Covenant House kids. *Daily News* columnist Bill Reel, who attended the mass with his son, was surprised and pleased that Ritter "seemed to be weathering the storm pretty well."

After Christmas and into early January, the charity appeared to have survived the worst of the scandal. Kite's father's coming forward had given the staff a real "shot in the arm," to use Kells's words. Father Ritter—although privately still shut off in his office and monitoring every heartbeat of the scandal—was publicly projecting an image of getting on with the "day-to-day functions" of his work.

Calls were flooding the charity's Nineline with reactions to the scandal. Ritter insisted that he be apprised of what the callers had to say. Late at night, the staff would slip small stacks of phone comments under Ritter's apartment door and watch him pull them through.

"It was pretty depressing," said one staffer. "It was like he was hiding. We just wanted to help cheer him up, so we'd only slip through the positive ones."

Kite was still depressed, but seemed to be through the worst of it. "I guess I just needed a rest. This whole thing is turning on me. I guess I expected that, I just didn't think it would be this bad," he said, unconsciously moving the small bandages that covered the tiny surface cuts on his wrists and gazing out the window of the psychiatric ward.

"But I'm not backing out. I'm going to stick with it."

The investigation seemed on the surface to be going nowhere, and the revelation about Kite's emotional instability seemed to confirm Covenant House's claims that he was not to be trusted. The D.A. was getting no cooperation from Ritter, despite his statements to the contrary, and Morgenthau was beginning to feel the heat from the news media to speed up the investigation.

On January 9, *The New York Times* ran an editorial titled "Father Ritter's Slow Bleed," which in not-so-subtle terms used the full weight of its opinion to admonish Morgenthau for dragging his feet.

"It is not the business of the District Attorney to issue certificates of good conduct but to determine whether a prosecutable offense was committed. Even so, given the importance to the community of Covenant House and the importance to Covenant House of Father Ritter, District Attorney Robert Morgenthau would serve everyone well by concluding his investigation quickly. Otherwise a slow bleed could become ruinous."

Daily News metropolitan editor Arthur Browne hadn't liked the story from the start. Browne felt the *Post* had given too much credence to the allegations of a disturbed street kid and "laundered it as truth" through the District Attorney's office. The *Daily News*—an important barometer of the story because of its large Catholic readership—began to steer its coverage in support of Ritter, culminating with a January 14 two-page spread in its Sunday editions titled "Keeping the Faith," a glowing account of the charity's good work and its continuing struggle to protect its founder.

Television news programs packaged emotional shots of the kids who would suffer as a result of the scandal. In mid-January, the tabloid TV show *Inside Edition* did a story with the logo "Anatomy of a Smear," in which the interviewer bullied Kite, slapping him with questions like "Are you lying?" No mention was even made of an active investigation by the Manhattan District Attorney's office. The interview—a hatchet job on Kite—was brokered by Kells.

New York Post editor Jerry Nachman was surprised that the press had turned against the paper. Even if it was the bad boy of New York journalism, he believed it had broken a legitimate story about a full-fledged investigation of a saint.

"I knew how to handle a kill-the-messenger strategy. That's simple. Just keep reporting," said Nachman. "But what I wasn't prepared for was to be turned against by our peers, to have them covering how the *Post* covered the story rather than the story itself. Suddenly, we were the story, not the allegations or the D.A.'s investigation.

"*Newsday* was gingerly treating the subject. But the *Daily News* went straight into the tank. I believe to this day that they whitewashed a story to save their Catholic readership," said Nachman.

Daily News editor Jim Willse said the reason was much simpler: "We got beat. Fair and square."

In the January 11 editions of *The New York Times*, A. M. Rosenthal, former executive editor, wrote in his "On My Mind" column a piece titled "Passage from Ezekiel."

". . . The headline and story appeared in the *Post* a month ago. They were based solely on the word of a young man whose own father later said he was a habitual liar. Now the young man has turned himself in to a psychiatric clinic. Father Ritter has denied the allegations," wrote Rosenthal.

He ended the column with the passage from Ezekiel that was Father Bruce's spiritual motto for Covenant House, which in light of the scandal was meant as an oath between Ritter and his believers: "I bound myself by oath, I made a covenant with you, and you became mine."

Nachman was furious about the column, which to him captured the reluctance of most of the press to look at the story for what it was. The *Post* story was not based "solely on the word" of a former male prostitute. It was a story based *solely* on the *fact* that the Manhattan District Attorney was investigating the former male prostitute's allegations concerning Ritter. The press had aggressively written about everyone from Lieutenant Colonel Oliver North to Richard Nixon, from hotelier Leona Helmsley to televangelist Jim Bakker when they were under investigation.

"So when did the rules change?" Nachman asked Rosenthal in an angry letter. "Why do we hold this story to a different standard? It is reminiscent of those who said don't do stories on Watergate because you will destroy the presidency. To which the press said, 'No, it might just be the wrong man in the presidency.' There were others who said don't do stories on My Lai because it will weaken the morale of the troops. To which the press said, 'No, it just means people like Lt. Calley shouldn't be in the army.' Now people are saying don't do stories on Father Ritter because it will destroy Covenant House. To which the *Post* is saying, 'No, it just means maybe Ritter should not be the one who is helping these kids.'"

The story had turned so decisively in favor of Ritter that donations to Covenant House came pouring in again. It was as if people had waited over the Christmas holiday to see what was going to happen and were now more than ever turning their support back to the founder of Covenant House.

Despite John Kells's repeated claims in the media that the scandal had dealt a devastating blow to their annual fund-raising effort, Covenant House revenues increased dramatically in January of 1990 compared to the same month the previous year. Covenant House was weaving gold out of the straw of scandal.

In late January, *Village Voice* writer Philip Nobile was putting the finishing touches on his explosive exposé of the interview he had done five years earlier with John Melican. In an interview prior to publication, Harnett asked Nobile, "How would you feel if your story destroyed Covenant House?"

Nobile, resenting the play on his Catholic conscience, shot back, "How will you feel when your continued defense of Father Ritter in the face of contrary evidence destroys Covenant House? After all, what's more important, Father Ritter or the truth?"

"The truth," said Harnett.

Nobile's cover story titled "The Secret Life of Father Ritter" in the January 30 edition of the *Voice* detailed Melican's story.

Covenant House dismissed the claims as a "copycat allegation," even though Nobile had painstakingly pointed out that the youth came to him five years earlier and that it was highly unlikely that Kite and Melican had communicated or somehow conspired to make a case against Ritter. Soon the Dobermans at Cravath were all over Nobile and the *Voice,* making veiled threats of "legal remedies." Covenant House's public-relations machine again kicked in, labeling Nobile a "pornographer" because of his former job as an editor at *Penthouse Forum* and calling the story a series of "unsubstantiated allegations" by a reporter with a "long history of hostility to Father Ritter."

Newsday's Dennis Duggan, still on his spiritual mission to defend Ritter's good name, blasted Nobile on Fox 5's *Newsline New York,* hosted by Jack Cafferty, the day the story ran. Duggan said he thought the stories "started in the *Post* and now carried forward by the *Village Voice* represent shoddy, reprehensible journalism of the worst sort.

"What it amounts to is really railroading a guy, a priest who does more good probably in one night than these people will do in a lifetime," said Duggan.

Maguire's Cafe on Second Avenue off Forty-second Street is common ground for many of the reporters and editors from the *Daily News* and the *Post.* Steve McFadden, affectionately known as "Pally," is a former schoolteacher turned bar owner, and an Irish shaman for a coterie of journalists. He usually knows a good story when he sees it. Like a barometer of the Irish neighborhoods in the city's heartland of Brooklyn and Queens, he has an intuitive sense of what the people care about. He hated this story.

One particular detail left even the faithful like McFadden shaking their heads in disgust. On February 5, the *Post* disclosed a new allegation: the name "Tim Warner" was an identity unlawfully provided by Covenant House officials to Kevin Kite. The real Tim Warner was a ten-year-old boy from Jamestown, New York, who had died of leukemia.

The real Timothy Warner's parents, a middle-class Catholic couple, were furious that the memory of their son was being dragged through the mud by a former male prostitute. When Betty Ann Warner first read the stories about Father Ritter and saw that the name of his accuser was "Tim Warner," she mentioned it to her husband over the breakfast table, but they forgot about it. It was just one more passing reminder of the son they had lost ten years before but still thought about every day.

Then in the middle of that afternoon a phone call came from a reporter, asking about her son, with a series of confusing questions about his baptismal records and whether she had been notified that his identity was being used by Covenant House. Bewildered, she called her husband, who worked in the printing plant at a local newspaper. He called the FBI and demanded an investigation. They met with an FBI official in their home several days later and were promised that it would be looked into.

"Who does this man think he is?" asked Mrs. Warner when she learned that Ritter had arranged to use her son's identity for a former male prostitute.

Harnett had misled the press about how Kite obtained the identity. In the rush to trash Kite, he had told reporters that the young man created the false identity for himself. He elaborated on how Kite had looked up the boy's name in obituaries at a local newspaper.

"If that gets out, Greg [Loken] is the one who is going to end up in jail," he told Anne Donahue, referring to Loken's role in creating the false identity. When presented with the documents, Harnett was forced to back down and admit that it was Covenant House that had unlawfully provided the identity.

To many Catholics, that Ritter would "steal the soul of a dead boy" was, as McFadden put it, "far worse than any sins of the flesh."

Behind the scenes, several different investigations were under way. The Manhattan District Attorney's office was on the trail of the accusers. By early February, they had already spoken to Paul Johnson, Darryl Bassile, John Melican, and at least one other former resident of the Faith Community. They had spoken with Mary Lane and Lee Meyers and were conducting a computer search of all federal and state records to find "Sergeant Pepper" and "Stevie," two of Ritter's fabled first six kids, who also had allegedly been sexually abused by Ritter. The investigators were corroborating the allegations with social workers and staff counselors. They discovered that people in the social-work community knew about Ritter's sexual indiscretions going back twenty years. The secret life of Father Ritter was cracking wide open.

Meanwhile, the investigation into the finances of Covenant House was widening. Assistant District Attorney Dan Castleman was writing carefully crafted requests to Ritter's prominent criminal attorney, Stanley Arkin, for all files and financial documents involved in the case.

The sixteen categories of documents requested filled nearly three pages. They included: all "current Finance Department procedures"; "payroll"; all "documents with respect to Office of the President"; the "Safe House" program; all telephone logs/messages for Father Ritter; all expenses pertaining to "Jim Wallace a.k.a. Tim Warner a.k.a. Kevin Lee Kite"; any "effort in which personnel arranged for, or participated in, changing the identities of individuals"; as well as all "personal or corporate credit cards used by Father Ritter."

The stacks of documents, hand delivered by Arkin to the District Attorney, were filling up filing cabinets and bulging cardboard boxes in Castleman's cluttered office. The investigation was going to take weeks, possibly months. Given the shocking revelations about his personal life, Father Bruce had incurred the righteous wrath of the Manhattan District Attorney's office. Ritter's life was being gone over with Morgenthau's fine-toothed comb. The admonitions from the *Times* to speed up the investigation went ignored, as the D.A. plodded along in tireless investigation.

There were, during the same period, a series of private investigations circling in different orbits. Peter Grace had hired his own expert P.I. to get to the bottom of the scandal. Grace believed it was a conspiracy by the "militant gay community" or other "anti-Catholic elements," said a board member, and was willing to spend whatever it took to find out who it was.

Ellen Levine had also recommended on several occasions that Covenant House hire its own private investigators and delve into the pasts of Kite and Melican. A mysterious former FBI man from Connecticut, who had been affiliated with Grace, the Knights of Malta, and IBM, was assigned to the case. He was a professional corporate investigator, and in early February Levine called him with some ideas about possible leads to help vindicate Ritter.

But he told her, "I've been taken off the case."

"By who?" Levine asked, surprised that she hadn't been made aware of that.

"By Father Ritter," he said. "Father Bruce said he doesn't think it's the right thing to do. He doesn't want me to damage the kids' reputations. He just told me to 'let it rest.' "

Levine hung up the phone and then called Ritter to ask him why he had called off an investigator who was appointed by the board without consulting them about his decision.

"Bruce, this is a mistake," she said. "If you are innocent you can't allow them to do this to you. If these charges are all false you can build your own case the way you would structure a law case in your own defense."

"Well, that's good, Ellen. I'll think about that," said Ritter, adopting a patronizing tone that Levine had heard before when he was politely putting people off.

Levine took Ritter's reluctance to allow the private investigator to pursue the case as the first clue that the allegations could be true.

"I can't tell you I had changed my mind, but I started to feel very uncomfortable. I felt the ice was getting very thin," said Levine.

Another pivotal investigation in Father Bruce Ritter's fall from grace was not by a private investigator, but by *The New York Times*. Initially, "the Gray Lady" treated the story as a sordid affair beneath its readership, but eventually, two top investigative reporters, M. A. Farber and Ralph Blumenthal, were assigned to discover whether the allegations were true or false.

They weighed into the story by delivering what they call their "journalistic *Miranda* warning" to Covenant House's chief operating officer, James Harnett.

"God help you if you tell us something that is not so," admonished Farber.

In early January, Farber and Blumenthal had a big break in their investigation. Out of frustration and anger that the Franciscans had ignored his calls, Bassile went to the *Times* with his allegation.

After interviewing Bassille, the *Times* contacted the Franciscan officials who had ignored him. The Franciscans were then embarrassed into weighing in with their own investigation.

As they neared the end of their reporting, Farber and Blumenthal requested an interview with Father Ritter. They met in Harnett's office. Dressed in a sweatshirt, jeans, and jogging shoes, Ritter looked at his watch as he walked in, "as if this was not the most important thing in his life," said Blumenthal. He sat in a straight-back leather chair behind a desk while Blumenthal drilled him with questions about Bassile, the false identity created for Kite, the trips to Rhinebeck, and the expenditures on Kite.

Then Farber began pacing the room—smoke from his pipe wafting behind him. He watched Ritter closely through Blumenthal's line of questioning and found him, as he phrased it, "unctuous, though not necessarily dissembling." There was a silence in the room before the interrogation shifted from Blumenthal to Farber. Forming his questions cautiously and thinking a good deal before each one, Farber slowly built up to his most direct confrontation.

"If you were standing before the good Lord today, and he asked you did you do anything wrong here, and if your Creator didn't want a ten-sentence answer, just a simple yes or no, what would be your answer?"

"No," said Ritter, growing impatient, and his cold blue eyes glaring at Farber as if to say, "Who the hell are you to ask such a question?"

Farber continued, narrowing his line of questioning and growing increasingly more prosecutorial in tone.

"Father Ritter, at that time wouldn't you have—"

Farber never finished the question. Suddenly there was a loud explosion. A fluorescent lightbulb directly over Ritter's head shattered. Tiny shards of glass came spraying down. The men stood up in shock.

"What the hell was that?" asked Ritter.

"It looks like the lightbulb just shattered," said Harnett, all of them bewildered, not knowing whether to laugh or read some larger significance into the bizarre occurrence. Ritter did not laugh. He looked annoyed. He dusted the tiny shards of glass off his sweatshirt and made sure his hands weren't bleeding. Harnett swept up the broken glass and dumped it in a trash can. They finished the interview.

"You better have that light checked," Ritter told Harnett, as they walked out of the room behind Farber and Blumenthal.

On Tuesday, February 6, 1990, *The New York Times* story landed on the front page. It was an article that stretched over three pages, providing full details of Bassile's allegations and putting into context the scandal that had been unfolding over the last three months. It disclosed for the first time that the Franciscan Order was conducting its own investigation into the additional allegations of sexual misconduct. The relative weight of *The New York Times* compared to the *New York Post* was obvious; the scandal had gone mainstream. It was all over for Ritter.

The same day the story appeared in the paper, Father Ritter announced he would temporarily step aside for a period of "rest and recuperation" during the scandal. Actually, he had been *directed* by his order to step aside and would never again return to the organization that he had founded. But for three long weeks, in a bitter struggle for the control of the direction of the charity, Ritter would relentlessly battle to hold on to his power.

In a press release sent over fax machines to newspapers across the country, Ritter wrote: "I am profoundly saddened by the allegations against me and the need to deny them constantly. I have no way of proving my innocence. My accusers cannot establish my guilt. . . . Therefore I have decided to take several weeks off to rest and recuperate to deal with the personal stress caused by this controversy as well as its impact on Covenant House."

His Franciscan brothers were shocked at the shrewd public-relations move by Ritter. Over the previous few days, Ritter had fought bitterly with the superiors of his order over their directive that he step down during their investigation. He told them that if he did, even temporarily, it would create a tremendous "appearance of guilt" in light of the accusations, and that it would undermine the charity's efforts to quell the storm surrounding the scandal.

Ritter's fellow Franciscans saw a need to clarify their own position, and just several hours after they heard about Ritter's press release, the Franciscan minister provincial, Father Conall McHugh, sent out a quite different statement.

On Dec. 12, 1989, [I] issued a statement of unequivocal support of Father Bruce Ritter. This statement was based on Father Ritter's assurance to his religious superior that he had not been involved in the fraudulent use of Covenant House funds nor in any other alleged misconduct. . . .

On Jan. 29, Mr. Bassile was interviewed in person by Father Canice Connors of the Franciscan Order. As of this date, the inquiry into this allegation is being continued. . . .

"The Provincial and his Council have *directed* Father Bruce to begin a period of rest and recuperation without responsibility for Covenant House until this inquiry is completed. [Emphasis in original.]

The Conventual Franciscan community has been and continues

to be proud of Covenant House and its dedicated staff. The Franciscans will continue to support the efforts of Covenant House to assist needy children during and after this inquiry. We pray that others will join us in this support.

The subtext of McHugh's terse statement was a war being waged between Ritter and his order. The one-page press release was the first acknowledgment by Ritter's fellow Franciscans that they would no longer publicly state their support for him, only the charity he founded. It was a subtle but significant difference and the beginning of a deepening rift between the Franciscan superstar and his family of friars. Father Bruce was—as he had always insisted he be—on his own.

Chapter 18

Church and State

IN the early evening of February 6, Ritter slipped past the reporters standing sentry in front of Covenant House and fled to the secluded cottage in Rhinebeck on the banks of the Hudson River. Board member Frank Macchiarola was at home, making a turkey dinner for his wife and children. Having had the day off from his job as a professor at Columbia University's Graduate School of Business, Macchiarola hadn't seen the explosive article in *The New York Times* that morning.

The phone rang. It was Father Ritter's secretary telling him there was going to be an emergency board meeting. When Macchiarola said he didn't think he could attend because he was preparing dinner, fellow board member Denis Coleman, former vice president of Bear, Stearns & Company and a member of Ritter's inner circle throughout the scandal, came to the phone.

"Look, Frank, there is a lot going on. I'm afraid you're going to have to come in," said Coleman. "Father Bruce is going to step down for a while for some rest and he may be going to ask you to do more."

"What do you mean 'do more'?" Macchiarola asked.

"He wants you to take over for a while, to run things," said Coleman.

Macchiarola arranged to arrive at the meeting late and left a note for his family not to wait for him. It was the beginning of three tumultuous weeks in which Macchiarola would be described by his fellow board members alternately as "the last man of integrity in the place" and "the biggest slime ball alive." As the former Chancellor of the New York City Board of Education and a prominent financial adviser to the city during the fiscal crisis of the mid-1970s, Macchiarola was a respected public figure, who had handled crises before. He had served four years on the finance committee at Covenant House.

When he arrived for the meeting, board members were putting the finishing touches on a press release and discussing ways to make it "look as if Bruce wasn't ordered to step down."

"Wait a minute, you mean he doesn't have a choice?" asked Macchiarola. "You mean the order is forcing him to step down?"

"Right, Frank," said Stroock. "But it's only temporary. Why should the media know that? I think it's real important to put the best face possible on this thing."

As Father Ritter had requested, the board quickly passed a motion allowing Macchiarola to take control of the organization as acting president. Some board members supported Harnett for the position, but the majority felt he was too close to Father Bruce to be objective. Whether Macchiarola was brought in as a reformer or a caretaker didn't seem to matter; the charity simply needed someone who could inspire confidence and carry the torch through crisis. Covenant House seemed safe in Macchiarola's competent hands.

By the next morning, he was lining up a team of loyalists and advisers to help him steer the ship, including Maureen Connelly, a top public-relations expert, and Dick Halverson, a policy consultant. But while Macchiarola was, as he put it, "thinking about the resurrection," the other board members were "worrying about the crucifixion."

Macchiarola's first move was to order an emergency strategy to hold onto the charity's major donors through the crisis. The goal was to confront Father Ritter's departure head-on through a massive telemarketing campaign. Senior staff officials, board members, and Macchiarola called the top five hundred "major donors."

The next phase of the strategy was to shift the focus away from the cult of personality around Ritter and begin "focusing more on the kids" and "those who work directly with the kids." Senior vice president for funding and development Chris Walton made it clear that the survival of the charity was going to have to be separated from the fate of its founder. It was a direction with which Ritter's loyal board was uncomfortable. They saw it as a betrayal of the man who had founded Covenant House. They bristled, but went along with it—at least for the time being.

Walton's projections for fund raising for the second half of the fiscal year were positive, based on January's "rally," but he did note that the reaction to the "smear" was unknown, and that the direct-mail-marketing loss could be as high as $100,000 per day through the end of March.

By Monday, February 12, Macchiarola was holding meetings with internal staff and desperately trying to get a handle on the burgeoning scandal. His hand-picked clean-up crew began requesting documents, asking for memos, and looking over shoulders. There was a sense of turmoil in Ritter's inner circle. Donahue, Kells, and Loken were furious. Who did Macchiarola and his henchmen think they were coming in and taking over?

Almost as soon as Macchiarola scratched the surface, dark secrets, conspiracies, and allegations came oozing out of the cracks of Covenant House. The investigation took him and his team down a hallway of funhouse mirrors that distorted all appearances of Ritter and his inner circle.

First, they began looking into the allegations about Kells's roommate, Tony Iacovazzi, who was purported to have a no-show job at the charity. Loken, they learned, was keeping a former male prostitute in the safe-house program—for which there was no clear documentation—in his Bronx apartment. There were allegations, later proven unfounded, that Loken was sexually involved with this youth. There were whispers about Covenant House employees assisting in the cover-up of the murder of Sean Russell, the former hustler who was killed by a transvestite in a bizarre murder-suicide. Later, there were allegations that linked Kells to Russell, including a memo from Covenant House lawyer Karen Staller to Harnett, dated February 16. The memo indicated that Kells's name was used "in reference to a sexual relationship with a resident" and that the issue should be taken "somewhat seriously" because its exposure to the press could "blow Covenant House out of the water." (These allegations were later dismissed as unfounded.)

Meanwhile, the District Attorney was still digging into the allegations of financial improprieties and their relationship to Ritter's alleged "private affairs" with at least five young former residents of Covenant House, as well as several members of the Faith Community. There were allegations by senior staff officials that ranged from Ritter's having used more than $3,000 in Covenant House funds to pay for a satellite dish at the cottage in Rhinebeck to the charity's connection with the Reagan administration's covert operation to fund the contras.

In the Latin America program, there were other swirling allegations of a separate scandal of sexual and financial misconduct by more than a dozen staff members in Guatemala and Honduras. The program, headed by Ritter acolyte Patrick Atkinson, was awash in allegations of a widespread pattern of sexual abuse and some questionable financial practices that went on with the knowledge of top staff officials.

Ritter, it was also alleged, had a puzzling relationship with Francis Pilecki, the president of Westfield State College in Massachusetts. Pilecki had been indicted for an alleged indecent assault on two male students at the college in 1986. The same month that Pilecki allegedly arranged a controversial pay-off with college funds to one of the parents of an accuser, he was meeting with Ritter in New York to establish a "relationship" between Covenant House and Westfield State, whereby the charity would send twenty street kids to a special study program at the college. (All charges against Pilecki were later dropped.) Regarding the relationship between the two men, Macchiarola said, "There wasn't much to it," certainly nothing to substantiate the conspiracy theory some reporters and fellow staffers had claimed. But, Macchiarola added, it was representative of the kind of bizarre terrain on which he was treading in his three-week ordeal as the acting president. The well-packaged mythology of Covenant House was deteriorating into darkness.

As the disturbing allegations emerged, Macchiarola made it clear that he would not serve as a "caretaker," as Ritter had defined his role. On February 13, Harnett called together nearly twenty executive directors and senior vice presidents of Covenant House operations throughout the country. They came to New York or listened in on teleconference from as far away as Anchorage and Guatemala for a crucial meeting that would address the direction of the charity in the wake of the scandal. Harnett was running the show, but Macchiarola quickly exerted control. He meant business. He told the senior staff employees across the country and throughout the world that "you need to assess what your contribution to Covenant House is going to be in the future."

"If there is anything you have done in the past that makes you feel you won't be able to contribute in the future," said Macchiarola, "you should resign."

It was a decisive moment—the point at which Macchiarola vowed to expose everything that had gone wrong. To the senior staff, the edict was confusing and elusive, an apparent warning shot before a war to rid the charity of its evils. Macchiarola was already moving to fire Loken and Kells, having deemed that, whether or not the allegations against them were true, the appearance of impropriety was so great that they were "no longer effective or useful" to the future of the charity. He ordered them both to take "vacations."

Macchiarola's aggressiveness must have scared Ritter. On February 16, he arranged a meeting at Columbia University's Academy of Political Sciences, where Macchiarola had his office. Trying to go unnoticed in the midst of the intense media coverage of the scandal, Ritter pulled his coat collar up and his hat down as he walked across the courtyard of the Columbia campus in the Morningside Heights section of Manhattan. They talked in Macchiarola's office over coffee.

"In terms of planning for the future, it would be useful to know if I am going to have the position on a permanent basis," Macchiarola said to Ritter.

Ritter was evasive on the question. He wanted to know more about what details Macchiarola had been uncovering in his investigation. Ritter was clearly still aggressively monitoring the unfolding scandal. Privately Ritter had discussed with Covenant House counsel Ed Burns the Franciscan Charitable Trust, which was the most glaring financial impropriety that, so far, had not yet come to light. But even though Macchiarola didn't know about the trust or the improper loans, he avoided Ritter's questions. The two of them were locked in an awkward dance around the truth.

"Put it this way, should I plan on teaching this summer?" asked Macchiarola, forcing some answer from Ritter on the length of his stay there.

"No," said Ritter, "this could easily take six months."

For Ritter, the loneliness and the want of power were setting in after only ten days away from the charity that he still believed was his. In veiled and confusing language, Ritter tried to define a future role for himself. He wavered back and forth. At times, he seemed to understand that he would never be in charge again, but then he would insist that his complete vindication was imminent and that he would return as president. Finally, Father Ritter rocked back in the wooden chair in Macchiarola's office and looked down. The lines on his face—deep horizontal lines that cut across his forehead—accentuated his depression in the bleak light of February.

"Look, you're in charge right now. There is nothing I can do," said

Ritter. "But you have to be careful to show compassion to the staff. . . . You cannot do away with open intake. I guess those are the two most important points we need to agree on."

Over the next week, Macchiarola ripped into Covenant House with plans to hire former Deputy Police Commissioner Patrick Murphy to investigate the list of allegations. He hinted at a purge of the charity and seemed to be lining up new directors to replace those who had become so close to the founder that it had "impaired their judgment." He asked Richard Shinn, a management consultant and president of Metropolitan Life Insurance, to come up with recommendations to set consistent compensation policies and to examine salary levels. He consulted with financial experts to set up new accounting procedures, and policy experts to establish an independent, internal system of accountability and a system for reporting allegations of misconduct.

He made bold pronouncements to the press that the charity had been "operat[ing] at the margins of appropriate behavior." He specifically stated that he intended to do away with the safe-house program, for which he incurred the wrath of Anne Donahue.

"The press bought Macchiarola hook, line, and sinker because he was telling them what they wanted to hear," said Donahue. "The stuff he was leaking to the press all turned out to be bull—the murder cover-up, the Loken suspicions, the Kells stuff—none of that was proven. . . . He was grandstanding for his own political career."

From Macchiarola's point of view "The place was filled with zealots." He felt Donahue typified the staff members who were unable to separate Father Ritter from the mission of Covenant House. For them Covenant House was a "form of sanctity," and they saw Macchiarola as "taking that away from them."

Throughout Ritter's hour of suffering Cardinal O'Connor was in contact with him by phone. Still rebelling against authority and skirting the rule of his order, Ritter led the cardinal to believe that he was staying at a "Franciscan House in New York State." He was actually spending most of his time at the private cottage in Rhinebeck. In the February 22 issue of *Catholic New York*, Cardinal O'Connor reflected on his conversations with Ritter.

"It would be deceitful to say his spirits are good. My spirits would certainly not be good if I were under the allegations he is," O'Connor said. "I think he's trying very hard to be a good religious and accept the poverty of spirit which is supposed to characterize Franciscan life. This situation would be difficult for anyone. It's difficult for him. . . . I'm sure he's doing a lot of praying and reflecting."

Macchiarola continued his investigation of the charity, his ferocity growing with each new outrageous allegation. On Friday, February 23, Macchiarola learned the first details of the personal loans made from Covenant House funds to Ritter and others. The details were sketchy, but from what he could gather there had been more than $20,000 in loans to Ritter, a $100,000 loan to Kells, and a roughly $60,000 loan to Jim Kelly. As a long-time public servant, Macchiarola understood fiduciary trust enough to know that the loans were at least improper, if not illegal. He met with Covenant House counsel Ed Burns to discuss the exact nature of the loans. What Macchiarola did not know was that Burns himself had had financial dealings with the Franciscan Charitable Trust. Without letting on, the attorney proceeded to tell Macchiarola, Stroock, and Denis Coleman that "there was absolutely nothing unlawful about the loans.

"It is absolutely legal for a corporation to give senior officers loans to help them relocate or to entice them to come to a company," said Burns.

Of course, Covenant House is a nonprofit charity, not a corporation. As a former head of the Attorney General's Charities Bureau put it, it is "ironclad" in state law that no officer or director of a nonprofit institution shall receive a loan from the institution. Although the loans to Kells and Kelly were not barred (because they were neither officers nor directors), they clearly should not have been made without board approval.

Burns and a group of investors had received a $100,000 loan from Ritter's as-yet-undisclosed Franciscan Charitable Trust to purchase undeveloped land in Long Island with a group of investors. For him not to disclose that to Macchiarola and the other board members during the inquiry about other loans was disingenuous at best.

Even though he did not have the full details of the loans, Macchiarola felt that they were the last straw. It was clearly improper for a charity to use money that donors had given to help kids for home-improvement loans and speculative real-estate deals by board members and senior staff officials. Macchiarola told the staff that Father Ritter, whether guilty or innocent of the charges of sexual misconduct, had to be severed from the charity.

But before Macchiarola could implement his plan, Donahue and Kells drove up to Rhinebeck to visit their exiled spiritual leader. It was Sunday, February 25, Ritter's sixty-third birthday, and they told him about Macchiarola's plan to sever him from the charity. Ritter would never let it happen without a fight. He immediately began

working the phone, lobbying board members to his side, and planning a last-minute palace coup to overthrow Macchiarola and replace
him with Jim Harnett.

First, he called Ellen Levine. "Things are not going well with Frank
at the helm," said Ritter in a tone of voice that was anguished and
conspiratorial. "I don't want my lifework, everything I've done, to be
in his hands."

Then he called Mark Stroock and asked him to come out to the
cottage to talk. When Stroock arrived, Ritter was standing in the
doorway in jeans and a sweater, with a gray stubble on his pale, drawn
cheeks.

"Can I ever come back?" Ritter asked his faithful adviser in a tone
that was earnest, but concealed a lot of pain.

"To be honest, Bruce, I don't know. I don't think so," said Stroock.
"There are two things that would permit you to come back. One is
if the kids recant. And two is if you agree to take a different kind of
role and vow never to be in a room alone with a kid again. To be
frank, I don't think either is realistic."

Ritter didn't say anything for a while. Then he began to ask questions about his financial future, about a possible "pension plan" for
himself. The queries caught Stroock by surprise.

"How the hell could he be thinking about his financial future when
the fate of the entire charity was hanging by a thread?" Stroock
wondered. It was calculated and presumptuous. Suddenly Stroock
was seeing a different side to Ritter. He felt the man was "beginning
to come undone."

"I've got to get Frank out of there," Ritter said, breaking into
another train of thought. "This is something I built my entire life. I
don't even know if people can see that. I spent my entire life building
this."

Desperate to keep his secrets hidden, Ritter succeeded in postpon-
ing for a day the board meeting that was scheduled for that Monday.
It was an eleventh-hour effort to replace Macchiarola with Harnett.
Macchiarola simply knew too much.

Late that Sunday, the phone rang at Macchiarola's home. He was
still up, planning the details for the meeting. He was prepared to
deliver his five-point plan for reforming the charity in the wake of
the scandal. He was nervous about the questionable loans. It was
going to be a bombshell.

It was Ritter on the phone, requesting a sitdown the next day to
"go over a few things." Ritter didn't tell him that the board meeting
had been canceled. These two men with fierce egos were set for a

showdown, while the future of the thousands of young people for whom the charity cared remained hanging in the balance.

But before that could happen, Ritter had business to take care of. He had to finalize the details of a deal that for days had been in the works between the Manhattan District Attorney's office and the archdiocese, with Ritter's attorney, Stanley Arkin, as the intermediary. Arkin apparently feared from the body language of the investigators that they were about to convene a grand jury on the charges and wanted to prevent that at any cost. It would escalate the scandal to a new level, from which they believed the charity and Ritter himself would never be able to recover. The priest and his attorney had to work fast—the scandal had come to a head.

The law was seated on the eighth floor of the Manhattan Criminal Court in the office of D.A. Robert Morgenthau. The Church was uptown on First Avenue at Fiftieth Street, where the executive office of Cardinal John O'Connor looks out over a panoramic view of midtown's skyscrapers and the East River. From these two offices, men of the law and men of the cloth were hammering out a deal, mostly by phone. If Father Ritter would permanently step down from the charity and vow never to work as a child-care provider again, certainly it would have great influence on the Manhattan D.A.'s decision as to whether to pursue the criminal investigation of the charity's conduct. Intermediaries for the prosecutor and His Eminence claimed there was no "quid pro quo." But as one official knowledgeable about the negotiations put it, "There had to be a clear understanding of where each side stood."

With the terms of the deal established, Ritter planned for a graceful exit from the charity. He would line up Harnett to replace Macchiarola, believing that there would be no aggressive investigation of the charity, that his philosophy of open intake would remain the cornerstone of the charity's policy, and that his core of loyalist staff would not be callously discarded in a reformist purge. And then Ritter would step down. Eventually the charges would be dropped, allowing him vindication without the appearance of a deal. Macchiarola was the only thing standing in the way.

When Ritter met with him in the late afternoon on Monday, Ritter told him quite bluntly that he wanted him to stay on as a figurehead, with Harnett to be in charge, temporarily, until things settled down.

"I think we need someone who is very knowledgeable of child-care policy and who has built a rapport with the staff. The morale has been severely affected by your moving so quickly," said Ritter.

"I don't think the issue is morale," Macchiarola shot back. "But if it is, I am surely not the one responsible for it."

Ritter explained that he would eventually be stepping down.

"Well, I think Mr. Morgenthau would be quite interested to hear that," quipped Macchiarola, quickly catching on to the fact that a deal was in the works.

Ritter glared at Macchiarola. There was little more to say. Each man understood precisely where the other was coming from.

"If I am not in charge and given the opportunity to carry out the reforms that I see necessary, I will simply resign," said Macchiarola.

Ritter had apparently wanted Macchiarola to stand idly by and sweep all of the allegations he had uncovered under the rug. Ritter even told him that if financial compensation was a problem he could arrange for the university professor to collect a $1,500-a-day consulting fee through the entire summer. Until then Macchiarola had still believed that Ritter was a Franciscan who took his vow of poverty seriously. The offer of such generous compensation only infuriated him more, making it glaringly apparent that the man in whom he had had so much faith was "morally bankrupt."

Sensing that Ritter was moving for a cover-up, Macchiarola made a preemptive strike. He told Ritter that either he accepted Macchiarola's long-term plan for reforming the charity and getting to the bottom of every allegation or he would resign and go public with all of the allegations that had so far surfaced.

Ritter's fury smoldered in a heavy silence in the room. He said nothing, but realized that his only move was to permanently resign the following day.

A board meeting was set for 5 P.M. Tuesday; Ritter and Macchiarola would make separate presentations to the board.

Ritter went first. Sitting around the polished mahogany conference table at Covenant House's Seventeenth Street building, the board members listened to his simple and direct speech. He had three conditions: that Harnett replace Macchiarola, that open intake be preserved, and that the leadership role be filled by someone from the Catholic clergy. The fact that Ritter did not specify that the new president be a Franciscan was significant and a reflection of his bitter falling-out with his fellow friars. Ritter concluded that, "after much thought and prayer," he had decided to resign.

Most of the board members were not surprised. They had all had their parts in the intricate dance Ritter had orchestrated throughout the weekend. Once Father Bruce said his last goodbye to the board members, Macchiarola was given the green light to come in and make his presentation. His plan for recovery included: launching a thorough investigation into all of the allegations that had been made; restructuring the policy of the organization to make it more accountable and to clearly state procedures; reviewing employee compensation policies; and establishing the board of directors as a separate and independent entity from the executive offices. He ended by saying that if his plan was not accepted he would resign. Macchiarola hinted that if there was a whitewash of the allegations he would consider going public.

He didn't know he had walked into an ambush, plotted by Ritter, who had already lobbied a majority of votes to have Macchiarola ousted. He did not know that at least two board members, Dr. Jim Kennedy and attorney James Maguire, had both received loans and, in Macchiarola's view, had a "vested interest in making sure that they were not found out."

Stroock told Macchiarola that he found his tactics unfair and abrasive. He was holding a gun to the board's head and none of them were going to go for it.

"You can't do that to your fellow board members," said Stroock, blowing up in the meeting. "We have enough trouble. You don't have to do that. For Christ's sake, you don't have to do it today. . . . If you go public with these allegations, you could do irreparable harm to Covenant House."

The board voted fifteen to one to remove Macchiarola as acting president and, as Ritter requested, put Harnett in control of the charity. They did tell Macchiarola that they would adopt some of his plans for reform. They took "the plan, not the man," as Levine quipped in a catchy sound bite for reporters. Donna Santarsiero, the lone holdout, resigned from the board in disgust the following day. Macchiarola went straight to the press and the State Attorney General with all of the allegations that had surfaced, especially the loans. By coming out with full disclosure of everything he knew, he prevented Ritter's plan to have loyalists, including Jim Harnett, sweep everything under the rug.

"I was the guy with the light," Macchiarola told the *Post* that night, "and they said, 'You know what? It's too bright in here.'"

It was dubbed the "Tuesday-night massacre," and Burns likened the atmosphere at Covenant House to "a meltdown." The charity was rocked to its core and the papers were having a field day.

Seventeen hours later, the Manhattan District Attorney's office held a press conference to announce that it would be dropping its criminal investigation of Father Ritter. Usually prosecutors drop a case and confine their comments to the bare statement that the case is closed for want of evidence. But Morgenthau showed no such restraint, as if he needed to expose the basis of his case to ensure that Ritter adhered to his end of the bargain. Morgenthau told the press that he was closing the case despite "some questionable financial transactions" and evidence of "violations of law," especially in relation to the falsification of Kite's identity.

It was a case study in prosecutorial discretion, whereby the prosecution, having found no crime, washed its hands of the scandal by convincing the Church it should force Father Ritter's resignation. "We wanted to make sure that the right thing happened here," said an Assistant District Attorney who worked on the case. "Clearly there were problems with the charity. The illegality did not reflect the seriousness of those problems, but we had to investigate every aspect of it that came to us. I think we did the right thing."

And so the law, the Church, and the press had pounded in different directions until eventually Ritter was toppled.

The fallen priest fled to New Canaan, Connecticut, and holed up in a guest bedroom at Bob Macauley's mansion. Macauley was one of the few remaining disciples. In a makeshift chapel in a second-floor study of Macauley's estate Ritter celebrated mass. Frequently, Macauley would join him, kneeling next to the Franciscan priest while he performed the Eucharist. The study was cluttered with framed commendations for Macauley's charitable work and political affiliations. On the walls, a shrine of photographs featured Macauley and Ritter with George Bush and Ronald Reagan and Pope John Paul. The smell of incense wafted through the mansion as they recited the Rite of Communion. They bowed their heads and prayed:

>"Deliver us, Lord, from every evil,
>and grant us peace in our day.
>In your mercy keep us free from sin
>and protect us from all anxiety
>as we wait in joyful hope for the coming of our savior,
>Jesus Christ."

For Father Bruce, the dream was over but the nightmare wasn't. New revelations kept spilling out—literally day by day.

Macchiarola had lived up to his promise. On March 2, the New York State Attorney General's office announced that it was investigating the legality of personal loans made by the charity to the Reverend Bruce Ritter and other Covenant House officials. The Manhattan D.A.'s office turned over its records to the A.G.'s office.

Ritter was not out of the woods by any means, nor were the charity's board members and senior staff who had benefited from the loans.

On March 5, board chairman Ralph Pfeiffer held a teleconference with all the senior staff officials. Saying that "serious errors were committed," Pfeiffer announced the board's plan to investigate the scandal and reexamine the charity's procedures in light of what had happened. Pfeiffer set the tone: The charity would rebuild itself with better internal controls and systems of accountability in the wake of the scandal. The charity was to be purged of its fallen founder, and would go to some of the biggest names in corporate America to do it.

William Ellinghaus was named chairman of a star-studded oversight committee, which included five of the most prominent and successful men in the country. Ellinghaus, former president of AT&T, was one of Ritter's fellow Knights of Malta and a friend of Bill Simon and Peter Grace. He had served on Simon's lay committee to attack the U.S. bishops' pastoral letter on the economy. The corporate kings on the board were in familiar company with the oversight committee. The other four committee members were the Reverend Theodore M. Hesburgh, former president of Notre Dame University; Cyrus Vance, former Secretary of State; Paul Volcker, former Chairman of the Federal Reserve; and Rabbi Marc Tanenbaum, an international-relations consultant.

Burns resigned as counsel. The law firm of Cravath, Swaine & Moore, which agreed to work on a pro bono basis, was named in his place. Cravath, along with Robert J. McGuire, former New York City Police Commissioner and currently the senior managing director of Kroll Associates, a prestigious private investigating firm, were asked to undertake a "full investigation of all allegations of misconduct relating to Covenant House."

The board also retained the accounting firm of Ernst & Young to conduct a review of the charity's financial procedures; Richard Shinn, executive vice chairman of the New York Stock Exchange and former president of Metropolitan Life Insurance Company, to review Covenant House's compensation and salary levels for its staff; and the Child Welfare League to review certain Covenant House programs for compliance with its own policies and generally recognized standards of care.

Before his departure, Burns released to the board the disturbing new information about the Franciscan Charitable Trust. Most members of the board had never heard of it. Those who had benefited—including Maguire and Kennedy—insisted that they did not know that the trust was connected with Covenant House. Father Conall McHugh, a board member and Ritter's superior, said he had never heard of the trust, even though it was listed in the name of the Order of Franciscan Minor Conventual. Harnett conceded to the board that he and Ritter and other top staff officials knew of the loans and that they should have been reported to the board. He called it "a big mistake."

Deciding to come clean about the Franciscan Charitable Trust, the board turned over all of the documents to the A.G.'s office. The complicated details of Ritter's secret $1 million Franciscan Charitable Trust and the loans it made were traced back to the board members and Burns.

"I thought I was doing a good thing to take care of the kids," Ritter told *The New York Times,* maintaining that he started the trust to help fund programs for youths that the charity could not otherwise afford.

The Franciscan Charitable Trust was created without the knowledge of Ritter's superiors and without the knowledge of most of the board members. Many of the check-request vouchers for money sent to the trust were countersigned by Harnett, Spanier, or Robert Cardany, head of Covenant House's finance department. In 1983, Ritter listed the donor of the initial $200,000 in the trust as the "Order Minor Conventual and Covenant House related sponsors," although it was actually $200,000 from the Greif Brothers stock. In 1984, Ritter, who was then sole trustee, applied through Burns to the Internal Revenue Service for an exemption under section 501(C) of the Internal Revenue Code, claiming not to be a private foundation and thereby entitled, along with any investors in the trust, to a tax deduction as well as a federal tax exemption of interest earned by the trust. It also freed the trust from certain limitations placed on private foundations, such as a requirement that a percentage of the trust be distributed annually.

The IRS filing stated that the purpose of the trust was to "support Father Bruce Ritter's ministry" and that "Covenant House and its related organizations have a significant voice in [the trust's] investment policies."

But there is no evidence that the trust made any significant disbursements for the purpose of Ritter's ministry. And there is no evidence that anyone other than Ritter had any say in the investment policies of the trust.

The only people who benefited from that trust were Ritter, several board members, Burns, and Ritter's sister, for whom he arranged an interest-free loan. Through a complex set of transfers, Ritter provided his sister with a bridge loan of $131,000 in October of 1987. The following year she repaid $108,000, with Ritter making up the $23,000 difference, or almost exactly the amount of interest owed at about 12 percent. That meant, in effect, that Ritter gave Wallace an interest-free loan on $108,000.

In 1986, board member James Maguire, who owned the former Astor Mansion in Rhinebeck and the private cottage that Ritter often used, had a "liquidity problem." In order to raise the cash, Burns created a special entity called Hudson River Views, to which Maguire sold five acres of land for $80,000. In 1989, the trust, acting through Hudson River Views, sold that land to Dr. Kennedy for $120,000, with Kennedy putting down $30,000 of his own money and the trust providing a 10-percent-interest mortgage on the rest.

Maguire again dipped into the trust in December of 1988, when he borrowed $100,000 for one year at 10.5 percent interest.

Burns, the trustee of the fund, and his group of investors were also beneficiaries, receiving $60,000 from the fund as well as $40,000 from Ritter (which included a $25,000 cash advance from Covenant House). The loan gave the group sufficient funding to purchase undeveloped land near Riverhead, Long Island, in October of 1989.

As Blumenthal and Farber confronted Ritter with the questionable loans and unethical use of charitable funds, the embattled priest grew defensive: "It was my salary. God help me, I earned it, seven days a week, year-round."

Dr. Jim Kennedy immediately resigned from the board to avoid any further appearance of impropriety. As the $80,000-a-year medical director of Covenant House, Kennedy had devoted fifteen years to the mission and was one of Ritter's closest personal friends.

James Maguire, who along with his wife had been involved with Covenant House since the 1970s and had spent weekends with Ritter in Rhinebeck, resigned and severed his relationship with Ritter, asking him to no longer stay in the cottage at the edge of their estate.

Board member James Makrianes, a partner of Ward Howell International and former president of Haley Associates, also resigned to "avoid any suggestion of conflict of interest." During the scandal, revelations surfaced that, while he was still president of Haley, the firm received compensation from Covenant House, with the board's knowledge.

Santarsiero had been the first board member to resign, after two decades of involvement with the charity. In a bitter letter to the rest of the board, she expressed her anger at being lied to about the abolition of the safe-house program by Kells and Harnett. She also stated that the highest echelons of leadership within Covenant House had been misleading on many issues, and as a result, the trust she had placed in the charity since its founding had been lost. She felt that the board was taking part in a coverup, and she wanted no part of it.

The board of directors' failure as an active and independent body was highlighted in the wake of the scandal. Questions were raised not only as to how much the board knew but about what it should have known. Clearly Macauley, Kennedy, and Maguire should have known or at least suspected that the trust was connected to Covenant House and brought this to the board's attention. The board should have asked more questions about the charity's expansion into Central America, about Ritter's sometimes reckless real-estate speculation, and about standard operating procedure at the charity, such as an independent system of accountability.

In hindsight, Stroock concedes that the board should have been more assertive and independent. But, he explains, Ritter's commanding personal presence and the faith they placed in his judgment led them to operate in a spirit of "great trust."

"I thought the guy was like every other Franciscan, out there with a begging bowl," said Stroock. "It never crossed my mind to ask about his salary or to ask, 'Hey, by the way, Bruce, do you have a one-million-dollar trust fund?"

Ralph Pfeiffer, Jr., former chairman of IBM World Trade, who was made chairman of the board a month before the scandal broke, said, "We wish we had done more and known more, and we've made as much a mea culpa as possible."

Edward L. Shaw, Jr., a Covenant House board member since 1987 and general counsel of the Chase Manhattan Corporation, said that the board had shown "too much deference" to Ritter. He said that many of the board members had felt that his work was "brilliant," that they trusted him and gave him the latitude to make the executive decisions.

Eventually, nearly half of the seventeen-member board would resign. A long list of staff members would follow, many of them handing in their resignations before they were asked to leave. The charity was being cleansed of Ritter's main loyalists, although some stayed on.

John Kells resigned on March 5, after he signed an agreement to return the $100,000 loan that he had received from Covenant House. Greg Loken resigned the same day.

Dozens of other resignations came between the end of February and April and included Jim Kelly, Pat Atkinson, John Spanier, and Monica Kaiser.

Harnett stayed on and was given the job of acting president. His only sin had been blind loyalty to Ritter. Although they had some ideological differences, Ritter believed that Harnett would continue his loyalty by keeping intact the spiritual mission of Covenant House, as Father Bruce had defined it. He was wrong.

Harnett announced a downscaling of the program. The Asian office, which had been about to launch a series of programs from the Philippines to Laos and Vietnam, would be closed; the New Jersey and Washington, D.C., programs would be limited to outreach services; open intake would be preserved but with qualifications; and the safe-house program was to be terminated.

"These have been difficult times for all of us. We've made some bad mistakes and errors in judgment. As Acting President, my commitment to our staff and kids is that these will be uncovered and corrected, and policies will be developed to insure this will not happen again," wrote Harnett in an internal memo to the staff.

The memo went on to say:

> there have been examples of behavior at Covenant House which were serious errors. I want to acknowledge them: It is wrong for anyone, including the Acting President of Covenant House, to fraternize with a resident outside our centers. It is wrong to provide a young man or woman an unsupervised apartment for personal use. It was wrong for residents to be employed by Covenant House as if they were staff. The policies and procedures of Covenant House must and will govern the conduct of staff equally from front line to top management.

Anne Donahue felt she was watching not only the downfall of Father Ritter and the abandonment of him by his own staff, but also the dismantling of the charity's foundation as a religious ministry based on Father Bruce's mission.

On March 9, she wrote her letter of resignation as executive director of the Los Angeles program:

> The decisions currently being made are too philosophically and personally painful for me to tolerate. The essence of what drew me to Covenant House has been destroyed, and a radical philosophical shift has been embraced. My colleagues and I no longer

share the same vision of Covenant House; those that did have been forced out.

I believe we sold out to media pressure from the very beginning of this crisis, and failed to defend the renegade, anti-institutional philosophy that created Covenant House and gave it its spirit, its vision, and its soul. . . . [A]s one who still believes in Bruce's vision, I have no interest in being a part of the new institution.

There was a battle not only for the "soul" of Covenant House but for its purse as well. And the archdiocese was making a bid for it. In the wake of Ritter's resignation, Cardinal O'Connor muscled the archdiocese's way into the role of interim leadership. The archdiocese had its eye on the nearly $100 million Covenant House raised each year, which was more than six times as much as the $15 million budget of Catholic Charities of the Archdiocese of New York. But that wasn't all the Church coveted. There was also Covenant House's impressive real-estate holdings and its sophisticated direct-mail-marketing machinery.

By the second week in March, O'Connor was directly intervening in the scandal and even arranged meetings with two of Ritter's accusers—John Melican and Kevin Kite.

On Sunday, March 18, during his then famous press briefings, which were traditionally held after the 10:15 A.M. mass at Saint Patrick's Cathedral, O'Connor told reporters that he was going to name a team from the archdiocese that would lead the charity in the wake of the scandal. O'Connor also said he wanted to examine Ritter's resignation letter to make sure that Ritter had "actually separated himself completely from Covenant House"—making a reference to the fact that Ritter was actually still clinging to his role as "sole member."

Ritter was suddenly facing a bleak future, powerless and penniless. He was watching the charity he had created engulfed by the forces he had fought against his whole life—the diocesan bureaucracy and the social-service establishment. But he clung to his last bit of power as long as he could. Even though he had announced his resignation, Ritter had not officially given up his status as the sole member of the charity. There was a great deal of worry in the archdiocese that Ritter could conceivably stage a coup d'état and reclaim control because it was technically his own private corporation. O'Connor's legal staff, including Monsignor William Toohy, a Harvard Law School graduate, examined the corporate structure of Covenant House, learning that the bylaws gave Ritter executive power over every aspect of the charity and that he had the full control of the Franciscan Charitable Trust.

While Ritter's last fight for power was going on, many of the hundreds of thousands of his supporters across the country, as well as board members, senior staff officials, and fellow Franciscans, were coming to terms with the fact that Ritter was not the man they had thought he was.

Others were standing steadfastly by him, seeing him as a martyr, a saint crucified by the press and eventually his own charity. One loyal donor from the Bronx, Bruce Snowden, even wrote a letter to *Catholic New York* comparing Ritter to Saint Gerard Majella, an eighteenth-century Redemptorist brother who was accused of lechery by a village girl he had befriended: " 'Blessed are you when people insult you and tell all manner of lies against you . . . this is how the prophets who lived before you were persecuted!' "

Like everyone else, Mark Stroock struggled to understand. He resigned from the charity as a board member in March. He had not been through anything more difficult in his life, Stroock said, except perhaps for a tragic fire in his family's home when his eight-year-old son was severely burned. But even that had caused Stroock and his wife to turn to their faith. The scandal at Covenant House shook the core of it. Stroock got a call from Ritter on March 12 in his office on Madison Avenue.

As Ritter talked, Stroock thought about the lies and deceptions that he had heard from Ritter over the last three horrible months. He thought about how much faith he had put in the man and his mission over the last fifteen years, and about his pride in the good work he had felt he was doing through Covenant House.

Ritter, not realizing that Stroock had resigned, launched into a pitch to rally the board to create a pension for him. Stroock could not believe that after all the agonizing soul-searching and with the economic future of the charity an open question, Ritter was concerned about his own financial future.

"Wait a minute, Bruce. I've resigned from the board," Stroock said, leaving a silence on the other end of the phone.

"How could you do that?" Ritter asked. "How could you leave without letting me know? How could you do it before I have my pension?"

Stroock was shocked at Ritter's arrogance and left him in midsentence on the phone. He hung up and never spoke to Ritter again. Stroock turned to the Old Testament for help in understanding how a man he had believed was so good could have belied so much dark-

ness. He found a passage that helped him understand what he called
his "crisis of faith." It was Psalm 146:
"Put not your trust in princes
or in any mortal man of power—
he cannot save,
he yields his breath and goes back
to the earth he came from,
and on that day all his schemes perish."

Ritter, clinging to whatever control he had, did not sign off on an
amendment to the charity's bylaws to transfer executive powers to
the board until a week later.

Chapter 19

The Door Closes

THE handwriting was a crooked scrawl that fell off the end of each line of the notebook paper. But for Darryl Bassile, the simple one-page letter he wrote to Father Bruce Ritter was a way to bring some closure to what had happened. Bassile—like Kite and Johnson and Melican and the many others betrayed by Ritter—was disillusioned by the Manhattan District Attorney's decision not to prosecute. He took solace in the promise that Ritter would never work with children again, but the final act to the tragedy was never written. No trial with a verdict. No admission. No apology. Bassile cried when he finished writing the letter. It was dated March 19, 1990.

Dear Bruce,
Well, here I am and there you are. I don't believe you will ever see me face to face so here I am writing you this letter. I am truly sorry that Covenant House has to endure this publicity because I believe the service it offers is a good one. The only thing I ever wanted was to let you know, or at least tell you, that you were wrong. You were wrong for inflicting your desires on a 14 year old. If you wish to have sex with a male, you should have chosen one who was old enough (at least 18). You knew the pain I was suffering and it was

your job to help me, not hurt me. I thought and believed your dream was to help kids and give them a fighting chance, a place where kids could feel safe and loved and with a better feeling about themselves. When you abused me, I lost what Covenant House had to offer, and that was a better life than I had run away from. You may deny what happened but we both know what happened. I know that someday you will stand before the one who judges all of us and at that time there will be no more denial, just the truth. I hope and pray that you seek help and forgiveness not just from God, but also from the ones you have hurt.

Survivor of your abuse,
Darryl James Bassile

Although Bassile never expected Ritter to reply, he gave the letter to the Reverend Canice Connors, the Franciscan priest who headed the order's own inquiry into the allegations against Ritter, to forward. Connors, who had known Ritter for some thirty years, was previously the director of a program in Canada for priests with drug addictions and/or sexual or emotional problems. Ritter continued to deny any wrongdoing, and even refused to cooperate with Connors's investigation, referring all questions to his own private criminal attorney, Stanley Arkin. The investigation was concluded on March 28, 1990. At the end of it all, Connors felt he understood the pain of those who came forward, especially in the absence of any public disclosure that validated their claims. Connors wrote this reply to Bassile:

Dear Darryl,
I received your kind note and the letter for Bruce. I have forwarded your message but I would be surprised if you get a response. This is the first Monday, my day off, that I have not spent in Union City in months. Frankly it feels good to have our inquiry at an end. Though I can well appreciate your quoted displeasure with the limited public outcome of our work, our lawyers had more to say about the contents than we did, but believe me your efforts had a deeper impact than we can make public. I again thank you on behalf of our community for coming forward. While your action brought a lot of pressure and pain to your life, I believe you did the correct thing in speaking out. You have our gratitude and prayers that your future may be happier than much of your past.

Canice Connors

Connors refused to elaborate on the specifics of the allegations brought forth in the Franciscan inquiry because of an agreement of confidentiality. But in his only open and candid interview about the investigation, he described the allegations of sexual misconduct against Ritter as "substantive" and "persuasive."

Despite Connors's letter, Bassile remained furious with the Franciscans, believing that they covered up Ritter's dirty little secret for years. After all, Father Conall McHugh and Father Juniper Alwell, the two highest-ranking officials in the provincial house of Ritter's order, were also respectively on the national and local boards of directors at Covenant House. They also participated in the inquiry, creating a perception of conflict of interest.

"Where the hell were they? Were they getting a kickback, a big salary, what was the reward for this? Why were they ignoring what was going on? Was their service for loyalty to Bruce Ritter, or a service to God? They have never offered to help in any way," said Bassile.

Ritter's case did raise a thorny question: Why hadn't the Church, and specifically the Franciscan Order, monitored Ritter more closely? And, perhaps more painfully, why, once Ritter was exposed, did the Church hide behind the advice of lawyers rather than emphasizing its pastoral role by helping those who were abused?

Ritter's superiors certainly should have known something was wrong. Suspicions about Ritter's sexual problems went as far back as the 1950s—when the incident with the young altar boy surfaced in the Italian resort town of Sabaudia, where Ritter was vacationing from his doctoral work in Rome. The warning signs reemerged in the late 1960s in the East Village, when at least a dozen social workers, members of various religious organizations, and streets kids all had heard about Ritter's sexual problems. In the 1970s, says Andrew Humm, a long-time gay activist who was a founding member of the Catholic gay-rights group Dignity, the rumors about Ritter were "common knowledge" among some Church officials. In 1979, Peter Calaghan, a Catholic priest who worked at Covenant House and eventually left the priesthood and died of AIDS, told Humm, "Father Bruce is screwing around with kids. Why doesn't anyone do anything about it?"

By the early 1980s, allegations of Ritter's sexual misconduct had reached the *National Catholic Reporter*. An editor there said that several reporters were assigned to track the story down. But with limited resources and without an accuser willing to speak out, the paper had to simply "wait for the time when it would all come spilling out."

In 1983, Ritter's own Franciscan superiors had more pointed complaints from several young male members of the Faith Community about Ritter's sexual advances toward them. The New York Archdiocese also had a string of complaints brought to its attention by the Reverend Terence German, who, in a document relating to Darryl Bassile's civil suit against Ritter and Covenant House, told Bassile's attorney, Jeff Anderson, that between 1986 and 1988, while he was working for the archdiocese, three separate allegations of sexual misconduct against Ritter were brought to his attention.

In a letter to Anderson, Father German wrote, "In all three cases when I mentioned it to someone, I was told to forget about it and be quiet. . . . I believe this should be part of the public record."

Although Father Connors denies there was a cover-up to protect Ritter, he concedes, "If they [Ritter's Franciscan superiors] had been more insistent or more perceptive, they would have seen it."

The problem, Connors explained, was that "the Franciscans backed off and gave Bruce a lot of space, too much space. . . . [The fact that Ritter demanded so much space] in itself should have raised questions."

And New York Archbishop Cardinal John O'Connor, who was quick to throw his public support behind Ritter in the early stages of the scandal, has been reticent about the matter since Ritter permanently resigned.

Humm, who now works at the Hetrick Martin Institute, which provides counseling and care to gay street kids in New York City, said, "O'Connor went out on a limb for Ritter, but at the same time he has vehemently attacked any homosexual activists in the Church. The message from that is simple: You have to loathe homosexuality, even if that means loathing yourself if you are a gay priest. You have to be in full denial for the Church to defend you or stand up for you."

The Church's pattern of concealing information, of shuffling priests off to new parishes despite knowledge of their sexual problems, and of showing a lack of will to thoroughly investigate allegations of sexual misconduct has become glaringly apparent in recent years. Dozens of highly publicized scandals involving sexual abuse by priests of young congregants have been splashed across the front pages of newspapers in Florida, Illinois, Indiana, Louisiana, Minnesota, Massachusetts, and Rhode Island.

But the case credited with first bringing the issue of sexual abuse by priests into the national spotlight was in 1985 in the rural parish of Lafayette, Louisiana. That case forced the Church to confront the problem and prompted the National Conference of Catholic Bishops to hold the first of several closed-door discussions on the subject. Louisiana's Catholic establishment was rocked when Father Gilbert Gauthe was convicted of sexually molesting at least thirty-five children and was sentenced to twenty years in prison. To date, the slew of lawsuits brought against the Church for its prior knowledge that Gauthe was a pedophile has cost the Church and its insurers an estimated $20 million. Jason Berry, who won a 1986 Catholic Press Association award for his coverage of Gauthe, has dubbed the priest pedophilia crisis "the Catholic Church's sexual Watergate."

Since Berry broke the Gauthe story, there has been one scandal after another. In the spring of 1992, two separate scandals erupted in Massachusetts and Chicago. In southeastern Massachusetts, a former priest who had married and moved to Minnesota was the target of civil suits and accusations by more than forty-five men and women who claimed they were sexually abused by him as children while he served at parishes in New Bedford and Fall River from 1960 to 1967.

In Chicago, the Reverend Robert Mayer was indicted and five other clergymen were removed from the archdiocese in a series of scandals involving allegations of sexual abuse of young parishioners.

The Chicago archbishop, Cardinal Joseph Bernardin, made a public apology during the scandal and appointed a special commission to reexamine decades of accusations against Mayer and dozens of other priests.

Even at the most respected Catholic institution of higher education in the country, the Church has suffered scandal. In December 1991, University of Notre Dame professor the Reverend James Burtchaell, a respected theologian and prominent spokesman against abortion, resigned from the faculty after complaints by male students that he had made sexual advances to them.

Another disturbing scandal erupted in New Orleans only two months later, when the Reverend Dino Cinel was revealed to have a collection of homemade videotapes of sexual encounters with teenage boys, some of which were filmed in the rectory of a New Orleans parish. The tapes were discovered in 1988 by another priest, and it took Church officials three months to turn them over to law-enforcement officials. But no public action was taken by the archdiocese or law-enforcement officials until a television news show exposed the scandal in March 1991.

In *Lead Us Not into Temptation*, Berry claims that some four hundred priests have faced criminal or civil charges over the last decade, forcing the Church to pay out $400 million in legal fees, and treatment costs for priests and victims, as well as damages. Since most of the criminal cases are eventually dropped or settled out of court, the records are often concealed. That means Berry's estimates are conservative.

As many as three thousand U.S. priests are estimated to be pedophiles, which would represent about 6 percent of the nation's 53,000 Catholic clergy. At the Villa Louis Martin in Jemez Springs, New Mexico, a special facility for priests with sexual problems, more than six hundred pedophiles have been treated in the last fifteen years. Internal Church documents have characterized priest pedophilia as a "major crisis" and warned that lawsuits may end up costing the Church as much as $1 billion by 1995.

The problem has become so extensive that the Church has recently been denied coverage by insurance companies on the issue of sexual molestation because of its pattern of cover-ups and its institutional failure to bring any allegations to light unless forced to by public scandal.

Father Andrew Greeley, a Chicago priest and sociologist who has written several popular novels about priests and sexuality and who has been an outspoken critic of the Church on sexual matters, said, "Pedophilia is the S&L disaster of the Catholic Church. The more that comes out, the worse it looks, and you begin to wonder if there's ever going to be an end to the mess."

Although most prominent Catholics, including Greeley, are careful to point out that they see nothing about the vow of celibacy that causes men to molest children any more than marriage causes incest, the spate of scandals across the country seems to disprove all that comforting Catholic simplicity. Humm, for example, said, "The Church fosters these sexual problems because they refuse to deal with human sexuality in any kind of mature way, so they often get people who are very immature sexually who act out in those repressed and destructive ways. That's how the Church ends up with priests involved in these exploitative relationships—it becomes a mirror of the institutional problems."

Despite the findings of the Franciscan report, Ritter continued to deny the accusations brought against him. He also continued to defy his order's directive to cease living outside the Franciscan community, a privilege he had been afforded for twenty-five years. And Ritter adamantly refused their orders that he undergo psychological counseling, seeing it as an admission of guilt.

"Look, Bruce, you're suffering," said Provincial Conall McHugh in one of a series of phone conversations with Ritter during the summer of 1990, when Ritter refused to let even his order know where he was in hiding.

"Anyone in their right mind who went through something like this would need counseling. You don't need to see it as an admission of guilt, you need to see it as healing," McHugh told Ritter.

"Absolutely not," Ritter replied. "There is no proof whatsoever to back up these allegations. You didn't support me. You were not behind me and that's the bottom line."

To his fellow friars, Father Bruce seemed more arrogant and righteous than ever in the wake of the scandal. There was not a hint of remorse and no acceptance that he needed help.

"Bruce, you are never wrong," McHugh said at the end of one phone conversation with Ritter from his secret exile. "It's always everybody else."

"I guess there is nothing left to say," Ritter said and hung up the phone.

The only time Ritter would surface was when he had to appear for questioning by the New York State Attorney General's office, which was still probing the Franciscan Charitable Trust he had created. Ritter would duck into the side door of the Attorney General's office at 120 Broadway in lower Manhattan, the thick gray beard that he had grown, keeping him anonymous. Only his eyes gave him away.

When he walked into the Charities Bureau at the A.G.'s office in the summer of 1990, an investigator sat at a long table amid stacks of documents, tracing the loans from Ritter's secret fund to the board members and Ritter's family. The investigator listened to Ritter's explanations about the confusing trust with a sharp pencil in her hand, taking notes on the margins of the documents, running arrows to trace the complicated money transfers that built Ritter's private $1 million trust. The problem was that few of the arrows traced back to any excessive spending by Ritter. He was not the PTL club's Reverend Jim Bakker, spending lavishly on himself. Ritter had built a temple of power, not greed. One Assistant A.G. put it perfectly when she said, "To figure this one out, you need a psychiatrist, not an accountant."

The Attorney General's investigation into Covenant House and Ritter's financial misconduct continued for months. Desperate to survive the scandal and win back disaffected donors, Covenant House nervously waited for the results of the investigation by the world-renowned private firm it had hired. Kroll Associates employed six investigators—two former FBI agents, two former New York City police detectives, two forensic experts—under the direction of former New York City police chief McGuire to sift through the charity's past finances and all of the sexual allegations brought against Ritter. Predictably, Ritter refused to cooperate with Kroll and referred the matter to Stanley Arkin.

Kroll's sixty-page report was based on documents of interviews with more than 150 people and done in cooperation with the Manhattan D.A.'s office. Its findings were a devastating confirmation of some ugly truths. Released to the media on August 3, 1990, it stated that the evidence of sexual misconduct was "extensive" and cited allegations made against Ritter by fifteen young men—eleven former residents of Covenant House and four residents of the Faith Community. As one investigator put it, "If we were able to find fifteen kids in a few months, you can bet there are a lot more out there."

A summary of the report concluded that "in view of the cumulative evidence found by Kroll supporting the allegations, if Father Ritter had not resigned from Covenant House, the termination of his relationship with Covenant House would have been required."

The evidence was particularly striking because the details of each independent accusation seemed to dovetail or provide a kind of "forensic match." In other words, each accuser described the same modus operandi used by Ritter in initiating the sexual advances. Almost all of the fifteen accusers whose allegations were investigated by Kroll said Ritter invited them to his apartment at night, typically to talk about their problems. Almost all stated that the initial sexual advance came slowly, after several occasions on which Ritter frequently touched or hugged them, before progressing to sexual advances. Specifically, Ritter would initiate the sexual activity while they were watching television. He would lie down on the couch or sofabed at the opposite end from the victim and then caress him with his feet. Ritter also fostered a relationship of codependency between the mostly destitute street kids and himself by offering them money and/or gifts in exchange for sex. They described the sexual encounters identically as mutual masturbation and oral sex. They all maintained that there were no words spoken before, during, or after the sex.

The reports established what was clearly unethical behavior, misuse of power, and consistent persuasive evidence of sexual misconduct, a violation of Ritter's priestly vow of celibacy. But none of the sexual relationships could be established as criminal, except possibly those with Bassile and Johnson, who at the time of their alleged encounters with Ritter were under the age of seventeen. However, by the time they came forward with the allegations, the criminal statute of limitations for such crimes had expired. Soon after the Kroll report was made public, the Attorney General also dropped his investigation into the workings of the Franciscan Charitable Trust. Showing the same kind of prosecutorial discretion exhibited by the Manhattan District Attorney, the A.G. decided that Ritter's exile from the charity and assurances that he would never again work in the field of child care were deemed sufficient punishment for the violations that had occurred.

But there were so many questions. The psychological experts could only help to define ways of looking at what happened. Although none of them could provide answers, most believe Ritter's behavior fits a classic paradigm of sexual pathology. They see Ritter as no different from the Boy Scout leader, the small-town minister, or the local schoolteacher who shocks the community when it is revealed that he has molested young boys in his care.

A starting point for piecing together the puzzle of Ritter was to look at how he fit in the "homosexual matrix." Was he a closeted priest who had relationships with young men, was he a pedophile with a pathological penchant for young boys, was he a man who manifested an obsession with power through a need to sexually exploit the very kids he claimed to be saving?

That young males were the target of Ritter's sexual pathology does not necessarily mean he had a homosexual orientation. However, if Ritter was in fact a closet homosexual, he certainly wasn't the only gay Catholic priest. A recent flood of literature has been written about homosexuality in the priesthood. Although there are no solid figures, estimates vary that from 20 to 40 percent of the priesthood is gay. The same research estimates that half of the gay priests are sexually active—all of which raises several thorny issues for the Church hierarchy. It not only exposes the Church's vitriolic condemnation of homosexuality as ridiculous, but it stirs questions about the vow of celibacy and the extent to which it is actually honored in the rectories and monasteries of American Catholicism.

In Catholic dogma, celibacy is intended to be a way for priests to emulate Christ by forgoing sexual intimacy in the name of a higher love. But nowhere in the Bible does Christ demand celibacy, and many Catholic theologians feel that the hierarchy had mandated celibacy without realizing that it is a very specific calling that only a select few are capable of living.

The vow was first instituted in the Middle Ages as a way for the Church—which was amassing large amounts of real estate—to keep priests' families from inheriting the land. But it has become a focus of fierce debate within the Church as the number of seminarians continues to dwindle in the United States and Europe, and an exodus of priests struggling with the vow goes unabated. Even in the conservative Catholic country of Ireland, more than two-thirds of Catholics believe priests should be able to marry. Dr. Eugene Kennedy, a psychologist at Loyola University in Chicago, has called celibacy an "eroding cornerstone" of the Church. He believes that the sexual scandals are precipitating the collapse of what he calls "the clerical society."

But the pattern of Ritter's behavior goes beyond a mere violation of his vow of celibacy. His public stance against homosexuality was that such acts were personally abhorrent to him, which some experts would say makes Ritter a "paraphiliac"—a clinical term that, put simply, means a sexual pervert. The textbook word for Ritter's problem is not *pedophilia,* but *ephebophilia*—a term for an adult who is obsessed with sexual partners who are postpubescent teenagers or those who look the part. The sexual acts that Ritter committed were attenuated and mild, never violent. But Ritter's psychological manipulation of his partners and his own self-loathing of the acts would be what made him pathological.

John Money, professor of medical psychology at the Department of Psychiatry and Behavioral Sciences at the Johns Hopkins Hospital and School of Medicine, is widely regarded as a leading researcher in understanding the intricate links between historical, cultural, and physiological influences that determine sexual orientation.

Money refers to a public-private split like the one in Ritter's personality as the "exorcist" syndrome—a "malignant" form of conflicted sexuality in which an individual is at war within himself, trying to purge his homosexuality by publicly condemning others who are sexually manipulative. By projecting a heterosexual disguise, he publicly becomes a "standard-bearer of traditional sexual values, conservator of virtue, and exterminator of vice." But privately, he is "a standard-bearer of idealized masculine lust, a devil-may-care playmate and a rebel, fearless of the consequences."

Dr. Judith Becker, a nationally recognized expert on the treatment of sex offenders and their victims and the former director of the sexual-behavior clinic at the New York State Psychiatric Institute, served with Ritter on the Meese Commission. She sat across from him at the hearings, in which he expressed his adamant disdain for homosexuality and his righteous sense of morality as a savior of youth from an adult world of sin. Although Dr. Becker emphasizes that she never counseled Ritter and that her views are based on her work in the field, she was not surprised when the allegations surfaced. Sex offenders, according to Becker, often put themselves in positions where they can seek out the type of victim they desire. That is not to say that people who work with children have a natural inclination to victimize. It simply means that pederasts will seek access to kids any way they can and frequently it is in a position of authority over young people. As their confidence builds, they begin to think they are untouchable, and take more and more risks until they get caught.

"Cognitive distortion" is what keeps them doing it, says Becker. They come to believe that what they are doing is not bad. Individuals who have fought so hard against something could have tremendous difficulty facing the fact that they are doing precisely what they are publicly fighting against. They can get so deep into the pathology that it becomes impossible for them to acknowledge the "splitting" of their personalities. If they are caught, many have to maintain full denial of their own actions merely to keep from taking their own lives.

The first step in healing this type of sex offender is to make him take responsibility for his actions, to make him realize that what he did was wrong. It is very common for ephebophiles to believe that they are saviors of the young people they abuse, Becker added. Most rationalize their actions by saying they helped the young men, that they brought them culture, that they fed them and clothed them and cared for them. Like Ritter, they often say, "Who knows what would have happened to the boy if it had not been for me."

The denial mechanism can also be selfish. That is, the victimizer won't admit he did anything wrong because he doesn't want to lose access to possible victims.

"Denial and minimalization are the hallmarks of a sex offender, but confronting them with what they did wrong is very important," said Becker. "One way to confront them is to bring a victim's state- ment" and "confront them with the overwhelming weight of the evidence."

Dr. Kennedy, who has treated many priests with sexual problems, didn't believe such a strategy would work with Ritter. "I don't think he'll ever admit what he did—the denial becomes his only way to survive," he said. "I have seen this again and again, the same kind of pink-faced piousness by priests who have been caught cold in what they are doing."

• • •

In the fall of 1990, buffered from New York City by the northern side of the Catskill Mountains, Ritter hid out in a small town in upstate New York not far from the Massachusetts border.

A friend of Macauley's provided him with a two-story wood-frame farmhouse on the gentle slope of a hill. Ritter spent the fall and winter fixing up the house, replacing and then staining the woodwork on the doors. The clapboards were freshly covered with a thick, shining coat of white paint. Three cords of freshly split wood were neatly stacked at the edge of the woods. Ritter kept his wood dry with a blue plastic tarp that was tied tightly over the top of the pile with nylon cord.

Through February and March of 1991, the frayed relationship between Ritter and his Franciscan Order was beginning to unravel completely. The Franciscans, after giving Ritter over a year to comply with their directive to return to living in the community and to seek professional counseling, were moving to oust Ritter from the order. A change in the leadership had occurred, with the Reverend Conall McHugh being voted out of his post as provincial and a new three-year term handed over to the Reverend Giles Van Wormer, who had known Ritter since their days together in the seminary of Saint Francis on Staten Island. Father Giles began the slow, painful process of severing Ritter from the order. Letters had been sent to Ritter through the winter and spring, warning him that if he failed to comply with their directive they would be forced to expel him from the Franciscan brotherhood. The correspondence was always sent to a P.O. box that Ritter had set up in Pound Ridge, New York. It was nowhere near where he was hiding, but, through a friend who lived in a town near Pound Ridge, he had his mail forwarded to his hilltop Elba.

Ritter did not reply to the letters. Instead, he began networking through several different archdioceses in the United States to find a bishop who would accept his request for a transfer. When the American Catholic hierarchy shunned Ritter's requests because he was violating the directive of his own order, he contacted a friend who ran a charity in Kerala, at the southern tip of India on the Arabian Sea. Through him Ritter was introduced to the archbishop of the local diocese, and his request for a transfer was accepted. Then Ritter moved for approval to resign from the order and be officially transferred to the Archdiocese of Kerala in Alleppey, India. The head of the Franciscan O.F.M. (Conv.) in Rome, General Lanfranco Serrini, and the Vatican's Congregation of the Clergy approved the request, despite Van Wormer's objection.

The transfer meant that Ritter remained a priest in "good standing." According to canonical law he is free to celebrate mass, though that does not, as Van Wormer pointed out, "eradicate any of the serious problems of his past."

Before Ritter disappeared into the farthest reaches of India, I knew I had to find him. I had not spoken to him since the first day I broke the news to him over the phone that he was being investigated by the Manhattan District Attorney. We had never met face to face. I had written several letters requesting interviews for the book, but had received no response. I heard through Macauley and Donahue that he would not speak with me, but I still set out to find him. Remembering that he had a history of reckless driving, I checked his Department of Motor Vehicles record, and it worked.

I drove from New York City through the Catskills on July 24, a beautiful sunny day. As the car climbed up the winding roads of rural upstate New York to the small town where Ritter was living, I thought about what I would say to the fallen priest, about Darryl Bassile and the letter he had written with no response, about the hundreds of thousands of people who had donated to Covenant House because they had believed in Father Ritter, and about the street kids whose last refuge was threatened by the public shame that Ritter had brought upon the charity.

When I arrived, Ritter was mowing a field on a hillside, making neat rows back and forth. I wasn't sure if it was he until I saw his eyes. No mistaking it. He waved cheerfully—greeting a stranger's car on the quiet dirt road. I kept driving, too shocked to stop and thinking that it would be better to approach him after he finished his work. I parked my car a half mile up the hill and listened to the faint sound of the lawn mower's motor until it stopped. Then I walked back down the road to the house.

It was clear that Ritter had kept himself busy by working on the garden. There were recently potted plants and rows of young perennials freshly mulched. An antique grindstone was carefully placed on display in the middle of the garden. I knocked on the door.

Ritter answered with a beaming smile. His face no longer had the ashen-gray pallor it carried for years through his tireless travels across the country while he built his empire. His forehead and cheekbones were toughened and bronzed by the sun. His forearms and biceps were once again powerful. His Hodgkin's disease had remained in remission and he looked fifteen years younger than he did during the scandal.

"Well, hello," said Ritter in a cheery voice. It was obvious he did not know who I was.

"Father Ritter, I'm Charlie Sennott," I said, and there was a long silence. Ritter's eyes were frightening. The sun played off the irises— a deep liquid blue. Through more than one year of interviews, I had heard people describe Ritter's eyes. They were much more unsettling in person.

"I have nothing to say," said Ritter, his face turning from a warm smile to a cold landscape of deep lines and dramatic ridges, like storm clouds sweeping over the sunlit hills. He stood with the door partially closed. He pulled on the choke collar of a large German shepherd that growled and lunged at the crack in the door.

"Easy," said Ritter, calming the dog. "Take it easy, it's okay."

"I think it's important for us to talk, Father Ritter," I said through the narrow opening in the door, his eyes becoming less intense as he retreated to the shadows of the house.

"It is something I've always regretted. We never sat down eye to eye to go through all of this," I continued. "The attorneys and the public-relations people always made sure that didn't happen. I thought it was important that I make the effort."

"I'm not going to talk to you. You've made your effort," said Ritter in a quick and cutting voice. "I have nothing to say to you, nothing whatsoever."

Ritter was caught without his guard up. It was far too beautiful a day for him even to think of having all that darkness brought back, to have been found out once again. He seemed furious and hurt. He shut the door tight. I left and walked back to my car.

Reporters get used to knocking on doors in difficult situations. There is a fine line between being aggressive and being callous. After a half hour of sitting in my car, I walked back down the hill and knocked on the door again. The German shepherd barked and growled. Ritter pushed aside a curtain on the front door and looked through the glass. He waited a few seconds and then opened the door. He nodded in a way that seemed self-consciously pious.It was holy but not humble. He pushed the growling shepherd behind him and stood in the door frame with his arms crossed.

Behind him was the sound of a television blaring abnormally loud. The six-o'clock news was coming on. The lead story of the day was the grisly tale of Jeffrey Dahmer's killings, torture, and cannibalism in Milwaukee.

"Father Ritter, first of all I want to let you know that I'm not planning on splashing this on the front page. That's not why I'm here. I want to be clear on that. I'm here because I have a lot of questions and I want to put them directly to you. I want this book to be fair. So much has been said . . ."

"May I ask how did you know I was here?" Ritter asked, cutting off my rambling and ineffective sales pitch.

His question was understandable. My unannounced visit had re-opened the wounds of pain and anger and betrayal. He was wondering if someone he knew, someone he trusted, had once again betrayed him even in his exile. He knew it would have been someone close to him. Very few people knew where he was, not even his Franciscan superiors.

"You should know that it wasn't anyone from Covenant House or anyone you know who told me," I said. "It was actually a very basic reporting step. I checked your records at the Department of Motor Vehicles."

"Okay," said Ritter, nodding his head and bringing down his guard a bit. "I hope you'll respect my privacy.

"I am sorry to have you come all this way," he went on, the anger fading and a rehearsed tone of priestly patience setting in. The anger seemed more honest. "I will never speak about this with anyone. It has been far too painful. I am sorry that you came all the way to hear that. I will never speak about this with anyone."

"Father Ritter, there are so many people who see you as someone who changed their lives and changed so many lives. There are people who are confused and some who are angry. I think they want to know what this was all about. What about the young men who accused you and the reports that confirm what they've said? You don't have anything to say to them? Do you think what you did is wrong?" I asked.

There was silence. He only glared, and moved to close the door. I reached for the door handle and there was a slight tension between the two sides of the door, with both of us gently pushing in different directions.

"I think there are also people who wonder how you have gotten along through all this, who wonder how you are doing," I said, still trying to get Ritter to open the door, to pry open the silence, to get some answers.

"Tell them I'm just fine," Ritter said.

"I'm just fine," he muttered again as he pushed the door shut and locked it.

Epilogue

THE sins of the father fell hard upon Covenant House. Two years after Father Ritter resigned in disgrace, the charity's flagship Under 21 crisis center in New York—which had always had the tidy look of a pleasant hotel lobby—seemed worn around the edges. In the reception area, the photographs of Ritter shaking hands with presidents and dignitaries had been removed, leaving faint outlines where the frames used to be. The color-coordinated furniture was threadbare, the walls needed painting, and the carpet looked grimy. The physical appearance reflected a crisis not only of cash but of confidence. Indeed, the charity has had a long struggle to pull itself out of the abyss of bad publicity suffered during the scandal. What is admirable is that the charity not only survives and continues to do good work, but that it went through a collective process first of self-doubt, then of soul-searching, and ultimately of much-needed change.

A disturbing truth of the Covenant House scandal is that had Kevin Kite never walked through the door of the Manhattan District Attorney's office the charity might still be functioning the way it was, and Ritter might have been moving on to his next victim. Rather than assuring donors that charities rarely get away with such antics, the criminal investigations seemed to illustrate the inadequacy of the federal, state, and local system for monitoring charities. Why hadn't they caught on to all this before?

Just as the Covenant House scandal quieted down, another major national charity, the United Way, became embroiled in a highly publicized exposé of its own financial misdeeds—some of which were remarkably similar to those of Covenant House. Both scandals underscored the need for a closer monitoring of charities. It seemed no one was watching these enormous not-for-profit corporations that prospered in the Reagan era. Reagan and Bush pushed for the greater role of charities in solving the nation's problems, but they had failed to implement agencies to monitor their unprecedented growth.

The Charities Bureau at the New York State Attorney General's office, for example, has a staff of six investigators to handle some 100,000 not-for-profit organizations based in New York City alone. And on the federal level, the IRS has been historically lax in examining the 990 tax forms for nonprofit organizations. The abbreviated forms also make it difficult to find financial irregularities, which are easily hidden through broad transactions within these agencies.

There are only two major national watchdog groups overseeing charities—the New York–based National Charities Information Bureau and the Virginia-based Council of Better Business Bureaus. The two groups are responsible for the independent monitoring of some 900,000 registered charities in the United States, at least 400,000 of which are considered "active operations." The NCIB has a staff of only nineteen full-time employees. The Better Business bureau has about twenty. That would mean each employee at the two independent agencies could be responsible for 10,000 charities. There are a series of smaller regional agencies that monitor charities, as well as a network of publications, including the *Philanthropic Journal* and *Fund Raising Management*. But clearly the American public needs more assurances that the hard-earned money it donates to charities is being handled responsibly.

In the wake of the scandal, the NCIB rescinded Covenant House's status as a qualified not-for-profit organization.* In its thirteen-page report, the NCIB focused on the national board of directors' failure to act as a vigilant and independent steward. It placed much of the blame for failing to root out the problems at the charity on the board's inaction and the charity's corporate structure, which gave Ritter unchecked authority and the ability to perpetuate it by hand-picking

*It was restored in the spring of 1992.

his board members. The NCIB also pointed out that Covenant House failed to meet its standards with regard to full accountability and safeguards against conflicts of interest. These were many of the same problems that existed at United Way.

But the real catalyst for change at Covenant House was its own internal report by the oversight committee and Kroll Associates. The private investigation was an admirable effort to get to the bottom of what happened and to study ways to effect changes that would prevent it from ever happening again.

The changes did not come easily or without pain. In the first year after Ritter's resignation, donors turned away in droves and caused a $22 million cut in its annual budget. With the fallout from the scandal as well as a deepening national recession, Covenant House's total budget has dropped more than 30 percent since Ritter's resignation. It went from the peak of $98 million in fiscal 1989–90 to a projected $65 million for 1992–93.

Along with this drying up of public donations came a massive downscaling of the charity's direct-mail campaign. No longer could Covenant House afford to invest in the mass mailings that fueled its rapid growth. Forced to give up on attracting new donors, the fund-raising department focused on retaining the faithful few who held on. The number of newsletters mailed out every month was cut in half—to only 500,000 a month by the summer of 1991. Poor attempts were made to copy Ritter's moving style, and as one senior executive put it, "No one has matched it. The loss of Ritter's newsletters has hurt us severely."

The turmoil also prompted a reexamination of the charity's programs and a shake-up of its administrative staff. Dozens of top administrators and scores of on-line staff quit over the way the scandal was handled. Budget cuts forced layoffs of more than four hundred executives and staff across the country, including some two hundred in New York City's Under 21 program.

Covenant House's plans for expansion were curtailed. New programs on the drawing board in a half-dozen cities, from Washington, D.C., to Manila in the Philippines, were scrapped. In the New York flagship program, crucial health-care services to the youths were cut back and the costly but desperately needed ward for HIV-positive youths was shut down. Meanwhile, the population at Covenant House was cut through attrition to more manageable numbers. At the Under 21 center and the mothers-and-children program in New York, the nightly population went from up to 350 to no more than 180 a night. At the New York Rights of Passage program, enrollment was cut from about 200 down to 120. In New York, two of the blue outreach vans were pulled off the streets, leaving only one van cruising for young people in need of help. Although Covenant House in New York was the most severely affected, subsidiaries in New Orleans, Houston, Fort Lauderdale, Toronto, Alaska, and Central America also suffered from the loss of funding from the corporate parent and the overall downsizing of the charity's mission.

Some ideological changes were also implemented by Covenant House under its new president, Sister Mary Rose McGeady. The philosophy of open intake, for example, was modified. Covenant House still vows an open-door policy to any young person who is coming to them in need of help for the first time. But it has gotten much tougher on a recidivist population of people coming back the third, fourth, or fifth time.

"We want to make sure that we don't have a revolving door," said McGeady. "There is a point where the rubber hits the road and maybe you need to say to a kid, 'You might as well go to a men's shelter and see how you like it.' "

Open intake—regarded as terrible social work but a true commitment to scripture—was, for many of the religious volunteers who worked there, the cornerstone of Covenant House. Many members of the Faith Community believe the charity has lost its religious orientation, and scores of them left—many in disgust with what happened and others out of dismay, feeling that the charity had betrayed its founder. Once integral to Ritter's view of the charity's Catholic missionary purpose, the Faith Community now provides a more service-oriented function. It has become more integrated into the staff and has less clout with the directors of individual programs and their on-line social-service workers. The key to this changed role was the abolition of the powerful ombudsman position that Ritter had created for a select few of the Faith Community.

The patriarchal structure within the charity was also dismantled. McGeady and the national board implemented changes that gave the executive directors of the subsidiary programs and their local boards of directors more autonomy and greater authority. Covenant House has also worked hard to shed its image as a kind of corporate raider of child-care services indifferent to small community-based programs. Della Hughes, director of the National Network of Runaway and Youth Services, said, "Covenant House is still in transition. But in some areas, such as Florida, we have seen the communication between agencies open up already. There is a long way to mend fences, but it is starting."

In many ways, the scaling down of the program has made it more manageable. Staff workers have a chance to provide closer monitoring of the troubled youngsters under their care. But there are some experts in the field who remain critical of Covenant House. William Treanor, a long-time child-care lobbyist and the director of the American Youth Work Center, which shelters young people in Washington, D.C., believes that the shelters are still too large and dangerous and that Ritter's influence remains pervasive because too few of his loyalists have been rooted out.

Nevertheless, Covenant House has successfully used the scandal as an opportunity not just to reevaluate its programs, but also to implement guidelines and internal audits that are now more comprehensive than those of any other charity in the country. Based on recommendations from the report of its independent oversight committee, stringent reforms at Covenant House were adopted. Those reforms created a model of accountability and internal review that should be implemented by all large charities. United Way, for example, could use the new Covenant House as a paradigm for its much-needed reforms as it looks to reshape the corporate structure in the wake of its highly publicized scandal. Covenant House's successful reforms came by clearly defining the stewardship role of the national board of directors. First, the makeup of the board was changed. Although still dominated by CEOs, bankers, and high-powered lawyers, there are now more minority representatives and a greater number of leaders in the fields of health care and social work. The board's mandate to be active, vigilant, independent, and thoroughly involved has also been made clear. Had it been that way from the beginning, many believe, the problems that nearly brought the house down could have been avoided.

What remains clear is that Covenant House is a desperately needed provider of services to an often forgotten segment of the population. Even after two years of turmoil, Covenant House continues to be one of the largest services of its kind in the country—providing care, counseling, and shelter to more than 22,000 young people a year. There are still hundreds of Covenant House staff workers from Toronto to Los Angeles and New York to Guatemala whose efforts to save young lives is nothing short of heroic. In the end, the scandal only proved that the mission of Covenant House was far bigger than the man who founded it.

Here's what has happened to some of the main characters in this book since the research was completed:

DARRYL BASSILE. When he first came forward with his allegation against Ritter in December 1989, Bassile received a letter from a woman who was also a survivor of sexual abuse at the hands of a minister. Bassile wrote back to her and the two arranged to meet. They are now married and live in New Jersey. Bassile has also taken an active role in a push for "delayed discovery" laws, which would allow the victims of sexual abuse to prosecute their abusers long after the abusive acts occurred; for many it takes decades to actually come to terms with what happened. In June 1992, Bassile testified in New York State Superior Court on behalf of a movement to repeal the existing state laws that prevented him from pressing criminal charges against Ritter because of the statute of limitations.

KEVIN KITE. He had a new black leather jacket with chains on the lapels and was carrying three suit bags after a Greenwich Village shopping spree in the winter of 1991. He had just been awarded an out-of-court settlement from Covenant House, before the papers were even completely filed on his slander suit against the charity. Kite said he felt that he had been vindicated by the settlement. He refused to disclose the amount, as part of the agreement, but sources say it was less than $200,000. Kite drifted in and out of New York and last called from Florida, where he was vacationing with a friend. He says he is going to use the money to complete his college education.

ROBERT MACAULEY still stands by his friend Father Bruce Ritter, and remains his close confidant. He insists that he doesn't believe any of the sexual-misconduct allegations against Ritter because of the "ilk of his accusers." He still suggests that there may have been a conspiracy by a militant gay group or another "enemy of the Church or of Father Bruce" to bring down the legendary street priest. Macauley resigned from Covenant House's national board of directors after the Kroll report was released. His relief agency, AmeriCares, continues to thrive, and Ritter reportedly participated in the agency's airlift to the U.S.-backed rebel forces in Afghanistan in the summer of 1991.

MONICA KAISER resigned from Covenant House. After spending some time with her family in the Midwest, recovering from the ordeal, she went on to work at God's Love, We Deliver, a Manhattan-based Catholic charity that delivers meals to AIDS patients. She describes Ritter's downfall as the most painful period of her life. But she maintains that in some ways it strengthened her faith by forcing her to reexamine it. She said though the experience ratcheted up her cynicism about the clerical hierarchy of the Catholic Church, it deepened her faith because she feels that ultimately the truth came out.

ANNE DONAHUE quit her position as executive director of Covenant House in Los Angeles in March of 1990. She says she was disgusted with the charity's national board of directors, feeling that they betrayed the spiritual founder of Covenant House just to salvage their own public reputations. She avoids the question of whether Father Bruce was guilty of sexual misconduct and instead employs her training as a lawyer to refocus the issue on what she calls a "perversion of the process of justice in America" that brought about Ritter's downfall. She insists the investigation was grossly unjust, and that in essence Ritter was unfairly convicted in the media by pure accusation and innuendo. She moved to Vermont, where she has spent the last year building a log cabin from foundation to roof with her own hands. She still has in the top drawer of her desk a neatly typed three-by-five card with the following quote from Solzhenitsyn: "What is the most precious thing in the world? Not to participate in injustices."

JOHN KELLS went back to Houston, where he works as a producer in the news department of a small television station. His comment on the scandal is the true confession of a yuppie public-relations man: "What I did was wrong. I should have had the integrity to defend the organization and not attack the messenger. The most important part is about how one goes about revealing the truth even when it hurts. Maybe it was all just too much public relations, too many manipulators and handlers. We lost the sense of a fact is a fact, and what is wrong is wrong. We ran so much on appearances and image that when we were presented with the truth it became very difficult to see it."

MARK REDMOND and his wife, Rosanne, were not surprised when the revelations about Ritter's sexual and financial misconduct came out in the press. In fact, they were surprised it took so long. They are now both involved with the Common Ground Community, a not-for-profit organization that received a loan from New York City to purchase the Times Square Hotel (the same one previously bought by Ritter). The Redmonds have turned it into a long-term residence for poor and homeless families, some of whom used to stay at Covenant House. Rosanne is the director of the Times Square Hotel. Mark helps out at the hotel but works full time at My Brother, My Keeper, a Catholic charity that helps the homeless in Brooklyn.

FATHER BRUCE RITTER remained in hiding in the small house in the mountains of New York State. His attempt to escape to India to work with a Catholic charity was thwarted by newspaper accounts exposing his plan. At one point he even experimented with trying to get back into fund raising by writing a letter on behalf of the Franciscan Family Apostolate, a Connecticut-based charity that helps the poor in India. But that too was stopped when the *New York Post* exposed it with a front-page headline that proclaimed: HE'S BAAACK. People close to Ritter say he is still planning a journey to India, but they are not sure when. He remains a priest in good standing despite the evidence of his sexual problems. He has refused counseling and shown no re-morse, according to his fellow Franciscan friars. The Church seems to be handling Ritter the way it has handled many priests with sexual problems, that is, by allowing the troubled priest to be shuffled off to a new assignment, where he may seek out more victims. Investi-gators at the Manhattan District Attorney's and the Attorney Gen-eral's offices, however, have stated that their investigations were dropped based on an agreement that Ritter should never work with young people again. They have told his victims that he is expected to live up to his end of the bargain. To this day, Ritter maintains his innocence.

Source Notes

All biblical references at the beginnings of the six parts of *Broken Covenant* are from the book of Genesis: *The Jerusalem Bible* (Doubleday, 1966). General editor, Alexander Jones. The Hebrew word "Yaweh" has been deleted and only "God" used.

PROLOGUE
Conversation based on written notes from the author's interview with Father Bruce Ritter, December 6, 1989, by telephone from New York. The description of the setting of the office and Ritter's movements that day are based on the author's visit to Covenant House in New Orleans on December 28–30, 1990, as well as interviews with the program's head of fund raising, Alex Comfort, and executive director, Phil Boudreau.

Part I

CHAPTER 1
21 On Covenant House's 1989 budget: From Covenant House's 1989 Annual Report.

22 Covenant House annually spent three times as much as the federal government's total yearly budget for similar programs: *The New York Times*, February 8, 1990.

23 On the national media interest in Ritter: From author's interviews with Covenant House public-relations officials George Wirt and John Kells.

24 Quotes from Reagan's speech at Covenant House: *The New York Times* and *New York Post*, November 15, 1989.

24 The description of the scene at the Reagan visit: From author's interviews with reporters who covered it, as well as author's interviews with Kells and Wirt.

26 On Manhattan Assistant District Attorney Linda Fairstein's prosecutorial record and background: From author's interview with fellow assistant D.A.s and from *The New York Times Magazine*, February 25, 1990.

CHAPTER 2

28 Scene of Kevin Kite being fitted for concealed tape recording: Recreated from author's interviews with Kite and from author's interview with a technician in the Manhattan D.A.'s office who was present.

30 Dialogue of tape-recorded conversation between Ritter and Kite: Based on author's interviews with Kite immediately after the taping and again several months later. Two investigators—one from law enforcement and one from a private agency—who worked on the case and had access to the transcript also confirmed that Kite's re-creation was substantively accurate. The author and a photographer from the *New York Post* also staked out the Covenant House headquarters that day and saw Ritter and Kite entering the car together. Ritter also confirmed some aspects of the conversation in the interview with the author on December 6, 1989.

CHAPTER 3

32 Under 21 shelters some 300 every night: From Covenant House's weekly *Service Report* for the month of February 1990. That month between 335 and 344 were registered weekly in the crisis center, but staff workers said numbers were unusually high that month and typically closer to an average of 275 to 300.

33 Description of Under 21 crisis center: From author's tour of the facility on December 7, 1989.

34 The stories of Mohammad, Felipe, and Lawrece are based on interviews with the author. Felipe and Lawrece also spoke at an annual dinner for Covenant House, and Mohammad later led a protest march to New York City Mayor David Dinkins's home to alert city officials to the need for Covenant House to survive in the wake of the scandal. The author chose not to use their last names to protect their identities.

37 Ritter's walk through the Port Authority was re-created through the author's interview with security supervisor Stan Ford and confirmed by child-care worker Rick Agcuili, who was also on duty that night. Also based on author's interviews with young homeless people who hung out at the Port Authority and remembered seeing Ritter that night, February 6, 1990.

Part II

CHAPTER 4

43 About history of Hamilton Township: From historical archives and author's interview with a township historian. About neighborhood and memories of Mrs. Ritter: Author's interview with Lou Peck, next-door neighbor to Ritter household for more than thirty years.

44 Ritter interview with *Current Biography*, June 1983. "We lost everything in the Crash. We moved out of a very fine home into a very poor one. My mother raised five kids by herself during the Depression."

44 Ritter "understood their pain": From author's interview with Greg Loken.

44 ". . . good old-fashioned Irish Catholic guilt": Ritter interview with the *New York Daily News*, May 17, 1987.

46 Information on Saint Francis of Assisi: *St. Francis of Assisi* by G. K. Chesterton (Image Books, 1957).

47 On life in the seminary: Author's interview with James Fitzgibbons and five of Ritter's fellow seminarians, as well as other priests who didn't know Ritter but provided general background. Interviews conducted in New York, New Jersey, Massachusetts, and Rome. For some general information, the author also relied on the novel *Prince of Peace* by James Carroll (Signet, 1984).

56 Description of Ritter's ordination and of the inside of the basilica: Based on author's interview with a Franciscan priest ordained with Ritter as well as author's trip to the same basilica in Rome.

60 Ritter's doctoral status: According to the records of the *Annuarium Academicum*, stored at the Franciscans' Collegio Serafico in Rome.

62 ". . . 45 million Catholics in America": *Saturday Evening Post*, November 28, 1964.

62 Information on the Catholic Church and Vatican II: *Modern Catholicism: Vatican II and After*, edited by Adrian Hastings (Oxford University Press, 1991).

CHAPTER 5

65 Ritter's sermon at Manhattan College: From *Covenant House: Lifeline to the Streets* by Father Bruce Ritter (Doubleday, 1987.)

66 Hugh O'Neill's remembrance of the same day: Author's interview with O'Neill, December 13, 1990.

68 On the early days of Ritter's street ministry in East Village: Author's interviews with James Fitzgibbons.

70 Ritter's version of the "first six kids": From *Covenant House: Lifeline to the Streets*, pp. 3–4.

71 The story of Mary Lane and Lee Meyers: The author found Lane and Meyers through the Reverend Jim Daniels, who contacted the author after the scandal hit the newspapers and television because he felt it was important that their stories be told. Eventually they told of their experiences in several lengthy interviews with the author. They also went on the record to the Manhattan District Attorney and to a private investigator hired by Covenant

House. Their stories are corroborated by several people, including the Reverend Jim Daniels, who worked as counselor in several different street ministries in the East Village at the time. Despite months of searching by the author and a full computer search by the Manhattan D.A.'s office, the other four of the "first six kids" could not be located.

78 On Ritter hiring thugs to take over abandoned apartments: From *Covenant House: Lifeline to the Streets*, p. 8.

78 Priest exodus in the wake of Vatican II: *Coming Apart: An Informal History of America in the 1960s* by William L. O'Neill (Quadrangle Books, 1971), p. 311, and *Modern Catholicism: Vatican II and After*, edited by Adrian Hastings, pp. 246–54.

CHAPTER 6

80 Image of young suicide victim in tree on East Seventh Street: From author's interview with S. I. Taubman, December 4, 1990.

81 ". . . focus on street kids was misguided": From author's interview with Jon Eddison, January 7, 1992.

81 On Stephen Morris: From author's interview with Morris, January 8, 1992.

81 "pedagogy": From Father John McNeil, author of *The Church and the Homosexual*, from an interview with *Village Voice*, January 30, 1990. "A lot of great teachers of children sublimate their [sexual] desires."

82 Allegation of Ritter's sexual relationship with Melican corroborated by Melican interview, *Village Voice*, January 30, 1990.

83 On Covenant House's state certification: From author's interviews with Donna Santarsiero and the Kroll report.

85 Covenant House charter from November 14, 1972, state certification: ". . . to identify and attempt to assist in solving the problems of the urban poor": From a five-page Covenant House document that records the history of the charity's origins. The information on the increase in funding and purchases of property from 1972 to 1974 is also based on this document.

87 "Ritter felt just like a politician": *New York Daily News*, February 7, 1988.

89 ". . . sixty to eighty hours a week": From *Covenant House: Lifetime to the Streets*, p. 7.

89 On Ritter's avoidance of diocesan and state control: From author's interview with Hugh O'Neill: "Having worked on both sides of the process, for Covenant House and for the state, I think he [Ritter] was right. The bureaucracy can be debilitating. It is a constant struggle to see how you can cut corners and avoid bureaucracy. . . . I don't think that Covenant House evaded state monitoring to any excessive degree. It did successfully evade archdiocesan control. In the end, Bruce decided that operating in that mode [as a state care provider] also involved a set of restrictions in dealing with kids that he didn't want."

89 According to the Kroll report, Ritter began tinkering with the administrative structure of the organization to give the illusion to state officials that there was an internal system of checks and balances. In May 1973, he resigned as a member of the board that he had hand-picked. But he continued to serve as president and as chairman of the meetings of the board.

The minutes of the meeting state that Father Ritter "wished to resign to lessen the conflict between his role as a board member [and] his other responsibilities as executive officer." Another reason was that Ritter found that Covenant House's contracts with New York City for foster care and the city regulations on the contract prohibited compensation to board members. The minutes of the November 14, 1973, meeting stated that Ritter "felt that the most important development of this year was the independence Covenant House had achieved from himself." By all accounts, however, Father Ritter continued to use his hand-picked board as a rubber stamp for his programs. *He* was Covenant House, and that was never going to change as long as he was in control. The minor adjustments served only to put on paper what the city officials wanted to hear. There were still no procedures for oversight and there was no established procedure to check Bruce Ritter's authority.

89 ". . . doing precisely what he claimed to be saving them from": There are at least three cases of sexual misconduct by Ritter with his young charges between 1971 and 1975 reported in the Kroll report (p. 15).

89 On Darryl Bassile: His allegations were detailed through extensive interviews with the author. He gave the same account to the Manhattan District Attorney's office, to Ritter's Franciscan superiors during their own inquiry, and in his own civil court case against Father Ritter and Covenant House. Bassile maintained in each of those interviews that Ritter sexually abused him on at least six occasions in the spring of 1973. Although his story can never be proven, the Franciscan investigator, the Reverend Canice Connors, who interviewed Bassile found his allegations "substantive" and "credible."

93 On Paul Johnson: His allegations were detailed through extensive interviews with the author from December of 1990 to November of 1991. Although his story can never be proven, Johnson underwent a lie-detector test on January 26, 1990, administered by Patrick Picciarelli of Condor Security & Investigations, Inc., and a member of the American Polygraph Association. Picciarelli determined that Johnson was "truthful" in describing his sexual relationship with Ritter. Johnson has changed his name, and the author agreed to use his original name, Paul Johnson, to protect his new identity.

93 On Bassile and Johnson: Allegations by both were brought to Ritter's Franciscan Order, which conducted its own investigation. On August 9, 1991, the author interviewed the Reverend Connors.

96 Ritter's use of money to trap his victims: It is a modus operandi similar to that of a Canadian priest who was at the center of the Mount Cashel scandal. The Mount Cashel Orphanage in Newfoundland was a Catholic boys' home, where scores of young wards suffered a kind of systematic sexual abuse at the hands of a coterie of pedophiliac Christian Brothers. It prompted an inquiry by the Royal Commission in June 1990. In *Unholy Orders: Tragedy at Mount Cashel* (Viking, 1990), Michael Harris documents the case and focuses one chapter on Father James Hickey, described as one of the most prominent and popular priests. Hickey allegedly used his position of trust to seduce and sexually abuse young boys under his care. Harris wrote: "Hickey would purposely leave money around the presbytery in small porcelain cups placed on the refrigerator and window ledges in full view of his impecunious house guests. 'It wouldn't be, like, a five-dollar or a ten-dollar bill. It would be, like, a twenty or a fifty,' a former altar boy testified. When the boys left and the money left with them, nothing was ever said. Jim Hickey was well versed in the sinister art of snaring his innocent prey."

CHAPTER 7

98 On Ritter's flying: From author's interview with Robert Macauley and from *Covenant House: Lifeline to the Streets*, p. 53.

99 "The inevitable process of assimilation into the child welfare system": Ibid., p. 51.

99 "Several members of the staff . . . wanted Covenant House to challenge the Church's position on birth control": From author's interview with Hugh O'Neill and the Kroll report.

99 On Ritter going to India: From *Covenant House: Lifeline to the Streets* (p. 52) and author's interview with Alan Oumeit, January 6, 1992.

100 On Ritter's changing the charity's bylaws to consolidate his power: The Kroll report and author's interviews with S. I. Taubman.

102 "I found myself in Times Square": From *Covenant House: Lifeline to the Streets*, p. 52.

104 Dialogue between Ritter and Cardinal Cooke: Ibid., pp. 54–55.

Part III

CHAPTER 8

112 Dialogue between Ritter and Macauley re-created through author's interview with Macauley, December 11, 1990. Also based in part on Macauley and Ritter interviews with *The Chronicle of Philanthropy*, October 3, 1989.

113 "I am not a fund raiser": *The Chronicle of Philanthropy*, interview with Ritter, October 3, 1989.

115 On Peter Grace: From *Catholic USA* (William Morrow and Company, 1989), edited by Linda Brandi Cateura, and "The Corporate State of Grace" by Joe Conason with Martin A. Rosenblatt in the *Village Voice*, April 12, 1983.

116 ". . . most active and dedicated private fundraisers": *Catholic USA*, p. 51.

117 On corporate giving: From Covenant House's 1983 Annual Report.

118 On Ritter's diminished reliance on government grants and subsequent lack of monitoring: From author's interview with Donna Santarsiero and review of charity's nonprofit tax forms.

123 On Grace and Governor Hugh Carey: Grace used his corporate might to push Carey along in the process of giving the property to Covenant House for an extended five-year lease at $1 a year, according to author's interviews with Taubman and O'Neill. Apparently Grace doesn't forget favors. After he left Albany, Carey was given a six-figure salary as an "environmental policy consultant" for W. R. Grace.

124 On purchase of the Manhattan Rehabilitation Center from New York State: *Covenant House: Lifeline to the Streets*, pp. 88–92.

125 "He who touches pitch": Ibid., p. 66.

CHAPTER 9

127 ". . . cornering the market in child care": From Ritter's "Message of the President" in Covenant House's 1983 Annual Report.

127 ". . . fired on the spot . . . nonnegotiable": From author's interview with Greg Loken.

128 "a cabal": From author's interview with Macauley.

128 Ritter replaced Taubman with Macauley as board chairman in 1984 without consulting other board members: From interviews with Santarsiero and Taubman.

128 On Toronto program: From Covenant House's 1983 Annual Report and author's interview with a former Covenant House official in Toronto.

129 On Houston program: From Kells's interview in the 1983 Annual Report. Also from author's interviews with first board chairman, John Kells and executive director of Houston program, Malcolm Host.

130 Republican circles in Houston: Author's interview with Host: "There was no question that the Texas board was aligned with George Bush and Jim Baker. This was their backyard. I would say many of the big contributors and some board members had relationships, either political or personal or in business, with Baker and Bush."

130 ". . . worst teenage runaway problem in America": *Houston Post*, September 1, 1985.

130 "When a slick priest . . .": Author's interview with former *Houston Post* reporter Dan Grothaus.

131 Cost $30,000 to recover furniture: *Village Voice*, March 20, 1990.

131 Kroll also noted that there was no evidence that Ellen Wallace Lofland received excessive payment or that her work was not satisfactory. In an interview with the *Village Voice* published March 20, 1990, she defended herself, stating that the "Covenant House portion of my income is minute. . . . I don't think anybody would do it for the price I'm doing it."

131 Tandy Lofland also had a minority interest in Intergroup Development, Inc.: Ibid.

131 Lofland reportedly had "little experience": Richard Derr, a purchasing director in Houston who knew Lofland, said he had only worked in the field for "several years" and had little experience running construction/renovation projects of that size. Lofland disputed the claim. Kroll also noted that there was no evidence he received excessive payment or that his work was unsatisfactory. *Village Voice*, March 20, 1989.

131 Proposed conflict-of-interest clause "would be an insult to Father Ritter": From the Kroll report.

132 On John Wetterer: He was publicly accused of sexually abusing many of the young boys in his care in an undercover investigation by CBS News' *60 Minutes* in 1988. Wetterer has denied the allegations. Although Guatemalan authorities cleared Wetterer, the U.S. Postal Service, in connection with the allegations of pedophilia, charged Wetterer with mail fraud in his fund-raising efforts. The allegations, which Wetterer denies, have been reported in several 1990 articles in *New York Newsday* and the *Miami Herald*. In the author's interview with Macauley, he said he and Wetterer helped start the Shoeshine Boys Foundation and that he helped Wetterer with his orphanage in Guatemala.

132 ". . . mother's milk": *Newsday*, October 7, 1990.

132 "You could support a kid": Author's interview with Macauley.

133 " 'Don't you understand?' Father Bruce asked": From author's interview with Santarsiero.

134 Alejos's alleged ties to right-wing death squads and the CIA are reported in several sources, including: *Gift of the Devil: A History of Guatemala* by Jim Handy (South End Press, 1984) and the *Village Voice*, February 20, 1990. But the *Village Voice* also points out that in recent years Alejos's "political views have moderated" and he has "even spoken out against the excesses of the right."

134 ". . . a tiny paradise": From Covenant House's 1983 Annual Report.

134 ". . . unearthed a shallow grave, where the bodies of nineteen people . . . each skull was pierced by a single bullet hole": *New York Newsday*, October 7, 1990.

135 The "model village" programs: *Gift of the Devil* (p. 261) and author's interview with Colum Lynch, freelance reporter for *New York Newsday* and the *Boston Globe*, formerly based in Guatemala; he researched Covenant House's ties to Alejos and the military.

135 "We are here to care for the children": From Ritter's August 1981 newsletter.

135 General information on Peter Grace: *Village Voice*, April 12, 1983, and *People of God: The Struggle for World Catholicism* by Penny Lernoux (Penguin, 1989), pp. 291–97.

135 "Grace was linked to many organizations": He served as head of a committee to evaluate President Kennedy's Alliance for Progress, which came up with the findings that corporations should receive more tax breaks and that the countries should receive less U.S. aid. He was also board chairman of the American Institute for Free Labor Development (AIFLD), which has been a "Trojan Horse" for several multinational corporations and the State Department in Latin America. AIFLD was reportedly involved in several U.S.-supported coups of elected governments in Brazil and the Dominican Republic. *Village Voice*, April 12, 1983, and *People of God*.

136 Alejos lent his land to the CIA for training for the Bay of Pigs: *People of God*, p. 295.

136 "Bill Simon was also": *People of God* describes Simon as "prominent in the *contra* private aid network." Simon later went on to found the Nicaraguan Freedom Fund. According to Lernoux, another source reported that Grace got the Knights of Malta involved in contra funding in the 1980s. Macauley's AmeriCares would later be linked by the press to contra aid, although Macauley has persistently denied these reports.

136 ". . . absolutely impossible to stay neutral": Marie Dennis of the Justice and Peace Office of the Maryknoll Society. *Newsday*, October 7, 1990.

136 Military bringing the orphans to Covenant House in Guatemala: From author's interview with Lynch and *Newsday*, October 7, 1990.

136 "The military did bring kids by": From interview with Atkinson in *Newsday*, October 7, 1990.

136 "That's a lie": From Russell W. Baker's interview with Alejos, *Village Voice*, January 8, 1991.

136 "It's like having Idi Amin": Ibid.

136 "There was a degree of cooperation": From author's interview.

137 "Ritter was safe because": *Newsday*, October 7, 1990.

138 On Ritter in Boston and purchase of the Avery Hotel: *Boston Globe*, January 16, 1983, and author's interview with Barbara Whelan.

139 Ritter exaggerated the prostitution and Mafia angle in Boston: " 'The Combat Zone in Boston is considered a minor version of Times Square. . . . Among the kids, their other options—mugging, ripping off people, knifing, and dealing drugs—prostitution is regarded by them as the safest because they are not so likely to get arrested,' Fr. Ritter said. . . . Many of the youth who seek refuge at Covenant House have also been involved in the child pornography business, described by Fr. Ritter as a 'highly profitable $1.5 billion industry on which the Mafia holds such a tight grip in Manhattan that no one can sell an obscene book, photograph or film without paying off the mob.' " *Boston Globe*, January 16, 1983.

140 Ritter and Whelan meeting at Bridge: Re-creation based on author's interview with Whelan.

140 "They scared me": Author's interview with Whelan.

142 On the clash with Ritter and the supporters of Boston's redevelopment plan: *Boston Globe*, February 6, 1983.

142 On Boston Redevelopment Authority and its director, Robert Ryan: *Boston Globe*, February 27, 1983, and author's interview with members of Covenant House R&D staff.

142 Marco Ottieri threatening legal action: *Boston Globe*, February 27, 1983.

143 Cost comparison of Bridge and Covenant House: *Village Voice*, March 20, 1990. If Covenant House served 25,000 kids a year in 1989, as it claimed (the numbers included a very high rate of recidivism), and its total annual budget was $89 million, their total expenditures figured out at roughly $3,600 a year per kid. Compare that to Bridge Over Troubled Waters, which cared for 4,000 youths a year on a budget of $1.5 million. That figures out to about $375 a head—a tenth the cost of Covenant House. And the Bridge finds homes for many of these young people, at a cost of $3,000 to $6,000 a year, compared to Covenant House, which has an average stay of about two weeks in which they provide mostly crisis care.

144 ". . . egomaniac": *Philadelphia Inquirer*, January 24, 1988.

144 ". . . very arrogant, very autocratic": *Houston Post*, September 1, 1985.

144 "The idea was to approximate": From author's interview with Linda Irwin, December 30, 1990.

145 "smaller programs . . . had success rates as high as 70 percent": Dr. Gary Yates of Children's Hospital in *Los Angeles Times*, April 10, 1989.

145 "the number of street kids increased dramatically during the first two years" of Covenant House in Houston: Based on a series of in-depth reports by Dan Grothaus in the *Houston Post*, September 1985.

146 "The next day I walked outside": Ibid.

146 "Covenant House brought me to the strip": Ibid.

147 "Covenant House had become the McDonald's of child care": Author's interview with John MacNeil.

147 On law-enforcement agencies' antagonism to Covenant House: From author's interview with Anne Donahue.

148 He bought off the police department's ill feeling: The Manhattan District Attorney eventually indicted several police officers on the scam in the spring of 1990.

148 $5,000 damage by vandals in Fort Lauderdale: Fort Lauderdale *News/Sun Sentinel*, September 22, 1985.

148 On cost overruns in Fort Lauderdale renovation: The investigators from Kroll Associates found no wrongdoing on the part of Lofland's company, but concluded a competitive bidding procedure might have provided them with a more qualified firm that could have finished the job without the additional costs.

149 On New Orleans Archdiocese: From author's interview with Sister Anthony Barczykowski, executive director of Associated Catholic Charities in New Orleans.

150 On Greenhouse: Author's interview with Linda Irwin, December 30, 1990.

CHAPTER 10

152 On Covenant House and Epsilon: Author's interview with Epsilon senior vice president Gene Henderson, January 27, 1992.

155 "The best writer of direct mail alive": From Covenant House senior vice president R. Christopher Walton's article in *Fund Raising Management*, June 1991.

155 Direct-mail fund-raising growth 1979 to 1983: Ibid.

156 The new right and direct mail: From Richard A. Viguerie: *The New Right: We're Ready to Lead*, revised edition (Caroline House, 1981). "Like all successful political movements, we must have a method of communicating with each other, and for conservatives in the 1970s it was direct mail. Frankly, the conservative movement is where it is today because of direct mail," p. 120.

156 Charitable giving from $22 billion in 1970 to $114 billion by 1989: From *Fund Raising Management* statistics compiled by William Olcott, editor.

156 The televangelists' scandals helped Covenant House: *Fund Raising Management*, November 1988, "Impact of Scandals on Giving," p. 32.

156 Viguerie sold lists to Covenant House, but never worked directly with the organization: From author's interview with Viguerie's assistant, Jerremy Squire.

156 Breakdown on Covenant House's rate of return with direct mail: Figures from 1983 Annual Report and analysis from author's interviews with Olcott and Stan Woodruff.

156 "In both categories—'ongoing donor base' and 'new donors'—no charity matched Covenant House": From author's interview with Gene Henderson (EpsilonVP), who qualified his statement to say that the U.S.O. during the Persian Gulf War did have a similar rate of return.

156 On Boys Town and St. Jude's: Estimation by Henderson.

157 ". . . ongoing dialogue with the donors": From "The Paradoxes of Covenant House," an in-depth article by Rosanne Haggerty Redmond and Mark Redmond, both of whom were Faith Community members and administrators in Covenant House. Rosanne also worked in donor communications. *Commonweal*, May 18, 1990.

157 "darkly fascinating images": Ibid.

162 "I've always suspected": *Village Voice*, January 20, 1990.

162 "He did that because it was the best way": From Russell W. Baker's interview with Treanor.

162 ". . . incredible burden": *Philadelphia Inquirer*, January 24, 1988.

162 "The real story": From author's interview with former Covenant House senior employee.

163 "Complex set of evils": *Commonweal*, May 18, 1990.

163 "Key-man life insurance policy": From Covenant House report on its assets to Lincoln Savings & Loan bank examiners, cover letter dated March 12, 1987. The policy was used as collateral against a loan.

Part IV
CHAPTER 11

167 On the Faith Community: From author's interviews with Redmond, Donahue, Loken, Spanier, the Reverend John Budwick, former director of the Center for Spiritual Development of the Laity, and from a lecture on "Laity: General Ministry in the Church at Large" at the Weston Theological Institute, Cambridge, MA. Also interviews with nearly a dozen other members of the Faith Community from New York, Houston, and New Orleans.

170 On the tension between the religious volunteers and the professional staff at Covenant House: From author's interview with Donahue and Linda Glassman, February 4, 1992.

170 "Network of spies": From author's interviews with John MacNeil in the fall of 1991.

172 On rift between Covenant House and the gay community: From author's interviews with Gabrielle Rotello, editor of *Outweek* magazine, and Dr. Joyce Hunter of the Hetrick Martin Institute.

175 Knights of Malta and Grace's network of private funding to the Nicaraguan contras: From *People of God*, p. 295.

176 AmeriCares's 1983 tax returns establish link to contras: Research project by John Spicer Nichols, a journalism professor at Pennsylvania State University, cited in *Newsday*, April 13, 1988.

176 Macauley flew shipment of newsprint to *La Prensa*, prompting allegations by Nicaraguan government that AmeriCares was a "CIA front": *Washington Post*, April 14, 1988.

176 Colonel Sam Watson made calls to Nicaraguan government for Macauley: From *Newsday*, April 13, 1988.

176 Copy of Lieutenant Colonel Oliver North memo mentioning Macauley: Obtained by author.

177 Knights of Malta connection to Guatemala's "model village" programs: From *People of God*, p. 295.

179 "I believed that I was doing something that mattered": Author's interview with John Kells, December 1991.

180 Projected income from telemarketing using Nineline: A 1989 internal report by Covenant House's Department of Fundraising and Development.

180 Importance of the Ad Council: From author's interview with Mark Stroock.

183 "Bill" is not the real name of the member of the Faith Community.

His story is based on the author's interviews with MacNeil and two members of the Faith Community who told him about Ritter's sexual advance. The allegation is documented in the Kroll report and by the Franciscan priests who investigated Ritter. The dialogue is re-created from author's interviews with MacNeil.

184 On "Bill's" complaint to the Franciscans: A priest who worked on the investigation of Ritter refused to elaborate on the specifics of the investigation, other than to point out that there was no allegation of any direct sexual contact and that the young man making the charge was not a youth under the care of Covenant House, but a member of the Faith Community.

185 Allegations of Ritter's sexual advances made by other members of the Faith Commmunity: *Commonweal*, May 1990, the Kroll report, and author's interviews with Faith Community members.

CHAPTER 12

186 The failure of the Great Society and the "collective despair that gave wide latitude to the Reagan administration's gutting of government programs": From *Within Our Reach: Breaking the Cycle of Disadvantage* by Lisbeth B. Schorr (Anchor Books, 1989).

187 Federal cuts in funding to New York City from 1981 to 1991: *The New York Times*, May 26, 1991.

187 On the new right and its "Catholic stars": In *People of God* Penny Lernoux detailed the Catholic Church's involvement in the new right. She placed Macauley, Simon, and Grace at the American core of a worldwide resurgence of religious fundamentalism that occurred throughout the 1980s. Lernoux wrote: "In the United States, fundamentalism is often associated with the movement of born-again Christians . . . but it is not limited to the United States or to certain Protestant churches. . . . It is a recurrent phenomenon in history, particularly in times of cultural stress when traditional values are challenged by political, economic and social changes. . . . Regardless of theological differences, religious fundamentalists share certain characteristics, such as a reverence for authority and a fear of secularization— or 'secular humanism,' as the Vatican and U.S. evangelicals call it. They also insist that they alone possess the truth, and they usually align themselves with the political right. In the United States they have been called the New Right to distinguish them from traditional forms of political and religious conservatism. Among the New Right's activists are fundamentalist Catholics who yearn for an 'old-time religion,' and who have made common cause with Reagan's evangelical supporters and the Roman Curia in the attack on liberal Catholic leaders."

189 Bishops' pastoral on the economy: From *People of God*, pp. 192–93, 195–200, and *Catholic USA*, pp. 57, 100–101, 135–36.

190 "There has always been the poor": From *Catholic USA*, p. 58.

191 Government statistics on poverty in America: From documents cited in *People of God*, pp. 196–97.

191 On Covenant House and tax benefits available to donors: From 1989 Covenant House manual called "Tales from Planned Giving: Examples of Well Planned Gifts." Criticism of such planned giving came in part from the text of the September 1989 Canaras Group Statement, an affiliation of planned-giving experts who drafted their own denunciation of promoting charitable gifts as tax shelters.

194 Background on the $500,000 federal grant from HUD: *Times-Picayune,* October 29 and November 28, 1989.

194 Kemp as "big fan" of Ritter: *Times-Picayune,* December 9, 1989.

195 ". . . the greatest needs of disenfranchised youth": *Commonweal,* May 18, 1990.

195 On distortion of the number of runaways by the National Center for Missing and Exploited Children: *The New Republic,* March 2, 1987.

196 Covenant House and Regnere's policy on juvenile justice declared "an embarassment" by the Justice Department: Ibid.

196 On Regnere's private collection of pornography: Exposed in *The New Republic,* June 23, 1987, by Murray Waas.

196 Covenant House federal funding: From public records of the Justice Department, Labor Department, Department of Housing and Urban Development, Department of Health and Human Services, and Federal Emergency Management Agency and *Federal Contracts Report* (July 30, 1984). Author's research was assisted by freelance reporter Russell W. Baker. Some grants from 1989 included: $118,682 from HUD, $80,000 from the Federal Emergency Management Agency, $156,000 from the Department of Labor, and a $59,000 award listed only as "Federal Food." Besides federal monies, Covenant House received nearly a million dollars in 1989 alone from state and city governments. Alaska and Louisiana gave Covenant House chapters in their respective states funding through school lunch programs. New York State agencies provided Covenant House with $513,000 for the year 1989.

197 Funding guidelines for Adolescent and Family Life Grants: From *Federal Register,* December 22, 1989.

198 Ritter's $98,000 salary and hiding it in the Franciscan Charitable Trust: From the Kroll report, which states that Ritter did the transaction because of "concern about the public perception" of his salary during his appointment to Meese Commission (p. 21).

199 "Sex Busters . . . a new moral militancy": *Time,* July 21, 1986.

199 On threats from the new right and letter from Russell Kirk to Ritter: From author's interview with Ellen Levine.

200 "This is terrible. This is terrible": From author's interview with Levine.

200 On Melican's allegation of sex in New Orleans: From transcript of taped interview with Philip Nobile. Also some information from fragments of other interviews with Melican published in *The New York Times* and the *New York Daily News.*

201 On Ritter's expenditures on Melican: February 8, 1990, letter from Ritter's attorney Stanley Arkin to Assistant Manhattan District Attorney Daniel Castleman spells out Melican expenses, including a $500 Chemical Bank check from Ritter's personal account dated July 7, 1985.

201 All dialogue at the Meese Commission hearing: From *United States of America vs. Sex: How the Meese Commission Lied About Pornography* by Philip Nobile and Eric Nadler (Minotaur Press, 1986).

203 On Nobile and Melican: Based on author's interviews with Nobile.

203 On the Meese Commission's findings and Ritter's point of view: *Final*

Report of the Attorney General's Commission on Pornography (Rutledge Hill Press, 1986)

204 First annual Charles Keating Award and $800,000 in donations for Covenant House in Scottsdale, Arizona: *Arizona Republic,* November 16, 1985.

204 Scene at Le Cirque and prayer: Re-created from author's interview with Macauley.

CHAPTER 13

205 Ritter and Kennedy dialogue re-created from author's interview with Bill Reel, who wrote about Ritter's cancer diagnosis in his *New York Daily News* column.

207 Ritter's May 23, 1988, letter to the Reverend John May: Copy obtained by author.

208 10 percent of the youths in its care would test positive for the HIV virus: From a study by Covenant House from a 1987 "double-blind test on blood drawn from a sample of teenagers in the New York program." Ritter's letter to the Reverend May detailed the findings, the results of which, Ritter writes, were "so shocking" that the Surgeon General, the Centers for Disease Control, and state health officials "begged us not to release them to the public because, as one said, they might cause widespread panic."

209 The battle between Koch and Ritter for the Maritime Building: Author's interview with Taubman and former Koch aide Maureen Connelly. Also: *New York Daily News,* September 23, 1987; *Daily News* and *The New York Times,* October 27, 1987; and *Fund Raising Management,* November 1988.

210 "Landmark" fund raising campaign: Chris Walton wrote a profile of the intensive effort in *Fund Raising Management,* November 1989.

211 Canceling health benefits of child-care workers: *Commonweal,* May 18, 1990.

213 "Don't let that collar fool you": *City Limits,* October 1987.

214 On racism among employees at Times Square Hotel: *Spy* magazine, April 1990.

214 On background of sale of Times Square Hotel: Ibid.

217 Ritter meeting Kite in New Orleans: From author's extensive interviews with Kite from fall of 1989 to fall of 1990. Details of the story also confirmed through author's interviews with Ritter and staff counselors in New Orleans.

224 The process of obtaining false baptismal documents through Father Duval: *The New York Times,* February 6, 1990.

224 Ritter and Kite at hotel in Reading, PA: From author's interviews with Kite, Ritter, and Kaiser.

226 Dialogue between Bush and the Covenant House kids: From ABC News footage, June 22, 1989.

229 "There were people": From author's interview with source who spoke on condition of anonymity.

230 Sean Russell's murder: *Newsday,* March 21, 1990, and *Outweek,* March 28, 1990.

230 "The Covenant House thing": *Newsday,* March 21, 1990.

Part V

CHAPTER 14

237 ". . . no adequate system of accountability at Covenant House": Based on findings of Kroll report (p. 19): "There was no formal procedure or mechanism in place for collecting or investigating such allegations or for taking such allegations outside the staff where they could be independently and objectively reviewed."

237 Kite called Andrew Vachss: Vachss's secretary logged his message on November 7, 1989. *Village Voice*, January 30, 1990.

238 On the possibility that Kite sought revenge for not getting enough money: Throughout the investigation, Kite turned down every offer of money, including one of thousands of dollars from a disco owner who wanted him to dress up as a priest and hand out condoms in front of the club. He rejected the $2,000 that he said *Penthouse* offered him to tell his story against its old enemy from the Meese Commission. He even turned down the "consulting" fee that Geraldo Rivera offered him to appear on a two-part show about pedophile priests. But in the end Kite did file a lawsuit, which he and his attorney, Aubrey Lee, claim was settled out of court. They both refused to disclose the amount, although Covenant House sources said it was less than $200,000. Kite said he only wanted enough to "pay for the college education I was promised."

239 Conversation between Ritter and Kite reconstructed based on author's interviews with Kite.

251 "I had seen a fair amount of homosexuality": From author's interview with John Scanlon. November 16, 1990.

252 About the law firm of Cravath, Swaine, & Moore: From *Reckless Disregard* by Renata Adler (Vintage Books, 1986).

CHAPTER 15

254 On the *New York Post*: Based on author's notes from the days of the scandal and interviews with John Cotter, Jerry Nachman, Valerie Salambier, and others.

260 Re-creation of dialogue at December 11, 1989, Covenant House board of directors meeting: From author's interviews with Stroock, Levine, Santarsiero, Macauley, and Taubman.

CHAPTER 16

269 Description and dialogue at Ritter's press conference, December 14, 1989: From author's own notes and from Covenant House video tape of the proceeding.

270 They would let Kells be the front man: From author's interview with Kells.

278 Scene after press conference: From author's interviews with Kells, Stroock, and Wirt.

280 On former Governor Hugh Carey wanting to bring Morgenthau before the Catholic Lawyers Guild: From *Newsday*, February 9, 1990.

280 "Awful mess": Cardinal O'Connor in *New York Post*, March 10, 1990.

281 On Bassile's psychotherapy: From author's interview with Bassile and *The New York Times*, February 6, 1990, for which the paper obtained copies of Matusiewicz's notes, with Bassile's permission.

Part VI

CHAPTER 17

289 "had a history of hurting anyone": From author's interview with Alton Kite, December 21, 1989.

295 "So when did the rules change": Author's interview with Jerry Nachman, November 1990.

299 On *The New York Times*'s investigation: From author's interview with Ralph Blumenthal and M. A. Farber, December 19, 1990.

CHAPTER 18

304 Dialogue involving Frank Macchiarola is reconstructed from his point of view based on author's interview with Macchiarola, July 31, 1990.

305 The inside view of land of the crisis and board meetings was provided largely through extensive interviews with Macchiarola, Stroock, Levine, Santarsiero, Donahue, and others.

313 About Macchiarola's crisis plan: From Covenant House internal report dated February 10 devising a "Three-Phase Strategy for Major Donors."

314 On the deal between the archdiocese and the Manhattan D.A.: From the author's interviews with both Church and law-enforcement officials. Also *Daily News*, *Newsday*, *New York Post*, March 1, 1990.

315 Franciscan Charitable Trust: IRS filing described the purpose of the trust as follows: ". . . [In] support of Father Bruce Ritter's ministry as reflected in Covenant House's and its subsidiary organizations' programs and purposes. For example, from time to time, sexually exploited children come to the attention of Covenant House in need of confidential 'safe harbor' sanctuaries which are imprudent to provide under the public auspices of Covenant House and its related organization. Such confidential 'safe harbor' sanctuaries for such sexually exploited youth which come to the attention of Covenant House . . . are a first priority for the Franciscan Charitable Trust, thereby providing a needed confidential resource for children known to Covenant House and its related organizations."

316 On who profited from the Franciscan Charitable Trust: The Kroll report.

CHAPTER 19

325 "common knowledge": Author's interview with Andrew Humm, April 20, 1992.

326 "O'Connor went out on a limb": Ibid.

327 On the national scope of the priest pedophilia problem: From extensive coverage on the issue in the *National Catholic Reporter*, which began with a series of reports and editorials in 1985 and continues to the present; "Unholy Alliances," *Vanity Fair*, December 1991; and 1985 articles for the *Times of Acadiana* Lafayette, LA.

327 Chicago priests' sexual misconduct and the formation of a special commission to reexamine the issue of how the Church handles such accusations, and the Notre Dame case: *The New York Times*, February 24, 1992.

327 Series of lawsuits in New York, Texas, and other states against the Catholic Church: *National Catholic Reporter*, May 3, 1991; and *Lead Us Not into Temptation* (Chosen Books, 1986).

328 As many as 3,000 U.S. priests: According to the Reverend Thomas P. Doyle, a Dominican canon lawyer, who worked at the Vatican Embassy, in a 1987 article in the *San Jose Mercury News*. A special segment on ABC's *20/20* in December of 1988 claimed "five percent" of U.S. priests were pedophiles. The number climbs higher, according to Jason Berry, when it includes ephebophiliacs, which is the clinical term for older men who are attracted to young postpubertal males, usually ranging in age from fourteen to twenty.

328 $1 billion: A 1985 internal report to the U.S. bishops recommended guidelines for pedophilia cases. It was written by Louisiana attorney F. Ray Mouton, Doyle, and the late Reverend Michael Peterson, who counseled priests with sexual problems at the Saint Luke's Institute in Suitland, MD, and died of AIDS in 1987. Mouton warned the Church that if it relied on "cover up" strategies by recycling priests with problems from one diocese to another, rather than confronting the problem, it faced $1 billion in losses over the next decade.

328 The Church has recently been denied insurance coverage: *National Catholic Reporter*, January 8, 1988.

328 "Pedophilia is the S&L disaster": *The New York Times*, February 24, 1992.

328 Ritter's conversations with McHugh: From author's interview with McHugh. August 1991.

330 Ritter refused to cooperate with Kroll: In a July 5, 1990, letter from Arkin to McGuire, the head of the Kroll investigation, he stated, "As you know, Father Ritter has on a number of occasions publicly denied the truth of the full range of accusations made against him in the past six months. In light of these denials, I see no constructive purpose to be served by submitting him to further inquiry now."

331 homosexuality in the priesthood: *Gay Priests: Research & Comment* (HarperCollins, 1989) is a collection of essays compiled under pseudonyms by four gay priests as well as data based on 101 questionnaires circulated

Index